THE MEN AND WOMEN WHO FIGHT
TO SURVIVE IN A HARSH WORLD
AT THE DAWN OF HISTORY

TORKA—The bold hunter of unsurpassed skill with the throwing spear, he leads his small band from the forbidden Corridor of Storms into a new land where other clans work their evil magic and hunt the mammoth—where he must fight again to save those he loves.

LONIT—She is Torka's beautiful round-eyed woman who has borne him children and loved him always. Yet she fears she cannot resist her powerful attraction to a man of evil who would destroy her to punish the man who long ago saved her life.

KARANA—Abandoned by his own people, he becomes Torka's adopted son and grows into young manhood as a brave and accomplished hunter. Gifted with vision of the destiny of his friends, he will risk much for the woman who can teach him how to use his great powers.

NAVAHK—The Spirit Killer, the Evil One, a magic man who uses his deadly charms to satisfy his dark desires and ruthlessly eliminate his enemies. He is sworn to kill the hated Torka, the one man who can stand against his evil powers.

SONDAHR—A woman of magic, tall and breathtakingly beautiful, she is desired by many men but gives herself only to the young hunter who needs her love and her knowledge the most—in order to fight Navahk.

BOOK 2 * THE FIRST AMERICANS

THE
FIRST
AMERICANS

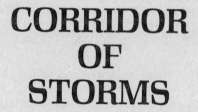

CORRIDOR
OF
STORMS

WILLIAM
SARABANDE

 Created by the producers of
The Holts: An American Dynasty
and **The Children of the Lion.**

Book Creations Inc., Canaan, NY • Lyle Kenyon Engel, Founder

BANTAM BOOKS
NEW YORK • TORONTO • LONDON • SYDNEY • AUCKLAND

THE FIRST AMERICANS: BOOK 2
CORRIDOR OF STORMS

A Bantam Domain Book / published by arrangement with Book Creations, Inc.

Bantam edition / June 1988

Produced by Book Creations, Inc.
Lyle Kenyon Engel: Founder

DOMAIN and the portrayal of a boxed "d" are trademarks of Bantam Books,
a division of Bantam Doubleday Dell Publishing Group, Inc.

ISBN 0-553-27159-8

Published simultaneously in the United States and Canada

Bantam Books are published by Bantam Books, a division of Bantam Doubleday Dell
Publishing Group, Inc. Its trademark, consisting of the words "Bantam Books" and the
portrayal of a rooster, is Registered in U.S. Patent and Trademark Office and in other
countries. Marca Registrada. Bantam Books, 1540 Broadway, New York, New York 10036.

PRINTED IN THE UNITED STATES OF AMERICA

OPM   19 18 17 16 15 14 13

for
Dagmaar
godmother, friend, and, if past lives be,
Eleanor of Aquitaine without a doubt!

Also, but by no means as an afterthought,
for
Paul and Lois
dear friends
I thank you for a lifetime of encouragement

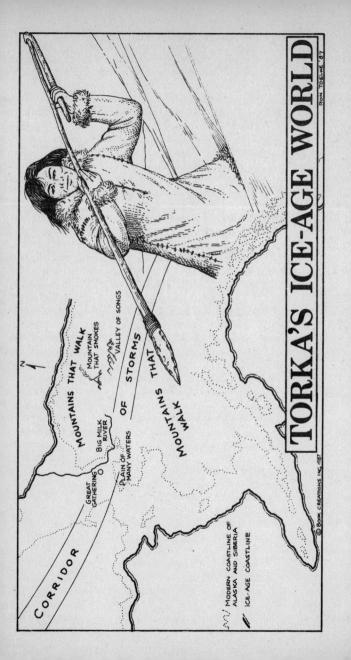

TORKA'S ICE-AGE WORLD

FROM TOELKE '87

© BOOK CREATIONS INC. 1987

N

CORRIDOR

GREAT GATHERING

MOUNTAINS THAT WALK

MOUNTAIN THAT SMOKES

Valley of Songs

BIG MILK RIVER

Plain of MANY WATERS

OF STORMS

MOUNTAINS THAT WALK

MODERN COASTLINE OF ALASKA AND SIBERIA

ICE-AGE COASTLINE

PART I

SPIRIT WALKERS

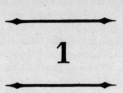

1

"In the beginning, when the land was one land, when the People were one people, before Father Above made the darkness that ate the sun, before Mother Below gave birth to the ice spirits that grew to cover the mountains, the wanawut was born to hunt the children of First Man and First Woman—to follow them as we now follow the great herds, to feed upon the People even as the People feed upon the meat and blood of mammoth and caribou and bison. For this alone was the wanawut born: to teach the People the meaning of fear."

The words of the magic man flowed into the night, into the wind that licked the perimeters of the communal fire, teasing the flames with its cold breath, circling the encampment like a stalking, invisible predator, and chilling the fur-clad people who were gathered into a circle. His words reminded them that although they were bundled close together, spears at hand and daggers ready, and swathed in their many-layered garments of skins and fur—their faces painted with ash to make them appear bold—they were nevertheless small and frightened and vulnerable beneath the vast and savage Arctic sky.

The magic man stood with his arms raised and his remarkably handsome face upturned to the night. He was a man in his prime. In fringed garments sewn entirely of the white belly skins of winter-killed caribou, he shone like glacial ice on a moonlit night.

"Fear . . ." He exhaled the word lovingly, as an offering to the night, while the low, hissing tide of cold, dry, Ice Age wind blew across endless miles of glacier-laden ranges and rolling steppeland. He alone seemed at peace with the night, a conspirator with the wind that swept into the gathering and streamed with dark portent through the minds of every man, woman, and child who listened as he spoke and gestured before the great communal fire.

As though at his command, the flames leaped high, feeding noisily upon bones and lichens and thick, dried sods cut from the shallow surface of the permafrost. It was a hot, hungry fire, which warmed the magic man as it sent sparks so high that they seemed to join the uncountable stars that sprawled across the taut, black skin of the sky. He smiled, master of the night and the stars, of the wind and the fire, and in absolute control of the people who sat in cross-legged, hunch-shouldered awe of him.

All except the newcomer.

Torka.

Something dark and malevolent moved within the magic man as his eyes drifted to the tall, powerful, physically magnificent young hunter who sat straight and unmoving in a black-maned, tawny outercoat of lion skin.

Torka.

Navahk, magic man, nearly hissed the hated name aloud. If only Supnah—his brother, and headman of the band—had not managed to persuade Torka to stay, he would be long gone and far away by now. Yes, Torka had been set to go. He had vowed to lead his infant-suckling woman and his cursed dogs and the boy whom he dared to call son into the unknown and forbidden country that lay to the east. He had told the people of Supnah's band that from a high promontory he had looked out across the forbidden land and had seen much game there. He had all but begged Supnah and his band to follow him; but the other man was not willing to commit his people to the unknown.

Supnah had spoken of a headman's responsibilities to his band with such persuasive eloquence that Torka had been sobered. Although he had already secured his pack frame onto his back, in the end Supnah had convinced him that for the sake of his woman and child, he must stay within the protection of the larger band, among those who would name him brother. In time, if the spirits of the game and the forces of Creation decreed that it might be so, perhaps they might yet venture into the forbidden land together. But for now the people of Supnah's band would remain in the land of their fathers. And so, although the woman had boldly urged him to go on, Torka had deferred to the wisdom of the older man and had chosen to remain with the people of Supnah's band. He had turned his back upon the far and forbidden country and had traveled west with Supnah's people to this night of fire and feasting.

The magic man's smile twisted into a leer of contempt and loathing. Before Torka had joined them, they had been starving. Now, suddenly, the land around them was rich in game. Many said that Torka brought the meat to die upon the spears of the hunters, and Navahk, who as magic man had always taken credit for bringing the game, did not know whom he despised more: Torka or Supnah.

Torka was staring back at him now, his face impassive and nearly as handsome in the firelight as the magic man's. Unused to rivals, Navahk hated him for that and because, while the thoughts of others were as easy for him to follow as mammoth tracks on a muddy outwash plain, the magic man found it impossible to know the thoughts of Torka. Unless Torka allowed him to know them.

Torka had made it no secret that he was a man who had endured much pain and suffering. He had lived with fear and had triumphed over it. It held little mystery for him; if anything, he was contemptuous of it. His body carried scars inflicted by wolves, bear, and mammoth, and by the lion in whose skin he walked. Why should he tremble at a magic man's tales of a legendary beast that he had never seen, when he had faced so many real threats and overcome them? Fear weakened a man and made him vulnerable to predators. And it was apparent from the way he observed the magic man that Torka knew that he was predacious.

Frustrated, Navahk looked away from Torka, determined not to be intimidated by him. He would drive him from the band or see him dead, along with the one Torka called son. The idea caught fire within him. He smiled. Then he actually laughed, and suddenly he leaped high and began to whirl in the firelight. He danced as gracefully as a hawk soaring upon the wind. He sang the high, wild, wordless songs of wolves and wild dogs and of stallions driving mares before them upon the vast, open grasslands of the summer tundra. He became prey and predator, bear and lion, mammoth and caribou, and then, hunching into a bestial crouch, he rocked himself on his heels and wailed and hissed, leaped and prowled, no longer flesh but spirit, the thing of which he warned his people—the wanawut.

He heard the women gasp with fear as the men murmured appreciation for the intricate savagery of his dance. He did not care about them. Instead he paused before Torka, smiling to mask his jealousy of the man's masculine beauty and unperturbable calm. The magic man raised his skin-beribboned ceremonial staff of office, a fire-hardened thighbone of a camel atop which the horned, oiled skull of an antelope gleamed and stared sightlessly at the newcomer. He shook the staff viciously at Torka, and all the claws, talons, and beaks sewn onto the streaming ribbons of skin rattled and clicked.

"Does Torka not fear the wanawut now that he has seen its spirit come to dance within the skin of Navahk?"

Torka did not move. He was startled by the rapaciousness he glimpsed within the magic man's eyes, and chose not to react to it visibly. "Torka is wary of all things he does not understand."

The magic man glared at him, hating him. Torka, having seen the threat in Navahk's eyes, was watchful as a grazing animal venturing to drink alone from a tundral pool where predators were known to lurk. But worse than that, his cool reserve toward the magic man was affecting Supnah, the headman of the band. *Supnah.* Navahk's lips flexed downward. His brother was such a wise and wary man in all things, except when it came to his younger brother. With Navahk, Supnah's credulity and gullibility had always been without bounds. Until Torka had walked into their lives. Now the magic man's words, gestures, and well-practiced performance had left the older man unimpressed . . . as he had been unimpressed with his brother ever since encountering Torka alone upon the tundra, pursuing slavers who had stolen his woman and boy.

The name of that boy was Karana. Abandoned with most of the children of Supnah's band during a time of famine, the boy alone had survived, to be later found and adopted by Torka, who had come to love him as a son. Torka had spoken Karana's name, imploring the hunters of Supnah to help him rescue his woman and the boy from the slavers who had stolen them and murdered his grandfather. The people of Supnah had cried out in surprise while the headman had stood in mute disbelief, a woman's tears welling beneath his lids.

Karana was Supnah's son—his *only* son—and Navahk was the magic man responsible for the children's abandonment; he had also sworn that he had seen a vision of the deaths of Karana and all the other children who had been abandoned with him.

"Do not look back," he had told their grieving parents. "This man has seen the children in his dreams, and they are food for beasts and for Spirit Sucker, the wanawut that howls in the time of long dark as it feeds upon the flesh of our abandoned little ones. Their life spirits are released to the wind, so those small, useless ones who have died in order that the strong among us would not starve may be born again to their people in better times."

But now Karana, the child whom Navahk had declared dead, sat alive and healthy beside his father, reunited with his people because of Torka. The boy stared at the magic man out of black, hostile eyes, which seemed to pierce straight to Navahk's heart.

The muscles of the magic man's jawline tensed visibly. Karana's eyes had *always* been able to pierce him. How he loathed the child and Torka and Supnah! How small and culpable they made him feel, even though he stood boldly against the night, working his magic for their pleasure while wishing that he could make the words strike all three of them dead.

His mouth grew taut over his small, white, oddly serrated teeth. If only he had been born *first*, brawny instead of beautiful, and with the potential to be even half as good a hunter as his brother! He would take his brother's place, and no man would ever question the validity of his dreams or magic again.

Not that they ever had . . . until Karana had walked back into their lives out of the world of spirits to which Navahk had consigned him.

Now, as a result, Supnah looked at his brother with speculation rather than adulation. He sat at the front of the men's side of the circle of his assembled people, in the full regalia of his rank. Because he was an unpretentious man, it was minimal: the headman's circlet of eagle, hawk, and teratorn feathers about his head; and around his neck, over his outer tunic, a collar of the downy breast skins of those birds, to which their taloned claws had been sewn. They hung like a fringe made of desiccated fingers, clicking dully in the wind as

Supnah sat stoically upon his lichen-and-down-stuffed sitting pad of bearskin, in the place where errant smoke was least likely to offend his nostrils or burn his eyes. He had seated Torka in a position of honor to his left and had placed Karana at his right. Now and then he looked down at the boy and slung a broad, powerful arm around his slim shoulders, drawing him close, hugging him with open and profoundly paternal affection, as though he could not believe that the child was really there; then he would lean forward slightly and look at Torka, nodding to indicate a depth of appreciation that no words could express.

Seeing that look, Navahk trembled with suppressed rage. The storytelling and magic were in celebration of Karana's miraculous return and in gratitude to Torka for having saved the life of the child. Since Torka had stepped into their lives, nothing had been the same. Wild dogs walked at his feet as though they were his brothers, and he had willingly shared knowledge of the miraculous spear hurler, which he had devised, with Supnah's band.

It was only an elongated shaft of bone approximately the length of a man's forearm, with a handgrip at one end and a barbed tip at the other. But with the sinew-wrapped grip held in the right hand, the butt end of the spear braced against the barb, and the narrowing, pointed end of the shaft facing back over his shoulder, a man could more than double the speed, distance, and power of his thrust. With this awe-inspiring weapon, Torka had led Supnah's hunters to a victory against the murderous slavers of the Ghost Band.

And now, thanks to Torka alone, a sense of power and self-determination had been reawakened within Supnah's band. The band had gaped at the newcomer as though he were a bright, warm sun rising on their world. As Navahk had stood by with murderous resentment, the people of Supnah's band had listened spellbound while Torka told them how a rampaging bull mammoth had destroyed his band—how he had dared to face its raging fury, been charged and lifted by its great tusks, fixed a spear in its shoulder, then was thrown and left to die, only to rise from death. Out of all his people, only he, his woman, and his ancient grandfather survived the appalling devastation that the beast had wrought. The three had fled eastward into unknown country, across the savage, twisted hills of a distant land, vulnerable to predators and the marrow-freezing cold of the endless nights. Nevertheless, they had survived the incomparable hardships until, at last, they sought refuge within a cave high upon a distant mountain. They had found shelter from the storms, and the filthy, stinking nest of a small, frightened child—Karana—who had also climbed the heights for safety.

Under Torka's leadership Supnah's hunters had killed many of the Ghost Band, which had preyed upon the people of the tundra for as long as any of them could remember, and had taken to their fires a dozen tattooed young women captives. The women's faces shone with pleasure in their new circumstances, and their eyes glowed with wonder at the overpowering physical perfection and astounding beauty of the magic man.

Navahk smiled. Their obvious adoration momentarily overshadowed his feelings of frustration. *They*, at least, were beguiled by his tales of enchantment, which had first been told at the dawn of his people's memory to drive back their fears and reassure them of their place within their world.

But sensing that his position within the band was in jeopardy, he had chosen another enchantment. Tonight Navahk had conjured fear and had danced with it through the flame light as though it were his lover. He had made it his ally, reaffirming his own status by loosing the beast of terror among his people—a beast that only he, as magic man, could control. It was a method he had long used to manipulate his brother to serve his own ambitions.

"Navahk says this to his people: In his dream times, this man had seen the wanawut walking in the mountains to the east. It hungers in the night. It longs to feast upon the flesh of those who would follow Torka into the new and unknown land into which he would lead us."

The magic man fell silent. Supnah was looking at him out of eyes that seemed to strip him to the bone. His arms folded across his chest, his weatherworn but still handsome features set into a watchful scowl, the headman seemed a stranger, his eyes fixed upon his brother with a mixture of contempt and pity. Seeing it, Navahk winced and felt his own smile disappear.

Navahk was no longer in control of his brother, and if he was not in control of his brother, then he was no longer in control of the band.

"Who has seen this wanawut?" Supnah's tone reeked of skepticism. "Who has found its hide or bones or any portion of its carcass upon the tundra? Who has seen its tracks or spoor or looked upon the living flesh of this wanawut . . . this spirit of the wind and mists that brings fear to the hearts of my people through the mouth of Navahk?" The headman's challenge was as powerful as the man.

Beside him, the boy Karana was startled and amazed. He was not certain if he had heard correctly. Had the headman actually spoken out to the magic man? Had Supnah, for the first time in his life, openly impugned his brother before the entire band?

Yes! It was so! The boy smiled for the first time since Supnah had insisted that he leave Torka to dwell with him and Naiapi, his third woman, as the headman's son again. He had not wanted to go, but Torka had allowed no argument from him. And although he had balked, he had actually been delighted when Navahk had glowered at him and proclaimed that the dead could not return to dwell among the living without dire consequences to all. Supnah had coldly replied that his son was alive, not dead, no thanks to his brother's mistaken portending. Then Karana had enjoyed smirking at the magic man but had not enjoyed his forced residence within Supnah's pit hut. He disliked Naiapi as much as she disliked him, although her little daughter, Pet, half smothered him with sisterly affection. She was looking at him now from across the fire, but he pretended not to notice. He wanted no part of her; she was one of only a handful of toddlers who had not been abandoned to the winter dark, because her mother, having just lost a sickly newborn, had breast milk to suckle her after the infant died. He had told her that she was not his sister, but Supnah had insisted that, although they had been born out of different mothers, they were nevertheless of his blood, and as he cherished them, so must they cherish each other.

Sullenly, Karana had kept his thoughts to himself. *If you cherished me, how could you have sent me off to die? How could you have sent any of us? No matter what Navahk said, you were headman and did not have to listen. In starving times Torka found enough food to feed his people and took in a strange band's child. We were hungry, but we survived. And now Karana is Torka's son forever. Karana will never be Supnah's son again.*

The boy sighed. He had loved Supnah once and been proud of the bold hunter. Yet there was now a bittersweet emptiness within his heart where filial love should have been. There was no way to tell the headman that he was, in fact, Navahk's spawn. When Karana had returned to his people, Navahk, for reasons the boy still could not fully understand, had sought him out and smiled maliciously as he had burned him with that unwelcome truth. It both revolted and shamed him.

Yet now, as he stared at the magic man in the flickering shadows of red and black and gold, he realized that he had always sensed the truth—even in those long-ago days of his childhood, when others would remark upon his resemblance to his father's brother. The similarity did not end there. He would amaze himself, as well as the people of his band, by knowing when the weather would turn, when the game would come, and where it would be found. He had often felt the magic man watching him, measuring him out of sharp, resentful eyes. His mother had warned him to keep his portending to himself and to be wary of Navahk. He was a dangerous, ugly man, she had warned. But Karana had been baffled because Navahk was even more beautiful than his mother, and she was the headman's woman, envied by all the females of the band.

A lump formed at the back of the boy's throat. His mother had perished the winter he had been abandoned. Her reasons for distrusting the magic man had died with her, and Karana was certain that if he were to tell Supnah the truth about his parentage, the headman would never believe him. Since the death of their parents, Supnah had been like a father to his much younger brother. To speak against Navahk to the headman had always been like shouting into the north wind at the height of a gale.

So it was that now Karana stared at Supnah, then at Navahk, incredulous. The headman's words struck the magic man like a well-placed spear, actually making him stagger. Supnah had never challenged Navahk, not even when the magic man had told the headman to abandon his own son.

A dark, intense warning sparked within Karana each time his eyes met his father's. He chafed each time the headman drew him close and called him son. *Torka is my father now. Torka will always be my father!* he wanted to shout. Loyalty and love made them father and son, not blood; blood was a thin, red thing that dried and blew away on the wind.

Karana knew that all too well, for he had watched the other

children slowly starve and freeze to death, one by one, crying for mothers and fathers who never came. He had been unable to help them, for he, too, was starving and dying—and all because Supnah had not been bold enough to challenge the spirits of the storms that spoke to him through his brother's mouth.

Karana wished he could spring to his feet and flee into the night. This was a bad camp, filled with bad people, and nothing good could come to any who stayed within it.

"Again I ask, who has seen the wanawut except Navahk in his clouded dreams?" Supnah's voice cut the night with an angry edge. The question settled heavily.

Navahk had regained his composure. He picked up Supnah's question and hurled it back at his brother. "Has Supnah walked the world of spirits that he may challenge what Navahk, magic man, has seen in his dreams? Or would the headman of this band listen to Torka, a stranger, before heeding the warnings of his own brother?"

"Torka has said that he has seen good hunting grounds to the east. Why should we doubt him? He has led us well against the Ghost Band, has brought women into our camp, and has twice faced Thunder Speaker, the great mammoth. Torka has given to us the knowledge of making and using the spear hurler. Torka has returned my son, when Navahk had sworn before all that Karana was dead. Torka has proved himself to be a man of unclouded dreams. So Supnah says *yes* to Navahk's question. Supnah *will* listen when Torka speaks."

Navahk stood dead still for a moment.

Supnah took the moment and shook his brother's world with it. "Perhaps it is time for the people of Supnah to name a new magic man. Perhaps it is time for Navahk—like the children of the people whose life spirits were eaten by his dreams—to walk away upon the wind, out of his band forever!"

"No!" Torka's declaration reverberated like the crack of thunder. He was on his feet, looking grimly at Supnah, then Navahk. They were like a pair of bull elk in deadly rut, antlers locked in competition for control of the band. Whatever the cause of their enmity, Torka wanted no part of it, nor would he take sides. He had his woman and infant to think of, and although he had instinctively recoiled from the magic man the first time he had seen him, he had no desire to undercut the man's status. His own grandfather had been what his people had called a spirit master—a magic man by this band's terms—and he knew the weight of the responsibility that went along with the title. The last thing he wanted was to assume the burden of such authority. If Supnah wished to deprive his brother of his rank, let him name another man to fill it. "This man is no magic man," he said.

The headman glowered at him. "This man says that you *are*! Have we not seen you do all that Supnah has just said? You faced the great mammoth Thunder Speaker before our very eyes, and when we fled in fear and Karana fell before the charging mammoth, was it not Torka who put himself between Karana and the beast? And did Death not turn away, gentled by the magic power of your will?"

Torka could not argue with the truth or allow it to be unchallenged. "It is so. But this man wonders if it *was* magic. The great mammoth once fell upon Torka's people because we had eaten of the flesh of its kindred. We are not strangers, Thunder Speaker and I. That one carries the head of one of my spears embedded within its shoulder. And this man carries the scars of its tusks across his belly. Across many miles Torka has carried the hope to kill the beast that killed his people. But perhaps, in the end, we are merely two bulls who are much alike, both of us willing to stand in defense of our own, and both of us so weary of killing that we are willing to walk away when there is no need for it."

The headman considered. "Perhaps. But not many men would be brave enough to stand unmoving before Thunder Speaker. In such bravery there *is* magic."

"Your son has become as a son to me, Supnah. We have endured many hardships together. To save Karana I faced death. But had you been at my side, you would have faced it in my place. A father's love *is* a thing of magic. But you must look to Navahk for guidance and wisdom. If sometimes his dreams are clouded, that is not because his magic is weak. It is because that is the way of the spirit world. No man may see into it clearly. If Navahk says that he walks with the spirits in his dreams, who may say that that is not the truth? Not Torka. This man is only a hunter. I have walked the far hills that open into an unknown land and have seen much game on broad grasslands that stretch eastward between the Mountains That Walk. But if Navahk says that it is forbidden country and that in his dreams he has seen the wanawut—whatever this creature may be—waiting to prey upon Supnah's band, then I would not go there. I would be content to follow Supnah, grateful for the protection that his people have offered to me, my woman, and my child."

Navahk growled. His eyes swept the silent assembly. The man *was* magic. He spoke with an eloquence that Navahk knew he could not match. He felt no gratitude to Torka. He glared at him in hate-engorged silence. Then, grasping at his sullied authority, he made the best of the moment.

"Torka has spoken wisely. One who has not seen the wanawut cannot be a magic man."

Torka seemed relieved, yet he felt obliged to reply lest he offend the headman. "As Navahk says, this man is no magic man. But if the wanawut is what my people call a wind spirit, then Torka *has* heard it cry in the long nights of the winter dark. It dwells in the land of the People, in the mists and clouds of high places. We are in as much danger from the wanawut here as in the unknown land that lies to the east."

A murmuring went through the gathering.

Supnah was pleased; Navahk was not. From his throat came a great cry and then low, snarling sounds such as wolves make when they devour their prey. He whirled and circled the fire, paused before the women's side of the gathering, stared at the watching women, caused the few children to cower, and deliberately lingered before Torka's woman until her unusually beautiful face blushed at the provocation in his eyes. Her reaction gratified him as much as it obviously angered Torka. When he turned back to face the men's side of the circle, there was open hostility on Torka's face. Navahk was glad. He would take Torka's woman if he could, to demean the newcomer and to make him pay for this night of humiliation.

Now Navahk stood splay-legged, with his shoulders back and his arms thrown wide before the flames as the wind combed through his knee-length hair and drove the long fringes of his sleeves outward like skeining mists. His voice seemed to come from outside himself. It was wind. It was fire. It was the voice of the cold, black, star-strewn infinity of the night. "The wanawut *is* a wind spirit. Its flesh is the substance of clouds. Its cry is the wind's. No man will ever find its spoor or follow its tracks! And no man who is not a magic man may see it until it leaps from the world of spirit to feed upon him!"

Again a murmuring sigh rippled through the gathering. Navahk had his people under his spell again.

"Karana has seen the wanawut."

Navahk stiffened and fixed the boy with eyes so filled with virulent hatred, anyone else might have withered away on the spot. But Karana did not flinch. His face was set, and hard for one who had lived to see the passing of only eleven summers. He was small and looked younger than his years in the multilayered, intricately stitched garments that Torka's woman, Lonit, had made for him. His face still bore the ravages of a great ordeal, but a restless energy and bold, resilient spirit shone from his eyes. "Karana has seen the wanawut. He has seen it in the storm mists and has heard it howling in the winter dark. He has looked upon it as it stood upright like a man, stalked like a bear, hunted like a lion, and followed the abandoned children of this band to feed upon us after Navahk's dreams sent us off to die."

From the women's side of the circle low moans of grief escaped a dozen mouths as hands flew to faces, and heads went down, unable to look at Karana. From across the circle hunters grunted against memories that they had long ago tried to bury deep within themselves. Karana's words had called unwelcome ghosts to the gathering, little ghosts in winter boots, toddling ghosts in coats of fur, brave tiny figures with hands lost in enormous mittens and chapped faces hidden within hoods ruffed all around with fur. The ghosts of abandoned children walked through the assembly, as they had once walked from a starving encampment into the endless night, into the ravenous storms of winter to become food for beasts while their mothers and fathers turned their backs in anguish.

Because Navahk, magic man of their band, had assured them that they *must* do so. And because Supnah, regardless of his professed love for his only son and his concern for the fate of the little ones, had not dared to challenge him.

"Karana has seen the wanawut," he repeated with the stern, unforgiving emphasis of one who, like Torka, had lived too long and seen too much of danger to allow it to intimidate him. "And he sees it now . . . standing before us all . . . in the skin of Navahk!"

"Karana!" Torka's voice was low, his tone sharp with unmistakable admonition.

The boy ignored it. He snapped to his feet, staring at the

fire-burnished faces that stared back at him in shock. It wa
forbidden for children to speak openly at gatherings, and
was unheard of for them to challenge their elders at any time
He did not care. Nor did he cower as he saw that Navahk wa
advancing toward him slowly, wearing a malicious smile tha
was somehow not a smile at all but a malignant leer. Karan
glared and smiled back at him.

Suddenly he could not breathe. Try as he might, he coul
not look away. It was as though Navahk were someho
sucking his spirit out of his body through his eyes and draw
ing it into himself. In black, bottomless sinks, the boy's min
waded through the dark suffocating depths of Navahk's mu
derous, mind-numbing hatred. He felt himself drowning i
it, choking, fighting for breath as, within the strangling dar
ness, light exploded—the light of vision.

Karana willed himself into it. Within himself a voice whi
pered, promised, warned. *He will kill you if he can, as he h*
tried to kill you in the past, because he is your father . .
because he knows that the gift of true Seeing is yours . .
because he knows you will grow to be a man who will ma
him small within your shadow . . . because he knows th
someday you will be a greater magic man than he has ev
been.

Karana shook his head. The light of vision faded. The voi
of warning fell silent. He drew in a deep breath, and the spe
of the magic man was broken.

Navahk stopped in his tracks. His smile twisted, and h
eyes narrowed. He knew he had lost the battle of wills th
he had initiated between himself and the boy.

Karana raised an arm and pointed accusingly at the mag
man. "*He* is the one to fear, not the wanawut. *He* is the bea
that will prey upon this band, as he preyed upon its childre
in the past and as he preys upon the spirit of its people nov
making you weak and indecisive and afraid. In your fear li
the power, and his power is a bad thing because it serves h
people only as long as it serves himself!"

2

Karana did not wait for Navahk's reaction. The night engulfed him as he turned and walked into it imperiously, eager to put the gathering behind him.

Voices called to him—Torka's, Supnah's, and a high, female voice that he did not recognize. Darkness surrounded him, and he wrapped himself in it as though it were a cloak that could hide him from the watching eyes that followed his bold steps from the encampment.

"Hrmmph!" He sneered and thought: *Let them stare! Let them gape! I have my dagger at my side. I am not afraid of the night. Thanks to them, I have lived in it alone and have learned to be wary of its dangers!*

He put the last of the conical, hide-covered pit huts behind him and skirted the last of the drying frames, where thin, wide fillets of a giant ground sloth were streaming stiffly in the wind like bloodred banners. He saw Grek, guardian of the meat, sitting cross-legged in the darkness. Karana, jogging past, startled the man, who was even more startled when the lean, wolflike shadow of a wild dog leaped over him in pursuit of the boy.

"Come back, you!"

Karana smiled, ignoring Grek's command, glad that the dog was following and that the hunter had not chosen to rise and give chase. Grek was no youth, but he was strong and agile; only Torka and Supnah could outrun him. And Aar.

The dog fell into step now with Karana, looking up at him in the darkness with blue eyes that reflected the starlight out of a wolfish, black-masked head.

The boy frowned. There was more than starlight in the eyes of Aar. There was also rebuke. Like old Umak—Torka's

17

grandfather, who had used his powers as a spirit master to befriend the dog in a far land—Karana's relationship with the animal was unique. There was an unspoken language between them, and understanding that bordered on the magical.

Again the boy harrumphed. "Karana will walk where he will! *When* he will. Better to be alone in the darkness than in the crowded firelight of an encampment with Navahk. There is less danger to this boy here. If Aar does not like it, he can go back to camp, to his pups and mate. This boy has not asked you to follow! This boy will not miss you if you go back!"

He knew it was a lie. Nevertheless, he lengthened his stride, glad that the dog ran with him but resentful that not even the companionship of the animal could brighten his mood. It seemed to Karana that somehow, impossibly, the eyes of Navahk were still watching him, following him, burning holes into his back.

"Karana!"

Within his multilayered fur tunic, beneath his undershirt of woman-chewed skins cut from the supple pelts of caribou fawns, hackles rose on his back. Navahk was calling his name. Navahk was coming after him.

Navahk will never catch me! Never! His thoughts were as black as the sky. Anger and frustration pricked him like the uncountable stars pricked the skin of the moonless night. He looked up for a moment and was dazzled by the shimmering beauty that lay above him. So many stars! Vast, swirling rivers of them, so thick that they formed blurred, cloudlike veils that, like the dog, ran with him as he loped across the world.

The beauty of the night took his breath away, then returned it to him as he tripped on a knee-high clump of tussock grass and looked down just in time to see the ground rush up to meet him.

Stunned, he lay flat on his belly while a bird squawked and, raining feathers, climbed for the stars on flapping wings. Something warm oozed beneath his palm, and he knew that he had been a fool to run so carelessly across the benighted tundra. He had come farther than he had realized. He could smell the pungent spruce groves in the not-too-distant hills and knew that he had blundered into the same expanse of tussocks that he and Torka had skirted earlier in the day. With Grek and a bandy-legged hunter named Stam, they had come out from the encampment to stand watch over the women as they went high-stepping among the mounded grasses to set snares for ptarmigan, the fat little partridge of the northlands that mated and nested in the tussock grasses. There were eggs to gather and snack upon, and this the men had done as they made certain that no predators would fall upon their females while they worked to make prey of the ptarmigans.

Now, levering up with his ungloved hands, Karana frowned. He seated himself and lifted his right hand. It was slimed with egg and pebbled with fragile, membranous shell. Aar nosed close and started to lick it clean, but the boy beat him to it. He was sucking his fingers when, suddenly, hackles rose on his skin again. They ran upward along his spine, stinging him like insects as he realized that he and the dog were not alone.

Aar's head went down. The dog made no sound; nevertheless, as Karana wrapped a slim arm about Aar's neck, he could feel the animal's tension as its hair bristled along its back and a growl began to form deep within its chest.

"Shhh . . ." he whispered imperatively, the sound audible only to the dog. Karana shifted his weight until he was balanced on the balls of his feet, left leg slightly forward, his right leg braced and ready to propel him outward into the night like a living spear if the need for flight arose. But for now, until the danger—if there was danger—was defined, his best defense was to hold his position and be as still as the night.

His right hand formed a fist around the bone handle of the nephrite dagger sheathed at his hip. It was a blade of many purposes. The greenish stone was beautifully flaked and sharp enough to lay open the toughest hide; but it was only a dagger, a working tool designed to flay dead meat, not to bring down living animals. For this a hunter needed a spear; especially when he was the one being hunted. With a tremulous, barely audible sigh of longing, Karana thought of his spears. He felt small and vulnerable and alone without them. For the second time he regretted his impetuosity.

Something *was* advancing toward him. Silhouetted against the starlight, the black form was the size of a mature bear. It hunched against the night, moving slowly, a hulking blur in the darkness. Was it man or beast? Still stunned by his fall, Karana's usually acute senses failed him.

He blinked and strained to see. Aar's heart was thumping beneath his left palm. The dog saw it too—what Karana knew he could *not* be seeing. That thing was man *and* beast! It was the creature he had heard howling in the winter dark long ago, when he had huddled with the other children, waiting to die, to become food for . . . the wanawut. Spirit Sucker. Beast of flesh and cloud and darkness, born to feed upon the People, born to teach the People the meaning of fear.

Karana gulped. His mouth was dry. The words of the magic man moved through his mind. *Fear.* He knew it all too well. The creature was close now, too close.

Illuminated by the starlight, it passed immediately ahead and to his right. It walked upright with a cautious, yet oddly rolling gait, bending slightly forward, like an aging man with a bad back. In the darkness it seemed to be clothed, for it was thickly maned across its shoulders and along its spine, and its entire body was darkly furred, with shaggy guard hairs of gray that gave it a frosted appearance. Its massive neck sloped into equally massive shoulders from which long, muscular, shaggy-haired arms swung with what, in a man, would have been considered easy grace. Impossibly, Karana saw that its hands were the hands of a man, except three times the size and clawed.

Staring upward out of the thick, deep lakes of shadow between the clumps of grasses in which he cowered, Karana saw the beast's outslung, bearlike profile. He caught glimpses of its features: a flattened, sloping cranium, a projecting brow, a flashing eye, a cylindrical muzzle, a wide, flaring, hairless nostril, a large, slightly pointed, grotesquely manlike ear set low at the side of its head, and a broad-lipped mouth that was pulled slightly back to reveal glistening, protruding canines that were longer than the boy's dagger.

Karana felt sick. The teeth of the beast were unmistakably the stabbing fangs of a carnivore. Coupled with its narrow hips and bunch-muscled, relatively short-boned thighs, they marked the creature as one that leaped upon its prey.

It paused for a moment. Karana's breath caught in his throat. His heart, like the dog's, was pounding so hard that he was certain the beast had heard it. But if it had, it gave no sign of it. It seemed to be resting as it turned its head and stared in the direction from which it had come.

Then, after only a few heartbeats, it moved on again, and Karana heard the deep, effortless suck of its breath and the soft pad of its broad, toed feet as it moved on between the tussocks. But its scent, like his own, was tangled in the gentle eddying wind of the night, mixed into the smells of crushed grass and bruised tundra earth, so that neither boy nor beast smelled more than only the vaguest inference of the other as the creature moved away into the darkness.

Karana nearly vomited with relief. Then, beside him, Aar shivered, and the boy saw that from the distances out of which the beast had come, others of its kind were coming toward him. He held his breath and gripped his dagger and the dog more tightly as, one by one, stooped, bearlike shadows as hairy as mammoths walked past him.

None was as large as the first beast that had passed. Some were much smaller. One limped badly. It was totally gray and so grizzled that it was almost white; from this, and from the strained, ragged suck of its breath, Karana knew that it was old and injured. As it moved past him, he grimaced with revulsion at the sight of hairless, unpleasantly human-looking breasts swinging pendulously against its shaggy chest and was puzzled to see that one of its scrawny, patchy-furred arms was linked through that of a powerful silver-backed male, as though the stronger were actually being solicitous of the weaker. The boy was immediately struck by the incongruity of their behavior and troubled by the realization that, among many of his own kind, the weak and the old were not coddled or cared for; they were abandoned. Memories of dying children and his own abandonment surged through him. As they passed, Karana observed that the long, hairless fingers of the old female were laced through those of a much younger member of her gender, who was suckling an infant as she walked on the old creature's other side.

For an instant the eyes of the suckling met those of Karana. Pale eyes. Filled with starlight. As clear as new ice upon which no snow has fallen.

The boy was stunned by their clarity and their undeniable but unexpected beauty. Then terror struck him. Had the thing seen him? Had it picked him out from the shadows? He squeezed his eyes shut, deliberately breaking visual contact with the suckling, knowing that if it recognized him as a living being, it had only to loose its lips from its mother's hideous teat and, through sound and gesture, indicate its presence to the others. Even with Aar ready to leap to his defense, neither he nor the dog would survive long.

But the thing kept on sucking. Its eyes were the wide, vacant, glossy eyes of the newly born, empty of all but starlight. Karana knew it was carried past him in the fold of its mother's hairy arm when he heard the soft whispering of her footsteps in the grass directly ahead of him.

Then, after a while, all was quiet except the hammering of his heart. Cringing with fear, he opened his eyes. With infinite caution he peered over the top of the grasses to see that the last of the beasts had gone by him, trailing southward.

For a long while, exhausted by fear, the boy and dog remained motionless and silent.

Until Torka came up from behind them. And although Aar's tail began to thump, Karana nearly leaped out of his skin in terror.

"I tell you, Karana, I have seen nothing." Once again, as when he had addressed the boy within the encampment, Torka's voice was stern with admonition. He stood frowning down at him in the darkness. "This country is crossed and recrossed by the fresh tracks of many beasts. Since Torka disregarded the advice of others and came out from the encampment in search of you and Brother Dog, this man has found it difficult to pick up the trail of one small boy amid the spoor of so many animals."

"But they were there! An entire pack of them! They came from the north and walked to the south, into mammoth country at the base of the distant hills. And they trod so lightly, it seems now to this boy that they deliberately laid no trail by which they might be followed. They—"

"Karana has seen only the flesh of his fear. Karana's arrogance and overconfidence have led him to see things that are not there. Torka says that this is good. Karana *should* be afraid. This man did not know whether he would find you alive or dead! Since Karana has cared nothing for the fear that his action has brought to others, it is time that he learns to fear for himself. Perhaps he understands why it is not good to challenge one's elders and then to run off alone, where no man can stand with him against the predators concealed within the night."

Karana was on his feet, facing the man, shaking his head in angry defense of his claim. "They were *not* concealed! I *saw* them. They were as close to me as you are now. I *saw* the wanawut! They were ugly and hairy and—"

The boy suddenly found himself seated again as Torka shoved him so hard that he knocked him down. A startled Aar jumped aside, ears back, as Karana, flat on his buttocks, his legs splayed and his mouth agape, stared up in befuddlement at the man he loved more than any other in the world. He could not understand what he had done to make Torka angry enough to strike him.

Torka shook his head at the boy's obvious confusion. "Can Karana have forgotten that among Torka's people it is forbidden to speak the name of a thing without respect? To do so is to dishonor the life spirit of that thing. And life spirits have wills of their own, be they the spirits of men or beasts, of stones, clouds, the smallest biting fly, or of Mother Below or Father Above. A dishonored spirit can become a crooked spirit—half flesh, half phantom—and who knows what such a spirit will do if it decides to punish the one who has shamed it? Torka says it is bad enough to be alone on the tundra with a foolish boy who has put himself at risk because he cannot control his temper, but it is worse to be alone with a boy who cannot control his tongue. Much worse. And much more dangerous to both of us!"

Karana closed his mouth. He looked up repentantly, knowing that Torka was right. The boy had forgotten the age-old taboo; it was a proscription among Torka's people, not among his own. It was easy to forget that they had not always lived together as father and son, that they were not of the same band.

"This boy meant no offense to Torka or to the spirits," he apologized.

The eyes of man and boy met and held. Torka nodded. His lean, handsome features relaxed as he offered a conciliatory hand to the boy. "It was wrong of me to strike you."

"It was wrong of me to run away," Karana admitted, gratefully taking Torka's hand and allowing himself to be pulled to his feet. "But Supnah's camp *is* a bad camp. This boy says that Torka's people should not stay there."

"Torka's people? I am one man, Little Hunter. One man, with a woman and a newborn daughter to care for. Where should Torka lead his 'people'? Into the unknown, where they would be alone and vulnerable again?"

"Torka has Karana. And Aar. He would not be alone."

"But Supnah is your father. His people are your people. Would you truly wish to be parted from them again?"

The question altered the boy's mood. Sullen hostility darkened his expression and thickened into bitterness. "Torka has forced Karana to dwell in the hut of Supnah. This Karana has done—to please Torka, not because Supnah has asked it. But Supnah and his people fed Karana's spirit to the wind, and this boy will not give it back to them. What they threw away, Torka has made his own. With his own mouth, Torka has called Karana *son*. And so now Karana says that he has no father but Torka. We are of one band. *Forever*."

The words touched Torka, and he grasped the boy's shoulder, wanting him to know it. "And so it is that for the good of Karana, my son, and of Lonit, my woman, and of little Summer Moon, my newborn daughter, that Torka says that we must *all* be of Supnah's band now—forever, if he will allow it—because alone upon the tundra we are prey to our darkest and ugliest fears, and even the strongest man soon grows weak when he is beset by dread. Within the protection of a band, even the weakest man may dare to be brave and strong."

Karana shook his head. "Supnah's band is a *bad* band. And Navahk has *always* been a bad man. And the wana— I mean, the beasts that I saw in the night *were* there. This boy saw them."

"As Navahk has seen them."

"Navahk is a liar. He has seen nothing."

Torka's dark brows came together across the high, narrow bridge of his nose. Far to the east the sun was rising beyond distant, glacier-smothered ranges. The faintest banding of light had appeared atop the mountains and was spilling over the ridges like mist, thinning the darkness just enough so that he could make out the intensely drawn face of the boy. Not for the first time, he was aware of Karana's marked resemblance to the magic man, but his awareness vanished as he saw how haggard the boy looked.

"Come," he said gently. "We must go back now. Lonit worries about you. When I left, little Mahnie, the daughter of Grek, was sitting with Pet, your sister, and both were crying from fear that you would be eaten by wolves."

"Pet is not this boy's sister! And Supnah's camp *is* a bad camp."

"When you are a man, you will understand that we sometimes must do what we do not wish to do—for others, not for ourselves." He let the words settle quietly, watching as the boy's face worked against them. Karana troubled him in many ways. He was headstrong, defiant, and often acted without thinking. But he always told the truth as he saw it. And sometimes in his dreams or with that strange sense that others did not possess, he *did* see things that others failed to see. Sight . . . sound . . . taste . . . touch . . . scent . . . these tools Torka shared with the boy. But not the sixth sense, that other, undependable, not-always-trustworthy power of knowing that was driving Karana to disobedience now.

Torka's hand patted his shoulder encouragingly. "No band is without dissension among its members from time to time, Little Hunter. And fear takes many shapes in the dark. Look now to the east, into the face of the rising sun, and tell this man that what walks there could not have passed you in the night."

Karana glowered. He saw tall, shaggy, reddish-brown humps moving on the horizon, tusks extended like branchless, horizontal trees. "Karana knows a mammoth when he sees one," he retorted, his feelings hurt by Torka's unwillingness to believe him. "They are *not* what I saw!"

"Then when you return to the encampment, you must tell the People that you have shared Navahk's vision. And that what he has seen has been a good thing for his people—a warning for them to be wary of the spirits that walk hungry in the night."

"Men must always be wary of the night. And this boy will *never* speak to Navahk."

"Hard words for a boy to utter. Karana should know that when he ran off from the encampment, Navahk asked the People if what was given to the spirits should be allowed to come back to live as flesh in the world of men again."

"Karana is not afraid of Navahk!"

"Karana had better be—for Torka's and Lonit's sake, if not for his own! This man has named you son! If you are put out of Supnah's band, I will not be able to watch you walk the wind alone. I will have to walk with you. Lonit will take our baby and insist upon walking with me. And soon she and I and our daughter and even you, Karana, will die upon the tundra, prey to lions or bears or wolves or simply to our own mistakes—all beasts every bit as terrible as the nightmare shapes of the wanawut that you claim to have seen."

Sobered, Karana frowned. "We tried to live among another band before and were forced to walk away alone. Has Torka forgotten how it was? How Karana said that we must go from the mountain cave where we lived with the people of Galeena? How Karana said that the mountain was a bad place and that Galeena's band was a bad band? Torka would not listen. But it *was* as Karana warned. And so at last we fled when they tried to kill us, and, as in Karana's dreams, the side of the mountain fell to bury the cave forever, and within it Galeena and all his people died. But we have survived—alone."

"Barely, and always at the risk of death."

"Then *do* as Supnah says. *Become* a magic man! Let Navahk be the one to walk the wind."

"No, Karana. Torka will not assure his place within the band at the cost of another man's life. What I have said to Supnah, I say to you: Torka is a hunter. No more."

Karana clamped his mouth tight against frustration. Torka was talking to him in the kind, condescending tone that adults often took with recalcitrant children.

Aar nuzzled his hand, to remind him that it was time to break the long hunger of the previous night. And from the west Supnah was trotting toward them with his spear raised in greeting and his voice crying out the boy's name with joy and relief.

Beyond the eastern ranges the sun was rising quickly now. Its face was still hidden, but its light had absorbed the stars and washed away the darkness. The night seemed long ago, its terrors muted by fatigue and distance. Karana sighed.

If he had been wrong to run away, perhaps his sight had been equally in error? Perhaps he *had* grown confused in the darkness and, looking east instead of south, had only seen mammoths after all?

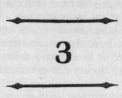

3

The tattooed woman smiled. She was as big and as brash as a man, but it was impossible to see her clearly, even though the sun was well up and the tundral world was awash in the sweet, yellow light of the spring morning. Like the other women of the band, she was armored against biting flies, in warm-weather leggings and a lightweight tunic of caribou skins that covered most of her body; but unlike the other women, every visible inch of her skin was blackened by tattoos.

Eyelids, lips, nostrils, earlobes. Even her filed teeth, fingernails, and the palms of her hands were covered with a mazework of dots and slashes that formed a blur of intricate, circular designs—unwanted gifts inflicted upon her by the tattoo-loving Ghost Band, to which she had been enslaved since girlhood. Then Torka, with the aid of Supnah and his hunters, had rescued her.

Now she knelt outside Torka's shelter, happily helping his woman, Lonit, to pound fat into oil that would be used to saturate the bundles of moss that lay at their sides. These would later serve as wicks for tallow lamps of hollowed stone and, in the days of the long dark, would light the pit hut of Torka during hours of endless night. The tattooed woman enjoyed both the work and the prospect of light in the winter dark, so she smiled; but because her teeth were as black as her face, her smile went unseen as she spoke with emphatic optimism.

"Aliga says that Torka and Supnah will soon return with the boy. Lonit will see. The spirits seem to be with Karana. His talk to the magic man was bad talk, but he *is* the headman's son, and Supnah is so glad to have him back, no harm will come to him because of his runaway feet and tongue."

"It is not Supnah whom Karana should fear. It is Navahk."

Lonit's long, graceful hands did not slow as she spoke. "This woman does not like the way the magic man looks at the boy . . . or the way that he looks at me . . . or the unspoken words that hide behind the things he says to Torka." Her beautiful, delicately formed features were grimly set as she pounded and scraped at the wedges of fat, using the grinding stone that she held in her fist to crush them within the concave mortar.

Aliga, the tattooed woman, envied Lonit not only for her beauty, which was unmarred by tattoos, but because she had a man to work for and worry over. A man beside whom most other men, including the powerful headman, Supnah, seemed inconsequential.

Torka!

Aliga's heart always beat a little faster when she thought of him. Until she had seen Navahk, the magic man of Supnah's band, she had not thought it possible that a more physically striking man than Torka could exist.

But Navahk existed. *Navahk!* In his fringed clothes of white, with the single winter-white flight feather of an Arctic owl braided into the forelock of his shining, knee-length hair. *Navahk!* With a face as finely made as a stallion's and eyes as black and lustrous as an obsidian dagger. That one, like Torka, could have any woman he wanted. He would never look at Aliga; and yet if he did focus his magic eyes through her tattoos to the substance of the woman beneath them, she would look back boldly and let him see how her heart quickened for him. He would know that he was the only man capable of shadowing Torka in her eyes.

What sort of an ungrateful female was she? Could she ever forget the way Torka had rescued her and the others from the Ghost Band? Or the way he had noticed her shame as all the other captives—younger, less tattooed—had found places beneath the sleeping skins of Supnah's hunters? What the men of the Ghost Band had found beautiful, the men of Supnah's band found amusing at best and repulsive at worst. Although she had a round, pretty face with bright eyes, a small, flat nose, and a pert mouth that revealed a pleasant nature and a propensity for sudden laughter, not one of them had offered to take the tattooed woman to his bed skins. To save her the humiliation of rejection, Torka had welcomed her to stay at his fire until another man spoke for her.

So far, no man had. She was not sorry. The only one she

encouraged with her smile and her looks of longing was the magic man; but she knew that she had little hope of winning so much as a glance from him. And, in truth, she found more than a little pride in the knowledge that the people of Supnah's band assumed that she was Torka's second woman in every way. She knew that Torka would never dishonor her by saying otherwise to his fellow hunters.

With a sigh, she recalled that from the first he made it quite clear to her that he was more than content with only one woman. His love for Lonit was absolute and without bounds. Aliga marveled at their relationship. In the night, when they lay in one another's arms, Torka not only made love to Lonit, he actually talked to her as though she were a male and thus his equal. He shared his thoughts with her as he would share them with a father or brother or trusted hunting companion. Aliga had never seen anything like it. Sometimes she found it unnatural. She told herself that it was this way because they had been long alone together, without other men and women with whom to form friendships. She was not certain if she would want such a relationship with a man; their thoughts were not woman thoughts, and their actions were often befuddling to her. She was more comfortable with other women, working, chatting, gossiping, and laughing together.

Although she was loath to admit it, she knew that her place at Torka's fire was puzzling to them. Sometimes she overheard "What does he see in her?" whispered behind her back. Bitterly, she would think: *He sees nothing! He feels sorry for me!* But she could never explain that to the women of Supnah's band. Pity was alien to them; indeed, she suspected that Torka's compassion, for which she was so grateful, would be viewed as a flaw in an otherwise praiseworthy hunter.

She cast a sidelong glance at Lonit, glad that she and her man were not uncaring like the others. She had become close to Torka's woman. Aliga knew her young friend well enough to be certain that Lonit would never knowingly speak words to bruise the spirit of another. Nevertheless, Lonit was fiercely possessive of Torka. She wanted what was best for Aliga but made no secret that she had no wish to share her man.

"Aliga is the best of women!" she would exclaim to the other females when they worked together within earshot of their men. "Such a hard worker! So quick at her tasks! How fortunate is Lonit to have Aliga sharing the burdens of her days!" And to Aliga she would say, "If Aliga would have a man of her own, she must try harder to make them see through the skin to the merits of the woman beneath!"

Aliga was not offended. Torka's fire circle was becoming crowded: Karana was often there, and Torka had taken the widow of Manaak, his murdered friend, to dwell within his protection. Poor, mind-blighted Iana, raped by the men who had murdered both her husband and her newborn son, had not spoken a word since she had been rescued from the Ghost Band. Torka insisted that Iana's responsibilities as a wet nurse for Summer Moon freed Lonit for other chores. Even now she slept within Torka's hut of bones and fur, with his daughter contentedly suckling at her breast, thus allowing Lonit the freedom to await the return of her man while she worked with Aliga, desperately trying to distract herself from worry.

"He *will* come back to us soon, and with the boy!" insisted the tattooed woman, herself distracted not by the work at hand but by her wandering thoughts.

For the first time in her life Aliga was happy. To share Torka's shelter was to hold the hope that someday, when Lonit was in her time of blood or again great with child, Torka would hold back his sleeping skins and welcome Aliga beneath them. She might never bear him a child, but the thought of pleasuring a man as powerful and handsome as Torka was enough to make her forget her years of sexual abuse at the hands of the Ghost Band.

Kneeling beside Lonit, Aliga's lustful thoughts of Torka caused her to blush with guilt. What if the younger woman could read her mind? The boy, Karana, sometimes did. She would find him watching her, and it was as though his mind had melded with her own. Startled, she would demand that he look away.

But someone else was watching her now. And, suddenly, as she met his glance, her thoughts flew from Torka.

Navahk *was* looking at her! He stood before the painted hide door flap of a pit hut covered in the white skins of winter-killed animals. A hut before which his ceremonial staff stood, butt end piercing the tundra, with its antelope skull gleaming and taloned, feathered skin streamers streaming gently in the wind. A hut he shared with no woman.

Aliga nearly swooned with disbelieving delight as his eyes

met hers, narrowing with what appeared to be almost sleepy speculation as he smiled. Yes! At the tattooed woman!

It was all she could do to remain seated as he began to walk slowly across the encampment toward her. As he passed the dogs that lay in the sun beside Lonit's and Aliga's drying frames, Sister Dog growled at him and the pups whimpered. Navahk proceeded as though the animals were not there. Aliga gave Lonit a sharp, meaningful elbow jab to the ribs and practically sang a joyous whisper out the side of her mouth as she held her head high, in the way of a woman accepting a man, and looked directly at her suitor. "Look! When Torka returns, he will have one less woman at his fire! Navahk comes! He comes for *me*!"

But when he reached her, acknowledging her presence with a gracious nod, his smile was more demeaning to her than death, for his eyes swept over her and rested upon the downturned head of Lonit.

"There are too many women at Torka's fire. Navahk has no woman. Lonit will come with me."

It had not been a question; it had been a command. It struck Lonit like a stone.

She heard Aliga stifle a sob. She looked up, not knowing whether to be flattered or angry. "My man is not here. Navahk has no right to ask for me."

His smile was barely perceptible. "A man may ask. A woman may accept or refuse. Only the spirits know if Torka will return."

Lonit allowed her anger to surface. "Do not speak so! Would you bring the words to life?"

His smile grew. It rearranged his features, softened them, warmed them, made them not only more perfect but infinitely likable and openly seductive; yet somehow the smile did not reach his eyes. They remained cold, raptorial, as hard and oily as the stone pestle in Lonit's hand. "With Torka here—or with him gone—Navahk says that it would be good for Torka's woman at the fire of the magic man."

"Lonit has a man! With Torka, she needs no other."

His smile did not waver. He extended a hand to her. "Come."

She stared up at him, her mind swimming in confusion, her body inexplicably responding to him, betraying Torka. From behind her Wallah, the woman of Grek, came from her own pit hut to see the cause of the young woman's exclamations. Her wide-eyed young daughter, Mahnie, peeked at Lonit from behind her mother's hare-trimmed skirt while the other women of the band followed from their own dwelling, including Naiapi, the woman of Supnah, and midnight-haired little Pet.

With his hand still extended down toward Lonit, Navahk's voice was as soft and low as a summer wind hissing through the ripe grasses of the tundral plain. "Come . . . Navahk will make magic for Torka's return—a magic he cannot make alone."

Lonit dared not move. Her hand was curled so tightly about the pestle that her aching fingers were growing numb with the resulting stress.

"Lonit *must* go!" insisted Wallah, appalled by the obvious hesitation of the younger woman. Did she not care for her man? Did she not understand that when it came to the making of magic, a magic man might ask anything and not be refused lest the spirits be offended and turn against the band?

The face of Naiapi, Supnah's woman, was unreadable. Her chin was up, and her long, generous lips were pressed so tightly against her teeth that they were devoid of color. Her eyes were fixed upon Navahk. They were unwavering and demanding eyes. "Has Navahk seen a danger, then, that Torka and Supnah will not return?"

He did not look at Naiapi. "Navahk always sees danger. That is why he is a magic man," he replied obliquely, his hand still extended to Lonit, his eyes holding hers, his smile unchanged and beckoning. "Come. We will make magic together. It will be a good thing."

Naiapi moved forward. "Navahk has no need of Lonit! She is Torka's! I am the *headman's* woman! Naiapi will make magic with Navahk! He needs no one else!" The eagerness in her words betrayed emotions that she had not intended to reveal. The color bled back into her lips, and she looked away from the watching eyes of the women of her band. They were no longer alone; drawn by the raised voices of their women, Supnah's hunters had gathered around. Flustered, Naiapi stared down at her booted feet until she became aware of Pet, her little daughter, looking up at her, perplexed. She made a rude noise at the child, then defiantly met the gazes of those who were staring at her. Her voice was unnaturally high, with an odd, brittle edge that cracked as she proclaimed: "For Supnah! For the *headman's* safe return to his people does Naiapi offer herself to Navahk! Come! Now, to assure the safe return of her man, will Naiapi and Navahk go to his hut, where we will make magic together!"

Navahk laughed. It was the merest exhalation of sound, but it was so ripe with derision that all who heard it were stunned—but none more than Naiapi. "Navahk and Naiapi will never make magic together."

A young girl ventured forward. "This girl will make magic with the magic man for *Karana*. Has everyone forgotten Karana?" The question was a peep such as hatchlings make, except that there was fear in it as Mahnie, barely eight years old, looked imploringly at Navahk.

The magic man's head pivoted and his eyes focused on the little one. He saw that she was shivering, and his smile grew liquid with pleasure. "This man could never forget Karana, little one."

"Nor does Karana need his magic!"

Everyone whirled at the sound of the boy's voice. Supnah was with him, and Torka, and the wild dog Aar, all returned safely from out of the night.

And as Lonit dropped the pestle, sprang to her feet, and leaped to stand joyfully beside her man, Navahk's smile disappeared.

Torka could not remember when last he was as angry as he was now. "What is this 'magic' that allows Navahk to walk into my fire circle and attempt to take any woman from me when I am not here to face his arrogance!"

The magic man raised his head with imperious disdain. He folded his arms across his chest and smiled. "Magic is not for hunters to understand. It is a thing of smokes and dreams."

"*Navahk's* smokes, made to cloud *other* men's dreams!" snapped Karana.

Torka looked at Supnah now. "Among Torka's people, custom demands that if a man wants another man's woman, he must first ask her man—not swoop behind his back like a vulture hoping to steal what is not his!"

Torka's statement had been so molten with anger that all who heard it stepped back lest they be burned when his temper burst into flame.

Supnah was taken aback by the intensity of Torka's feelings. He shrugged his shoulders apologetically and spoke in the tone of a born conciliator. "Among Supnah's people, if a

man wants another man's woman and the woman wants him
also, the woman may go with him . . . if her own man is not
man enough to keep her. This is the way of Supnah's people.
From time beyond beginning."

The headman's words stung Torka but did not drain the
anger from his heart. "It is a bad way," he said.

Beside him, Lonit was trembling. Her tall, slender body
pressed against him, and he could feel the opulent curve of
her hip and the softness of her shoulder. Her wide eyes, as
deep a brown and as thickly lashed as the eyes of a frightened
steppe antelope, looked up at him. "Torka *is* man enough!"
she said loudly for all to hear. "This woman looks at no
other!"

The magic man, apparently unperturbed, was smiling again.
His arms unfolded like the wings of a graceful white bird, and
his hands swept outward in a gesture of conciliation. "Torka's
people are *dead*. Their ways and customs died with them.
Torka is of this band now. He will accept the ways and
customs of Supnah's people, or he may walk away into the
wind. The choice is his. As for this man, Navahk only sought
to make the magic that would bring Torka safely back to camp
with the others. To make this magic, it was necessary to seek
the assistance of Torka's woman. Ask Naiapi if this is not so.
She and little Mahnie, Grek's girl, were both willing to speak
to the spirits through Navahk's magic smokes on behalf of
Karana and Supnah. Would Torka not have permitted his
woman to do the same for him?"

Torka glared hatefully at the man. He had seen the way
Navahk had been looking at Lonit and had not misread the
sexual provocation that underlay his seemingly innocent invitation. And he had clearly heard him refuse Naiapi's almost
panting offer of assistance.

"It *is* so," Naiapi quickly affirmed. Her face was unnaturally pale as she looked at Supnah, hoping that he would
believe her lie. He had been several paces behind Torka and
Karana when the gathering had parted to allow them through.
Perhaps he had not seen the wanting in her eyes or heard it
in her voice.

But the headman was not looking at his woman. He was
observing his brother with stern-eyed speculation. A guileless
and pragmatic man, Supnah usually heard what others wanted
him to hear, accepting as truth that which offered the least
resistance to argument. But Supnah *had* seen the look of

wanting in his woman's eyes, and he was emotionally torn by the realization that last night, for the second time, Navahk had been in a position of control over the life of Karana, and he had chosen once again to negate that life.

After Karana had stalked away from the gathering, Navahk had portended a thousand dangers to all who would walk after Karana and into the "night of the wanawut." He had the hunters cowering and the women moaning in fear for them until, in frustration, Torka and Supnah had said that two men were all that was needed to find one small boy. Navahk had shaken his staff at them, warning them to beware lest they offend the spirits, and had said that for the good of the band they must not put themselves at risk for one useless, disobedient child. But they had gone despite his warnings, leaving him to chant and whirl in foul smokes of his own devising.

There had been a moment, as he had watched his brother perform before the feast fire, when memories of their boyhood had risen within him, and he had been ready to forgive Navahk everything. But then he had seen Naiapi looking at his brother across the flames in a way that no man ever wants to see his woman look at another. Resentment and jealousy congealed into pure loathing, inspiring Supnah to suggest that Torka, a stranger, might better serve as magic man in Navahk's place. His public humiliation of Navahk had cleared the way for Karana's misbehavior.

The recollection made Supnah feel ashamed. Naiapi *had* looked at Navahk, but then *all* of the women looked at him; his beauty was that rare, that perfect. Supnah had to admit that he had never seen Navahk look back. *Never.* Navahk had not openly taken a woman to his bed skins since he was barely more than a boy and had lived with a wandering magic woman.

Supnah looked at Navahk now, hoping to see that young boy somewhere in the lean, magnificently imperious, hawklike face but failing. In his weariness, with everyone making him the focus of their attention, he himself felt like a boy trapped within the skin of a man. As often happened, he longed to be free of a man's responsibility, to be a youth again, with elders to tell him what to do and when to do it . . . as Navahk had so often done.

Guilt rose in him again. Since Torka had come to the encampment with Karana, Supnah's behavior toward Navahk had been hostile and belligerent. He had actually enjoyed making his brother suffer and ground the fact of Karana's homecoming into Navahk's pride at every opportunity.

By now Supnah had no doubts that Navahk was capable of seeing clearly into the spirit world. When he and Torka had separated in their search for Karana, Navahk's warnings had been proved right—there *had* been a thousand dangers. Supnah had seen lion and wolf sign and strange spoor that he could not identify. Just before joining Torka, he had seen shadows moving upon the horizon—shadows that had so defied his understanding that they made him feel old and weak with fear. He had seen the wanawut.

How long would it be before Navahk's words were once again fulfilled? *No man may see the wanawut . . . no man may find its spoor or follow its tracks lest it leap upon him from the world of spirits to feed upon him.*

Was he marked for death by the wanawut? Or by his own brother?

No! He would tolerate no further suspicions! Navahk was of his band! Of his flesh! When he spoke, he spoke with the wisdom and the power of the spirits, and although Supnah would never again follow him blindly, neither would he impugn his authority.

In the tone of one who has been severely wronged, the magic man was speaking earnestly to the headman. Startled, Supnah realized that he had not heard a word. Again he felt old and weary and wished that he were a boy.

". . . must tell Torka that if he is to dwell among Supnah's people, he must accept Supnah's ways. The things that Torka says are bad, crooked things that enter the thoughts of Supnah's people to make them question the ways that have been their ways since time beyond beginning."

The magic man's words fell into the receptive soil of his brother's mind. Supnah nodded. The weariness was growing in him. He thought of his bed skins. "Torka has heard the words of Navahk?"

"Torka has heard," said the hunter.

"Then Torka will obey. Or he will walk from this band as he came into it—alone."

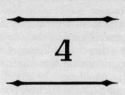

4

Alone.

Torka's pit hut was filled with sleeping women and a suckling child, yet he was alone, isolated amid the dreaming females, tormented by his thoughts, unable to sleep, and suffocating in the all-confining darkness in which he lay . . . alone.

It was late. Darkness would fill the sky for hours before it yielded to dawn. Torka lay on his back, naked beneath the bed skins that he shared with Lonit. She was warm against him, curled close, her breathing deep and even, perfectly synchronized with his, as though one being lay beneath the skins, not two.

He lay still, listening to the cool, mild wind move through the encampment. He could hear it prowling around the exterior of his little conical hut, slap-slapping gently as it searched with invisible feelers for gaps in the layered bison skins that covered the shelter's arching framework of caribou antlers and mammoth ribs. The wind might find breaches in the coverings of other huts within the encampment, but Torka knew that it would find no entrance here because Lonit had been responsible for the skins that formed the walls of his shelter. With the help of Aliga, Lonit had sewn seams and patched where there was need. Then, while Iana sat crooning to the baby as she nursed it, Lonit and Aliga had lashed the dark, thickly pelaged skins down with strong thongs laced crosswise and secured them to fire-hardened stakes of bone that he had helped them to drive deep into the permafrost.

Them!

How had he come to have so many women? Mad Iana. Tattooed Aliga. Lonit of the antelope eyes. And his tiny daughter, as precious to him as her mother, and both of them as warm and beautiful as the golden summer moon for which the child had been named.

Nevertheless, the presence of the women and child was strangling to him now. He drew in a breath, found no air within it, gasped soundlessly, and rose, desperate to be outside, beneath the night, within the wind, and alone.

A man could think when he was alone. A man could *not* think when he was surrounded by females.

Lonit sighed in her sleep, sensed his absence, and reached for him, whispering his name.

Carefully, not wishing to wake her, he bent and tenderly drew the bed skins back over her smooth, tawny form, pausing just long enough to look upon the relaxed grace and suppleness of her body. The sight of her soothed him a little as, even in the darkness, the beauty of her profile against the pale, spotted lynx fur of their pillows illuminated his heart.

Taking his clothes from where they lay in a jumble next to his moss- and down-lined sleeping pad beside Lonit's meticulously folded garments, he straightened as much as the height of the pit hut would allow and, his mind filled with images of his first woman, began to dress.

It never failed to amaze him that once, long ago, his people had considered Lonit ugly—a too tall, coltish girl who should have been exposed at birth. Females were considered beautiful only if they were dull eyed, short limbed, broad hipped, capable of working endlessly, bearing children with minimal complaint, walking long miles under heavy packs, and eating only as much as their men allowed them . . . and never of prime portions.

Torka knew that Lonit's father had allowed her to live only out of pity for her mother; the woman had never before been able to bring a child to full term. Kiuk had spent the rest of his days and nights regretting his weakness and later had done all he could to abuse and degrade the living proof of his unmanly generosity to a lowly female. After the death of Lonit's mother, Kiuk's other women found endless uses for her as a drudge, and the child became Kiuk's vessel for the outpouring of his lust. It was his right to mount the child in the night and to abuse her verbally and physically by day. Old Umak, Torka's grandfather, had observed that by so doing, Kiuk degraded not the girl but himself and the band.

The other members of the band had found amusement in his brutal degradation of the unusual-looking little girl and had mocked Torka when, pitying Lonit but admiring the way she clung to life regardless of its adversity, he occasionally went out of his way to encourage her. Umak had advised Torka to remain aloof from the child. As magic man for the People, Umak had already spoken to the spirits on her behalf; but she was only a female, after all, and would live or die according to the whim of her father. This was the way of the People. From time beyond beginning.

As he pulled on his buckskin boot liners, Torka's mouth worked bitterly at the memory of that statement. How many times had he been confronted with those now-despised words? *This is the way it has been . . . always has been . . . from time beyond beginning.*

He jammed his feet into his boots, and as he began to lace them, memories swam in the darkness. One night Thunder Speaker, the great mammoth that his people called the Destroyer, came to the band's encampment to fulfill its name in death. Its tusks had hurled them high, and as its trumpeting, man-hating shrieks had cracked the sky, it had ground their lives into the tundra until it was not possible to tell where earth ended and the flesh of Man began.

In the end only Torka, Umak, and Lonit had survived.

And it had seemed as though it were time beyond beginning. They were First Man and First Woman, with a spirit master who was only a frail old man. Together they had fled across a savage, unknown land, without the protection of a band, learning new ways, forgetting the past except for that which served the present. And so, against all odds, they had survived.

In time Torka discovered the truth about Lonit, when he had looked at her with eyes free of the blinding, insular conventions of others. He had seen that she was beautiful.

As he saw her now.

As Navahk had seen her. And had dared to try to win her away from Torka to his own fire circle!

In a sudden, so injudicious but righteously seething rush, the anger that had caused him to challenge the magic man pulsed behind his eyes. It was a fire-heated bone lodged at the back of his throat. Again he could not breathe. Again the darkness was suffocating him. If they stayed in this camp, in time Navahk would find a way to have his woman. And nothing Torka or Lonit could say or do would stop him.

On the piled furs that she shared with Iana and the baby, Aliga made smacking little sucking sounds in her sleep as, with a sigh of contentment, she hefted herself onto her side.

The wave of anger crested within Torka as he focused on the tattooed woman and the sleeping form of mad Iana. Why had he accepted the responsibility for their lives? Did he honestly believe that the responsibility was only temporary? No man would ever invite Aliga or Iana to leave Torka's fire. They would be upon his back like a sodden pack filled with boulders forever! If starving times came to this band again, Navahk would send them both to walk the wind, and if Torka tried to stop him, Supnah would send Torka with them . . . and Navahk would have Lonit and would never let her go. *Never!* Torka had seen this in his eyes.

With two long steps he crossed the dark confines of the hut, pulled back the door skin, and stepped out into the night.

To the south, far beyond the pit hut, a lion roared from out of the tangled hills. The sound rolled across the tundral world and echoed through a thousand unseen glacial canyons. Wolves answered—and something else, something deeper than a wolf cry and less scraping then the scream of the lion. Something as full of latent power and threat as the wind whistling across the land from out of the north. Something familiar somehow, something almost human.

Wah nah wah . . . wah nah wut . . . wah nahhh . . .

The wanawut! He stiffened, listening, unable to believe what he heard. Words? Had he heard *words*?

The sound rose and fell, not one sound but many, calling, answering.

Wah nah wah . . . wah nah wut . . .

In his boyhood he had heard these strange howlings and mewings in the night. And later, crossing the tundra close to the mountains, he had heard them moaning and roaring in the long, burnished twilight of autumn or whispering on the winds that blew down from the heights in the depth of the winter dark.

Men did not go into the mountains, which were the realm of wind spirits. Men hunted the open tundra, beneath the open sky. And Torka, who had stood against wolves, wild dogs, lions, bears, and the great mammoth Thunder Speaker, wondered why he should fear phantoms that existed unseen within the misted mountains.

Yet now, as the voices of the wind spirits began to fade, he feared them, as all men instinctively fear the unknown. He stood listening until the voices melded into the dark and wind-combed night.

A mammoth trumpeted somewhere to the east. Torka looked toward the sound. The Mountains That Walk bulked against the horizon. Two miles high, they glistened blue on either side of broad grasslands that stretched into the infinity of the forbidden country that Supnah's people called the Corridor of Storms.

Navahk had said that the wanawut lived there. Navahk lied.

The wanawut was in the southern hills, close to this encampment. Karana *had* seen it, and Torka had heard its song. He stood very still, feeling the night, drinking in its sounds and scents. His eyes strayed over the sleeping encampment, past the smoldering bones of fire circles, to linger on the charred rubble of the feast fire where, not for the first time, Torka had observed the virulent antagonism that lay between Navahk and Supnah. That hatred would erupt someday, and one or both of the brothers, and perhaps their entire band, would be destroyed.

In the days that followed, Supnah and his people broke camp and moved south in search of new hunting grounds. If any men or women saw sign of the wanawut, they remembered Navahk's warning and spoke no assent to their sighting lest wind spirits leap from the shadows to take their lives.

At night, although weary from the day's trek, Torka slept fitfully, his question demanding a decision from him. *Is it wise for Torka to stay with Supnah's band?* It was not the sort of decision that a man made in a night, or a day, or a week of days. It was made and unmade a dozen times.

He could not say that he did not enjoy their daily treks. It was good to walk across the land in the company of men, with Lonit at his side. She held little Summer Moon close to her breast, while a distraught Iana often plucked at the wrappings of the baby's sling to make certain that the child was safe in her mother's arms. Aliga trudged behind, the dogs at her side. She would kick out at them if they came too close. The big blue-eyed male, Aar, walked with Karana, tongue lolling, tail up and curled forward over his rump as he proudly carried side packs loaded with the boy's belongings. Sister Dog, Aar's mate, and her pack of pups had taken a liking to Aliga, and nothing that she did, short of tethering them and leaving them behind, could keep them from romping at her heels and trying to grab at the loose ends of her boot ties.

It was an amusing sight. After the tension of the camp that they had put behind them, the sight of the tattooed woman kicking and cursing at the mischievous pups for mile after mile lightened Torka's mood more than a little. Although Aliga never stopped complaining about the dogs and openly feared the older pair, she had an obvious soft spot for the pups. Her kicks were as ineffective as her curses.

The people of the band began to point and laugh with merriment at her predicament. Supnah was openly amused. And for the first time in longer than he could remember, Torka laughed with unrestrained delight when the most tenacious of the pups, a blue-eyed, black-masked replica of Aar, sunk its molars into a boot lace and, pulling hard, ran a neat circle around Aliga's ankles, effectively hobbling her. Seeing the big, bold woman go to her knees amid a swarm of licking, yapping puppies—one still tugging on her boot lace, his bottom up, tail curled, head down, growling as ferociously as a bear in rut—brought everyone to pause with laughter.

Then the magic man turned to see the cause of his people's unbidden happiness.

"It is not natural for people to walk with dogs. Look. See how Torka's woman slows our trek. It is not a good thing! Perhaps, in this night's camp, we will eat the meat of these dogs. The little ones will be tender."

They did not eat the dogs. Although Navahk would have liked to do so, Supnah acquiesced to Karana, who swore that the dogs were his brothers. No one seemed to know what to make of such a ridiculous assumption, but the dogs *were* like no others that they had ever seen: The big male carried a pack like a man, and the female cared for her pups as diligently as any woman.

It was early evening. The women had formed what Torka had come to think of as a chatter circle. He heard the sound of Lonit's laughter as she sat with the other women, enjoying her baby and the company of other females. He watched her with troubled eyes and thought: *If I take her from this camp, she will be alone with only mad Iana and a tattooed woman for company. Here the number of women makes the workload light for all.*

His eyes strayed to Hetchem, an extremely pregnant female who, judging by the gray strands in her hair and the many lines about her eyes, was very old. She claimed to remember seeing the sun rise to eat the winter dark over thirty times, and her teeth were showing signs of wear. Torka could not help but notice how Lonit and Aliga and the other females of the band doted upon the older woman. In the morning they brought special boot pads to soften her step on the long trek of the day. In the evening they brought poultices for her swollen ankles and charms to string about her enormous belly. They would break stride with their men to walk beside her during the day, offering to share her load, entertaining her with hours of idle female chatter.

Torka recalled the long, dangerous days that he had shared with Lonit, Karana, and his grandfather upon the distant mountain and the open tundra. *It was not good for Lonit to be alone with only one hunter, a boy, and an old man. She must have been lonely. She must have been frightened when she began to shed a woman's blood. Or thought about giving birth to the baby. Torka cannot ask her to bear such fear alone again! It is good for a woman to live in a camp with others of her kind.*

It was early evening. A temporary camp had been set up for the night—a careless jumble of packs and lean-tos, of fire circles over which the last meal of the day had already been prepared and eaten. The men gathered to work their weapons and talk of the next day's journey. In the thin, remaining light of the long Arctic dusk, while an unnaturally sallow-looking, exhausted Hetchem lounged on her sleeping skins, the females kept her company while working happily at their various sewing tasks, talking of those things that were a mystery to their men, until Navahk walked into their circle.

Nearby, Torka watched from where he sat cross-legged before his lean-to, instructing Karana in the best way to reknap a damaged spearhead. Within the chatter circle Navahk paused before Hetchem. He waved his staff above her. He spoke words that Torka could not understand. After a moment Torka realized that they were not words, they were some sort of chanting no man or woman could understand. They were for the spirits. The women were impressed.

Karana was not. He made a low harrumph of deprecation. Torka elbow-jabbed him to silence. Navahk was smiling now, inquiring with utmost solicitude into the state of Hetchem's health. She beamed at him out of a clammy face, assuring him that all seemed well with the spirit within her. The magic man nodded. He told her that he had made good smokes for the baby spirit.

"Hrmmph!" This time Karana's exhalation was a little louder, and Torka's following elbow jab a little harder. The boy looked up at him, frowning. "What good will the burning of green sticks soaked in rancid fat do for Hetchem's baby? It is Hetchem who is sick! Look at her skin. And her eyes. The whites are as yellow as egg yolks. Umak told this boy that when eyes look like that, it is a *very* bad thing. Hetchem should be drinking much bearberry juice. This boy told her that, but she would not listen. As long as Navahk makes his smokes, his magic is enough for her. She will be sorry."

The boy's words had been audible only to Torka, but Torka was not listening. Navahk was smiling at the other women. They were smiling back at him, even Lonit. It was impossible for a woman not to smile back at Navahk; he was a cool, magnificent winter moon shining down upon them out of the dying warmth of the springtime sun—and he knew it. He deliberately held the eyes of Lonit and offered an open, if unspoken, sexual invitation with his smile until Naiapi glared resentfully at Lonit and the other females tittered. Flustered, her face afire, Lonit stared into her lap.

Navahk turned to face Torka. He smiled at him, but it was not the same smile that he had bestowed upon the women. It was a malignant leer of contempt and daring. He raised his staff and held it out toward Torka. The horned skull of the antelope atop his staff stared sightlessly, grinning as though it were somehow an extension of the man who held it. Torka shook with revulsion, jealousy, and then anger as Navahk took something from his medicine bag and dropped it into the pool of shadows that lay in Lonit's lap.

Startled, she lifted a thong of highly polished, perfectly matched white stone beads. While the other women exhaled in envy, she looked up at the magic man, not certain what he intended her to do with them.

"They are a gift!" he exclaimed. "From Navahk! To Torka's woman!"

Her blush deepened. She looked to Torka, saw the anger

on his face, and quickly turned back toward the magic man. She did not look at him as she handed the beads up to him, stammering, "Torka's woman can accept gifts from no other man."

His smiled deepened. "I am Navahk. I am Magic Man. You *will* accept gifts from me!" He turned then, allowing no further dispute from her as he strode across the encampment to stand alone, arms raised to the setting sun, head thrown back in communion with the spirits.

If Torka's spearhead had been attached to its shaft at that moment, Navahk might have entered the spirit world permanently. As it was, Torka was shaking as his eyes moved back to where Lonit knelt, holding Navahk's gift as though it were a living thing capable of stinging her from each of a dozen polished round heads.

"*This* woman will wear it if Lonit finds it so repugnant!" said Naiapi, greedily reaching to snatch the necklace from Lonit's hands. "Naiapi would not insult the magic man of her people by refusing to accept a gift from one who—"

"Take it!" agreed Torka's woman, looking not at Naiapi but at Torka with confusion and apology as she gratefully yielded the unwanted gift to the headman's talkative woman.

But Supnah had risen. He stalked to the women's circle and jerked the beads from Naiapi's hands so abruptly that she cried out in protest.

"What Navahk has given to the woman of Torka, Lonit, not Naiapi, will wear!" He ignored the petulant glare of his woman as he put the necklace roughly around Lonit's neck.

Torka saw his woman tremble as the weight of the stones fell heavily upon her shoulders and over her long, plaited hair. He was so angry that he rose, holding the spearhead in his hand as though it were a dagger.

Supnah was coming toward him. The dogs that lay near his fire circle tensed noticeably. Slowly Aar got to his feet and walked forward to stand, tail tucked, ears back, beside Karana.

The headman distrusted the wild dogs that were always close to Torka's fire; and in particular, he disliked the big male, Aar. He paused and indicated the dog with a sideward nod of his head. "Tell the spirit of the dog to hold."

Karana hesitated.

"Tell him!" commanded Torka, for the boy's sake, not his own. Were it up to him, now that Supnah had twice chosen to encourage Navahk's advances toward Lonit, he would have allowed the dog to leap for the headman's throat. But Supnah was Karana's father, and he had risked his life and the lives of his hunters to help Torka to rescue his woman from the Ghost Band. He owed him something for that; but the headman was stressing that debt nearly beyond its limit.

Karana obeyed, frowning up at Supnah as the headman extended a hand to him.

"Torka is not the only man who knows how to rework a damaged spearhead. Come! Karana spends too much time at Torka's fire."

Things went badly after that.

They continued southward toward the River of Caribou Spring Crossing, traversing a barren land of broken gullies and long, windy hills. There was little sign of game, and when at last they reached their destination and made camp, it was under leaden skies that promised rain, and all signs told them that the caribou had crossed the river many days before. In the ever-shortening night, the people murmured with frustration, and Supnah assured them that it was the way of the caribou to pass in a segmented line: first cows and calves, then bulls. Days of intermittent rain made the herd signs difficult to read. Perhaps the bulls had not yet passed this way?

"This man will make the songs that will call the caribou to the river and to the spears of the hungry people . . . *if* the spirits of the caribou are close enough to hear." Navahk looked meaningfully at Torka, reproaching him before the entire band. "Did I not say that it was a bad thing when Torka's dogs and women slowed the trek? Because of Torka the caribou have crossed the river. Because of Torka this band may go many days without fresh meat."

Men hunkered by smoky fires of dried sod and bones that they had brought with them from their last camp. They ate traveling rations of dried meat and fish and berries that their women had pounded into cakes of fat. Tomorrow, when the women had rested, they would seine for fresh fish in the river and set snares for ptarmigan. By tomorrow night Navahk's magic might call the caribou; then they would feast upon real meat and drink hot, nourishing blood beneath the cold and threatening sky.

But although he chanted and danced and made magic

smokes that rose from within his lean-to like clouds boiling on a mountaintop when a storm is due, the caribou did not come to cross the river. The only thing that came to the River of Caribou Spring Crossing was rain—steady, cold rain.

"Torka's rain," Navahk called it. "Just as Father Above has driven away the game, he has made rain for Supnah's people because Torka and his women walk with dogs. This is not a good thing!"

All day the rain fell. Navahk said that Father Above remained angry. He told his people that he had heard spirit voices in his magic smokes, telling him that it was not a good day to hunt. Supnah's women murmured with worry, but Supnah's men said nothing. They were not in a mood for hunting. Torka chafed against the watchful, wary way that they looked at him. Navahk smiled at his discomfort.

Angry and frustrated, Torka fought down the desire to challenge the man physically. He put on his waterproof rain cloak of oiled bison intestines instead, took up his spears and his spear hurler, and without so much as a word to his women stalked out from the encampment alone. No one except Lonit tried to stop him. Aliga knew better than to try to change his mind once it was made up. From where he sat like a captive within Supnah's lean-to, Karana made to jog after Torka when he saw the hunter stride purposefully past the last of the lean-tos, but Supnah pulled the boy back by the fringes of his tunic.

In the end only the dog Aar left the encampment with Torka. They returned by nightfall, the dog with the limp body of a fat ground squirrel held proudly in its jaws, the man with the carcass of a steppe antelope slung across his shoulders and several hares and a ptarmigan hanging from his bone carrying stick. With the dog at his side, he stalked to the headman's lean-to, glad to find that the magic man was there talking with him. It was a spacious shelter, well braced against the weather and wind, with Naiapi and Pet sewing at the back and Karana playing a moody game of bone toss in a corner.

Torka interrupted them all without ceremony, dropping the game that he had taken at the entrance to the shelter. It splashed water inside. He was not concerned. They stared up at him, amazed by his rudeness; somehow this did not concern him either. If anything, it pleased him.

"Torka brings fresh meat for Supnah's hungry people. As he has said, he is *not* a magic man. He cannot call the game to die upon the spears of men. But Torka *is* a hunter who can go out and kill it." He hefted his spear and shook it meaningfully at the magic man, as Navahk had once too often hefted and shaken his staff at him. "*This* is a good thing!" he said, and taking none of the meat for himself, turned and walked to his own lean-to.

The people were glad for the gift of Torka's kill. The headman divided it among the families, and all savored a share. All except Navahk, who would partake of not so much as a bite.

The rain fell for two days and nights, and for more than half of that time, Hetchem screamed against the pitiless agony of childbirth. Navahk, glad to be distracted from the food that Torka had so generously provided, danced naked for Hetchem in the rain. Within her damp and frigid lean-to, while the women gathered outside, watching as best as they could, he made magic smokes for her and brought forth from between her legs the bloodied heart and entrails of the bad spirits of her pain. He held these things up for the watching women to see. They marveled as they beheld his powerful magic and stared wide eyed as he threw the small heart and finger-thin, ribbonlike guts of Hetchem's pain into the flames of his magic fire. Sizzling like any other meat, they made good smoke. Comforted, Hetchem slept and did not cry out again.

The next morning, while the sun rose into clear skies beneath which Karana searched and called in vain for a missing pup, Hetchem died while giving birth to a hideously deformed baby.

The women wailed. The men were silent.

"We will go from this camp," announced the headman. "The River of Caribou Spring Crossing is a bad camp for Supnah's people."

No one spoke against moving on. They broke camp eagerly. Hetchem was put to look at the sky forever. The women dressed her in her best furs and favorite adornments. They placed her fire-making bag at her side, with her sewing and working tools, and each woman brought a little something from her own fire circle as a gift for Hetchem's spirit. When finally they turned and walked away from their friend for the last time, she was resplendent in nose and lip and ear rings of pebbles and bone and precious wood . . . and a necklace of polished, perfectly matched white stone beads glistened like a collar of hailstones around her shoulders.

Torka smiled when he saw it, and hugged Lonit as Navahk glared hatefully at them both.

A wind had risen out of the east as they gathered to perform one last ritual before taking up their belongings and putting the camp of the Caribou Spring Crossing behind them. Rhik, Hetchem's man, would not go with them. He would stay behind to keep the mandatory five-day death watch for his woman, lest predators come to devour her body before her spirit had a chance to decide whether it really wished to leave her. When the necessary number of days had passed and he was certain that her spirit was free to be born again within the next child of the band who would be given her name, he would follow and rejoin his people.

But first he must expose his deformed infant according to custom. It lay quietly sucking its fingers on the floor of the bloodied birth hut where the women had been forced by tradition to leave it after its father had refused to look at its face. He did not look at it now. He brought it into the light of day, holding it outward toward the magic man with an expression of abhorrence upon his face.

The people of Supnah formed a circle around Rhik and the baby and the magic man as Navahk shook his staff over the infant, proclaiming its life invalid.

"This life has never been born! This life has no spirit! This life is *not* life! The People put this dead thing out from among us!"

In absolute silence and solemnity, the members of the band symbolically turned their backs upon the child.

Now the father knelt. He lay the baby upon the sodden, spongy surface of the permafrost. Naiapi brought a small basket of woven grass and placed it into his hands. It was full of freshly gathered tundral mosses. As Naiapi turned away, the father stared at the contents of the little basket; then, with grim determination, he proceeded to pack the infant's mouth, nostrils, ears, and anal as well as vaginal openings with moss so that whatever twisted life spirit it might possess would be trapped within its body and incapable of being born again.

Torka stood with the other hunters, his back to the ritual killing of the child, an unwelcome litany of words moving like fever-chill within him. *This is the way of the People. From time beyond beginning. This is the way it has always been. This is the way it will always be.*

In silence the circle broke. The people of Supnah left Rhik alone with his dead woman and his dying child. Packs were hefted. People shuffled off after Supnah without a word. Even the dogs were unnaturally quiet, although Sister Dog walked whining, nervous circles, searching for her lost pup, until at last Karana came and, with only a touch, caused her to follow the others.

As the band walked on, Torka looked back, troubled as his eyes fell upon the solitary figure of Rhik, hunched forward, rocking himself in grief. All semblance of dignity and composure had left him as he was wracked by lamentation for the death of one who had walked beside him for a lifetime, his back turned upon the naked infant that tradition had forced him to suffocate with his own hands.

The people of Supnah walked in silence, bent beneath the weight of their traveling packs. All except Navahk, whose belongings were hefted by Grek and Stam, so that he might walk ahead of his people unencumbered, free to sing a death song for the woman and to shake his staff at the world while eagles and teratorns and other carrion-eating birds began to circle in the sky above and behind him.

Torka watched him. Torka knew that he enjoyed his song, and that, somehow, he was kindred to the carrion eaters of the world.

This is a bad band, thought Torka, and knew at last and without doubt that he must leave it.

For many days Torka kept his decision in his heart. For as many nights he lay awake with it, measuring its worth as though it were a new woman whose merits must be carefully considered before at last allowing her to share his bed skins. He wished that he had taken as much care before he had first taken upon himself the double burden of Iana and Aliga; but what was done was done. He would not dishonor them, or himself, by turning his back upon them now—as he must turn his back upon Karana.

The thought of leaving the boy was like contemplating the amputation of his spear arm. Karana was as a son to him, but Supnah was his true father. And the more Torka watched them together, the more convinced he became that it would be wrong to take the boy from his people. Karana was as stubborn as a musk ox and as unforgiving as the storms of the winter dark, but Supnah's doting display of protective concern and paternal affection would eventually make their mark upon the boy. Karana might become headman of his band one day, and in time he might even become a man who would put his dagger-eyed uncle in his place; but in the meantime Supnah would see to it that no harm came to the boy, and most assuredly the headman would never allow his son to walk out of his life twice.

The initial awe the band felt for Man Who Walks With Dogs had lost its luster. After he had allowed them to see that his spear hurler was not a magic stick but only a tool that all the hunters might learn to make and use, he became only another man in their eyes, an outsider who had walked into their band to bring shame to their headman, magic man, and themselves as well.

When they looked at him, they saw a man who had survived the terrible long winter of the starving moon without abandoning his woman, his ancient grandfather, or another man's child. When they looked at him, they remembered the old people and the children whom they had turned out of their encampment to walk the wind forever.

And at last he understood why Supnah and Navahk had put aside their enmity and focused it upon him. Yes, he had brought Karana back to them alive from the spirit world, but as long as he stayed among them, he would be a constant reminder of the fallibility of Navahk's powers, and Supnah would always see him as the stranger who had saved the life of the beloved son whom he had sent to die.

Inside his shelter Torka lay quietly in the dark, with Lonit asleep in the curl of his arm. His thoughts no longer distressed him. He had made his peace with them. Like a hunter who has come to a fork in a game trail, he had carefully analyzed the signs and had made up his mind as to which trail would most benefit him.

To continue on with Supnah would lead him to the loss of his woman and, inevitably, to the loss of his own life. He would never give her up. *Never.* Torka and Lonit were like the great dark swans that flew together, male and female, hearts and lives bonded until death. He would fight for her against any man, as he had fought for her in the past, barehanded against wolves and with spears and bludgeon against men. Unless she asked to go. And then his life would be over.

He closed his eyes. Beside him Lonit murmured against
dreams. They had come far since leaving Rhik to sit death
watch for his woman. Only this afternoon he had rejoined the
band as Supnah had led them on a more easterly course, out
of the tundral barrens toward familiar hunting grounds that
lay at the confluence of two rivers, in a country that his
people called the Land of Little Sticks.

They would be there tomorrow. The hunters said that it
was good hunting country, with many streams and groves of
dwarf willow from which the women could gather generous
supplies of sticks for burning and twigs for the making of
baskets. They had killed moose there in the past, and sloth
and horse. There were fish for the taking, and good birding.
Men could hunt in the Land of Little Sticks for many days
before being forced to move on in search of fresh food supplies.

Then they would turn back. Beyond the Land of Little
Sticks the tundra stretched away to the southernmost extension of the Mountains That Walk. There, in a wall of ice two
miles high and no man knew how many miles wide, the
world ended.

Or did it? Torka closed his eyes. Memories filled him, of a
land that Supnah, at Navahk's insistence, had refused to
enter. It lay behind them now—or perhaps, as an eagle flies,
it lay somewhere ahead, hidden within the mountain vast-
ness. It was a river of grassland ten to twenty miles wide
running due east between the towering, transversely aligned
glacier-ridden mountains. Supnah had called it the Corridor
of Storms. Navahk had said that it was forbidden country, the
realm of the wanawut, the end of the world. Yet, as Torka
allowed the memory of that land to grow within him, it was as
though he stood again on the bare, black-boned ridge looking down at an undulating sun-washed land so thick with the
first new grass of spring that it rippled in the wind like the fur
of a green animal. And everywhere upon that land he saw
herds of grazing animals. So many animals that he was overwhelmed by the hunting potential of the land that was forbidden to Supnah's people. Navahk had said that it was the end
of the world. To Torka it seemed to hold the promise of a
new beginning.

He opened his eyes. A mammoth trumpeted in the night.
Torka stared into the darkness as the high, shrieking cry
reverberated through a thousand distant, unseen canyons

Lonit stirred against him. He drew her closer, listening as the last echoings of the mammoth's cry faded into the night.

She sighed, awake now. "Listen. Did you hear it? Was it Thunder Speaker? Was it Life Giver?"

Life Giver. She called the great mammoth that. No longer the Destroyer. It had killed their people and set them to wander alone. It had killed the men of the Ghost Band, but it had turned away and allowed Torka to keep his life when he had dared to place himself before its charge to save the life of Karana. No one could convince her that something magic had not happened in that moment, that a covenant had not been made between man and mammoth. And although he claimed otherwise to all who had witnessed that encounter, within the deepest recesses of his spirit he knew that she was right. He and the beast had been one in that moment when life and death had hung in the balance. He had not thrown his spear, and the mammoth had not charged. The Destroyer had not destroyed him; it had given him the gift of life instead, and in his heart he had named it totem. He would never hunt it, or its kind, again. "Life Giver is far away," he said to the woman in his arms. "In lands from which Supnah has led his people."

"There was game there. Beyond the country where the Ghost Band died. In the long land of grass between the Mountains That Walk. There was *much* game." Her hand strayed upward across his chest, stroked him softly. "The women say that if hunting is good, we will winter in the Land of Little Sticks. The women say that if the hunting is not good, we will walk northward again, crossing the Plain of Many Waters, following Big Milk River to winter at the place of the Great Gathering. It is far, beyond the country of the Ghost Band. Wallah, Grek's woman, says it is a big camp. Many bands come there in the last days of summer, to settle in for the duration of the time of the long dark, to trade and share news and to barter women and children and goods. Naiapi says that Supnah gave her father a robe of bearskin, two of his best spears, and a marmot-skin bag filled with his favorite fishing hooks in trade for her. Naiapi is proud to speak of that and says that the Great Gathering is a good camp. Wallah says that there are games, much storytelling, and competitions between the women to test their cooking and sewing skills. But mostly, in the last of the days of light, there is . . . mammoth hunting." She paused. "Would Torka hunt mammoths in the last of the days of light?"

"Torka will not hunt mammoths in days of light or darkness."

The answer was what she wanted to hear. She lay quietly in his arms, her hand continuing to stroke him. "Navahk will be angry if Torka does not hunt. He will say that it is a bad thing for his people. Supnah will agree. He will *make* you hunt."

"No matter what Torka does, or does not do, Navahk will always say that it is a bad thing for his people. Supnah will always agree. But no man will ever make Torka hunt mammoths."

Her hand paused, lay open over his heart. She moved closer, her bare body suddenly tense against his. "Navahk has looked at me again. Always he looks at me. Awake or asleep, even now, in Torka's arms, Lonit sees his eyes and knows that if she stays within Supnah's band, Navahk will have this woman behind Torka's back. Again and again he has said that this will be so, and if Torka tries to keep her, Supnah and his men will turn upon him like wolves turn upon any member of their pack who breaks favor with the head wolf! They will drive him away or kill him. And without Torka, Lonit's spirit will not want to live!" She pressed even closer, trembling against him. "Sometimes in the dark this woman dreams of the faraway land of grass that lies between the Mountains That Walk. She dreams of game walking into the face of the rising sun. She dreams of a land that is forbidden to Supnah's people, and she wishes that Torka would lead her there, beyond the end of the world, away from Navahk and out of a band that is not a good band for us."

Her words startled as much as pleased him. Until this moment he had been hesitant to share his decision to leave the band with her, knowing that when the time came, she would follow him, but not without apprehension and certainly not without regret. "Lonit would leave this band?"

"Lonit *would* leave it."

He moved to kiss her, in the way of the People—an exhalation of the breath of his life into her nostrils. She drew it into herself and, with open lips, returned it to him with one of her own. Her arms reached to embrace him. Her hands moved like a warm summer wind over his back. Her touch roused fire within his loins as she opened herself to him, eagerly melding the heat of her passion with his. Heat became flame.

Together they were one, burning wild like a summer grass fire until the fusion of their passions became molten, surged, and glowed, cooling at last and sweeping them away into the warm black river of exhausted sleep.

They awoke in the thin blue light of dawn and lay joined in each other's arms at the edge of the river of sleep, listening to the sound of Summer Moon sucking at a sleeping Iana's breast and to the dry clacking of bones as Aliga, who was already up and dressed and out of the shelter, gleaned reburnable fragments from the fire circle and tossed them onto a skin in which they would be wrapped and carried to the next camp.

Torka propped himself onto an elbow and looked down at his woman lovingly. Several strands of her long hair lay across her face. He reached to draw them tenderly away. Smiling, she arrested his hand, drew it to her lips, and kissed his palm. Then, suddenly, her smile vanished, and she hurled herself upward, throwing her arms around him, holding him desperately. "Lonit is Torka's woman. Always and forever."

Her heart was beating like that of a terrified bird caught within a snare net. Gently he put his hands upon her shoulders and held her away from him so that he might look into her face. "Always and forever," he said, wanting her to see the affirmation in his eyes. He drew her close, loving her more in this moment than words could ever say. "Lonit would not be afraid to walk the world alone with Torka, with only mute, mindless Iana to help her with Summer Moon? To be without the protection of a band again?"

She held onto him as though he had just pulled her from an icy river and she was terrified that if she relaxed her grip, she would surely fall into it again and be drowned. "Lonit is afraid *now*! There is more danger to us here, within this band, than we ever faced alone upon the open tundra!"

"Lonit speaks Torka's thoughts."

She relaxed instantly. Releasing her grip, she looked at him with hopeful incredulity. "It is so?"

"It is so. From this day Torka walks with Supnah's people no more!"

The band made no move to stop him. They did not even ask him in which direction he would go. They watched as he helped his women break their encampment and ready their belongings for transport. Only Naiapi came forward to help Lonit in a poor pretense of friendliness.

Wallah, standing with her little daughter, Mahnie, puckered her lips as though she had just eaten something sour. "Look at that. Glad to get rid of the stranger's woman, Naiapi is. Now she'll be free to look hungry eyed at the magic man whenever his brother isn't around!" When Mahnie grimaced and snapped her head hard to the left, Wallah's round face blushed as red as an autumn bearberry, and she silently cursed her own thoughtlessness; two other little girls sat in the shade of her lean-to, playing with dolls made of leftover fragments of skins from her sewing bag. She had invited the girls to play with Mahnie's dolls, and there they sat: Ketti, Stam's little one, and Pet, daughter of Naiapi. Ketti, as bright as a polished bone bead but not nearly as pretty, had clapped a grubby little hand across her mouth to stifle her giggles. Pet, as pretty as her friend was bright, stared at Wallah with hurt puzzlement upon her face.

Wallah tittered, trying hard to sound innocent of her slur against the child's mother. "And don't we all cast a glance at Navahk when our men aren't around! As handsome as the first sunrise at the end of the time of long dark is that one. Perhaps someday he will choose one of you girls to warm his bed skins, eh? What an honor that would be!"

Little Pet's dirty face went as blank as a moss-haired doll as she threw the lichen-stuffed figure of skins onto the ground and, rising, fled to her own fire circle.

"She is afraid of the magic man, Mother!" said Mahnie in the tone of an adult reprimanding a child.

"Look!" instructed Ketti, her small eyes wide as Karana burst from Supnah's lean-to, rubbing sleep from his eyes as he strode across the encampment, Aar at his side, and paused before Torka. "There'll be trouble now," whispered the girl. Beside Wallah, Mahnie protectively clutched her doll to her skinny little chest.

"Karana will go with Torka!" the boy announced.

Supnah, standing with arms folded across his chest, stoically observing Torka's preparations for departure from the band, frowned. "Karana will walk with his own people."

"Hrmmph! Torka's people *are* Karana's people!" replied the boy coldly.

From beside Supnah, Navahk's smile had never been broader

or more malicious. "All three of them. What an impressive band!"

Torka had been tightening the thongs that held his antlered stalking cloak to his pack frame. He straightened. No wonder the magic man smiled! The look on Supnah's face was appalling. Once again the headman was shamed before his people; his son preferred to walk off into the unknown with a stranger rather than stay within his own band.

Torka fixed his gaze upon Karana, and as he spoke, the words half choked him. But he knew that Supnah was so engorged with jealous hatred that he might well send the boy off and then, when his anger cooled, pick up his spears and come after Torka to kill him and the boy. And then Navahk would have Lonit. So he spoke the hated words and put such strength and command in them that all who heard them winced and took an inadvertent step back from the anger he was directing toward the headman's son. "What sort of boy is this who tells a man what to do? Has Torka asked Karana to come with him?"

Karana blinked, startled, confused, and dismayed all at once. "I—"

"No! Torka did *not* ask Karana! Nor would he have him! *This* is Karana's band! *These* are Karana's people! Torka has stayed with them long enough. It is time for him to take his women and child and walk his own way, but *not* with Karana!" He turned his gaze to Supnah. "Why does this boy hover in Torka's shadow like a gnat on a summer day? This man has brought him to his people. Now it is time for Supnah to swat him into place so that he remembers always that he is a headman's son who must show respect to his people and to their traditions!" Then, to the boy again: "Go! Take your place at your father's side!"

Karana was so shocked by Torka's hostility that he could not react to it. His hand reached to his shoulder, remembering the night on the tundra when Torka had been so angry with him that he had shoved him down. But that had been between the two of them. This was different. Now he had made a display of his anger for all to see. The boy's face burned with shame, but only when Torka shouted "Go!" once more did Karana obey.

For three days Torka led his little band north, then east, toward the Mountains That Walk, avoiding the barrens through which they had come with Supnah. With Sister Dog and the pups at her heels, Aliga walked with them, for although Torka had given her the opportunity to stay, without a man to hunt for her, she would surely have starved in the lean, dark days of winter.

It rained on the fourth day and again on the fifth. The rain beat in Torka's heart. He missed Karana and brooded over the way they had been forced to part. Perhaps when the boy became a man, he would understand that Torka had acted for the good of all.

In a sodden camp, while Aliga, Iana, and the baby slept, Torka listened to dire wolves howling in the distant hills and briefly wondered if he had done the right thing.

"Those wolves," said Lonit, "are more constant and trustworthy companions than the ones we left behind who walked upright on two legs."

"And Karana?"

She heard the longing in his voice and shared it. "He will live in this woman's heart forever."

Restless, he stood in the rain, looking eastward, thinking: *If Karana truly has the gift of Seeing, see now into this man's heart. Know to what land Torka would lead his people and come to us there. Come to the river of grass that runs between the Mountains That Walk. Come to the end of the world to be a son to this man again.*

"Come." Lonit's whisper startled him. Her hand rested gently on his forearm, drawing him back into the shelter of the lean-to. "This woman and this man will make a new son."

And so they traveled for many days under clearing skies, with Aliga seining for fish in rain-swollen creeks and Lonit hunting beside Torka with her four-thonged bola of braided sinew, with weights contrived of the strange shells of stone that they had gathered in a far land.

The tundra was adorned with summer color by the time they reached their destination and made camp amid mountain avens, heather, and flameweed in the high, bony foothills that Torka remembered. Night was little more than twilight now. Mammoths called to one another within deep, ice-gouged canyons. And into one such cleft in the bare bones of Mother Below, Torka led his women through familiar corridors of stone, higher and higher, until, at last, with the dogs panting at their side, they reached the crest of a wide, black ridge and looked down at the end of the world, at the Corridor of Storms, at the river of grass that ran toward the face of the rising sun for thousands of miles between the soaring, glistening blue walls of mountains that towered two miles high.

These were the Mountains That Walk. This was the end of the world. And as Torka led his people into it, the dogs ran forward, alerted to the barking of one of their own kind, and Torka paused to see a small, fur-clad figure walking toward him with a spear in his hand.

It was Karana.

He was smiling. "What took you so long?" he asked. "This boy and his Brother Dog have been waiting many days to be reunited with their father."

PART II

CHILD
OF MIST,
MOUNTAIN
OF FIRE

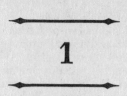

1

They ran together against the wind, into the high, tangled refuge of the glacier-ridden mountains where they had always found safety from the beasts before. But there would be no safety for them now. They were alone, a mother and a child, and although they were well into the mountains, the beasts were still following, matching them step for step, climbing out of the tundral lowlands like a howling, yipping pack of blood-maddened dire wolves.

The mother stumbled. She gasped against the pain of a wound that she had managed to conceal from the child until now. Blood bubbled at the back of her throat. Welling from her thorax, it filled her mouth and seeped in rivulets from the corners of her lips.

The child smelled the hot redness of it. It stared, startled, its gray eyes wide with disbelief. Bending close, it mewed with concern and tenderly reached to wipe the blood away.

The mother stayed the gentle, caring hand. There was no time for tenderness. The beasts were closing on them. She forced herself to rise, spat out a mouthful of blood, and pulled her child on.

And on. Higher into the mountains, deeper into the familiar labyrinthine canyons that cleft the sprawling, glacier-straddled range. The air was cold. Gray and bitter with the scent of ice and shadows, it was nonetheless sweet to the mother's pain-ravaged senses, for it was the smell of home. Now she took comfort in the knowledge that the way she had chosen *was* proving too difficult for the beasts. The distance between prey and predators was increasing. As she had hoped, the beasts, being creatures of the open tundra, were intimidated by the soaring walls of stone and ice across which she led her child with the sure, fleet-footed abandon of a mountain ewe.

At last, light-headed from pain, exhaustion, and loss of blood, she paused and looked back from the spine of a bare, precipitous ridge. Beneath wide, prominent brows, her pale eyes squinted against the sun's glare. Although each ragged suck of breath seared her senses, her mouth curved into a smile of satisfaction. She could see no sign of the beasts. Far below, the vast, rolling tundral hills lay awash in the green-gold glow of spring. Suspended between the earth and the savage blue of the cloudless Arctic sky, a teratorn shrieked as it spread its huge, condorlike wings and rode the wind into infinity.

Upon the heights the wind was a constant tide sweeping across the mountains from the north. The mother breathed in, tensing against pain as she held the wind captive, then released it slowly through her nostrils and analyzed every cold, invisible fiber of it. If the beasts were still close enough to pose a threat, the wind would tell her; she would smell the warm, ochre odor of their soft, oiled flesh. Her belly would turn, as it always did, at their rank brown stink.

Beside her the child sighed with exhaustion and leaned into her powerfully muscled, gray-furred limb. A strange, bewildering weariness was filling her. Her heart was beating erratically as, with her free hand, she stroked the head of her little one, soothing it. The wind bore no discernible scent or sound of the beasts; her touch conveyed this to the child. It relaxed at her side, comforted by the knowledge that, somewhere at the base of the ridge, the beasts had abandoned the chase. Mother and child were alone upon the mountain now, safe from prey that had unexpectedly become predacious and nearly home from a hunt that had gone so terribly, unpredictably wrong.

She shivered. Her memories were misted now, bitter, recalling a time when the child was but an infant . . . when she had first learned what the beasts and their flying sticks could do. Visions filled her head. . . . Howling beasts driving her family ahead of them into a dead-end canyon with cold stone walls through which they could not flee . . . flying sticks and yipping beasts and crying babies and blood . . . being pushed hard against the wall as the dead fell against her and the dying screamed . . . her mate somehow pulling her and the child away from the carnage, through a narrow fissure in the stone that scraped their bodies raw as they forced their way through it and into the dark heart of the mountain.

The sound of death had followed them as they went on until the mountain turned to ice beneath their probing feet. Suddenly the ice gave way, and they fell into rushing water so cold that it was fire against their scraped and bleeding skin. She had held onto the child, and her mate had held onto her, and together they were swept away through underground corridors of absolute blackness, into the roaring channels of a river that ran beneath the glacier.

Gradually the world had turned gray, then blue as the river carried them into the light of day to a strange land, far away to new hunting grounds. To a new range of mountains where, after many days of sun and many nights of endless dark, her mate died and their child grew strong.

They wintered with bears and voles and marmots in the deep, sheltering, wind-protected canyons of the mountain, sleeping away the time of the long dark, dreaming of the return of the great herds upon which they would feed through the days of endless sun.

But with the herds came the beasts with their flying sticks. In the skins of the animals that they killed and ate, the beasts hunted in packs like dogs and wolves. The mother and child had watched them from the heights, curious and amazed as they surrounded entire herds of musk oxen and killed them to the last calf. Working together, they drove bawling, panicked herds of bison and caribou over obstacles of their own devising and then slaughtered every animal that fell to injury. Like lions, they dragged their prey away from the killing site; unlike lions, they fed upon only a portion of what they killed and left the rest for scavengers.

And so it was that she and the child, along with wolves, wild dogs, leaping cats, and foxes, began to follow the beasts across the summer tundra to feed upon their leavings. And when they were careless or abandoned their weak and young to die, she fed upon *them*, as her kind had always done; only now their meat was the sweetest meat of all to her, and when she ate of it, she remembered the way her band had died and how she had been warned long ago that wherever her kind lived, the beast would either run from them or seek them out and kill them with their flying sticks. . . .

Now, as her weary eyes scanned the tundra, she was

puzzled. Where were the herds? They had vanished at the onset of the time of the long dark. Ever-moving in their constant quest for food, vast, rivering herds of bison, camel, and elk, of musk ox, horse, and mammoth, and of moose, yak, and caribou had always returned to graze the seas of summer grass and tundral scrub. Their antlers, tusks, and horns pricked the horizon of the Ice Age world like a forest of living bones on the move. But the time of light had returned to the tundra, and still they had not come. The time of the long dark had seemed longer than usual this year. The beasts had returned to the tundra to wait for the coming of the great herds, as she herself waited, with wolves and lions, and a winter-lean child that needed to be. fed.

Thus she had come to hunt the beasts, certain that she was well out of range of their throwing sticks. But when she had noticed the straggler, hunger had made her bold; hunger and the hatred she bore for their kind. When they saw her leap at her prey, the other members of the pack had not run away; they howled and stomped and shook their sticks at her. Yet she had sensed more fear than hostility. Only one of them, who walked ahead of the others, had hurled a stick at her. That one had been encased within the white belly skins of winter-killed caribou, and its narrow, hideous face was bald except for a lateral strip of white fur that encircled its elongated brow. Black hair grew in abundance upon its skull, falling downward over its back to its knees; rather like the mane of a horse, yet so thick and glossy that, at first, she had thought the beast possessed wings and would fly at her. It had thrown its stick instead. And the stick had flown with the speed of a plummeting eagle attacking its prey. But the attempt had gone wide, striking the straggler instead, making her kill easier.

Any other animal would have backed away then, granting deference to a superior hunter, allowing her to take what she had slain. But again the beasts had howled and stomped and shaken their sticks at her, and then, led by the one in white skins, they had advanced even though she waved her fists and displayed her teeth to warn them away. The entire pack had run like bears moving downhill, crouched forward, heads out, forelimbs dangling. They were dangerous, unpredictable creatures, but she knew their ways and was not afraid. Then the beast in the white belly skins had stood erect, reared back, and hurled yet another stick, screaming like a bull mammoth.

Never had she seen a stick fly so far or so fast or with so much power. It had struck her before she could turn away. The child had not seen it happen; she had sent the little one running ahead when the beasts had not fled from her. Her cry had been more an exhalation of surprise than of pain. That had come later, after she fled. . . .

A single sharp, bright tangle of red pain put an end to her thoughts. She felt as though the core of her body was filled with molten light. It pooled outward and filled every portion of her body, expanding with excruciating brilliance within her head. Then it ebbed like a river at full flood, flowing backward into the stone-headed tip of the flying stick that was embedded all too close to her heart.

She shivered. Her heart lurched, then beat madly as the stone tip invaded it and drew blood. Unable to pull the stick from her chest, she had broken it instead, leaving its stone tip buried within her breast. She could feel it now, the source of her pain and bleeding as it worked deeper and deeper . . . into her heart.

There was no pain, only coldness. She was desperately in need of rest as, with her free hand, she nudged the child. They went downward now, into the narrows of a dark, spruce-shaded ravine. Soon they would be home. Soon they would rest together within their nest of branches, bones, and lichens. Soon they would feed upon the forelimb and head of the beast, which she had managed to rip from its body before the others of its pack had driven her from her decapitated kill.

She was suddenly warm with hunger and intensely aware of myriad, multicolored scents of the mountain: time-scoured rock and alpine glaciers . . . a pair of marmots cautiously observing from beneath the protection of a lichen-flowered boulder . . . a wolverine prowling far below the ridge . . .

Despite her weakness she still clutched the forelimb, carrying it tucked high beneath her thickly furred upper arm while the straggler's head dangled from her hand by its hair. Both would nourish her child while she herself rested and recovered. When stripped of the skins of dead animals in which it covered itself, the meat of the beast man was the best meat of all.

*　　　*　　　*

"Let it go, Navahk. It and its little one. Let it die. *If* it can die."

Grek's voice was an imperative whisper, yet it struck his fellow hunters as though he had screamed. They murmured, intimidated by his audacity and by their surroundings. Mountains were not a place for men. Nevertheless, Grek was risking the anger of the magic man by urging him to turn back from his purpose.

"Navahk—your brother, Supnah, is dead. We will die, too, if we go on. Let us go back now, before the wind spirits kill us because we have succeeded in spearing one of their own."

"*We?*" The magic man turned with the sharpness of movement of a man in his prime. In garments cut entirely from the white, silken belly skins of winter-killed caribou, he seemed larger than his followers, although he was actually smaller and leaner. Starving times had threatened his people twice in the three long years since Torka had left their band, but the cutting edge of hunger had only sharpened and more fully defined his beauty. His body and face were still as finely honed as the most perfectly chiseled spearhead . . . and as hard and as dangerous. He looked at the older, stockier hunter out of eyes that were as black as obsidian, as if measuring whether Grek was worthy of his contempt. "It was the spear of Navahk that struck the killer of my brother. Would Grek, would any man, contest that?"

They would not. Navahk's spear hurler *had* loosed the weapon that had struck the wind spirit and driven it away from Supnah's mutilated body. The had all seen it: Grek and Stam, Mond and Het, and aging, albeit still wiry-legged, Rhik. They had also seen Navahk's first throw miss its intended target and strike the headman instead. It was this wounding that had made the hapless Supnah unable to escape the wind spirit.

The creature's first attack had been a sudden, bold leap out of the willow scrub in which it had lain in wait for unwary prey. A heavy ground fog lay upon the tundra. The hunters waded through it, knee deep, as though through the shallows of a river. As Supnah had paused to relieve himself, the wind spirit had hurled itself at him. It was the wanawut of legend and nightmare, the beast that no men saw unless they were marked for death at its hands. With one terrible, ripping swipe, it had torn the headman's arm from his body. But Supnah was strong and quick and unwilling to die. With blood spurting from his horrendous wound, he had run with a speed fueled by panic until Navahk's spear had struck him. He had fallen with the wanawut at his heels, and Navahk, raging in anguish, had then made his second throw. It was this spear that had struck the spirit's hairy, grotesquely human torso. It had been shaking huge, hirsute fists at them and displaying canines that rivaled those of the feared saber-toothed leaping cats. Its hairless chest had been bared to them, with two spatulate breasts swinging. When Navahk's spear had found its mark, the men had cheered even though Supnah was dead by then, his head torn from his body.

Their cheering had stopped as abruptly as it had begun. The wind spirit did not die. They watched in silence as, shrieking, it ran off after its child. Navahk had struck it a heart wounding, but still it ran! Sobered, they remembered that men could not kill spirits. That was why only Navahk had done a forbidden thing and risked loosing his spears against the creature that had killed his brother. If the spirits turned upon him, perhaps Navahk, as magic man, could fight them in ways that other men could not.

Now, as Grek deferred to Navahk with a grunt and a nod, he knew that the magic man was justifiably mad with grief and rage and, yes, shame for his failure to save his brother's life. If Navahk insisted upon following wind spirits, he and this small group of the band's bravest hunters would shadow him, ready to spring to his defense, until his madness passed, lest the wanawut fall upon Navahk and deprive the band of its magic man. Navahk had been brave this day. They owed him an equal display of courage. Although all of them would have preferred to turn and flee from the mountainous realm of wind spirits, their pride kept them at Navahk's heels . . . pride and the knowledge that Navahk's powers were great and that he was not a forgiving man.

In the shadowed narrows of the cold, spruce-choked ravine, the child crouched over its mother. With wide, long, hairy fingers, it mewed with compassion as it probed the extent of its parent's devastating wound. Blood was everywhere, darkening her chest, forming a black skin over her bare breasts, and bubbling in a warm, pulsing spring around the child's fingertips as it pinched at the stem of the spearhead, trying in vain to dislodge it.

Once again the mother stayed the child's gentle hand. The

little one was too cautious, too afraid to be the cause of pain. The mother's massive, hirsute hand formed a fist around the projecting end of the shaft. She must be rid of it; it was the source of her pain, and to be free of her agony, she must first increase it. Her powerfully muscled arm, apelike in proportion to her broad, foreshortened torso, wrenched the spearhead free, hefting it high. Colors flared, merged, and became one searing flame of white. Her pain neither decreased nor increased; instead, she grew smaller, fell into it somehow, and became the pain. Disoriented, as frightened and confused as her child, she howled as though in supplication to the bright hole in the springtime sky. It seemed to be sucking her upward, out of her body, drawing her into distances where the teratorns had flown and disappeared.

The child cowered. Beneath its sloping, bony brow, its small, gray eyes were wide. Fear and perplexity lived in them. Its mother had never made such a sound before. Suddenly the contorted body went limp. The spearhead fell to the ground. The mother stared, gaping at the sky, not breathing.

The child jumped away, then ventured close. It picked up the bloodied spearhead, sniffed it, cut its soft, hairless palm on the sharp edges of the flat bit of stone, and cried out, dropping it. The child whined a little to itself, sucking its wound and wondering why its mother did not rise to offer comfort. It bent over her and sniffed her open mouth. Bewildered, it breathed into her. She did not breathe back. Puzzled, it hunkered on its strong, gray-furred limbs and whimpered, then carefully picked up the projectile and reinserted it into its mother's gaping wound. It still bled, but thickly, smoothly, no longer pulsing. The child pressed the spearhead deep, as though the killing stone might somehow draw death back into itself and thus restore life to the mother.

A cold wind gusted through the narrow, stunted, misshapen trees of the spruce grove. Although the naked child was as heavily furred as its dead mother, it shivered. Unable to rouse its parent, it made a series of high, thin little shrieks of near panic, then fell to silence, listening. Its head turned upward upon its thick, maned neck, and it sniffed the air with broad nostrils that flared beneath the elongated bridge of a nose that gave its heavy-jawed face an almost bearlike appearance.

Beasts.

The child could smell and hear them. They were ascending the ridge. Soon they would stand high above the ravine, beneath the hole in the sky. Then they would descend into the gorge, where beasts had never dared to come . . . into the high vastnesses of the tortured ranges where their kind were unknown . . . where the child had been safe with its mother until now.

Mother. Safe. The child began to whimper again. The beasts were coming, with their flying sticks and stones that cut flesh and took away the breath of living beings. Of mother. How could the child put the breath back into her, if not through the offending stone? It jabbed it in and out, in and out, desperate now. The mother *must* breathe, *must* be roused, to show the child what to do and where to hide, for surely the arms of her little one were not strong enough to rip the beasts limb from limb, nor were the clawed fingers and stabbing canines of the child long enough to open their bellies or slash their hairless throats in order to suck them dry of blood. This was the way of the hunt, but the mother had just begun to teach the child. This was the way to defend against predators, but the mother had always defended the little one. Always. Alone, the child had no defense—none except its raw instinct for survival, and in this, the child was strong.

The beasts were close now. Through the deep-green shadows of the trees, it could see straight up along the wall of the gorge. Stone and ice reached to the sky. The beasts stood high above, upon the ridge, blocking the light given off by the hole in the sky. The child shivered so hard that it was afraid the beasts would hear; but they were vocalizing in the odd way of their kind, briefly and in whispers, as though to prevent the child, with its small, intricately lobed, batlike ears, from hearing them. It heard them clearly; it could even hear the turn of a larva wriggling within the skin of the land. Although language was alien to its kind, it sensed their intent.

Panic screamed for release, momentarily winning over judgment as the little one screeched an echo of its mother's dying howl. *"Wah nah wa! Wah nah wut!"* The sound had that deep, flat resonance of a creature twice the size of the child and a thousand times more dangerous. It was the roar of a trapped lion, of an enraged bear, of a wind spirit shrieking across the world—a threat of power that would not come to fulfillment until the child was grown.

In spite of his multilayered garments, Grek was colder than he had ever been in his life. In a meticulously stitched patchwork of the skins of caribou, hare, dog, wolf, bear, and yak, he stood beneath the oblique glow of the springtime sun and was as cold as if he stood naked in the depths of the storms of the winter dark.

The voice of the wind spirit reverberated within the gorge. Grek could not tell if it was the sound of one creature or a dozen. It rose from the darkness, from the lake of shadows far below. Trees rose from that lake, and Grek, a man of the barren tundra, did not like trees, especially when they formed groves. Predators could hide within the woods, and the trees were conspirators with them, concealing them. A man was at risk when he walked among trees, and it seemed to Grek that the trees knew it as they stood as tall as a man, many armed, their twisted bodies stinking of pitch and needlelike foliage palatable only to mammoths—and to wind spirits; they were creatures of the mountain groves, of the misted heights where the people of Grek's band never ventured. Until now.

"To go farther . . . this will not be good." Grek's statement was spoken casually. It was not the way of his people to reveal the depth of their inner feelings, and it was not the way of any man of any band to admit to fear. Now that Supnah was dead, Grek was almost certain to be named headman when he returned to the encampment of his people. His woman, Wallah, would smile and say that this was only as it should be, and his daughter, Mahnie, would be proud. When Supnah's daughter, Pet, came to her womanhood, she would come to share Grek's bed skins and dwell once again at the fire of headman of the band. These prospects were pleasing to Grek; the prospect of the gorge was not. But if he wanted to be named headman of his people, he must display no fear of it.

Nevertheless, he *was* afraid, of the mountains, the trees, the shadowed gorge into which the wind spirit had fled with its little one, and of Navahk, who still had the madness of pursuit in him.

At first it had seemed to be a maned man clad in the skin of a strange, never-before-seen kind of bear; but it was too massively boned for a man, and it leaped and ran with the power and speed of a lion. When it had stood over Supnah's corpse, they had seen that it was naked, furred, female, and more terrifying than any beast that stalked a hunter's dreams to mock his boldness. It was its striking similarity to themselves that roused a terrible outrage within them because somehow it was not a beast. It was human, and yet not human.

Apprehension in their dark eyes, the hunters looked at Navahk, then at Grek. Their silence conceded leadership to the older man. It was a sudden and unexpectedly heavy burden, as though they had slung the invisible carcass of a slain bison upon his back and now waited to see if he could carry its weight alone.

At this moment Grek was no longer certain that he wanted to be headman. His fellow hunters wanted to go back; the magic man wanted to go on. If he spoke for the hunters and against the magic man, he was certain that Navahk would accuse them all of being fearful and would never approve of Grek being chosen as headman. If he sided with Navahk against the hunters and urged them to go on, they would have to face their fear or be shamed by it; either way, they would never forgive him for forcing them to make such a choice. If they survived their encounter with the wind spirits within the gorge, they would not elect Grek to lead them. They would boast of their bravery, and when the time came to choose a new headman, they would turn their backs upon Grek and name one of their own number. That man would have the right to bring Supnah's women to his own fire and Pet to his bed skins. Grek would have to turn away in silence and see the disappointment in his own woman's eyes.

The older man scowled, drawing the back of a brown, unsteady hand across his mouth. He had already challenged Navahk once and had been ignored. He understood why the magic man wanted to risk his life and the lives of the hunters to take his brother's head and arm back from the wanawut that had stolen them—without its head, Supnah's body could not be laid out to look upon the sky; without an arm, his spirit could not hunt in the spirit world until it was ready to be reborn into the band through the birth of a new child. In time, when what was left of Supnah's body was consumed by predators, the wind would transform his spirit into a crooked spirit, a ghost that would haunt those who had failed to retrieve its head and arm, a phantom that would tear them limb from limb as Supnah had been torn. Not one of them would be born again. They would wander the wind forever, and future generations would forget that they had ever lived at all.

Navahk had told them how it would be. He had said that in his dream times, when he walked with spirits, they revealed their world to him. It was a desolate, lonely world that no man would wish to enter, except for a magic man who must commune with the spirits on behalf of his band.

Frustration pricked Grek. Navahk was responsible for Supnah's death. It was his spear that had flown wide, causing his brother to fall prey to the wanawut. And it was Navahk who had wounded the wind spirit, causing it to flee into the mountains with Supnah's head and arm. By right, the responsibility and the risk for reclaiming his brother's parts should be his.

Yet what was a band without a magic man? Weak. Vulnerable to the whims of the weather spirits, unable to anticipate the coming and going of the game or to protect itself against the vengeance of the crooked spirits of its members when they came from the spirit world to take the lives of those who had prevented them from being reborn into the world of men.

This spring the great herds of grazing animals had not returned to the tundra. The newborns were crying with hunger, and mothers had little milk for them. The People had been reduced to living off birds and vermin, camping closer to the mountain realm of the wind spirits than they would normally have dared, so that they might set snares for marmots and dig pit traps for sheep and wolves and bears. It was dangerous hunting, and their rewards had been small. It was not a time to offend the spirits of the mountains or to leave the mutilated corpse of their slain headman to become a crooked spirit.

Grek sucked in a deep yet reluctant breath. His course was clear now: For the good of the band, for Wallah and Mahnie, and with the hope of a future relationship with Pet, Navahk must be followed and protected as he challenged the wind spirits. The band must have its magic man. And if Grek were going to be headman, this was the time to take the lead.

Having accepted it, the weight of responsibility seemed lighter; although, for the first time, he knew that authority was not without disadvantages. As he spoke with the unfamiliar tone of command, he saw the expressions on the faces of his fellow hunters harden toward him. "We will walk with Navahk into the shadow lake of spirits. Together we will bring back the head and arm of Supnah."

Grek was as startled as the others when Navahk turned abruptly and, with a single word, robbed him of command. "No," he hissed. His face was raptorial, black eyes fixed upon them, broad mouth set. "I am Navahk, magic man. I alone walk the spirit world. No man may follow."

The child held its breath. Through the green, fragrant spruce boughs, it could see that one of the beasts was descending into the ravine. The others, remaining where they were, still blocked the light of day; and yet somehow the beast that was coming closer walked in the light, as though the radiance of a winter moon emanated through his body and shimmered in the white skins. That which had seemed ugly and repulsive from a distance was transposed into beauty within the eyes of the watching child. There was a lithe, fluid grace to the beast's movements, a raw, savage tension in the way he held his head. He was like a white lion walking upright, picking his way downward along the dangerous, precipitous face of the gorge. The child sensed his intent. Danger walked in the skin of the beast.

Navahk paused in his descent of the wall of stone. This was the abode of wind spirits, yet the wind was absent. Within the gorge the air was heavy, cold, unnaturally still. He could smell blood and death in the shadowed depths, and he smiled, pleased. High above, Grek and his fear-wracked companions stood watching. What gullible, easily manipulated fools they were to believe that the creatures they pursued were somehow more than mere flesh and blood and bone. Whatever they were—and Navahk had never seen their kind before—they were not spirits. Spirits were things of wind and air, clouds that formed in the substance of men's minds and drifted through their dreams to gnaw upon their reason. Spirits did not bleed. They did not cry out against pain or flee in blind panic, leading their pursuers to their lair.

Navahk's smile widened. Whatever the beast was that had attacked his brother, it was so devastated by its injury that its poor judgment had betrayed it. Navahk would seek it out and, if it was not already dead, he would kill it. And its child. As he had killed his brother.

Now Navahk's smile flexed against memories. Supnah had always been the superlative hunter, so powerful and fast that he could run down a fleeing horse or antelope. Navahk knew that Supnah's wound would have healed in time. Afterward, although maimed, Supnah would have been held in awe for having survived an attack by a wind spirit. Men would have hunted for him; women would have vied for the honor of sharing his bed skins. Word of his miraculous encounter with the beast would have spread from band to band until his reputation outshone that of his younger brother.

Navahk frowned. He could not have allowed that to happen. As magic man he had worked too hard and too long to maintain the subtle balance that allowed him to be the driving force behind the band. As headman Supnah controlled the band. As magic man Navahk controlled Supnah. It had been a comfortable arrangement until Torka had come to the band and caused Supnah to challenge his brother.

Even though Navahk had succeeded in driving Torka away, increasingly there had been bad blood between the brothers. Now that starving times had returned to the band once again—despite the best of Navahk's chanting and dancing—it would have been only a matter of time before Supnah saw into Navahk's heart and, recoiling, stripped him of his status. He had nearly done it once before. Three long years had passed since that night, but Navahk had not forgotten the heat of the feast fire before which his brother had shamed him by suggesting that Torka become magic man. Had Torka not refused, Navahk might well have been driven from the band. He trembled with rage at the memory, which had fed upon his pride for too many years.

So when the wind spirit had leaped at Supnah out of the mists, Navahk had deliberately aimed wide. He had feigned remorse when his spear had struck his brother squarely in the back, and he had loosed a cry when Supnah had fallen and the beast had hurled itself upon him. As his fellow hunters had howled and stamped their feet and ineffectively threatened with their spears, Navahk had known that they would make no move to help his brother; they were terrified of what might happen to their own hides.

Wind slurred briefly in the gorge, stirring the treetops that created the surface of the shadow lake below. Was it the wind? No—something moved within the shadows. Navahk's mouth pressed against his serrated teeth. Again he caught the mell of blood and death, and he felt the eyes of something watching him. Something . . . or some*one*?

His mind was filled with the image of the beast that had straddled the fallen body of his brother. Never, even at the heights of image-making that he reached during the telling of his tales, or in the worst of the childhood nightmares that had often sent him bolting upward out of his dreams, had he seen anything to equal it. It had stared at him out of eyes that were the color of gray mist, out of a face that was neither beast nor human but something in between. And, unable to look away, unable to move, he had stared back, appalled by its ugliness, enthralled by its physical power.

Incredibly, he had been aroused by it. It was female. The awe she inspired reminded him of Sondahr, the magic woman who had stayed with his band long ago. Old Beksem, the band's master of magic and deception, had died just before her mystical arrival in the aura of assurance that surrounded her as visibly and impressively as her cloak, which was sewn entirely of the black and white flight feathers of the giant teratorn. She had singled Navahk out so that he might learn from her and share the secrets of shamanism. Her teachings had been planned to summon up both man and mystic from within the body of the youth, challenging, nurturing, and inspiring.

But he had always been frustrated by her because he could never fully satisfy himself upon her body and could only grasp inferences of the complexity of her spirit as she spoke to him of good and evil, light and dark, blood and water, fire and ice, earth and sky, and meat and grass. And she would speak of men—men of flesh, and men of spirit. She said that the latter were rare, able to transcend their bodies and walk the world of dreams, where they communed with the spirits of all things, animate and inanimate, living and dead. He asked her if she was a spirit woman, and when she said yes, he said that he would be a spirit man.

Sondahr was mother, sister, lover, and prodder to him. She posed endless riddles but never told him if his answers were correct. She taught him the chants and magic that called upon the spirits of the game to come to die upon the spears of the hunters of his band. It was so for her but not for him, and when he grew restless and frustrated, she gave neither rebuke nor encouragement. He watched her bring forth babies from women whose time was at hand. He wit-

nessed the way she expelled evil spirits from the sick an
sang sad, gentle songs of mourning with the old who kne
that death was near. He had little concern for learning thes
things. Seeing this, she told him that a shaman must be
living fire for his people, to brighten and clarify the cloude
world of the men of flesh. A band without a shaman was
band that must live in darkness.

He had grown impatient with her words about spirits an
shamanistic light and asked her to tell him instead about th
powers of magic. She told him that magic was a false an
distorted thing and that a magic man who was not also
shaman was a man of smoke; he blinded those who would b
warmed by his fire so that they could not see where, or t
what, he was leading them. She had made him know that a
his skills would amount to nothing when compared to wha
they might be if he were a man of spirit instead of flesh.

Those were her last words to him. Like a late-summer mi
that lay upon the tundral lake at dawn and was gone by noor
she vanished. She had lain with his brother before she ha
left the band, to honor its headman, to give to him the gift
her presence, and to leave with him a feather from her cloa
as a token of her favor. To Navahk she had left nothing bu
shame, for when Supnah had given him the sacred medicin
bag of Beksem shortly after Sondahr's departure, thus be
stowing upon him the rank and responsibility of magic mar
he had worn Sondahr's feather in his hair. Navahk had know
then that dull, uncomplicated Supnah had pleased and satis
fied Sondahr when he, Navahk, had failed. He had hated he
for that. . . .

Memories pricked behind his eyelids like the beaks c
carrion-eating birds. Everyone loved his brother. People fo
lowed Supnah as naturally as grazing animals followed th
greening grass of summer. The steady warmth of his natur
was like an inner sun that drew the loyalty of women an
fellowship of men while, for all of Navahk's cleverness an
extraordinary handsomeness, women feared him as much
they desired him, and men tended to be wary of him, observ
ing him from a distance.

Navahk hated his brother for this. He had hated him sinc
the death of their parents, when Navahk was sent to shar
the fire of old Beksem. Supnah, already a young man, had
woman and a fire of his own. The boy begged to live wit
him, but Beksem had chosen him to be the future magic ma

of the band. This was an honor, although Navahk had not wanted it then. Old Beksem had used him as other men used their women. Supnah was oblivious to his brother's plight, and Navahk would not be further shamed by speaking of it. As the years passed, he found other ways to deal with his disgrace: by humiliating others and by learning to make them fear his magic. This was when he came to realize that his brother's status was nothing when compared to the power that was held in the hands of a magic man.

When old Beksem continued to use him into manhood, Navahk surreptitiously fed him contaminated portions of the spleens and livers of carnivorous animals. The old man died slowly of the poison. Navahk had smiled; he liked to kill. He had wanted to kill Sondahr and Supnah when he saw her bright feather shining in his brother's hair, but he contrived a new and better game—finding perverse pleasure in insidiously undercutting his brother's natural dignity and gradually overshadowing his status.

Everything had gone according to plan until Supnah's first woman had died and he had bartered several of the band's superfluous females in exchange for a new woman, whom he adored. She was a virgin. Violating all taboos, Navahk had secretly entered the small, conical hut of purification that the women had raised for her. There the intended bride of Supnah sat naked for the entire cycle of a single moon, amid smokes of wormwood and fragrant grasses, cleansing her body and spirit, preparing herself to enter a new life and to put her girlhood behind.

He had not desired her; he had desired to possess and impregnate that which was to have been solely Supnah's. He whispered that his body was not his own but that of a spirit hunter who walked the wind, entering the bodies of living men in order to enjoy the bodies of living women. He told her that she must yield or be consumed in the fire of the spirit's anger. He warned her that to speak of the mating, even in her dreams, would result in her becoming barren forever. Her eyes, brown and soft, had gone wild with terror as she had spread herself for him.

The fear in her eyes had aroused him—that and the thought of Supnah, in his own pit hut, longing to lie with her, to bloody himself with her virginity even as Navahk was secretly taking it for himself. He had laughed to think of it and had pierced the girl with no concern for her pain as he whipped

himself into a frenzied passion, riding her to heights of ec
stasy that he had not thought possible.

Again and again Navahk secretly entered the hut of purifi
cation and lay with Supnah's bride, thinking of his brother'
disappointment when he at last penetrated his new woma
only to find that she was not tight around his shaft but a
pliable as an old skin basket. But the moment of victor
never came. Supnah's bride had used female trickery so tha
her husband was given no cause to suspect that he was no
the first to lie with her. As the woman swelled with life
Supnah spoke often of his love for her, and when she looke
at him, he saw his love reflected. The woman had not looke
at Navahk like that. She spurned him, and months later
when her child was born and Navahk prowled close to se
what he had spawned, she warned him away. She called th
magic man ugly and devious and misshapen. Then she hel
up her beautiful son, Karana, and said that in the infant's fac
she learned the truth of Navahk's treachery. Karana was *hi*
son, not put into her by any spirit, but by a brother who, fo
all his beauty, was not fit to walk in Supnah's shadow.

Karana had been a bone in Navahk's throat ever since
Because Supnah and Navahk shared a physical resemblance
Karana's true paternity was not suspected. But as time passe
it became increasingly evident that the little boy possessed a
the precognitive genius that Navahk pretended to own. Navah
had jealously watched the power maturing within the chil
until one day, like his mother, Karana had looked into Navahk
eyes to see the core of deceit and treachery.

The magic man had known that it was only a matter of tim
before Karana's powers eclipsed his own. And so it was that
in the midst of one of the longest, coldest winters eve
suffered, he began to contrive omens that would dispose c
his unwanted child, his brother's beloved only son. Althoug
weakened by starvation and illness, the boy's mother ha
sensed Navahk's intentions but had been unable to convinc
the guileless Supnah of his beloved brother's treachery. Soo
after, she died.

Child abandonment was the way of his people during star
ing times, and although Karana was no longer an infant o
toddler, Navahk had seen to it that he was among those to b
abandoned. When Supnah had balked, Navahk had only t
suggest that a headman who must ask his people to sacrific
their children for the good of the band must not be unwillin

to offer his own child to the spirit of the storms. He had almost laughed when Supnah had agreed. In an unprecedented vow, one made in memory of the boy's mother, Supnah promised to seek out the children in the spring.

Karana, standing tall, had strode off bravely with the other children, as if he would somehow protect them until the band came for them. Navahk smiled, knowing that the hated child was as good as dead.

Weeks later game was sighted. The men of the band hunted. The people ate. Supnah took up his spears and prepared to go after his son.

It had not been difficult for Navahk to convince Supnah that any effort on behalf of Karana and the children would be in vain. The magic man swore that he had seen their deaths in a vision.

Supnah was a man broken by his losses. Navahk virtually ruled the band until Karana had walked back into his life with a story of survival that had set the band to murmuring that Karana surely had been favored above all men by the spirits.

Nothing had been the same since the boy's return. For the first time Supnah had been unsettled by Karana's resemblance to his brother, a likeness that had been strengthened by the passing of time. The headman had begun to brood over the accusation he had refused to believe when his woman had finally told him of it. His loyalty to Navahk rapidly deteriorated into open resentment.

But Supnah was Supnah. The older man still held a hope that he had misjudged Navahk. Even after Torka had left and the boy disappeared, Navahk would be aware of Supnah watching him out of brooding eyes, and he would respond by secretly lying with Naiapi whenever he could, despising the woman except as a vessel into which he could pour his contempt for his brother, and with a brotherly smile for the headman, which overlay a sneer of disdain.

After three long years of good hunting, starving times had returned, and Navahk's chanting and dancing and magic smoke had failed to call the herds to come to die upon the spears of Supnah's hunters. The old questions were back in Supnah's eyes. His lack of faith in the powers of the magic man was growing. The people of the band had begun to sense it.

And so Navahk had killed his brother. Supnah had left him no choice.

* * *

The child huddled in the shadows. Hidden beneath the thick, tangled undergrowth, its body was a dark, shivering, shapeless blur within the gloom.

The beast was there, just ahead, standing over the body of the child's mother. With all but his head and hands hidden within the white skins of caribou, he seemed to be a creature composed of light, so beautiful that, for a moment, the child was almost drawn out of hiding.

Then the beast smiled, and the little one saw his ugliness—a hideous twisting of his naked face as he drew a stone from a double-sided length of tree bark that he carried attached to a thong wrapped around his midsection. The child stared, squinting through shadows as it tried to get a better view without being seen. The stone was black, shaped like a willow leaf, and as shiny as river ice after a sudden freeze. It was similar to the stone that had been embedded in its mother's chest; the stone that now lay at the feet of the beast beside the motionless body.

The child sucked at the gash that the stone had made in its own palm. The stones of the beast were sharp. The child did not like them or the way the beast was looking at its mother. He was kneeling now, and poking. Suddenly the child nearly cried aloud, and only the pure, raw instinct for survival kept the little one from leaping out of hiding in order to stay the beast's hand.

In the dim, filtered light at the bottom of the gorge, Navahk lay his head upon the corpse. He could hear his own heart beating, feel his blood throbbing as his nightmares dissolved and he realized that the dead thing was no spirit. She *was* of flesh, bone, and blood, animal and human all at once. And still warm. His hand lay open upon her chest, a large island of bare, bloodstained flesh exposing now-flaccid breasts and a portion of massive rib cage. The rest was furred, as gray as the skin, wolf-toned, and as sleek, with a short, thick nap underlying the longer, stiffer guard hairs.

Navahk stared down at the creature, appalled by her ugliness and fascinated by the power that now lay stilled forever within her extraordinary musculature. If only such physical power were his! He would not need magic to manipulate the lives of men.

He looked up through the gloom, along the wall of the gorge to where his fellow hunters stood peering down at him in awe and terror. His smiled intensified. *They shall have their magic now!*

Working quickly, he skinned the corpse, leaving its hands and head attached. The work excited him. Pausing briefly, he looked for Supnah's head and arm. Neither was to be seen. He was glad. His brother's soul was doomed to wander the spirit world forever, but Navahk had no fear of him. Dead or alive, Supnah's gentle, guileless spirit would never be a threat to such as Navahk.

Standing, the magic man donned the skin of the creature as though it were a robe of honor taken in a particularly dangerous and difficult hunt. Balancing her heavy head atop his own, wrapping her gory arms around his neck and folding them across his chest in a grotesque embrace, Navahk danced in her skin and felt her power rising within him, as sweet and heady as blood sucked from the wound of a living beast.

Navahk's eyes glittered at the idea. Bending, he savagely tore open the chest of the mutilated corpse, ripped out its heart with his bare hands, then consumed it, gnawing and gulping like a wolf. No man would contest his right to become headman now. He was Navahk, the magic man who dared to kill a wind spirit and dance in its skin! The mystical force of the wanawut was in him now. No man would ever stand against his will again.

Suddenly aware of being watched from within the tangled shadows of the stunted grove surrounding the little clearing in which he danced, Navahk stopped.

He saw the child—a hairy, heavy-featured, misshapen thing as ugly as its parent. Nevertheless, its eyes were as rarely beautiful as the softest gray of the clouds—but clear, without threat. Yet they cut Navahk to his soul as he stood in the skin of its mother as though he, and not the creature, were mute and unintelligent. But he knew in that moment that somehow the creature's intelligence was as fully advanced as his own; and in its grotesque, half humanness, he had glimpsed a reflection of himself.

For a long time after the beast had wheeled and fled from the gorge in the skin of its mother, the child barely moved, barely breathed. Around it the world seemed to be holding its breath, too, as though in sympathy with the plight of one of its creatures.

Bereft and stunned by what it had witnessed, the child

slowly returned to what was left of its mother. Mutely it mourned. The image of the beast was seared into its brain. Hatred for all beasts of its kind burned within its heart. For a long time it sat, moaning softly.

After a while hunger caused the child to stir and look at the arm and head of the beast, which it instinctively had taken from its mother's side before the beast in white had come into the gorge. Man meat was good; its mother had taught it that man meat was the best. Weak with exhaustion, the child began to gnaw upon the meat that its mother had provided at such great cost.

Darkness filled the gorge. The wind stirred softly. The child slept and dreamed terrible dreams, then awoke, thinking of the beast in the skins of winter-killed caribou . . . thinking of how someday it would hunt him and dance in his skin as he now danced in the skin of its mother.

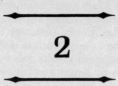

2

In the shadow of the Mountains That Walk, Torka and Karana stalked antelope with the dog Aar. They moved slowly, hunched forward, concealed by the deep, sweet grass of spring. The land sloped upward beneath their feet. Everywhere was the smell of grass and wind and open, sunlit spaces. They paused at the top of a knoll and lay on their bellies in the shoulder-high grass, so content with the moment that they decided to savor it before going on.

"It is good," said the youth, still breathing hard from the long, unbroken trek out of the valley in which their encampment lay.

"It is good," affirmed the man as his hand parted the long, tender stalks of grass and his eyes scanned the land that lay before them.

It was like no other. Even now, three years after entering it, Torka remained awed and amazed by it. Neither valley nor plain, it was a twenty-mile-wide swath of undulating tundral steppe that ran southeastward for uncounted distances between towering mountain ranges. On either side of the river of grass, the Mountains That Walk, unlike other mountains, were not the exposed bones of Mother Below. They lay atop those bones, clothing them in ice that stood some two miles high.

The grassland rolled away before them, pooled here and there with tundra lakes, which sparkled silver in the sun, and veined with the meandering rivers of meltwater cascading out of the surrounding, glacier-buried ranges. Westward the land rose into high hills, which led off into familiar country where dark fingers of shadow spilled out of canyons. Hardy, weather-stunted spruce forests grew there, and a scabrous, heavy-shouldered peak devoid of ice stood tall against the sky. Smoke rose from its summit as though, somehow, a band of men were camped within and building ill-made fires.

Neither Torka nor Karana paid heed to the lambent smoke that clouded the distant volcano. They had passed within its sulfurous-smelling shadow on their way into the new land, when they first had left the protection of Supnah's band. The volcano had been an object of fear and wonder then, but no more. Its plume was no longer remarkable; they found it no more threatening than fair-weather summer clouds drifting before the sun.

"Look," whispered Karana, his strong, sun-browned hand pointing off through the grass. "Can there be so many?"

Torka gestured the youth to silence; but beside him even the dog seemed incredulous as it stared straight ahead, salivating, its body tense, its blue eyes fixed and dilated in its black-masked face.

Torka's broad, powerful hand flexed about the bone haft of his spear. He counted the various species that grazed ahead of him and thought: *For three passings of the time of light this man has hunted in this land, and still the game comes, always walking eastward into the face of the rising sun, vanishing into it at the beginning of the time of the long dark and leaving my people with meat to feast upon beneath the rising of the starving moon. And now the time of light has come again. Again the cycle begins. And again this man wonders how a land so rich with game could have been forbidden.*

The question troubled him, but only for a moment. A panorama of life spread before him. Bison, black maned and long horned, huffed and bellowed and pawed up the fragile skin of the tundra, cropping the grass in a vast, dark line of life the size of which Torka had not seen since he was a boy hunting the broad hills of the high Arctic with his grandfather. They were miles away, but he could see the black blur of them upon the horizon, feel their movement in the earth, and smell their good, rich, acrid stink mixing with the smells of other animals.

Close to the western hills a moose stood shoulder deep within a tundral pool, its head underwater as it browsed upon the bottom. Nearer to the knoll, antelope were grazing, and Torka could see a small herd of elk, antlers furred with velvet, high stepping across a broad stretch of tussock. Nearby, a group of three camels, tall-humped and as irritable as always, observed the elk and brayed with the coughing, hacking, phlegmy sound that old men make after too many years of breathing winter smokes. It was a sound designed to drive the elk away; when it did not, the camels hacked more loudly than before and scattered, indignant.

Karana supressed a laugh. When Torka looked at him, the youth smiled, and Torka smiled back. To share in the sighting and observation of game was a good thing, as was the love shared by this man and the youth.

The dog sat up and cocked its head. Karana reached out and slung an arm around the neck of the animal, drawing it close with rough and well-appreciated affection.

Torka looked across the land. He saw a ring of musk oxen on a not-too-distant rise and knew that if the shaggy beasts formed a circle, there must be wolves about, or lions.

Or bears, he thought, recalling the enormous paw prints that he and the boy had seen earlier in the day while crossing one of the refugium's innumerable outwash streams. Once again he was troubled by his thoughts. He and Karana had been only a short distance from their encampment when they had sighted the bear tracks.

For three summers they had lived in that camp, which lay within a wide, wind-protected valley he and Karana had discovered while pursuing a gut-wounded goat into one of the many canyons that cut deeply into the glacier-smothered ranges. Almost perfectly circular, its high, stony hills stood between the valley floor and the surrounding ice-capped mountains. Sweet, warm springs bubbled from the earth, and the pools remained liquid even during the coldest days of winter. It had proved a perfect refuge from the nearly incessant wind that ripped across the game-rich grasslands upon which he and the boy did most of their hunting.

Finding the paw prints of the great, short-faced bear so close to the entrance to the valley had set him on edge, for no other predator was as agile, aggressive, or unpredictably dangerous. The short-faced bear was almost exclusively a meat eater. When Torka had knelt and measured the paw prints, he had felt a terrible hollow expand within his belly. Only because the prints had been leading away from the valley had he continued on with Karana instead of turning back to make certain it was not on the scent of the encampment.

"Torka . . ."

Karana's whisper drew him back to the present.

"You still worry about the great bear?"

It was not unusual for the youth to know his thoughts. He nodded. "It is so."

"The entrance to the valley is staked against predators. If the great one walks there, he will turn back or blunder into the pit trap that we have dug and die upon the sharpened stakes within it. He will be food for us. It would be a good thing. Bear meat is fat. It gives much oil. We would have plenty of tallow for our lamps in the winter dark."

The boy was right. Nevertheless, the concern stayed on Torka's face.

Karana shook his head. "Torka worries too much these days. All is good in this land."

"Yet we are alone—one man, a boy, three women, a child, and a suckling."

"Karana is not a boy! Karana will soon have seen the passing of fourteen summers. He is a man! Torka does *not* hunt alone!"

"No, but Torka *does* worry. When we walked from Supnah's band, it was in this man's heart that we would soon find a new band—a better band—but not once has this man seen a sign that even a solitary hunter has ever passed this way."

"We are a band. We need no others. We have taught the women well. Aliga is good with a spear. Lonit is better, and deadly with her bola."

"And Iana is hopeless with either."

"Iana does not need her spear. We will hunt for her and protect her."

"And if something should happen to one or both of us?"

Karana shook his head and smiled, then leaped to his feet, spear braced and nocked to his spear hurler. "Torka must stop worrying! Torka has done the right thing by leading his people into this new land! Look! There is so much game waiting to be taken, the spirits will be offended if we sit here talking like a pair of fat old men! Come! A blind man could make a kill this day!"

On the horizon the plume of smoke that rose from the distant volcano thickened visibly. The moose raised its head from the tundral pool, and its ears swiveled as it nickered loudly. Then, with a wheeze, it broke into a run, its nose and antlers dripping moss and water as it disappeared into a grove of scrub spruce and alder. Birds flew up and wheeled screaming overhead, while foxes, lynx, wolves, and lions ran with squirrels and hares, voles and lemmings, and made no attempt to catch and eat them.

But Torka and Karana did not notice the odd behavior of prey and predator, nor did they pay heed to Aar as the dog frantically attempted to gain their attention by pulling at the fringes of their leggings. In frustration they kicked out at him, and the dog, despairing, whined and circled and hunkered close to the ground, yapping like a disoriented pup.

The attention of the hunters was focused on the frightened herd of antelope that skittered past them, circling and leaping and trampling the high grasses, making pathetic bleats, oblivious to the man and boy who had not even had a chance to position themselves downwind before each of them had made a kill.

Amazed, Torka and Karana whooped with pleasure, raising and shaking their bloodied spears . . . until Aar leaped with the power of a saber-toothed cat and roared not like a dog but like a lion. With tail tucked, ears back, teeth bared, and every hair along his shoulders and spine standing on end, Aar flung himself past the hunters as they whirled to see the great, short-faced bear that had emerged from nowhere to charge them out of the silken camouflage of the grasses.

"I tell you, this woman does not like the look or the feel of it. It is too quiet, much too quiet, except for the fish in the weir. Even from here you can see them jumping, as though trying to leap from the pool and escape. You would think we were standing over them with a net, ready to scoop them up for dinner! And have you ever seen the dogs behave like this?"

Lonit tried to make light of Aliga's words, but the tattooed woman was right: No birds sang. No insects hummed. The ground shivered beneath her feet. The water in the hot springs lapped at the embankment of the pools, bleeding quietly into the surrounding earth. The lashings of the pit huts rubbed against the thongs that held them fast, and the huts themselves, as well as the many drying frames upon which meat and skins were stretched to cure, creaked and chafed against their trembling frames.

It was as though a strong wind was blowing through the camp, but there was no wind. The air seemed suddenly heavy, and the dogs whined and sniffed around in directionless confusion. Sister Dog had disappeared, carrying two of her newest litter of pups, with the rest trotting after her, tails up, milk bellies half dragging on the ground. Aliga supported the distention of her advanced pregnancy with her hands, fingers laced protectively beneath it, as she rose with great effort from where she had been sitting outside the main pit hut, cracking marrow bones.

Lonit looked at her and tried not to betray her own trepidation. It was not easy to do, since she had already reached for a spear with one hand and held her bola at the ready in the other. Aliga's advanced pregnancy made Lonit feel increasingly protective toward her. The tattooed woman wanted this child desperately, not only because she longed for Torka, who lay with her only when he sensed that she needed reassurance that she was his woman in every way. She wanted this baby because she had been so sure that she was barren. Lonit had borne only daughters to Torka—first Summer Moon, and then, in the last time of the long dark, precious, plump little Demmi, who had been named for Torka's long-dead mother—and Aliga wanted to be the first to bear a son to Torka, in gratitude to him for having taken her to his fire circle when no other man would have her. And she wanted it for herself, because she had never borne a child, and because she could not forget that, among the People, it was said that a woman who has never brought forth life can never truly call herself a woman.

"Look, the dogs are quieting," Lonit said, relaxing a little. The wind was rising again. The moment of unnatural stillness was passing. From within the shadowed interior of the main pit hut, little Demmi's baby laughter bubbled like a warm spring as Iana resumed a happy song.

Summer Moon's face appeared at the door flap, a little hand holding the intricately seamed hide aside. "This girl cannot nap! Mother Below make belch!"

The little one's statement brought a smile to Lonit's lips. The child saw it and dimpled, rubbing sleep from her eyes as she ambled naked from the pit hut to seek comfort in her mother's arms. Lonit lifted her firstborn and held her tightly, glad that the strange moment had passed. Perhaps she had imagined it. The earth could not move. Yet she could have sworn that it had shifted beneath her feet. No. It could not have been. The dogs were relaxed now, birds were peeping from the willow grove behind the pools, and the blackflies were back.

Summer Moon winced and began to cry as one of them pierced her tender skin. Lonit slapped it away, and to Aliga's consternation, rather than going to dress the little one, Lonit put down her weapons and began to take off her own clothes.

"Come," she said to the tattooed woman. "Join us in the pools. The day is warm, and the steaming water will keep away the curse of the biting flies."

As always, Aliga's face flushed at this invitation, the merest suggestion of color seeping between the black swirls that covered her face. "This woman is not a fish! This woman does not strip naked to flop and splash in water! What would others say?"

Lonit laughed. "But there are no others in this world that we have made our own!" Even now she thrilled to think of their golden days in this valley, where Torka had taught her to use a spear, to hunt beside him, as finely honed to the dangers and excitement of the hunt as any man.

"One day others may come," snapped Aliga. "One day we may choose to walk out of this far land where there are no people! What will others say then, if Lonit forgets herself and takes up a spear as though she were a man or encourages her children to peel off their clothing and leap into water to splash like fish in a net?"

"Too much does Aliga speak of leaving this valley! Does she long for the Ghost Band? Does she yearn for such bands as Galeena's people, who smelled like fresh dung? Or does she miss the peaceful life within Supnah's band, when each night the headman and the magic man thought of new ways of shaming Torka!"

Aliga's head went up. Her eyes narrowed, and her mouth turned down. "When this woman's baby comes, it would be good to have wise women and a magic man beside her to help her bear it."

Now Lonit's head went up. Her mouth narrowed and turned down. "Lonit will help Aliga, as Aliga has helped Lonit. We have learned much woman wisdom. We need no others. Because we have chosen to walk with Torka, we are the wisest women of all!"

"But we have no magic man," lamented Aliga piteously.

"Then, indeed, we *are* wise!" retorted Lonit, turning her back upon the tattooed woman and heading for the pools with her child.

*   *   *

Suddenly, sharply, the world moved. It flexed like the skin of a living beast, knocking Torka, Karana, and the dog off their feet while the great, short-faced bear went running by them, disappearing into the sea of grass, not to be seen again, as the earth rolled like the surface of a turbulent lake.

And then the roaring came—a terrible, all-pervasive growl that rose from deep within the earth, far below the fragile skin of the permafrost that now buckled and cracked. One crevice yawned wide directly below the hunters, and they fell into it, fighting desperately for footing in a world that allowed them none, reaching and grasping for holds that were not there. Paroxysms of heaving earth pressed in against them until they were certain they were being buried alive.

Then, as suddenly as it had begun, the earthquake was over. Torka and Karana scrambled out of the fissure and, spitting earth from their mouths, reached down to help the frantic dog. They stood amid the broken grassland, too stunned to retrieve their spears or the carcasses of the antelope that still lay within the fissure; too shattered by the enormity of their experience to realize how fortunate they were not to have been pierced by their own weapons when they had dropped into the heaving earth.

Dust gauzed the air. On the western horizon the smoke that issued from the bare, scabrous mountain was a boiling cloud of steam and ash that filled the sky as it rained fiery fragments of its inner core on the world.

"We must go!" Torka commanded, his mind filled with images of a ruined camp and of his women and children consumed by the earth that had nearly swallowed him and the boy.

Lonit screamed.

The pool dropped. The water rose, covering her, then fell away, rolling out of the pool entirely, while just upstream, in a broad, shallow pond she had created by raising a semicircular dam that captured many fat, lazy fish, the fish were leaping and splashing madly. The earth shook as though it would never stop. Summer Moon clasped her little arms about her mother's neck and matched Lonit scream for scream. Lonit saw Aliga fall as the fish in the weir pond were washed onto dry land and the pit huts and the drying frames collapsed and the sods that lined the fire pit tumbled into disarray.

Lonit found her footing, and with Summer Moon gripped

under one arm, leaped from the now-empty pool. The earth threw her down. She rose again, holding the sobbing child as, sobbing herself, she forced her way across the rolling earth, staggering to where her baby and Iana were trapped within the collapsed pit hut. The framework was heavy enough to stun a woman or crush a child. They had built it of caribou antlers from recent kills and of mammoth ribs and tusks that they had taken from the long-dead carcass of a woolly mammoth they had discovered in the willow grove behind the pools. Lonit's heart was in her throat as she fell upon her knees before the rubble of hide and horn and bone, calling to Iana, crying her baby's name.

When Aliga joined her, relief flared in her heart that the tattooed woman was all right. The convulsive movements of the earth had lessened. She put Summer Moon down and told her that she must be a big girl and help to save her little sister. The child gulped down her tears.

Together they ripped away the hides and hefted the massive bones until, at last, Iana's face stared up at them, blinking, and they saw that little Demmi lay curled in the protective fold of Iana's arms, still gurgling happily, as though the rolling of the earth and the collapsing of the hut were a new game devised for her pleasure. With a cry of relief, Lonit lifted her infant, and as a dazed but unhurt Iana was helped to her feet by Aliga and Summer Moon, Lonit wept with joy.

Then her eyes swept over the ruins of the encampment, and her happiness faded. Everything had been leveled. With the huts and frames down and the small, ordered world of their encampment a shambles, a terrible sense of vulnerability fell upon Lonit. Where was Torka?

Roarings now reached her from the distant mountains.

"Look! Mountains come down!" exclaimed Summer Moon, clutching Lonit's bare limb and pressing close.

Lonit's eyes widened. The white plumes of enormous avalanches tumbled from the heights. Far to the west a great, gray cloud was filling the sky like smoke rising from an impossibly huge fire. The smoke was dark as though with grease, and the wind that now blew into the valley from out of that cloud was foul and reminiscent of the sulfurous mists that occasionally lay upon the pools.

A blackfly found the bare skin of her back and bit deep. She hardly felt it as she held her little one, tensing as the world once again rolled beneath her feet. It was not enough to throw her off balance, but her mind expanded with fear.

Aliga stepped cautiously across the jumble of fallen drying frames, meat, and skins. She was holding her belly again, as though afraid that her unborn child would fall out. Her eyes were dilated, and her tattooed lips were pinched against her filed, tattooed teeth. She paused beside Lonit, took off her doeskin apron, and wrapped it around little Summer Moon. "Lonit had best cover herself. Her skin is as black with biting flies as this woman's is with tattooing."

Lonit saw that Aliga was not exaggerating. She handed Demmi to Iana and hurried to retrieve her garments.

"Will Torka come back?" Iana asked.

Lonit was wiggling into her undertunic when Iana's question caused her to pause, startled. Iana had not spoken to anyone except the children since she had been rescued from the Ghost Band. Lonit ran to embrace her. "Of course he will come back!" Any other answer was unthinkable. And yet her mind swam out across vistas of broken, earthquake-devastated land upon which she visualized her man and Karana both lying dead. No! She would not let herself even think it!

Torka barely said a word when he returned to camp with Karana and Aar. His face spoke his relief when he saw the children and Lonit safe. She ran to him, declaring that she and the others were well. He held her as though he would never let her go, but his features tightened when she declared that all would soon be made right again.

"It is so!" Karana agreed, fending off the welcome of the pups, Sister Dog, and other members of Aar's ever-growing canine clan. Over half of the once-wild dog's progeny had run off to join the wild dogs in the valley's distant hills, but Aar and his mate and the rest of their strong, eager-to-learn pups stayed. The unnatural alliance between the dogs and the people of this band was strong; its roots lay deep in the bond that Aar had forged with Umak, spirit master and Torka's grandfather.

Torka gave no sign of having heard Karana. The man's eyes had taken on a sudden guarded look as he looked at Aliga, sitting cross-legged and mumbling to herself on bed skins that Lonit had dragged out of the ruins of the main pit hut. Rocking herself and her unborn child, Aliga still supported the weight of her belly within her folded arms. As Torka walked toward her, she did not even look up at him.

"It is well with you?" Torka knelt before her, placing a gently questing palm across her abdomen. It was not like Aliga to sit when others were on their feet. She was usually up before the dogs in the morning and the last to close her eyes at night.

"It is well." She shivered and looked up at Torka reproachfully. "As well as it can be for any woman with child in a land that shakes! Lonit has brought to this woman a horn of brewed willow, and she has cracked a marrow joint for me to eat—as though these things would make me forget what has just happened! Lonit is so determined to live forever in this land, she is willing to overlook everything."

Lonit came to stand beside Torka. She had put the children into Iana's doting care in order to bring Aliga's favorite robe to her, which she had made when they had first come to the valley. Lonit had worked long hours to sew the many strips of fur, which were taken from the prime skins of animals that she had stalked and killed herself, for the express purpose of making a gift for Aliga that would be a gesture of sisterhood. Aliga loved it so much that she wore it even on days when it was really too warm to wear such a garment; but now, even though the late afternoon was still warm, she was trembling against an inner cold. Draping the robe around her shoulders, Lonit stepped back, not understanding why Aliga had taken such a hostile tone.

"But this land has been good to us," Lonit told her. "We have known no hunger. This valley has sheltered us against storms. We have filled it with songs of praise and have shared it with all the creatures that warm themselves beside its hot springs in the time of the long dark. We have seen Life Giver lead his children and his females close to our encampment, and we have seen him walk away, leaving Torka and his people to live without harm from him and his kind. How can Aliga have forgotten these things?"

"Aliga has *not* forgotten," the woman responded thoughtfully. "Torka *has* led his people well, and this *has* been a good land. But now this woman is troubled. We are wanderers . . . seekers . . . who should join other bands to make great hunts together. Navahk told us before the great feast fire that we must prey upon the weak and the unwary among the game animals, so that always they will be strong and able to flee before the hunters who, in turn, are made strong by the chase! Aliga says that Mother Below has grown angry with Torka's band! She has shaken the ground to tell us that it is not good to stay in one place. Torka's people must go back into the country from which we have come. If we do not, Mother Below will shake the world and swallow Torka's people, and we will be spirits moaning forever within the earth and—"

"Say no more." Torka's words were gently spoken as his hand moved from Aliga's belly to her mouth, closing her lips. "Be cautious, Aliga. Remember that among this man's people, to speak of a thing is, sometimes, to make it happen."

Karana was angry. "Be wary, woman! Do not let your female fears control your tongue!"

"Female fears? Watch your *own* tongue, boy! The next time you are pregnant in a land that shakes, with no wise women or magic men around to help you, then you may talk of 'female fears'!" She disliked Karana these days. He was beginning to look too much like his father's brother, and Navahk walked her dreams in ways that Torka would not have approved. Somehow, she had the feeling that Karana knew this. His wide black eyes saw too much for a boy, private things that were not visible to anyone else—sometimes not even to her until he made her aware of them. She knew that he was angry enough to speak his inner thoughts, and fearing them, she attempted to silence him with her glare.

Karana would not be intimidated. For all of his pretentions to maturity, Karana *was* a youth; wisdom was as alien to him as the apprehensions of the pregnant woman who sat before him. "Aliga fears giving birth in a band with no wise women or magic men to attend her. It has been on her mind since she first knew that she was with child. She does not care about Torka or his people. Aliga cares only for herself!"

"Karana!" Torka exploded. Although the youth had displayed remarkable intuition on a hunt, had seen the yellow sickness in old Hetchem, and had warned of her death, Karana had failed to note the unnatural dilation of Aliga's eyes. Torka had learned enough about healing to know that something was wrong when eyes looked like that in the light of day. How deeply wrong, only time could say. He felt sick with worry, remembering how she had wept and laughed with incredulous delight when she had found herself to be pregnant. Then, in the days that followed, her mood wilted and she had grown ill.

He could not blame her for wanting to go back. "Would

Aliga truly have Torka lead her back into the land of other people, where women are not allowed to hunt beside their men, where one band preys upon another, where babies are eaten in the winter dark or thrown away at the word of a headman? Does Aliga believe that the birth of her baby would be less painful or dangerous, or that her child would be better off among strangers in a starving land than here, among those who love her?"

Aliga chewed her lower lip petulantly. "Torka has met bad people. But not *all* bands are so. Supnah's band was not so bad. There were wise women among them, and a magic man."

Karana's mouth curled into a sneer. "All of the women of that band who were old enough to be truly wise were sent walking the wind long ago. Supnah's band *is* a bad band. And Navahk is no magic man at all!"

"He is!" she retorted, as though flying to the defense of a maligned loved one.

Torka did not miss the underlying implications of her reaction. He felt no jealousy, only a sad, oblique pity. He had come to like the tattooed woman. He was sorry that she could not have had the man of her choice. "Navahk is far away, and this baby is very near. It sleeps now, as Aliga should sleep," he told her as he placed his open palm across her distended belly. If his unborn child stirred beneath his hand, he could not feel it.

The earth trembled. On the western horizon the Mountain That Smokes sent up an enormous plume. Even from this great distance Torka saw the glow of falling debris that must have been the size of boulders. It was a sight that allowed no argument. "The land of Navahk and Supnah's people and of the Great Gathering lies there, far to the west, beyond the Mountain That Smokes, beyond the cloud that rains fire. We cannot go back, Aliga. Neither Mother Below nor Father Above will let us."

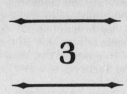

3

For three days the distant mountain smoked, but the earth did not shake again. Soon the pit huts, drying frames, and fire circle were reassembled. The sky cleared and the encampment looked the same except for a thin, gray ash that continued to fall from the sky, coating everything. Torka and his small band remained on edge. Only the little ones slept well through the ever-shortening nights.

The days passed, and the weeks. Now there was no night, and after the first summer rain, the dust disappeared and the Mountain That Smokes became dormant. Its summit was no longer conical but concave, rather like a grinding tooth with a great cavity in one side.

Torka stood with Karana at the edge of the rebuilt encampment. Although the hot-springs pools had filled again with warm, steaming water, no fish swam downstream to become trapped in Lonit's rebuilt weir, and it seemed to Torka that the waters smelled more consistently sulfurous than before, so he could not bring himself to bathe in them. Lonit displayed none of his reticence. Now she bathed with Iana and the children, and it did his heart good to hear laughter echoing across the land.

Aliga sat glumly in the sun. Torka had not heard her laugh or say a positive word since he had told her that she must bear their child here. Torka wished that the baby would be born. Its time was near, and it would be good to see Aliga smile again, even if her teeth were filed and black.

A soft, cooling wind blew across the valley from the distant, snowcapped ranges. It was gentled by the encircling hills, yet still strong enough to keep the biting flies at bay. Not for the first time Torka noted that the wind was un-

tainted by the stink of smoke from the far mountain; it had
been many days since ash had fallen from the sky.

"The wind will be strong on the sea of grass," said Karana.
"It will be a good day to hunt. In his dreams this boy has
heard the great mammoth walking in the hills to the east.
And where Life Giver walks, the spirits of the game are
strong with favor for Torka's people!"

With Aar, Sister Dog, and three of the older pups at their
sides, they hefted their spears and loped through the narrow
arm of land that bent out of the valley and through the
encircling hills, to open at last onto the wide, windswept sea
of grass.

Torka had learned long before that Karana's visions of
where the game would be were usually correct; as a result,
he rarely challenged them. When they skirted the pit traps
and snares that lay at the entrance to the valley, they headed
east, into the wind.

The sound of battling horses drew them on, and although
they ran, it was with the measured pace of experienced
hunters alert to danger. The grasses grew tall, as golden and
brittle as the manes of young lions. Torka drew his razor-
edged bludgeon of fossilized whalebone from its sheath of
tanned leather at his side. He scythed the grasses aside with
it; the blade cut through them as easily as it cut through
warm fat. It was a unique weapon, one that he had brought
with him from a wide, rolling land that smelled strongly of
salt. It, too, had been rich grassland, yet troubling somehow,
rousing nightmares of great, roaring black waters that swept
across the world, drowning all that lay before them. They had
found the carcass of the great fish; but it was stone—as were
the shells Lonit had found—and it was from one of the
whale's ribs that Torka's bludgeon was made.

As he walked now with Karana and the dogs upon the sea
of grass, he tested the weight of the bludgeon within his hand
and thought of that strange land across which he had come.
There was no way for him to know that it had once lain at the
bottom of a shallow strait that connected two oceans and was
a bridge between two continents—or that, in millennia to
come, it would lie at the bottom of the sea again. He could
only perceive some difference in that plain, as he sensed that
the Mountains That Walk on either side of the sea of grass
were not mountains at all but the leading edges of glaciers

larger than any that had ever lain upon the world. He could not know that three-fourths of the moisture of all the seas and oceans and rivers on earth lay captive within their appalling mass, or that most of the northern half of the North American continent, into which he had led his tiny band from Asia, lay entombed in ice.

The sound of the horses was close now. At the crest of a low hill Karana signaled to the dogs with the flat of his hand, and as one they hunkered in the grass beside him. Torka joined them, watching through the screen of summer gold as, below them in a narrow depression in the sea of knolls and hillocks, two stallions fought savagely for dominance over a small herd of shaggy, blocky mares.

The dominant stallion was unusual not only because it pursued its older, less aggressive foe even when the other horse attempted to run away, but also because its uniformly pale coat was devoid of the dark stripe along the spine that was characteristic of its species.

The frenzied, bleeding animals screamed and reared, kicked and bit and pawed the air. The older, more sturdily built stallion wheeled and ran; the younger, leaner, fleeter animal pursued it and turned it back to the battle. The older stallion was clearly losing ground. Torka marveled at the beauty, power, and persistence of the pale horse. Beside him Karana's head dropped a little as his pleasure ebbed. Where Torka saw beauty and power, Karana saw beyond the animal's physical perfection to its unrelenting savagery and cruel and merciless power. It reminded him of his father.

When suddenly a leaping cat sprang from a thick stand of scrub into which the dominant horse had driven the exhausted older stallion, the fight ended. The lion-sized cat sank fangs that were nearly as long as Torka's forearm into the hindquarters of the stallion. Battle-weakened and bloodied, it screamed but had no strength to flee. Its rear legs went out from under it, and in a moment the cat was at its throat while the pale horse wheeled and raced away, neighing triumphantly. It drove its newly acquired mares ahead of it, viciously kicking and biting at them as it ran, brutalizing them so that any that were pregnant with the other stallion's foals would miscarry. This was the stallion's way of assuring that only its offspring would survive.

"Navahk would do that," hissed Karana.

But Torka was not listening. The sudden, brutally quick

death of the stallion had worried him. *Torka could die in such a way—quickly and without warning. What would happen to my women and children then, with only a boy and a pack of dogs to protect them?*

As they went farther east, Torka could not keep his thoughts on his tracking. Karana scouted ahead with the dogs, but Torka stopped and looked back, thoughts of Aliga haunting him. Poor, frightened woman. If she did not bear her child soon, she would die of it. He had seen the sickness and weariness growing in her. And the fear of death.

"Torka! Come! It is a good day to hunt!" The youth was beside him now, gesturing. They could see for miles, where great herds of awe-inspiring numbers and diversity grazed. "There! Do you see? As in my dreams, Life Giver walks ahead, into the sun, leading us to the game."

But Torka was still looking back, toward the world out of which he had come, toward a distant land where mountains did not smoke, the earth did not move, and where, if a man were killed, there would always be others to care for his women and children. "We *will* hunt for the last time in this land without people," he declared, looking at Karana with stern and uncompromising authority. "Tomorrow we will gather our women and children and return to the land of men."

PART III

THE OTHER SIDE OF THE SKY

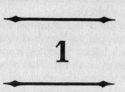

1

A frigid wind stirred the stunted, misshapen trees that choked the bottom of the gorge. The shadows were warmed by the light that seeped into the world through the hole in the sky, but the child shivered amid the scattered remnants upon which it had been feeding for weeks—the bones of its mother . . . of Supnah's arm . . . and his skull—smashed in the child's attempt to extract marrow and the brain. The bones were no longer distinguishable; they were only splinters and jagged fragments, rubble from which meat had been gnawed and all juices extracted.

For some time now there had been nothing nourishing left except the small comfort that the child found in gnawing and sucking them. It lived on bark and spruce needles, insects and unwary birds, and the body of a lemming that it had managed to root from its burrow beneath the spruce trees.

It chewed the lemming now, grinding it between molars adapted to masticate heavier, more nutritious bones. The child trembled as it ate, dizzy, its body craving more meat and blood than the stringy, sweet flesh of the rodent could provide.

Mother! I am alone! Mother! I am hungry! Mother! I am afraid!

There was no comfort for the child in the bones and meat of the lemming nor in the warm, yellow wind that blew across the world from out of the hole in the sky. The child rose and climbed out of the gorge to crouch upon the ridge that allowed an overview of the tundra. Comfort came as it stood, where it had once stood with its mother, and thought of her. It leaned forward, head out, the wind ruffling its gray fur and filling its nostrils with the scent of the beasts that camped far below upon the plain. Comfort came as its gray eyes drew in the sight of the ones who had killed its mother. Comfort came with hatred, which nourished the child more than meat, bones, or blood.

They had moved their encampment once. The child had watched them, perplexed, as they had dragged their shelters with them upon their backs, plodding across the grasslands as slowly and ponderously as sloths. They went several miles, to a spot more protected from the wind and closer to water. For a brief time the child had panicked, fearing that they would keep on walking, right off of the edge of the world, leaving it alone with no one to hate. But they had paused and raised their odd shelters and built their smoky fires and lifted their voices in the peculiar ululations. The child found these sounds strangely soothing, as beautiful as star song murmuring across the sky in the depths of the winter dark. For weeks it had watched them from the heights, salivating each time it saw the blur of white that was the object of its hatred, knowing that someday it would hunt him, kill him, and dance in his skin, singing its own celebration of his death.

Now, light-headed with hunger, the child exhaled a hoot of frustration. The encampment was gone! The beasts were trailing off into the distance, all bent beneath their packs, except the mother-killing one in white, who led them.

The child whimpered at having lost the deep, perverted comfort from knowing that those who had killed its mother were near. Bereft, it shifted its weight from one foot to the other again and again. It beat its curled, hairy fists against its hairy thighs. If the beasts were to walk off the edge of the world, how would it find them again? How would it someday leap from the mists onto the one in white, as its mother had leaped, to rip him apart until he was red with blood and shrieking?

As the focus of its existence began to disappear across the eastern horizon, the child screeched, enraged. It knew instinctively that it would die if it was deprived of its sole reason to live. It hunkered, apelike, then rose. Supremely agitated, it swung its torso back and forth as it waved its long, hairy arms. It shook its fists at the departing beasts, screaming in frustration and anger.

"Wah nah wah! Wah nah wut!"

The beasts did not slow their progress, although the child saw the one in white pause and look back. The child drew its hand across its mouth, erasing the blood of the lemming and hungering for the blood of the mother killer.

The beast shone gold in the light of the hole in the sky as, slowly, he turned and disappeared into the haze of distance.

Now the child's solitude was absolute. Again it mewed for its mother, for any of its kind, but all were gone—killed by beasts.

That thought gave the child courage. The way down from the heights was difficult, but the little one was undeterred. Drawing energy from its hatred of the mother killer, it left the familiar territory of its past behind, coming out of the mountains and walking across the tundra alone, to follow the band of the one in white, in whose skin it longed to dance.

Karana bolted upright on his sleeping skins. "No!" he cried, still tangled in his dreams. Howling dire wolves raced across the tundra, pursuing him. He looked back, and as he did, the wolves turned into hideous, half-human beasts that loped after him, with Navahk in the lead—an amalgamation of magic man and wild stallion and something else . . . something dark and terrifying that he had seen long ago . . . a shadow silhouetted against distant, glistening mountains of ice . . . a form moving in the night, furred, massive, and powerful, with glinting eye and bearlike snout and broad-lipped mouth pulled back to reveal protruding canines longer than Karana's dagger.

The wanawut.

Spirit Sucker.

Navahk.

His *father!*

He blinked. The dream vanished. And yet he did not think it would ever vanish. He sat shaking, his sleeping skins tumbling down from around his shoulders into his lap.

It took several days to dismantle the camp and prepare for the long trek ahead. Each time he slept, Karana dreamed the same dream. But each time he spoke of it to Torka, leaving out no detail except the fact that Navahk was his true father, the hunter silenced him with grim admonishment.

"This man also dreams, and his dreams have been untroubled since he has made up his mind to return to the world of men."

"It is a *bad* world."

"Karana left it as a boy and will return to it as a man. Perhaps he will find it better."

Karana harrumphed. "Why? Because there are *girls*? Karana cares nothing for girls!"

"*Yet*," replied Torka, finding it difficult to suppress his smile when the youth stood chin up, arms folded belligerently across his chest, taking on all of the mannerisms of Torka's beloved grandfather. In moments like this he wondered if, when old Umak had died, his life spirit had entered Karana to live again within the flesh of youth. It was not an unpleasant thought; but, as always, he was startled when Karana responded to it as though he had spoken it aloud.

"Umak has said that Karana would be a great spirit master someday. Umak would have listened to Karana!"

"Torka listens. But we must go. Aliga is sick. We have not the magic or the medicine to cure her. Her baby should have been born weeks ago."

"Babies come when they are ready."

"And if they do not come, then death comes to them and to the woman who carries them."

Torka put a reassuring hand upon Karana's shoulder. "Perhaps we will come back to this place someday. We have cached the meat and supplies that we cannot carry. If we meet with others who would wish to return with us, we will tell them that hunting is good in this land. But Karana is quick to forget that beyond this Valley of Songs, within the Corridor of Storms, the winter wind is cold and constant and crueler than any storm wind that this man has ever known. If, for any reason, the game did not come to winter in our valley, we would be forced to follow it into the sea of grass, and Torka wonders if a band could long survive the winter dark within the Corridor of Storms."

"Longer than we will survive among Supnah's band!"

"It is not this man's intention to seek out Supnah's band. Long and hard Torka has thought on it. If we leave our valley now, we should easily reach the Great Gathering before summer's end. There will be wise women, spirit masters, and magic men there from many bands. Think of all the healing knowledge that Karana will learn from them!"

"They are mammoth hunters," the youth reminded sourly.

"We need not join in the mammoth hunting. We can hunt for our own fire and provide for our own needs. Our women will savor women talk with others. Summer Moon has never seen little ones her own age. And this man longs to hunt and talk with other men again!"

Stung, Karana wondered if Torka would ever consider him a man. "If Aliga is sick, she should not make such a journey."

"Aliga feels better just thinking about it. She will travel by sledge and will be no worse for the traveling than she is for her worrying."

The boy shook his head, refusing to hear logic. "Lonit does not want to go."

Torka sighed. Discussing this subject with Karana was like talking to a mountain wall. In time he would see the wisdom of Torka's decision; in the meantime, there was no use arguing. His hand opened as he patted the youth's shoulder with paternal affection. "Lonit, unlike Karana, has learned that it is not good to challenge one's headman once he has made up his mind."

"But will Torka *remain* our headman in the world of men?"

The question was sobering. Since Torka had no answer for it, he turned away.

Lonit knelt holding her spear across her thighs, sliding her curled palms along the sleekness of the bone stave. She had made the weapon herself. Torka had taught her how to soak the bone until it was malleable, how to harden it and define its shape in fire, and he had helped her to work the long, broad-ribbed, heavy head of shining, lanceolate obsidian. She remembered the laughter that they had shared over her many mistakes, and how at last, when she had accidentally cut the heel of her hand, he had kissed it, then taken the stone and finished the work himself, while she sat back and marveled at his skill. After securing the projectile point to the shaft, they had begun her training, and after weeks of practice, she had, with this spear, made her first kill.

She sighed and set it aside. She would not be able to use this spear or any other in the future. Beyond the Valley of Songs women did not use spears, nor did they hunt beside their men. She sighed again, turning her attention to the tools and clothing before her. These were the things she would take with her on the long trek into the world of men. Winter things and summer things, all neatly arrayed on separate skins, would be rolled into individual packs, then combined into one main roll, which would be secured by thongs to her pack frame of caribou antlers. There was so much that she wanted to bring, and so much that must be left behind. Never had she stayed long enough in one camp to enjoy the luxury of accumulating personal belongings that were not essential to the daily routine of nomadic life. Never before had she come to love a *place*, not only because it offered good and sustained hunting but because it seemed as though she had somehow become a part of it.

She leaned back on her heels, resting her palms upon her thighs, savoring the sleek texture of her beautifully tanned dress of unusual pale-gray elk skin. She had worked for weeks upon this dress after Torka had brought the skin back to camp as a present. She had slept with the skin hair-side out, raw flesh pressed to her naked body so it would absorb the precious oils and sweat of her own skin as she lay bundled for the night under as many furs as she could bear. Torka had laughed with amusement, saying that she, instead of the elk skin, would be soft and ready to be scraped by morning. But she had survived the night, greedy to begin work with her scraper.

She had used a sharpened caribou scapula to stretch and soften the hide. With good-natured deprecation Aliga had teased her, asking why anyone would need so soft a dress. It had seemed wrong to say that she simply *wanted* it. She had the time to spend on such a luxury and considered it a challenge to her skill. But primarily her reason was that Torka had brought the skin especially for her pleasure. She was proud of this, and when she wore it, she wanted the touch of it to pleasure him as much as he had pleased her by bringing it to her.

After she had scraped and stretched it, she moistened it with urine steaming hot from her own body, then left it to freeze in the early autumn night. She kept watch over it herself so that no predatory rodent would nibble on it in the dark. For three nights she sat guard beside her elk skin, and on the morning of the fourth day, she whisked frost from it, meticulously cut away the thin, fleshy layer of subcutaneous membrane, and began the final scraping and thinning process. For days she kept at it. Karana observed her with interest, saying that he had not thought it possible for Lonit to make better hides than she already did.

"We can always make things better," she told him. "And Lonit remembers what our old Umak used to say: 'In new times, men must learn new ways.' It is so with women too."

He had nodded, reminiscing that his own mother had once worked hard like this to make special clothes for him. "The tunic she made for my first hunt was of many skins—one strip for each kind of animal that a hunter may hope to kill in his lifetime."

She had not missed the sadness in his eyes when he spoke of his long-dead mother. Without slowing the stroke of her scraper, she had promised herself that when she was finished with her dress of gray elk skin, she would make Karana a tunic of many skins—perhaps not of all the species of animals that a man might hope to hunt in a lifetime, but at least of those animals that a woman might kill with her spear and her bola.

And this she had done. It had taken her over a year to collect the skins, and Karana, Torka, and Aliga all agreed that they had never seen a finer tunic. Lonit still preferred her dress of elk skin because Torka had brought the skin as a gift to her.

She smiled with pleasure at the recollection of that shining moment. Whenever she wore the pale-gray dress—with its long-fringed seams to which she had sewn many of the tiny, spiral, shell-shaped rocks that she had carried with her into the Corridor of Storms—Torka not only enjoyed touching the dress, he enjoyed touching it so much that, whenever they were alone, he peeled it off her and began to enjoy touching her much more.

How could a woman not love such a dress or the man who loved her above all others?

But he did not love her enough to stay in the land where they had been so happy.

He was coming toward her now, his eyes looking at her but not seeing her. He paused, knelt, and focused on the traveling bags and bladder flasks of oil that lay at her side and the objects arrayed upon the traveling skins. He nodded approvingly at the adze and awls and scrapers, the fur comber and antler straightener, and the bow drill of bone and the little bag of dried lichen and moss that would be used for wicking and kindling, then at the multipurpose loops of thong and sinew, the birding nets of braided musk-ox hair, the fishing trident and lures and hooks of bone, the skinning knives, and at the feather shafts filled with dried blood, which could later be liquified with spittle and used as glue.

He frowned when his eyes fell upon the smaller of her two soapstone lamps. Both were oblong, flat-bottomed vessels for the holding of oil, in which moss wicks were laid and burned. He shook his head. The little lamp had been the first one that he made for her when they had come to the valley and discovered soapstone in the encircling hills. Summer Moon had accidentally dropped it, and the little lamp, badly cracked along its right side, had leaked oil ever since. He had assumed that she had tossed it away when he had carved the new one for her.

"Our journey will be long," he said. "That lamp is damaged. Leave it. Lonit's pack will be heavy enough as it is."

He reached to take it off the skin, but her hand stayed his. "This was the first tool that Torka made for this woman when we came to this valley. This woman would keep the lamp always." She hesitated, barely daring to speak the next words. "As she would stay in the Valley of Songs always."

"It cannot be. For Aliga, we must go back."

Her heart sank. "Yes. It must be so."

His hand caught hers and gripped it. "Is Lonit not afraid to stay in this land that walks, where the mountains rain fire?"

"The land walks, but no one was hurt. We have raised our huts and drying frames again. The mountains rain fire, but far from this valley. Who can say that the land did not also walk to the west, or that mountains did not rain fire there too? In this valley, *Torka* is headman. The band may be small, but it is strong because Torka is strong. Life is good because Torka is good. For the first time in her life this woman has been completely happy. As long as Torka is beside her, Lonit is not afraid." She knew from the expression upon his face that she had spoken the wrong words.

"And when Torka is *not* beside her? If someday Torka should go from this valley to hunt within the Corridor of Storms and not return . . . ? Would Lonit be afraid then, alone with her children and two other women in this far land, with only an inexperienced youth to protect her?"

She wanted to lie. She wanted to reply boldly, saying that with her bola and spear she could face any danger, but he would see the truth in her eyes. Without Torka she *would* be afraid—and not for herself. Were it not for the children, Lonit would have no desire to live without him.

Or would she?

The question terrified her. There were worse things to fear than a lonely death—things she could not speak of to her man or admit to the other women. There was the memory of a flame-lit night and of a man in white, more beautiful and mysterious than the night itself, dancing and whirling before her, telling her that she was beautiful, inviting her to turn her back on Torka and join with him at his magic man's fire.

And there was the memory of wanting to join with him, of longing to rise and take his hand and walk into the fire-lit night with him and lie with him and never look back.

Never. Not for Torka. Not for Summer Moon. And *that* was more frightening than death. Knowing that for one shattering moment she had been close to abandoning all that she loved, all that made her life worth living.

He nodded at her silence, misunderstanding it. He saw the fear in her eyes and kissed her lightly on the lids. "It is good that Lonit has been brave in this land. As for Torka, he *is* afraid for all of us, and he will not stop being afraid until we have found protection within another band at the Great Gathering."

He held her. He *loved* to hold her, to smell the sweetness of her skin and the long, fragrant swan-black strands of her hair into which she rubbed the pungent oils of artemisia . . . to feel the full, swelling firmness of her breasts against his chest and the warm sleekness of her elk-skin dress against his palms. She never failed to stir man-need in him, especially when she wore this dress. His hands slipped downward along the bend of her back, enfolded her hips, swept back upward to her shoulders, began to work at the laces of the dress, then paused. The pit huts were down. Aliga, Iana, Karana, and the children were watching from where they were assembling their own traveling packs and awaiting his inspection of them.

He put Lonit away from him, suddenly understanding why she had chosen to wear this dress instead of her heavier, more serviceable hunting and traveling clothes. He shook his head as he looked at her with eyes filled with love. "Lonit must change into traveling clothes. This man will not turn away from his purpose. And never will he consent to allow Lonit to go to another man's bed skins. In this valley, or in the world of men, in the dress of elk skin or out of it, you are Torka's woman, always and forever."

She bowed her head, devastated by the love that she had seen in his eyes, terrified that he would see the indecision and betrayal in hers. If Navahk came to the Great Gathering to join with the other magic men, if he danced before her in the firelight beneath the whirling stars, if he held out his hand to her again and asked her to come with him, she was not certain that she could refuse.

She was not certain at all.

* * *

Beneath the endless day of the Arctic summer, Torka led his little band out of the Valley of Songs. The terrain did not easily accommodate heavily burdened, sledge-dragging travelers. Their progress was slow, and they walked in silence. The dogs trotted ahead of them, Aar and Sister Dog and three of the older pups carrying side packs, looking back often, as though they could not understand what was taking the men and women of their pack so long.

They plodded on, deep into the narrows of the valley that opened into the Corridor of Storms, against a wind that seemed determined to shove them back to their encampment.

"You see?" Karana asked. "The spirits of the wind wish us to stay."

"And the spirit of survival tells Torka that it wishes us to continue."

On they walked, pausing at last on the other side of the stakes and pit traps that had kept large carnivores from entering their valley. The great, glistening walls of the Mountains That Walk lay before them, silent sentinels flanking the vast, rolling river of grass. Ahead and to the west, the Mountain That Smokes was without its usual plume. Above, the sun watched them, as did the great woolly mammoth, Life Giver.

Eighteen feet tall at the shoulder, it loomed directly ahead of them, about a mile away at the crest of a broad, tundral rise. Life Giver's massive, twin-domed head was raised, its ears twitched forward, its tusks were extended, its trunk upcurled.

"Look! Big Spirit has come out of the valley," said Aliga, pointing from where she lay upon the fur-padded sledge of crossed, sinew-bound caribou antlers.

Karana set down his end of the sledge, and Torka did the same. "The Great Spirit wonders why we are headed out of the valley and into the world of men—men who would hunt him and *us*, if they had the chance."

Torka cuffed the youth hard upon the shoulders. The boy stood firm against it and dared to challenge the man again.

"They *will*, you know," he pressed. "Torka is not like other men; he cannot live within a band. He must lead it. And so other men will always try to bring Torka down or drive him out from among them."

The words of the youth were heavy with a truth that Torka had no wish to acknowledge. "Torka has no desire to challenge the authority of men older and wiser than he. Torka *will* live within a band again. This time, Torka will walk with caution, lest he cause offense."

"Hrmmph! If Navahk is at the Great Gathering, he will find a way to trip you."

"Amid the throng at the Great Gathering Navahk will be only one man among many. This man will not misjudge him again—nor will he fear him. Navahk may be a magic man, Karana, but he *is* only a man."

"He is a very bad man."

Torka shook his head, giving up on the conversation. "Come," he said sharply, annoyed with the youth for having visibly upset Lonit. "Torka has thought much of this, and so he says now to Karana: Just how bad can one man be, after all?"

They walked until their need for sleep caused them to stop. Beneath the light of the endless day they put down their sledges and packs, ate a light meal of traveling rations, and, except for Karana, slept.

With Aar curled and dreaming at his side, he sat with his arms folded around his knees, his back to the wind as he looked back across the miles toward the Valley of Songs.

The mammoth was still there, far away now, grazing alone at the base of the tundral rise that stood before the neck of the canyon that led into the valley. Karana could not have said what motivated him to rise, waking Aar, and to move toward the animal, but it seemed that the warmth of the sun was rising in him, blinding him to all but the mammoth.

Well away from his sleeping fellow travelers, he broke into a lope. With Aar bounding at his side, he ran through molten gold—the gold sun above and golden grasses all around. Karana ran until the miles that lay between him and the great mammoth ceased to exist.

The mammoth raised its head, watching him come. The creature swayed restlessly, raised its huge tusks so high that they seemed to touch the sun.

Karana stopped less than a spear-throw's distance away. But he had come unarmed and stood with his arms hanging loose at his sides, his heart pounding and his breath coming in deep, even rasps.

The mammoth lowered its great, twin-domed head and fixed the youth with its ancient eyes.

Karana stared back. He was so close he could clearly see the discolored tips of the mammoth's tusks and the crooked scar high on its shoulder where Torka's projectile point had struck it so many years ago. Karana could see the jagged tip of the spear shaft that the mammoth had broken off, extending from the animal's tough hide.

Beside him, Aar looked up, curious. His blue eyes moved from Karana to the mammoth. The dog saw the animal through the tall golden grasses, a towering, mountainous form. He smelled the beast and knew through its scent that there was no threat in it—as long as Karana stayed where he was.

But slowly, raising his arms, the youth began to move forward. He softly whispered for the dog to stay, and Aar, trembling in confusion and frustration, reluctantly obeyed.

Karana was warmed by the sun. Its light filled him as, across the golden land, he walked entranced, his mind as wide as the sea of grass, as free and light as the spirit wind that whispered within his head.

"I will come back!" he shouted to the mammoth, to the land, and to the surrounding mountains. The wind took his voice and sent it rushing on, on, back into the Valley of Songs, where it caressed the familiar hills and pools and rushing stream.

Behind him Aar whimpered and hunkered back, tail tucked, hair bristling. Karana seemed a stranger to him in this moment—no longer a youth, but a man . . . a man of power . . . a magic man, a man without fear.

The mammoth was moving toward him, but Karana stood unflinching. As his arms were raised, so, too, was the trunk of the mammoth raised. And in the golden light of the sun, his body aflame with the spirit wind, Karana reached, *touched*, set his splayed hands upon the tips of the great tusks, and named the mammoth Brother.

"I *will* come back!" he vowed again. "And in the land of men I will raise no spear against your kind, nor eat of your flesh, nor drink of your blood. You are totem to me. Life Giver, forever!"

2

For a thousand miles the wind moaned across the land, and
the people of Navahk moaned with it. Although tradition
forbade it, the magic man was also headman now. He had
won that right when he had walked into camp wearing the
skin of the wind spirit, explaining that Supnah's arm and head
had vanished and that the former headman would never be
reborn into the band. Navahk had not explained how a spirit
had come to have a skin or earthly form, but no one had
asked for an explanation; Navahk's power was incontestable in
this world and the next.

His face and arms upraised to the sun, he stood now
clothed only in ornamental feathers: the white owl feather that
adorned the forelock of his knee-length hair; the headman's
circlet of eagle, hawk, and teratorn feathers about his brow,
wrists, and ankles; and the broad downy collar that had once
been Supnah's, with its grotesque fringe of taloned claws
draping his shoulders and chest.

His people sat around him, making a song of their moaning, slapping their hands upon their thighs in a slow, desul-
tory rhythm that matched the low, resonant hum of the flies
buzzing around the drying frames that held wind-stiffened
ribbons of meat, fish, and whole, gutted, unfeathered fowl.

It was the time of year called time when the caribou
change hair, long past the time when the caribou came to
familiar crossings en route to northern calving grounds from
winters spent to the south and east. Navahk's band had
wintered at such a crossing, but they had still been the
people of Supnah then, and now they knew that it was
Supnah's fault that the caribou had not come. Navahk had
assured them of that; he had told them that the spirits had
not favored Supnah for a long time—that was why they had

sent the wind spirit to kill him and had sent the spear of the magic man flying wide so that they might commune with Navahk now, as he stood naked beneath the sun, listening expressionlessly as his people's songs of adoration droned around him as atonally as the flies droned around the meat.

They sang of Navahk, story-chanting, as was their way at festive occasions. They sang of how he had returned from the mountain of the wanawut wearing the skin of the spirit that had killed his beloved brother. They sang of how he had kept the mandatory five-day death watch for Supnah and of how, to prove his merit as a hunter to his people, he had led them to hunt successfully once again. They sang of finding the smaller herds of caribou that broke off from the main thrust of the migration to forage until signs of the impending time of the long dark called the small groups into a single river of life, and together they walked southeastward into the face of the rising sun.

The rhythm of their chant quickened. The men boasted of following Navahk from one hunting camp to another, of killing caribou until there were no more. They did not add to their song that their kills were small, a cluster of cows and calves here, another cluster there, not once equaling the great kills on which Supnah had so often led them, kills that enabled them to stay in one camp for months on end and sometimes for an entire season. The chant did not ask the spirits why the great herds of caribou had not returned to this portion of the tundra. They did not ask the forces of Creation why the spirits of bison and elk and ox grazed not upon the grass where the band might find and hunt them. Instead they praised the spirits of the caribou, without embellishing their songs with the information that by late in the season the animals were fly bitten, their valuable winter pelage long since replaced with the stiffer, shorter hair of summer, suitable only for making boots and pouches. Instead they sang of how, at any time of year, men were grateful for meat and for magic men who led them to it.

They praised the changing season that had brought two of their girls to womanhood and chanted to the spirits of the owls, ptarmigans, hares, and foxes, which had completely shed their coats of winter white, exchanging them for less conspicuous tones of brown and gray. The rhythm of the chant grew faster still, the words more boastful, warning the creatures of the tundra that their new hiding coats would make no difference. Navahk was headman of this band! The animals of the tundra must be wary, or the magic man would call them forth to die within the snares and nets and upon the spears of his people. No animal or spirit could refuse the command of Navahk. Not even the wanawut!

And certainly not the new women, Pet and Ketti, who now waited within the blue smokes of the hut of first blood, which the women of the band had raised for them. Within it they had passed their first time of blood. The hut would be burned at the end of this day's ritual, during which both new women would be ritually deflowered by their magic man, whose portendings would determine their new status within the band.

Mahnie was afraid. She sat beside her mother on the women's side of the circle and watched as Ketti and Pet were led stiff-legged with fear from the hut of first blood to stand before the magic man.

Across from her the faces of the men of the band were rapt, strangely hungry eyed, as though they were viewing game instead of girls. Their chanting was strident now, tensely drawn, like their faces. One would think that they had never seen a naked female before.

Mahnie licked her lips and felt the sun's heat beating upon the top of her head, rousing a dull ache. She reached to rest an open palm protectively upon her head and was startled to feel how hot her hair was. She was equally startled when Wallah grabbed her wrist and forcefully returned her hand to her thigh. She looked up at her mother, saw a warning in dark eyes that communicated the need for self-control, and felt afraid again as she forced herself to clap and chant with the others.

Mahnie did not like the chant; it reeked of insincerity, and the men had all the words. The females merely accented them in low, tedious sucks and exhalations of air, rather like dull-witted animals giving birth. Beneath the thin, light-weight buckskin of her skirt, her thighs were growing numb from the repeated slapping of her palms against them. Still the chanting went on and on.

And still the magic man stood motionless in the center of the circle, his body greased to prevent biting flies from piercing his skin, his head back, the paraphernalia that he would soon use arrayed at his feet upon the terrible skin of

the wanawut. He stood so still that had she not seen the
pulse beat at his throat and the subtle, throbbing movement
of his engorged, erect penis, she might have taken him to be
dead and stretched upon an invisible drying frame.

She stared at his organ, not liking what she saw. Nudity
was common among her people within the confines of their
pit huts, not flaunted beneath the blazing eye of the summer
sun. She had seen all of the men of her band naked at one
time or another—as they had seen her—but never had a man
displayed himself like this . . . nor had she ever seen an
organ so engorged that it stood upright, above the magic
man's navel, moving slowly, as though it had a life of its own.

The sight of it unnerved her, as did the entire atmosphere
of the impending ceremony. It had been the talk of the band
for days now, ever since both Pet and Ketti had come to their
menses simultaneously and the women had hurried to raise
the hut of first blood for them. She had been jealous at first;
at eleven she was nearly as old as they. Her mother had
consoled her, saying that it was difficult to predict when
blood would come to a girl, and starving times could delay a
girl's time indefinitely. Under the starving moon many women
did not bleed at all. And in a band where most of the children
had been abandoned years before, everyone doubly rejoiced
when first Ketti, and then Pet, had announced within hours
that at last their time of blood had come.

Mahnie had found it unfair. The three of them always did
everything together. Wallah had hugged her and said that
her time would come soon enough, and in the meantime
Wallah would enjoy having her little girl for a bit longer. But
Mahnie did not want to be a little girl when Pet and Ketti
were women. She had pouted as she watched the hut of first
blood go up and saw the special treatment accorded to her
friends.

Everyone was so happy, especially Grek. Her father had
been eyeing Pet, Supnah's girl, for years. And for years the
two girls had giggled about it.

"If I bleed before you, I will come to share the bed skins of
your father. We will share the same hut, and you will have to
call me Mother!"

It had been a great joke between them. When Grek was
not within hearing distance, Mahnie often teased Pet by
calling her Mother. Pet teased her back by calling her Daughter, turning up her pert little nose, and ordering her to do as

she was told or Grek would hear of it and Worthless Daughter would be punished. Overhearing, Wallah had been amused. She liked Supnah's gentle, pretty daughter. There would be no jealousy at Grek's fire; the more women in a man's camp, the less work for all.

For three long days Mahnie had been angry with her friends and the blood spirits, who denied her the privilege of sharing the hut of first blood with Pet and Ketti. Then, slowly, as the days passed and the women came and went from the hut, their rejoicing became a quiet introspection. Sometimes, if someone spoke too loudly, the women jumped and skittered off across the camp like frightened antelope. The men were different too, watchful, full of unspoken secrets. And the magic man was not seen for days after he retired into his own hut to do whatever magic men did when they were alone and preparing for a ritual ceremony.

Mahnie asked her mother why the other women were so tense, but suddenly Wallah was nervous and flighty like all the others, with no answers at all. So she asked Grek, who grunted, looked for Wallah, and not finding her, explained as best as any man could about woman wisdom.

"It has to do with the acceptance of the girls into the band."

She sensed evasiveness, which was not her father's way. Even when Navahk had become headman, when everyone had known that eventually Grek was to have been chosen, he had dealt with the matter in a straightforward way. He made no attempt to hide his disappointment, but he did not brood on it either. When Wallah had attempted to console him, he had brushed her away, saying simply that the spirits had chosen who would lead the people; a man did not argue with the spirits.

And girls did not argue with their fathers. But Mahnie was Grek's only surviving child. She was only a female, but he adored her, and she knew it. So she pressed him. "The girls are already members of the band? . . ."

The statement was a question. From the look on her face, he had known that she needed an answer from him. "As girls, yes. As women, no. Since time beyond beginning, it is up to the headman of each band to accept each daughter of his people into the protection of the band—to blood her, or, by refusing to blood her, to deny her that protection."

"Blood?"

"First piercing. It must be done by the magic man. Then the headman makes second piercing, as a man. And if he does not choose to keep the woman for his own bed skins, then her father may at last be rid of her by giving her to the man who gives him most for her."

"Does Grek long to be rid of Mahnie?"

"Of course! You are a girl, aren't you?"

She saw his love through his scowl, but her heart had not been lightened by it. The ritual of first blood no longer seemed a thing to be envied. "Grek has said 'deny.' Do you mean, turn her out to walk the wind forever?"

"Something like that, but that has not been done among this people since time beyond remembering."

"But it has been done?"

"Not in this man's memory. Not in the time of Supnah."

"Navahk is headman now."

The sky bled heat.

Navahk looked up, directly into the molten eye of the sun—then *through* it, to the other side of the sky, to the endless, burning lake of power that lay beyond.

Heat and light poured into him, burning his eyes, but he did not flinch. He drew his strength from them, as he drew strength from the flame light of feast fires, from the cold, distant fires of the uncountable stars, and from the dazzling color displays of the aurora borealis that so cowed and intimidated his people. And from their fear he drew his strength.

He closed his eyes. The sun shone beneath his lids, pooling outward in red and orange, in yellow and white-hot evanescence; like the glimmering lake of heat he had glimpsed beyond the eye of the sun, on the other side of the sky, it was power . . . pure, mind-consuming power. If it were possible for him to fly up into it, piercing the eye of the sun, then to swim in that lake of fire, he would do so. He would not be consumed by the flames; he would be transformed by them, like a spear shaft is strengthened when it has been subject to the searing heat of coals.

The imagery pleased him. He felt the power of the sun engorging his maleness, his pride, and his sense of control over his people and the two young women whose fate lay within his hands. He opened his eyes again, still daring to stare into the eye of the sun, opening himself to its heat, filling himself with its light as though it were blood that might be sucked hot from a living beast.

It burned. He smiled. Pain was sweet to him. Slowly his eyes focused upon the two girls. Ketti, bright and eager in her fear. Pet, wide eyed, trembling lipped. He despised Pet. He saw his brother in her face.

She saw the hatred in his eyes. Her lips went white.

His smile broadened. He knelt. The chanting of his people stopped. Absolute silence was a song of its own, beating its portent in his ears as, from the skin of the wanawut, he lifted the horn of First Man, a heavily greased phallus that was said to be the penis of the first man in all the world. It was not a penis; it was the bonelike protuberance that once grew atop the nose of what must have been a massive woolly rhinoceros. The wide base had been cut away. All that remained were twelve inches of narrow-tipped, upcurling, deadly looking horn. Smoothed by age and generations of handling, it was black with a patina of oils and fat, body fluids and dried blood.

Navahk rose, holding it as though it were his own organ, working it, walking a circuit around the two girls, then pausing before Ketti.

Behind him he heard murmuring as Ketti took the position the women instructed her to take. With knees bent, hips arched, and limbs splayed, she waited.

He looked at her with interest only because her bravery annoyed him. Her bare body did not excite him; if his organ was erect, that was due to the thrill of power that the ceremony was granting to him. He did not look forward to sharing his bed skins with either of them, but he did look forward to the moment of blooding. The horn was smooth and warm within his palms. His lips were taut across his teeth. He raised the horn high above the girl. He saw her grit her teeth and close her eyes, readying herself for pain.

The magic man saw no reason to disappoint her. Nor did he see any reason to prolong the blooding for the pleasure of the girl or the watchers. When Supnah had lived, Navahk had done it that way, to please his brother. Now Supnah was dead, and Navahk pleased himself. His arm arced down. The horn went in fast, hard. If the girl had moved, it might have pierced her womb. But she did not move; the women had warned her that she must not move.

Navahk was disappointed. He snarled as he raised the bloodied horn. A jubilant cry went up from the People.

Ketti's entire body blushed pink with relief and pride. She had survived! She had survived bravely, without a sob or a tear! Her eyes sought Mahnie among the women. Finding her girlhood friend, she beamed with pride as Navahk announced to all that Ketti was now accepted as a woman of his band.

And now it was Pet's turn. The girl was deathly pale. She fought to take the required position of submission. She shook so badly that balance was difficult; her knees buckled, then locked, then quivered pathetically. Beside her Ketti stood as tall as her plump little figure would allow, her posture and expression informing Pet that the worst would soon be over. *Be brave*, her eyes said. *Do not be afraid. It is not so bad.*

Navahk read the reassurance in her eyes and reacted perversely to it. He looked from Ketti's plain, round face to Pet's more defined, infinitely prettier one. Again he saw his brother in the girl. And himself. And Karana. The same eyes. The same nose. The same mouth. Cut to feminine dimensions, but the same. It occurred to him then, as it had before, that she might be his get. He had secretly joined with Naiapi enough times to make it a distinct possibility.

His head eased to one side, his eyes lingering on the girl's face as he recalled that both he and his brother were the sons of many generations of magic men. How many of their fathers had stood where he stood now, holding the sacred horn of First Man? Karana would have known. Karana would have stood beneath this same sun, and the power would have come to him from the other side of the sky, as it had yet to come to Navahk—fully, effortlessly. Karana would have seen through time as Navahk had never been able to see. Karana would have been able to give his father an answer. Karana had the power.

He had not thought of the boy in many days, but he saw Karana now, in the face of Pet. In his dreams the boy walked the other side of the sky and was still too innocent to realize it. He saw a similar innocence in the eyes of Pet. Looking at her now, he wondered if, although Supnah had possessed no precognitive powers, it was still possible for the girl to have inherited those powers through his brother. Or, if she had inherited them, had they been a gift from him, if he were her real father? She had none of the bold inquisitiveness of Karana, but she was only a female. Females were deceitful creatures. Perhaps her fear of him was feigned, and she was a latent force waiting to overshadow him before he managed to hone

his abilities into the perfection and absolute power that still
eluded him? The possibility reminded him of the magic woman
Sondahr.

The sun was very hot on his back. For the first time since
he had come to stand naked in its light, it began to sap him of
energy. Anger rose in him at memories of Sondahr, and of
Lonit, who had shamed him before his people by preferring
to walk into forbidden country with Torka than to share the
fire of Navahk.

Anger fused with hatred and jealousy. Now he was strong
again. His arm rose, holding the bloodied horn of First Man
high. The power was in him—the power of headman, the
power of magic man, the power of life and death. His arm
arced with the force of a spear thrust, driving twelve inches
of rhinoceros horn straight up through her belly into her heart.

Naiapi screamed. She did not break from the women's side
of the circle, nor did she run to her only child as Navahk
ripped the horn from the dead girl's breast. Pet's death had
been quick, although she had shamed herself by crying out at
the moment of her unexpected impaling, an unforgivable
offense not only for her, but for the mother who had borne her.

Navahk was advancing slowly toward the women's side of
the circle, to where Naiapi cowered before him. The woman
expected to be killed. Death was in his eyes. She met it
boldly with her own. Since Supnah's death Naiapi had lived
at the fringes of the band. Pregnant with a dead man's child,
no other man welcomed her to his bed skins. She had gone to
Navahk, offering herself, saying that the child she carried
might well be his and that she would be his woman on any
terms, on any day or night he wanted her. But he did not
want her, or the infant, or her daughter. She and Pet had
lived apart, grateful for Navahk's sufferance, knowing that
soon Pet would be a woman at Grek's fire, and that once
Naiapi's infant was born and exposed—if it was not male—
one of the hunters of the band was certain to welcome such a
comely woman into his protection . . . if Navahk allowed it
. . . if Navahk did not take her for himself.

But now that would never happen, for Naiapi had screamed
at the moment of her daughter's death. Despair growled at
the back of her throat. If only she could bring herself to break
tradition once again by daring to tell them all that her scream

had not been a protest; it had been a cry of surprise and joy.
She would have exposed the girl at birth, as she had exposed
all the others—four little girls—had Supnah not insisted upon
her keeping the child. Pet—another daughter—had been
living proof that Naiapi could bear no sons. But Supnah had
insisted upon accepting the child. Her mouth twisted. How
she loathed the girl! Navahk should have killed her years ago
instead of allowing her to live to soften the headman's grief at
Karana's abandonment.

Her eyes held upon Navahk now. If only he and not
Supnah had seen her first, when their band had come to the
Great Gathering! She was glad Supnah was dead.

The magic man paused before her.

The band watched, waited, for Navahk to loose Death once
again. Instead the magic man smiled. The woman at his feet
impressed him. She was unflinching, brave, hungry eyed,
and distractingly brazen with open sexual invitation even at
the moment of her death. She was beautiful, even though she
was no longer young and her body was distorted with pregnancy. Many men were eager to have Naiapi free of Supnah's
child so that they might attempt to win her.

Navahk's eyes left the woman and scanned the men's side
of the circle. There was no missing the resentment on Grek's
face; he had wanted Pet badly, just as others wanted Naiapi.
Frustration twitched visibly at the corners of Navahk's mouth.
His blood was up for dealing death. But while the death of
Pet had served him, the death of Naiapi would not. Too many
lusted for a chance to win her, and he would alienate them if
he deprived them of that chance.

His smiled expanded. Naiapi would live, but Navahk, like
the wild stallions of the steppe, would suffer no offspring of
Supnah to survive, lest it grow to sap him of his powers. The
men of the band would not object to the expulsion of the
child from her womb. If she survived, they would thank
Navahk for cleansing the woman for their use.

As the woman herself seemed to be thanking him. Her
eyes had seen the subtle change in his expression, telling her
that he was not going to take her life—unless she died as a
result of his killing of her unborn child. She shivered, but he
knew it was not with fear. Her eyes were wide and shining
with expectation, as though what must surely follow would
pleasure rather than pain her. He knew her reputation for

being a woman who had, with her own hands and a notable absence of grief, willingly exposed four of her own infants. At the height of the great killing winter, she had come to him behind his brother's back and asked him not to spare the life of her daughter. She had even dared to imply that he might be the father. She had taunted him with that and suggested that if he was asking Supnah to abandon his child, he should be willing to offer up his own as well. She had told him that she was sick of daughters, and she had offered herself to him then, suggesting that he put a son in her. He had considered killing her and was sorry that he had not, as once again she offered herself to him. She knelt, limbs spread wide, hips arched forward, moving with slow, deliberate provocation. As she threw back her arms and exposed the great, mounding expanse of her belly to him, her mouth expanded across her teeth into a mad, salivating smile of anticipation.

"Kill it!" she whispered with low, hissing ferocity.

Her insane sexual eagerness for pain excited him. His organ swelled and throbbed as he obliged her. Once, twice, half a dozen times, his foot struck into her belly.

Although she fell onto her side and gasped against the pain of his blows, she smiled up at him. "With the *horn* . . ." she begged, opening herself wide to him.

As the members of the band watched in stunned silence, again he obliged her, straddling her now. Slowly the horn of First Man entered Naiapi, to pierce the unborn infant without undo injury to the woman who accepted it and moved on it as though it were the organ of the man who held it. Then he suddenly removed the horn, and it was his organ that penetrated her, thrusting deep, savagely seeking to rouse pain, then withdrawing in disgust as she cried out with the anguished delight of orgasm. Bloodied, his penis still hard and upright, he got to his feet. As the women turned away and Mahnie sobbed into her mother's lap, Navahk smiled and held out his hand to Ketti.

"Come," he said. "It is your turn now."

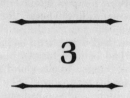

3

They put the Corridor of Storms behind them and walked westward into familiar country. They traveled most of the day, resting only when necessary. This was a haunted land for them: In the low, rolling country to the south, they had encountered the Ghost Band and had seen their loved ones murdered; here they had walked with Supnah's people, and witnessed the death of Hetchem and the abandonment of her poor, misbegotten child.

In the high hills that stood between this open land and the Corridor of Storms, Torka had stood before the great mammoth and been given the gift of life.

And now he walks away from that life! thought Karana, begrudgingly dragging Aliga's sledge, plodding grimly beside Torka. It was as though the sky were a great, gray blanket, weighting all those who moved beneath it. The land seemed gray, and the mood of the youth was even grayer. It seemed hours since anyone had spoken. Even the dogs were subdued, their heads down and tails sagging.

As they came to the bones of the encampment that they had shared with Supnah's people near the Land of Little Sticks, they veered away into unfamiliar country, until the sun disappeared behind the high, glistening blue walls of the Mountains That Walk. At last they shrugged off their packs and gratefully began to make camp in stony, broken country beside a wide, shallow tributary of the River of Caribou Spring Crossing. From here they would continue toward the northwest until they came to the broad outwash plain at the base of the high, forested hills, where they would join the Great Gathering.

Torka and Karana raised shelters against the rain that they

knew would come before morning. The wind had changed. The clouds had thinned to mere streaks. Tomorrow, thicker, darker, more potent clouds would follow. Now the sky glowed. It took on the color of clear water into which blood has seeped. Only if they looked very hard could they see stars at all. This was the time of light. There would be no night, except in their bones and muscles when fatigue told them that it was time to sleep.

Lonit, Iana, and Summer Moon searched for additions to the traveling rations of dried meat and cakes of fat into which berries and bits of wind-cured fish had been pressed. In the shade of scrub willow, birch, and alder growing along the river, the women speared graylings with their fishing tridents.

Lonit and Iana used digging sticks of fire-hardened bone to uproot tubers and picked the crisp, deep-green leaves of mountain sorrel, munching as they worked. Summer Moon followed them eagerly, imitating their every move as Lonit instructed her tiny daughter in the names and uses of the growing gifts of Mother Below.

They feasted upon fish, fragrant leaves, and sweet roots, saving their less desirable traveling provisions for another camp. Aliga sighed, rose weakly to her feet, stretched her great girth, then leaned on Lonit for support as the younger woman helped her to hobble off to a private place within the shrubs where she could relieve herself. This done, Lonit helped her back to the campsite again and gently assisted her as she seated herself.

Seeing that Torka and Karana had gone off to attend to their own needs, Aliga leaned close to Lonit. "Do you think that Navahk will be at the Great Gathering?"

Lonit frowned at the ever-deepening sallow color that she saw within Aliga's swirling tattoos. She touched Aliga's brow, testing for fever. "This woman has no wish to see that one again," she replied. Her fever was still there, but low, barely perceptible, like a tiny ember glowing within the ash of a well-banked fire. She wished that Aliga would drink the bearberry brew that she made for her at Karana's advice, or at least chew on fever-eating willow leaves. But Aliga was not willing to give much credence to either Lonit's or Karana's attempts at healing.

"That one was the most beautiful man that this woman has ever seen," exhaled the tattooed woman, closing her eyes, smiling at memories. "And so powerful, so strong in his magic. Navahk called the bad spirits out of Hetchem. He called them out of her and held them up for all to see! He could do that for this woman!"

Again Lonit frowned. The mention of his name caused an unwelcome and instant quickening of her heart. "Aliga's memory does not see beyond the face and smile of the man! Has she forgotten that Hetchem died? Navahk's magic smokes and chanting did not save her."

"He *could* have. But Hetchem was too old for baby bearing. Aliga is not so old. The magic of Navahk could help this woman. Aliga is sure of it."

"Karana says that his magic is trickery, that there is a darkness in him."

Aliga's blackened lids fluttered open. She shook her head weakly and smiled conspiratorially at her friend. "What does a boy know of how a woman sees a man, eh?"

"We are Torka's women!" Lonit replied defensively.

"Yes, but we would have to be blind not to respond to Navahk or want to be with him, at least once."

"This woman *never* wants to see him again!"

The intensity of Lonit's reply did not pass Aliga unnoticed. "Not even if he could save this woman and bring forth her baby?"

Shame and guilt burned Lonit's face. She wondered if Aliga had seen into her heart. "There will be many magic men at the Great Gathering, Aliga," she responded evasively. "This woman asks the spirits every day that one of these healers will help her sister. Also she asks that it not be Navahk. Navahk's magic is bad."

Aliga measured her out of jaundiced eyes. "Bad for whom?" she pressed, then shook her head again and clucked her tongue knowingly. Sighing, she drifted into sleep, leaving Lonit to ponder a question that she had no wish to answer.

Karana first saw the strangers, although the dogs were on their scent long before the youth pointed toward them. Alerted by the frenzied barking and circling of the animals, Torka rose from his sleeping skins, hefted his bludgeon, raised his spear, and stood tall, unmoving, and silent as the interlopers advanced.

Lonit was instantly awake, alarmed by the dogs and the tension that she saw in Torka's back. She sat up beneath their lean-to and called out to Iana, who shared another shelter with the children.

"Keep the little ones close!" she commanded as she shoved her bed skins aside. Jamming her feet into her boots, she took up her bola from where it lay close to her lynx-skin headrest, and clambered to stand beside her man, thankful that they had not all stripped naked before retiring.

The strangers were clothed in well-worked skins. Theirs was a small band, not more than thirty people. But next to Torka's tiny company, the number seemed enormous, as was the noise that they made. Bent forward under heavy pack frames, they boldly sloshed across the shallows of the river.

Then they paused, transfixed with amazement and terror as they saw the pack of wild dogs that threatened them from the far embankment. They stopped dead, squinting, trying to make sense of the fact that the dogs seemed to be a part of Torka's tiny band. The women began to murmur against grave misgivings. A child began to cry. The hunters took their spears and waved their arms, shouting and hooting, pretending they were not intimidated.

Under Aar's leadership the dogs were entering the river, heads out, teeth bared, entire bodies straining forward as if about to leap to the attack. A single word from Torka caused the animals to hold. When one of the younger males moved forward, Aar and Sister Dog leaped upon him and sent him yipping back to join his siblings.

"Aiyeeeh!" The cry of amazement went out of every mouth in the strange band. The threat of the attacking dogs was less frightening than the specter of a lone man controlling a pack of wild animals with a single word. As one they stepped back, stumbling over themselves until they were safe on the far shore. The women clutched their children while the men again raised their weapons and shook them violently. One of their number levered back and hurled a spear at Torka. It was an impressive throw but short of its target. It landed near the water, its head embedded in the riverbank, its painted shaft quivering as though with embarrassment for having failed to serve its master.

Torka did not move. Behind him, kneeling within her lean-to, Iana struggled to hold the children while Summer Moon was straining angrily to be free. From beneath the skins of her own shelter, Aliga peeked with groggy curiosity from her jumbled sleeping skins.

Karana stood brazenly with spear in hand beside Torka, who was proud that neither of them flinched when the man hurled his weapon from the far shore. Three long years of hunting together had taught them that a spear thrust from such a distance could be no threat. From the way that the stranger balanced and hurled his weapon, Torka was certain that the man must have known it too; it was simply his way of keeping his pride.

"A fool's throw," Karana sneered. "The spearhead will be ruined, and from the way the shaft quivers, the bone is cracked."

Torka nodded. "Nevertheless, the spear spoke well for the man. He does not want us to think that he is afraid."

"But why does he fear us?" Lonit asked, herself fearful.

"I would imagine that he and his people have never seen men walk with dogs before," Torka answered. "It was so with Supnah's people until they learned that there was no special magic to the relationship. But this man will not make the same mistake twice. The few are always weak among the many unless the many have cause to fear them. Karana, bring this man his spear hurler. We'll show them some real magic."

It was a graceful, elegantly carved tool. Years of refinement had made it much more accurate and easier to handle than his first design. This hurler was of caribou antler, considerably lighter than the first, made from the pelvis of a bison. He smiled in anticipation of the strangers' reaction to the spectacle to which they were about to be treated.

"Are you going to kill him?" Karana asked eagerly.

"Not unless I've lost my eye and touch," responded Torka, and knew that he had lost neither as, commanding Lonit and the youth to stand aside, he balanced himself squarely on both feet, pivoted to the right, then leaned back, back, until all of his weight was on his right leg. And still he twisted his body back until he felt his power burning along his entire right side—the exquisite pain of absolute control—as he took meticulous aim, and in a sudden burst of energy, whirled around and felt his power uncoiling, releasing up through his body as he hurled himself forward, caught his balance on his left foot, steadied it again on his right, and threw the spear, not just with his arm, but with a sharp snap-and-fling motion. The spear hurler effectively became a second forearm and wrist as it launched his weapon with twice the speed of any normally thrown spear and across twice the distance.

The headman jumped straight up as Torka's spear landed at his feet. He stared, gape mouthed. No spear could fly so far! But this spear had. It could have struck a killing blow. But clearly the man who had thrown it had not intended that.

"Aiy yah!" cried the women.

Every man and boy of the band sucked in his breath with wonder and covetousness while their headman tentatively touched the powerful, magical weapon.

And so, with the thrust of a spear, an alliance was begun; for in that moment Torka raised his now empty spear arm in a sign of greeting and, alone but not unarmed, waded out across the river.

"You hold the spear of Torka," he offered, striding out of the shallows. His right hand was open and extended imperiously toward the headman, his left curled about the haft of his bludgeon.

The man had pulled Torka's spear from the ground at his feet. He was small and burly. His large head, puffed along his right cheek and jaw, seemed even larger from a turbanlike helmet of bison skin, to which the time-worn, fly-bitten body of a fox had been stitched. The tail trailed down the man's back, and the ferretlike face stared with eyes of polished stone over his brow. From beneath the fox's snout the man's heavy features were lean with hunger. There was wariness and fear in his eyes as he stared at Torka, but no malice, anger, or cruelty. A chapped, chunky hand shot outward, fingers curled about Torka's spear. "The point will need reknapping, but the shaft is still sound. Here. You take! Torka is a man of much power to walk with beasts and tell them what to do! To throw a spear so far, so fast, with so much strength! The spirits of hunting magic must be strong in Torka, says this man, Zinkh!"

Torka held his tongue, letting Zinkh think what he wanted him to think. Torka looked past him to his equally lean-looking people. He counted children of varying ages, infants, women, and several faces so seamed with age that, were it not for their clothing, it would have been difficult to guess their gender. *This band is lean, but it has not sent its old to walk the wind so that its young might grow fat upon their leavings.* He scanned the watchful faces of at least eight strong hunters—young men in their prime, all with eyes like their spokesman. Watchful and wary but without guile.

Torka allowed himself to relax a little. Had he found the band he had been seeking? "Zinkh will keep the spear of Torka."

"Ahhh . . ." The man's face puckered with pleasure. Then he winced, his free hand flying to his swollen jaw, where his fingers pressed to relieve pain. "And what does this man Zinkh have to give in return to Torka?"

"Torka asks for nothing."

"Good. Zinkh and his band, we have nothing. Has been bad season for hunting. Not much meat. Many say passes to far north and west are closed by walking snow. Game cannot come through to eat spring grass. So now in lean days of summer, Zinkh and his people, we journey to make winter camp at Great Gathering. It is good place to winter. Hunt mammoths if nothing better turns up. Phuggh! Stinking mammoth! Taste like trees! Torka of much power, you like mammoth meat?"

"This man does not hunt the mammoth. It is his totem. But Torka also journeys to the Great Gathering, to winter there and to find a wise woman with healing powers for one of my women who is slow to give birth. But Torka knows no hunger. My people walk out of the east with bellies full. And Torka's camp across the river is filled now with fresh fish and much dried meat. Gladly would we welcome Zinkh and his people to share meat. And perhaps, among your women, there are wise ones who could ease the worries of my woman who is with child?"

The man's face expanded into a smile that seemed to split his face. "We travel to Great Gathering together! Make one band. Zinkh and his people could use a hunter of much power like Torka! We tell old Pomm to make baby-come-forth songs for woman of Torka! Old Pomm, she knows everything about babies!"

Old Pomm thought she knew everything, but she knew nothing. She possessed such absolute and aggressive conviction, there was no arguing with her. She was not a wise woman in any sense of the word, nor did she pretend to know magic; but she was the closest to wisdom and magic among her simple, straightforward people. They were proud of her, and she marinated herself in their pride like a prime, plump fillet of haunch meat set to soak in fermented berry juice at summer's end. She absorbed it and grew fat upon it—so much so that when Zinkh called her to cross the river with him, fear of the strangers was absorbed by her pride. Great indeed must her knowledge be, if such a man as Torka asked for her!

The people of Zinkh stared with solemn anticipation of the worst as their headman escorted Pomm across the shallows. Not one wished to make the crossing, even for the promise of food. They were intimidated by the large, wolflike dogs and murmured respectfully of the unprecedented bravery of their headman. But that was what headmen were for; after Zinkh had tested the waters of Torka's camp and found them safe, only then would his people follow.

So Zinkh and Pomm came alone and were greeted with friendship. Custom demanded that strangers be given food, so Lonit stood by, ready to offer leftover roasted grayling to the headman and the fat woman the moment they sloshed out of the river. Both eyed the fish as though it were offal. Iana held out a skin basket filled with cakes of fat and long ribbons of dried meat. Zinkh and Pomm greedily took handfuls of both, and while the fat woman grunted her approval and appraised Karana with eyes as ravenous and bold as her appetite, the headman nodded with exuberant appreciation of the food.

"Not taste bison, fresh or dried, for long time now," said Zinkh. "Eat fish, all the time fish—and bird and rodent. Phuggh! Not man meat! Woman meat!"

Lonit was glad that her eyes were downturned, lest the stranger be offended by what he saw in them. After three long years of living with Torka in the Valley of Songs, she had forgotten how rude other men were to their women. The grayling she had offered were whole and untouched. Each weighed well over five pounds, gutted, and had been prepared with care, stuffed with sorrel leaves and slow-cooked over the coals. Now, although they were cold, they were still fragrant and tender. Anyone who claimed to be hungry but dismissed such well-made food was not only rude, he was stupid. Lonit gritted her teeth.

Both Pomm and Zinkh eyed the well-packed basket as they stuffed their faces, chewing with infinite pleasure, as the headman asked through a mouthful: "Torka of much power has much man meat to share?"

"Torka has packed much man meat out of the east. Bison, camel, antelope, horse—"

Zinkh's small, bright eyes went round with surprise, then narrowed with speculation. "East! Where east?"

"Between the Mountains That Walk, within the Corridor of Storms."

A well-chewed spattering of food exploded out of Pomm's mouth. She choked. Zinkh slapped her on the back hard enough to drop a horse; she did not fall.

The headman stared at Torka. "No man hunts there," he whispered, as though he feared being overheard.

"Torka hunts there."

Lonit cast a sideward glance up at her man, proud of the disdainful authority with which he spoke to the overdressed, rude little headman.

"It is forbidden." Zinkh was still whispering. "No man has ever walked into that far country and come back to tell of it."

"Torka has come back to tell of it and to share its man meat with Zinkh."

The man gulped, no longer certain that the meat was as tasty as before. But he had already eaten it, and it would be an offense to the life spirit of the game animal that had died to provide it if he vomited it up now. Besides, it was the tastiest dried meat that he had ever eaten. Even the disgusting white flesh of the river fish had given off a tempting aroma. He wondered if Torka's women cooked with magic. Perhaps Torka himself was a spirit man. He gulped, wondering what powers the spirits would grant to him and to his people if they walked with such a man. "Torka is a man of much power?" The question trembled with excitement.

Torka's face was expressionless. "Torka is what Zinkh sees," he replied obliquely. "And now, if Zinkh would bring this woman. . . ."

It was obvious from their behavior that they would do whatever Torka asked. They followed him obediently to where Aliga lay, and while Pomm winked at Karana and flashed a snaggle-toothed smile that caused the boy to blush to his hairline and turn away, Zinkh openly admired the neat lean-to.

The little man in the enormous headdress eyed the sky. "Torka think rain will come soon?"

"Rain will come."

"Soon?"

"Soon."

Zinkh nodded thoughtfully, rubbing his cheek, wincing again against pain. "If Torka say it will be good, Zinkh will make one camp here with Torka's people. If Torka's dogs will not eat us—?"

The question reeked of deference and fear. Torka looked down at the little man in the elaborately constructed garments and the absurdly overwhelming helmet. Zinkh had deliberately taken a tone and position of subservience. He stood with his head twisted to one side, his throat bared, like a wolf or dog cowering before a dominant member of its pack. Startled, Torka realized that the little man was relinquishing his position as headman, yielding his authority to a man whom he feared capable of taking it and leaving him nothing in the bargain.

"The dogs are this man's spirit brothers. They will do as Torka commands," he said, and knew that Zinkh and his people would do the same, as long as it served them. "Go. Bring your people across the river. Torka says that, until we reach the Great Gathering, it will be a good thing if we be one band."

Pomm laid her hands upon Aliga's belly. She raised her voice in what she called a song. It had the yapping cadence of a dog when its tail has been stepped upon. As the members of her band crossed the river, set up their lean-tos, and gratefully fed upon Torka's rations, Pomm sang and sang until she grew tired and asked that more food be brought to her.

While she ate, she could not sing, and although no one said as much, everyone was glad for the silence—especially Aliga, who midway through Pomm's caterwauling looked beseechingly at Lonit and asked, "This is the healer you would bring to me instead of Navahk? This fat one will sing me to death." With that she pulled her bed skins over her head and lay moaning while Pomm continued her song.

Now she knelt beside the sick woman's fur-covered form. Lonit watched Pomm, who stared at Aliga. Her weather-savaged face would have been as runneled as an outwash plain except that her fatness absorbed her lines. Lonit wondered how she stayed so fat when the rest of her band was lean with hunger.

Pomm belched resoundingly, then patted her belly, which was rounder than Aliga's. "Good food in this camp," she commended, nodding at Lonit. Then she sighed and looked to Aliga again. The tattooed woman had drifted back into sleep. Pomm made a tisking sound with her tongue. "Pomm says that we talk quiet. Sleep is good for woman with baby in belly. Baby sleep long enough, it wakes up and says, 'Too long has this one dreamed alone in the dark. Now will this child be born! Now will it come forth into the world of people, to be alone no more!' "

"Karana has tried to convince Aliga to drink bearberry tea, for the yellow in her eyes and skin and—"

"Karana?" An unmistakable glint of interest sparkled in the woman's eyes. "Karana be handsome boy that Pomm sees with Lonit's man? Who sits now alone—"

"Yes. And Karana says that Aliga needs—"

"*Shhh!*" Pomm's fat index finger flew to press warningly against her small, childlike mouth. "Not say name! This is the most powerful medicine of all. Teas? Bah! Bearberry juice? Bah! Lonit, listen you good what Pomm she tells you now: Tattooed woman, she sick with bad spirit. Bad spirit loves that woman whose name you speak, and it will live forever in the belly of that woman unless we confuse it . . . unless we make it want to go away."

"How?"

"Give woman new name! Never more call her by old name. Spirit will mourn, then it will go across the world until it finds another woman with the same name! Is great magic, Lonit! You learn from this woman, you will be wise someday, and all people will look to you for healing magic! Pomm is greatest healing woman in all bands! At Great Gathering Lonit will see how big is Pomm's magic!"

"Lonit sees that now," she said quietly, and turned away, despairing for Aliga, who grew weaker daily, and for the unborn child, whose chances were slim indeed if its life lay in the hands of such would-be healers as Pomm.

They slept as one band beneath the light of the midnight sun. Then suddenly Zinkh jumped straight up from beneath his sleeping skins, his hand pressed to his jaw. He cursed and paced. As everyone stared at him in stunned amazement, he took up a bone awl and shook it at the sky. With the index finger of his left hand hooked into his cheek, he exposed his teeth and, and with his right hand, gouged the offending member from his mouth.

"No more will that tooth cause this man pain!" Blood seeped from his mouth. He stamped upon the tooth, grinding it into the tundral earth. "There! Now Zinkh laughs at you! Ha!"

Blinking, Karana shook his head. The headman was bleeding badly. His laughter had vanished as suddenly as it had come. He had removed his tooth but caused greater pain. He slapped his hand against his jaw and moaned in abject misery.

Karana waited for Zinkh's wise woman to rise and bring him a paste of ground willow shoots to pack into the wound; this would slow the bleeding and ease the pain. But the little headman began a frenzied dance, blood bearding his chin and staining his clothes while Pomm watched, unmoving. With a sigh, Karana rummaged through his supplies, found what he needed, and went to the headman with it.

"Here. Take this. It will stop the bleeding. It will drive away the pain spirit." He was suddenly aware of everyone's rapt attention. Old Pomm was frowning. Zinkh, holding his jaw with one hand, opened his mouth like a baby waiting to be fed.

Grimacing, Karana stuck a finger into the narrow ointment bag, took up a generous amount of the efficacious pulp, and obliged Zinkh by administering it directly to his wound.

It was instantly soothing. Zinkh's eyes widened. He embraced the embarrassed youth. "You! Pain Eater! Magic Maker!" He kissed him on both cheeks, looking over his shoulders at Pomm. "You! Why does Woman Who Knows Everything not know this?" His hands gripped Karana's shoulders and enthusiastically shook the youth. "Zinkh to Karana give great gift of thanks! To Karana, this man gives Pomm! You teach Woman Who Knows Everything. Together your magics be big."

Karana was flabbergasted. "It is only the pulp of willow root, ground with oil from—"

"You teach Pomm, not Zinkh!" She was at his side, grinning rapaciously.

Karana had not imagined that anyone so fat could move so fast. She was on him as voraciously as a leaping cat. Her strong arms went around him, and she hugged him so hard that the air went out of his lungs.

"Come! Karana teach Pomm later! Now Pomm make Karana happy. Pomm will make Karana give *her* big gift!"

Everyone except Karana laughed at her brazen lewdness. He was appalled and horrified. She had him by the hand and was pulling him toward her sleeping skins. "Wait!" he implored, his eyes seeking Torka's, his heart sinking as he saw that Torka was as amused as the others.

"There must be a first time for every man," Torka jibed with paternal affection.

"Perhaps," Karana retorted, anger giving him the strength to jerk away. "But this will *not* be the time for me!"

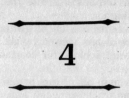

4

In all of her years, Mahnie had never seen her parents so preoccupied. The entire camp was quiet—too quiet. Now and then, from beyond the walls of her family hut, the whispering voices of a man or woman would rise slightly, then ebb away, and Mahnie would try to sleep again; but when she did, she saw Pet and Ketti and Naiapi and the horn of First Man and blood . . . everywhere . . . blood.

She sat up and leaned back on her palms, staring and blinking, trying to obliterate her memories. Three little dolls stared back at her from the far end of her sleeping skins. Three little dolls of remnant fur and hide, with eyes of dried cloudberries and mouths of sedge seeds, with bodies of doe-skin stuffed with moss and encased in summer dresses and trousers, and tiny boots, and long hair made of cuttings from Wallah's own hair, so that Mahnie and her friends could enjoy combing it with the tiny bone combs Grek had carved for them.

A sob of grief shook the girl as she reached for the dolls and drew them into her protective embrace. A doll for her, one for Ketti, one for Pet. She buried her face in their softness and let her tears fall as she mourned for days of childhood happiness that could never come again.

"Leave the girl alone."

Grek's voice was soft, but Mahnie heard it and knew that Wallah had moved, wanting to comfort her.

"There is no consolation," he said bitterly. "Not for what she has seen. Or for what she will fear until her own time of blood has come and gone. And even then . . ."

Her father's words trailed off into a sigh. Bed skins rustled, and she knew that Wallah was comforting him now.

"It was his right," whispered the woman tremulously.

141

"*Right?* To kick Naiapi's unborn child to death in her womb? To take the life of Pet before the entire band, with the *children* watching?"

"Your sadness over the loss of the girl talks for you, Grek. First-blood rites are always viewed by all. It is just that this band has had no one to blood for so many years, we have forgotten how—"

"Forgotten? Never in all of this man's years has he witnessed anything like what happened today. Never in Grek's memory has the horn of First Man been blooded by anything but the first blood of a woman. To take more than that, to take a life—such a thing has not happened since time beyond beginning. And yes, this man thinks of Pet. She was like a daughter to you, Wallah! Like a sister to Mahnie! And Navahk knew that she was for me. He knew it!"

The bed skins rustled again. Mahnie heard the whispered soothings of her mother and the infuriated, restless breathing of her father. She looked up at them through her laced fingers, where they sat together upon their piled sleeping skins. Although the time for sleep was nearly over, neither had undressed or slept. Mahnie doubted if anyone within the entire encampment had slept. She frowned. Grek looked old and haggard. His face was drawn with grief, his eyes focused inward in solemn introspection. Wallah rested her head against his shoulder, one arm beneath his and draped around his back, the other held across his chest, her hand idly stroking.

"This woman wishes that Grek had been named headman instead of Navahk. Grek would have been a good headman. He is a better hunter than Navahk, and Pet would be alive to come to this hut. How Mahnie had looked forward to that. Mahnie—" Her words caught in her throat, and her hand froze. "When the time of first blood comes to our little one, the magic man would not—"

Mahnie's heart stopped. She shared her mother's fear. Her inevitable trek to womanhood would unavoidably bring her to where her life and death lay in the hands of a magic man who seemed to loathe all women.

She could hear him howl now like a wolf from within the hut of purification into which he had disappeared with Ketti hours before. Mahnie shivered. The howling stopped. It had not been Navahk—it had been Ketti. A single high cry answered by the baying of wild dogs that roamed the distant hills.

"Sometimes this man thinks that he would have been wise to have taken his women and belongings and followed Torka. Torka was a good man. But Navahk is new to woman making. By the time it is Mahnie's turn, he will have learned how to be gentle."

Grek looked with love at his distraught woman and thought of Pet. His heart bled. Something deep and basic to his nature had changed within him when he had witnessed her death. He felt drained of himself, somehow, as though a stranger filled his skin and all that was trusting and open bled out of him, leaving him hard, unforgiving, and infinitely protective of those who were dearest to him. When he thought of Navahk and all that had been conceded to him, Grek's eyes narrowed. "The magic man had better learn how to be gentle by the time this man's girl comes to first blood, or Grek will teach him another lesson: He will teach him how to die."

The horn went deep, moving, probing. Ketti fought to be free of its invasion. She screamed again, but this time the sound was forced back down her throat by the smothering kiss of the magic man. His body lay splayed across her, pinning her down while he worked the horn deep between her thighs, deliberately tearing her womb so no child would ever take root.

His tongue entered her mouth, stabbed rhythmically, keeping perfect cadence with the jabbing, circular movements of the horn. She was too tired to fight him. He sapped her of life.

"Move!" He rammed the horn deep and smiled when she went rigid against it. "Dance in the way you were taught by the women, in the way you first danced naked before me when we entered this hut. Dance! Open yourself, offer yourself. But we will see who is weakened by your women's dance, you or this man who takes his pleasure as he sees fit, not in the way that you would give it!"

She nearly fainted as he knelt back from her. She could breathe again, but only for a moment. His left hand slipped beneath her buttocks, forcing her hips up while the other hand still worked the horn, rousing pain, not the pleasure that her mother and the other women had promised.

She felt blood upon her thighs and through the daze saw him smile as the horn slipped out. He bent to browse between her thighs, to lick her blood, to suck, to bite until she

could bear no more of him. Summoning all her strength, she
lurched up screaming, pulled herself away, and kicked him
hard in the face.

He caught her ankle and pulled her back. Impossibly, his
smile had broadened. His nose was bleeding; he seemed
strengthened by the pain.

"Ketti is bold. Ketti is brave to defy Navahk. Would *you* be
like Torka's woman, then? Yes, like Lonit. She would be
bold. She would dance bravely against the pain that I would
give her."

For the first time in all of the hours of abuse that he had
inflicted upon her since entering the hut of purification, he
penetrated her with his organ. He was hard, engorged, impossibly huge for a mere man. But he was not a mere man,
he was Magic Man, a dark and perverse power that defied
her understanding as he called her by another name—Lonit—
and hissed with pleasure, thrusting deep, swelling within
her, shivering as he heard her sob. He smothered her cries
with his open lips, invading her mouth with his tongue.

She could not breathe. She wanted to die. Perhaps he was
leading her to that, and she would be with Pet soon, a spirit
woman, free of him, and that would be a mercy.

"Dance!" The word was an imperative snarl. His organ was
shrinking as he gripped her hips and rode her brutally,
viciously, to a release that would not come. He cursed and
rode her harder.

A terrifying howl suddenly pierced the silence of the encampment. It was the cry of a wild animal, followed by the scream of
a fear-maddened child. Yet the scream was not fully human.

Navahk, still joined to the girl, stopped and lifted his head,
listening. "Wanawut . . ." He exhaled the word with reverence, visualizing the shadowed gorge, the female corpse of
the massive, half-human thing with the breasts of a woman
and a musculature powerful enough to rip off the arm of a
man with one casual swipe and to remove his head with
another. The vision thrilled him. He looked down at the girl.
So small. So weak. So shattered by his power.

Sensation flooded back into his organ, swelling it until
suddenly, as he closed his eyes and imagined how it would be
to couple with the wanawut . . . to ride it as he rode the girl
. . . to lick its blood . . . to draw its power into himself,
release came, and he poured himself into the girl while
crying out with the pure, savage ecstasy of ejaculation.

He slept then and did not wake until the girl's pathetic mewing roused him. Her hands were pressing against his shoulders.

Far away within the distant hills the howling had begun again. Navahk listened, transfixed and envious, knowing that the beast-child that he had chosen not to kill would someday grow to dimensions that equaled its parent's.

He felt suddenly weak. He rolled off the girl, hating her. She had sapped him of the exquisite feeling of power that had swept through him just prior to ejaculation. If only he had been able to maintain the strength that had been in him at that moment, his power would equal that of the wanawut—a power greater than any man could ever hope to own.

Just thinking of it made him potent again, but this time he wanted no part of the girl. Her very femaleness disgusted him. Tomorrow he would give her to Rhik, who was old and a widower and would appreciate having a young girl to ride again. And tomorrow, if Naiapi was still alive, he would give her to Grek lest she continue to come mewling after him. That would repay the aging hunter for daring to challenge him with his eyes when he had killed Pet. Oh, yes, Grek deserved Naiapi. She would be a bone in his throat to the end of his days or hers. He got to his feet and left the bloodied bed skins that the traditions of his people had forced him to soil through his use of the girl. Impatiently he backhanded the hide door flap away and left the hut to stand naked in the watery, bloodred glow of the midsummer morning. The sun was rising from above the eastern ranges.

Trembling, his organ fully erect again, the magic man raised his arms and invoked the forces of Creation. As though in response, the wanawut answered him out of the distant hills.

PART IV

THE GREAT GATHERING

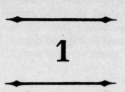

1

The child huddled within a stand of scrub willow, shivering against the cold of an early, wind-driven snow. Weak with hunger, it drew aside a frost-brittled screen of yellow-leaved branches with hairy-backed, snow-dusted fingers. Beyond, falling snow gauzed a rolling, tundral world, which had only moments earlier been aflame with the colors of summer's end as the sun's last rays had pierced the cloud cover. The child drew in a thousand tawny scents: shrubs, grass, bogs, rivers and ponds thickening with ice, ripening berries sheened white with frost, distant forests of climate-stunted spruce and hardwoods, open miles, and ranging glacial vastnesses . . . all masked now by the impending night, the stinging white smell of the snow, and the overriding smell of that which the child feared—the beast.

He was hunting alone again, walking boldly with the wind at his back and making no attempt to hide either his scent or his presence. As he had done for several evenings now at the end of each daily trek, the beast in white was coming away alone from the traveling camp of his kind. And the child, exhausted at the end of each day of following the beasts, put aside its desire to seek a nest in order to watch the one in white.

The child trembled, frowning against the now familiar smell of smoke on snow, which tainted the evening wind. The beasts were making day-end fires and building their odd shelters against the stormy night to come.

Cowering within the meager, ice-rimed protection of the willow grove, the child instinctively knew that the beast was hunting it. For days it had been so. The child could see him clearly now, walking slowly, head up, scenting the wind, then stopping, bending, checking the earth for sign, finding it, and moving forward. Closer . . . ever closer.

Trembling with hatred, the child wished that it could break from its hiding place within the willows and run forward to pounce upon the beast to kill and devour him, but even if it was brave enough to do so, it was still too small to inflict enough damage.

Yet.

Again it trembled, this time not so much against cold and hunger but with the frightening knowledge that it was growing. Slowly, inexorably, despite the ravages of hunger, the child sensed bewildering changes within itself. Its head moved to one side as its hands rose to lay open upon its chest. Not only did its body ache with hunger, it seemed to be transforming itself, sprouting two hot, painfully tender lumps that were forcing its once-flat nipples outward. Its hands seemed bigger, its limbs longer, and often it whacked the top of its head upon branches that it could have walked under with ease only days before.

Now, staring through the ice-rimed branches of the willow grove, the child hunched forward, one hand pressing its breasts, the other resting upon the top of its bruised head. It shivered violently against the cold, confused by it. It was too soon for snow; the luxuriant, downy undercoat of thick, silvery fur that kept the child warm through the long, brutal storms of the dark times was only halfway grown. The wind combed through the shaggy gray guard hairs that covered nearly all of the child's emaciated body. It parted them, found the child's pale, delicate skin, and made no concessions to its youth or pitifully weak condition. Again the child shivered, this time so violently that the spasmodic movements actually warmed it a little.

Its body's battle against the cold brought a sudden, overwhelming surge of exhaustion. The child slumped to its knees in the thick, resilient layer of faded, crinkly leaves and deep-orange moss that carpeted the floor of the grove. Because the trees grew so thickly, there was only a thin veining of snow despite the driving wind. Impatiently the child whisked the snow away and, moving quietly, dug itself a burrow within the insulating blanket of vegetation. Its work accomplished, it scooted gratefully into the nest, covering itself entirely as fatigue allowed it to forget that it had sought the grove not only for shelter against the impending storm but as a place to hide from the hunting beast. It dozed blissfully, then came up abruptly out of sleep, sitting upright, shaking leaves from its shoulders as it remembered that it was in danger.

Groggy, dizzy with fatigue, the child stared out of the grove. The beast, although a good distance away, was still there. It had paused, scanning the rolling hills that were rapidly losing their color to the thickening snowfall and ebbing light. Above, wind-driven snow clouds skeined across the darkening sky, now and then revealing the full, staring face of the moon.

The child looked up just as it disappeared behind a thickening bank of swirling cloud from which snow hurled itself vengefully at the earth.

Snow. The child had loved it once, and scampered through it at its mother's side. Together they had rolled and played in it, savoring its coolness against their bare faces and chests and the thick, callused padding of their feet. They had lifted great handfuls of it and tossed it high, hooting with delight.

Mother!

The child's longing was almost unbearable, until it realized that the snow had caused Mother Killer to pause. The beast had evidently lost all trace of the child's sign. He stood like a stallion, with his head raised and nostrils wide, drawing in the wind.

The child, confused by its emotions, salivated. It *wanted* the beast to come, to kneel, to stare into the willow grove, to make eye contact, as he had for the past five dusks, and then to go away, as he had also done, speaking low and leaving tiny morsels of meat before turning away. The starving child was always transfixed with terror and bewildered by his behavior, while thinking of the miserable stalks, leaves, berries, insects, and occasional rodents that had formed its diet since its mother's death.

Better to go hungry than to eat the leavings of Mother Killer, thought the child stubbornly. But it was not easy to go hungry; it was painful and weakening and frightening. And each time the beast looked into the child's eyes and then turned away, the child was filled with a strange, half-remembered, oddly calming recollection of a star-strewn night, of being carried across the world as an infant at its mother's breast while others of its kind paraded silently ahead . . . of staring into eyes that observed it from the tangled blackness of the earth—eyes that it knew now were the eyes of a beast—frightened, awestruck, filled with the wondrous reflection of the night; and in those dark, starlit eyes there was no threat, no threat at all.

Not like the eyes of Mother Killer. Not like the eyes of the beast that had eaten its mother's heart and danced in her skin.

Or were they? Mother Killer brought meat. Mother Killer walked alone out of the encampment of its fellow beasts, hunting the child and finding the child, not to kill it but to feed it. *Why?*

Confusion, coupled with exhaustion, muddled the child's memories. It lay down onto its side, assuming a fetal curl as it worked itself so deeply under the leaves that only one side of its head was visible. It was warm under the leaves, and the child relaxed a little, still watching the unmoving beast, as though he were somehow a man of ice, frozen solid. Frozen beasts were no threat.

The child's eyelids drooped. Far off, wolves howled at the storm-veiled moon. Sleep filled the child, and in its sleep it moaned and cried softly, longing for its mother, drifting into a delirium of dreams . . . images of its mother hunting, killing, savaging, leaping out of the shadows at unwary travelers.

Its stomach contracted, lurching with hunger. It awoke, listened to the wind and the wailing wolves, and stared out of its lonely bed of leaves and moss—into the watching eyes of the beast.

Navahk smiled. The mist-gray eyes that stared at him out of the tangled scrub did not smile back. They were wide, filled with fear and hatred.

Navahk's smile deepened. Above and behind him night absorbed the last pale glow of dusk. Now the world, lit solely by the rising moon, was silver and black with deep, rivering shadows. Other hunters would have turned back for the comfort and firelight and company of an encampment. Men did not hunt the tundra alone at night. But Navahk was a magic man, and unlike other men, fear was a food to him. He felt emboldened by it.

The wind was gusting from the north. Hard, thin pellets of snow stung his face as the nocturnal animals of the tundra began to stir. He listened, his senses alert. He was one of them now, and only his concern that the creature that cowered before him might bolt away kept him from howling with pure, animalistic pleasure.

Navahk looked down at the half-human face buried amid the leaves and shadows. His smile faded. He saw a double image of the moon swimming in the twin lakes of the creature's eyes, and within those moons he saw himself—a part of the beast, a part of the moon and the night, a part of the savage storm wind. It was a startling vision—absolute beauty held captive within the eyes of a creature of absolute ugliness.

Instinctively Navahk's hand tightened upon the haft of his spear. His smile returned. He could hear the shallow rasp of the creature's breath; he could smell its fear and see that its hideous, hairless, bearlike face was gaunt and haggard. Yet as it moved uncomfortably under his scrutiny, he caught sight of its furred shoulder and arm and knew that, despite its obvious near starvation, it had grown since he last saw it, and that was only yesterday. Navahk frowned, envious of the power within its musculature.

Soon it will become a beast like its mother. Soon! It does not mature like a human child. In one summer it has grown as much as a man would grow in half a lifetime!

He stared at it, enraptured by the thought that had driven him to find the beast at the end of each day. Hunting had not improved since the ceremony of first blood. Although he had led his people down all the old, familiar game trails, along none of them had they found the game that he had promised: enough game to provide meat for a winter camp, enough to guarantee his people's survival through the coming time of long dark. So it was that they were slowly traveling toward the place of the Great Gathering.

Navahk knew from Grek's continuing, thinly veiled hostility that the older hunter would never forgive him for killing Pet, and that if hunting did not improve, Grek would remind others that Navahk had broken tradition by becoming their headman as well as their magic man. He would say what others were already thinking: *If Navahk is strong in the favor of the spirits, why do the life spirits of the game not come to die upon the spears of his people, and why does the wanawut follow us to howl in the night in mourning for the one of its kind that Navahk has killed?*

Navahk trembled with frustration. "Why?" he hissed to the terrified thing that crouched within the shadows.

The sound of his voice caused the creature to stiffen and

widen its stare. Its eyes were opaque with fatigue. *"Wah? . . ."* it mewed pathetically.

Navahk sank to his knees in shock. It was the magic man who stiffened now. The beast had spoken! It had echoed him, the way an infant echoes its parents. For days now he had heard it howling beneath the midnight sun, always the same dirgelike *"Wah nah wah . . . wah nah wut . . ."* And for days it had followed his people across the tundra, had run from him when he had sought it, and had refused the food he secretly offered. He had wondered how his people would react if he simply killed the thing and dragged its corpse back into their encampment to prove to them that it was no phantom but an animal that could be meat for them, to be feared no more than any other predator. But that would lessen the murder of its mother. He had held back, thinking of its power, wishing he could possess it, control it, and bend it to his will while it was still a small, weak child. What would his people say of his magic then? No men would dare to challenge his powers, or he would bring forth the wanawut and command it to feed upon their flesh! The concept inspired a radiant smile.

Now, from the leather sack that he carried wrapped in a larger sack of oiled bison intestine, he drew a handful of bloody antelope meat and guts.

"Wah nah wuh . . . wah nah wut . . ." Navahk whispered, slowly extending his hand, holding the meat toward the half-human thing, repeating the sounds softly, encouragingly, lovingly, as a parent might have spoken them.

The thing mewed pitifully and edged back from its nest into the deeper shadows that filled the grove. As the gentle lulling of the magic man whispered on, the beast hugged and rocked itself, making weak, fretful sounds of confusion and indecision. Its senses were obviously dulled by malnutrition. Navahk knew that his voice was both soothing and befuddling it at the same time. Was it Man or Mother who offered it food and spoke to it in its own tongue?

"Wah nah wuh . . ." he repeated, then ate of the meat himself, slowly, pausing to smack his lips. He offered it again, making low sounds of invitation.

This time the creature's need for sustenance outweighed its caution. It sprang forward, snatched the meat from the hand of the man, and began to eat ravenously.

Navahk could have roared with triumph. Instead he remained absolutely still—watching and smiling. The beast had eaten from the hand of the man! And when the meat was consumed, Navahk offered all that was left within the sack.

"Wah nah wuh . . . wah nah wut . . ." he whispered.

This time the creature did not echo him. Nourishment had brought clarity back into its eyes, and Navahk, meeting its gaze, was startled to see tears of frustration brimming over as, with a grunt of self-revilement, the thing grasped his offering and began to devour it, hating the magic man for putting before it that which hunger would no longer allow it to deny itself.

Tears? What kind of animal cries? he wondered, incredulous.

And as he watched the creature finish the last of the meat, he saw the moon in its eyes again, and his own image, shining and white and beautiful, and knew that in all of his life, he could not remember ever having shed a tear for anything, or for anyone.

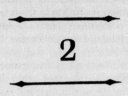

2

Two days after a thin, driving snowstorm left the tundra as white as the grizzled beard of an ancient musk ox, Torka led his people and Zinkh's to the place of the Great Gathering. The dry snow had been followed by a day of severe cold, then by clear, windy skies and a brazen sun that melted the snow in less time than it had taken it to fall. It was on this day, beneath this sun, that Torka and his women and children, with Karana and Aar's pack, and the hunters of Zinkh at his side, walked across broad, well-traveled land toward the great encampment.

They walked with purpose, lengthening their stride as their destination came into sight . . . and sound . . . and scent. Beneath their traveling packs, they were dressed in their finest ceremonial attire. Lonit had donned her gray elk-skin dress. Torka was clad in his parka of golden, black-maned lion skin. Around his neck he wore his necklet of wolf fangs and paws. The clatter and jangle of their traveling gear, their women's bone jewelry, and the stone-beaded fringes of their own garments would have been audible for miles had it not been for the cacophonous din of the vast encampment they were approaching.

They paused, transfixed. Completely encircled by a massive windbreak of mammoth bones, it occupied the entire western edge of the plain. The air trembled with the sounds of song and whistles and lap drums, of laughter and argument, of haggling and baby cries. The smoke that rose from over a hundred fires fogged the sky and imbued the wind with the rich smells of roasting meat, charred bones, burning turf, and human refuse.

"Bigger camp than last time this man winters here!" exclaimed Zinkh, nodding with such enthusiasm that his head-dress slid to one side. Only hasty adjustment kept it from falling off. He grinned up at Torka from beneath the scabby-looking fox head. "Here for certain, Zinkh says, we will find healing magic for Aliga, and maybe even Iana will find her tongue again, yes!"

"Bah!" Pomm snorted rudely from where she had paused next to Lonit and Iana at the front of the line of women. "No one make better healing magic than *this* woman!" she insisted under her breath to Lonit. "You see soon! Pomm will have great rank in this camp!"

Bound securely inside Iana's pack frame, little Demmi made baby noises that, under different circumstances, would have told Lonit that her infant daughter's swaddling of moss needed to be changed. But Lonit was so overwhelmed by the enormity of the encampment that she neither paid heed to her infant nor heard Pomm's boast. She held Summer Moon tightly. The child's slender, trousered limbs encircled her waist. Lonit could feel the excitement of the little girl as she strained forward, pointing to the scene that held Lonit's eyes.

"Look! Big bones! Stinky smoke. Many people! There be children there?"

"Yes, little one. Many children."

"We play?"

"If they are good children." She could see them now, coming out of the encircling wall of bones with their mothers and fathers. So many people! Never in all of her days had Lonit imagined that there were so many people in the world!

She felt ill and longed to be far from this place where there might be a man in white who had danced before her one flame-lit night and held out his hand to her and told her that she was beautiful. . . . No! If he were at the Great Gathering, she would not allow herself to see him. She would stare at her feet and not lift her eyes from the ground. She was Torka's woman. Always and forever.

And now Torka, frowning as he stared at the wall of mammoth bones and tusks, was urging his people onward. Beside him Karana shook his head dubiously. "This place has too many people, all surrounded by the bones of our totem's kin. We are sworn not to kill mammoth. This is not a good camp for us."

Without slowing his step, Torka cut him short. "This is the last time that Torka will hear those words. This man has come to think that there is not an encampment in all the world that Karana will ever find to his liking!"

The youth shrugged. "The Valley of Songs was a good camp."

"This will be a good camp too. You will see."

Through a haze of eye-stinging, drifting camp smoke turned orange by sunlight, Torka led his people closer to their destination, then signed for them to stop in front of the many people who had come out to meet them. He gripped his bludgeon in one hand and raised his spear upright in the other in the sign of peace. Those who first saw him striding boldly at the head of the respectably sized band, with a pack of ferocious, burden-carrying dogs running alongside his women, made gestures of awe and wonder to the spirits they most feared as they spoke in many dialects of a root language that had once been universal.

"Another man of magic comes to gift the Great Gathering with his powers!"

"Eh yeh! The weatheh chenges as he khums!"

"Look! Dogs walk with him as though they were his brothers!"

"Not brothers—*slaves*. Man speaks . . . dogs listen . . . dogs obey!"

"See there, hey! Animals carry women burdens!"

"Impossible!"

"Man khum . . . sun khum . . . and snow melts beneath his feet!"

"Great must be the magic of that man!"

"Great yes!" affirmed Zinkh, seeking and finding a few familiar faces in the crowd that surrounded them. "So great that even Zinkh—and many here know how much great hunter Zinkh he be—has said: Man Who Walks With Dogs, his band and Zinkh's band be one band! Together, we have much magic! Together, Torka and Zinkh we journey far to Great Gathering. We share our magic and meat and furs with many there!"

"This is so?"

The question came from an old man who headed what was evidently a contingent of magic men, for all were elaborately dressed and carried themselves with an air of condescension. The speaker was easily the eldest of the lot; perhaps the oldest human being Torka had ever seen. Judging from the crenelated escarpments of his craggy face and from his oddly flattened, grotesquely high-veined, twisted hands, Torka guessed that he had lived to lament the passing of at least fifty summers. He was gray of hair and skin and dressed entirely in the pelts of birds, with layers of dried, outstretched wings cut from varying small raptorial species arrayed along his sleeves. His face, eyes, and mouth were hard. Even though he squinted up at Torka, he seemed to be looking down at him from either side of a nose that was as beaked as a teratorn's, and the query that he had directed to Torka had been every bit as sharp.

"This *is* so."

Startled because he had not spoken the reply, Torka saw a tall, astoundingly beautiful woman step through the ranks of the assembled magic men. Her voice had been as low and languorous as a river moving beneath the turgid warmth of the summer sun. She stood as straight as a well-made spear; like the elder, she exuded confidence and authority. Her garments were constructed of the pelts of birds: a black and white cloak made entirely of the flight feathers of the great condorlike teratorn fell over her shoulders, and a circle of snow-white swan's down crowned her head. The thick, intricately plaited forelock that fell gracefully over one shoulder to her waist was gray, and there were long streaks of silver in the remainder of her loose, knee-length hair. When she smiled, little fans appeared at the corners of her eyes, betraying the fact that the days of her youth lay far behind her, but her teeth were still strong and straight and white between lips as soft and full as a young girl's.

"There are many kinds of magic," she said, speaking to Torka but looking directly at Karana, as if puzzled to see in a stranger someone she had known before.

The youth blushed red under her glance.

Torka was stunned not only by her beauty but by her easy assumption of equality with the males among whom she had seemingly taken a dominant role. Beside her the supreme elder bristled.

"Sondahr honors us with her insight," he said, sneering.

Her head went up. "Sondahr thanks Lorak for his words of confidence," she replied evenly, returning sarcasm for sarcasm as, not without difficulty, she forced her eyes from Karana. She observed Torka and the wolflike, blue-eyed dog that stood between him and the youth. Aar cocked his head.

Her eyes moved past him to the people of Torka and Zinkh. Showing no fear of the dogs that stood as sentinels beside Aliga, Sondahr regally swept out of the ranks of the magic men and walked to where the sick woman lay upon her sledge.

When Sister Dog lowered her grizzled head and growled, the woman merely looked at her and the dog relaxed, allowing her to come near, watching as she drew the furs away from Aliga. She touched her belly and her brow, breathed in the scent of her breath, then turned back to Torka, her troubled eyes seeing no one else.

For a long moment she said nothing, then: "Torka has not come to the Great Gathering to hunt the mammoth. He will not eat of the meat of great tusked ones. He has come to seek healing for this woman." She spoke casually, as though it were the most natural thing in the world for her to know the reasons behind the stranger's arrival. "Come, Man Who Walks With Dogs. Bring this tattooed woman to the fire of Sondahr. I will do for her what I can."

As Pomm glowered resentfully beside Lonit, Aliga stared at the magic woman out of eyes filmed pink by fever. "You are not Navahk."

"No," assented Sondahr obliquely, her eyes straying to where Karana stood gaping at her as though he had never seen a woman before. "That man is not in this camp."

Lonit was so relieved by Sondahr's revelation about the magic man, she forgot to be jealous of her. Pomm, however, was jealous enough for the two of them. One of Zinkh's burliest hunters took up the burden of Aliga's sledge, and Karana followed Sondahr like a moonstruck shadow. With the strong little headman happily basking in Torka's reflected glory, Lorak and the magic man led Torka and his people through the mammoth bones and into the encampment of the Great Gathering.

Terrified of the dogs, children stopped in the middle of their games while the adults cleared a path, murmuring, pointing, and whispering in awe.

Torka's band passed innumerable pit huts and crude lean-tos of bones and hide and thatch before which small groups were gathered at various tasks and games. A twosome of half-grown girls tossed a toddler high; the little one flew up, laughing ecstatically, his pudgy arms and legs akimbo as he fell and was caught in a tightly held skin. The girls snapped the skin so hard that it cracked the air as the toddler again flew upward, giggling and shrieking. This time when they caught the little one, the girls saw the strangers and their dogs. The girls put the skin down, and the toddler peered out of it, as incredulous as his playmates.

Lonit smiled at them as she passed. In her arms Summer Moon stared wide eyed, amazed by the sight of so many children and as dazzled as her mother by the many cooking fires, row upon row of drying frames, the aromas of food, and the presence of so many diverse people. For a moment Lonit half expected Iana to cast off her lethargy and speak delightedly about the many happy, noisy children. But the sad-eyed woman walked on as before, in silence, with Demmi asleep upon her back.

Lorak spoke as he walked, naming the various bands and headmen, their attributes and shortcomings. He complained of a season of poor hunting, explaining that this was why so many were assembled at the Great Gathering.

"In lean times many come into this country, forgetting that they are eaters of bison, caribou, and the grass-eating game that they say is sweet of meat and blood. They say that mammoth meat is strong with the taste of spruce, bad meat, except in lean times." He deliberately let Torka know that he held those with no preference for mammoth meat in disdain. "It is from the meat of the great tusked ones that true men draw their strength," he said, eyeing Torka sideways to see his reaction.

Torka smiled at Lorak's obvious baiting. He would not give him the satisfaction of rising to it. Faces were looking toward them from countless fires. He was aware of the dogs slinking under the burden of their packs as they walked with tails tucked, sensing the fear and potential hostility. A boy suddenly leaped from the sidelines to touch one of the larger pups—to prove his bravery and to assure himself that he was not seeing things. With a shriek he fell back as the pup leaped straight into the air, snarling and puncturing the boy's offending finger with a well-placed canine before Torka's single command brought the animal into line with its siblings.

"Forbidden!" Torka echoed the dog's snarls to the boy who had shrunk back, looking much like a startled pup himself as he sucked his injury.

"These be spirit dogs!" shouted Zinkh, emphasizing Torka's

warning to all within earshot. "Only Torka's people and Zinkh's people may walk as brothers and sisters with these dogs! All others stay away from the magic dogs of Torka!"

Torka rolled his eyes. Zinkh, obviously enjoying his newfound, much-elevated status, was making the best of a good thing.

Lorak looked with misgivings at the dogs but said nothing. He led the newcomers on, pausing at the base of a sparsely populated rise of tundral earth amid a broad clearing, upwind of the latrines. "There. Ahead in that place may Man Who Walks With Dogs build his fire and raise his pit huts," he commanded.

"Great honor!" cried Zinkh, grinning at Torka with obsequious adoration. "This be Hill of Dreams! Best place in camp. Rain comes, it runs off into other men's camps! Wind blows, it carries flies and stink of offal pits away. A place of shamans!"

"But not for you!" Lorak added with relish. "This man has seen Zinkh and his people at his camp before. No magic walks with you!" He looked again at Torka with wariness. "But by Zinkh's words, Man Who Walks With Dogs is a shaman, so he and his women and son must camp in this place. Zinkh and the rest of this band, you may camp wherever you can find a spot!"

Torka saw Zinkh wilt with disappointment, and he resented the way the little man had been deliberately demeaned by the supreme elder. "Zinkh and the rest of this band, they are Torka's people now," he protested. "We will make one camp together. We will camp here."

"Come," urged Sondahr. "Bring the tattooed woman to me upon the Hill of Dreams. Others will help your women and son to raise your camp." She pointed to the hunter who had been carrying the sick woman's sledge. "You will stay here. Her man will come with her—only her man."

Torka obeyed. Slinging off his traveling pack, he lifted Aliga gently from the sledge and carried her as he walked with the magic woman onto the Hill of Dreams, past several small conical, hide-covered huts, and one larger one that was completely covered with the black and white feathers of teratorns. He assumed that this was her hut and paused, but she looked back at him over her shoulder and shook her head, smiling.

"That is Lorak's place of dreams. If the wind is right, perhaps someday it will fly away and take him with it." She continued on.

He followed, marveling at the wondrous views that the hill afforded: He could see for miles in all directions, across the teeming encampment to the vast, river-veined, lake-pocked land that lay beyond. He could see the glistening, northernmost edge of the Mountains That Walk and followed their towering blue-white splendor east and south until distance shrank them into insignificance. Had he not walked there, into the land of grass that lay between them, he would have thought them to be not mountains at all but clouds piling high into the sky. Briefly he thought of the Valley of Songs, of the sweet, warm pools where he had laughed and loved with Lonit. A pang of longing struck him.

He turned his eyes away and, hefting Aliga's weight, drew his thoughts out of the past and looked westward to closer, craggier, deeply cleft ranges of stone that formed the horizon of the world of men—a world where his women and children were safe at last within the protective circle of another band . . . where he would find healing for Aliga. He stared into those dark and spruce-shadowed canyons. Soon mammoths would come to them, along with other game that sought refuge from the savage winter storms that whipped across the tundral grasslands. With Aar and the other dogs he would hunt with his spear hurler and show the people of this encampment what *his* kind of magic could do—a magic of practical inventiveness that had nothing to do with smoke or dreams.

"Come." Sondahr beckoned to him.

He walked on.

At the summit of the hill was a great longhouse built entirely of mammoth bones and tusks. The bleached and polished skulls of two massively tusked bulls sat on the ground at either side of a high, arching entryway made of two upright tusks braced at the base by stabilizing bones. The tips of these tusks were lashed together by a lacing of intricate thongwork, while four tusks extended out from the two skulls on the ground formed a walkway. Sondahr skirted it and continued on, at the crest of the hill, where she stopped beside a small mound covered by the shaggy, weather-darkened red hide of a mammoth. She bade Torka enter through an arching entryway composed of a single unusually curved tusk.

Torka stooped as he entered. The dark interior was redolent of a well-banked fire in which wormwood had been recently burned.

"Torka may place his woman here."

He paused, squinting until his eyes gradually adjusted to the dark interior. He saw that the walls of the mounded hut were composed of mammoth ribs. The central fire pit was ringed not by stones or turf but by the grinding teeth of mammoths. Similar teeth formed the understructure of the hut. The pallet was also covered with shaggy red mammoth hide. He crossed the little room and gently placed the barely conscious Aliga onto the pallet.

Sondahr removed her cloak and brow circlet. She knelt, pressing her cheek, ear, and open palm against Aliga's belly. Her hand moved, questing, then lay still. Her eyes closed.

Torka frowned. The magic woman seemed to be sleeping. Then she exhaled and spoke as though out of her dreams.

"How long has this woman been with this child?"

"Too long."

"I can feel no life in her beside her own heartbeat and breath."

"Aliga feels it."

"Your woman *longs* to feel it, and so, perhaps, she does. It will take time for me to tell." She sighed again and rose to her feet in one graceful unfolding of limbs and torso. "You will leave her with me for the passing of a day or more? To rest, to drink strengthening brews, to—"

"For as long as you need to bring forth the child."

"There may be no child."

He was stunned.

She saw his reaction and stepped close, guiding him out of the hut. Together they stood in the sun, yet as she spoke, Torka went cold. "There is no form, nothing I could feel within her belly. None."

"But she has felt it move! Many times."

"She has never borne a child and so feels what her soul has need of feeling. It is Spirit Sucker that lives in your woman's belly, Torka. It is draining her of life as it feeds upon her. I have seen it before. There is no healing for it. But she is lucky; she has a man who cares enough for her to keep what I now tell him a secret and who has brought her to live her last days among other women. That will be good medicine for her. It is what she has wanted. Until the end she need not know what is to come. No one need know except Torka, so that until the end a caring man will hunt for her and hold her in his arms at the moment when her spirit leaves her body to walk upon the wind forever. That is more than most women will ever know."

He turned away, wanting to hear no more. He would have left the hill, but she lay her hand upon his forearm and caused him to face her again. "You are no shaman," she said quietly.

"Zinkh has said it, not I."

"You have not denied it."

"As you have said, there are many kinds of magic."

"The youth who walks at your side, he can work them all. He is not your son?"

He heard a question in her voice, and fear. "He *is* my son," he said, meaning it; no son of his flesh could mean more to him.

Her hand moved quickly to touch his loins. "Not the son of *this!*"

He slapped her hand away. "You assume too much, Sondahr."

A look of terrible sadness moved across her incomparably beautiful face. "I assume nothing, Torka! I *know*. As the birds rise from the waters at summer's end and fly into the face of the rising sun, as the game moves eastward into that same sun as night grows to feed upon the day, I *know* when winter is coming—before the hunters know it, before the geese and the swans know it, before the spirits of the sky and storm and cloud know it! The winter I see and foretell is not a season, Torka; it is a winter of the spirit, a cold, clouded remembrance of things that have happened and *will* happen. And for this knowledge there is no healing—*none*. Like your woman, there is no help for me."

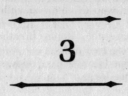

3

"Rhino!"

One word and the hunt was on. From every hut and shelter within the encampment, men and youths took up their spears and ran eagerly toward danger.

"Now we show them what magic is, yes?" asked Zinkh as Torka came down from the Hill of Dreams to find his camp already nearly set up. He nodded, pleased to see that Zinkh and his men had dug the ground for their pit huts as well as for his own. Lonit, Iana, the other women, and children were busy gouging trenches to assure that rain would be channeled away from their shelters and into pools from which they would be able to draw fresh drinking water. He smiled to see Summer Moon doing her best to help the others, while Lonit overlooked the fact that the child was succeeding mainly in scattering soil all over herself.

Nearby, a sullen, dreamy-eyed Karana had the dogs under control, which was no easy task because, until the cry of "rhino" had gone up, every youth in the camp was hunkering in the vicinity, trying to learn by what magic the dogs obeyed the commands of a human being. Now, in their enthusiasm for the hunt, they had vanished as quickly as flies before an early summer gale, and Karana was left looking at Torka with the strangest expression on his face. Torka had seen it before, on the faces of other men, but never before upon Karana's: jealousy. But of what?

"Where is Aliga?" Lonit asked.

Torka frowned. The same jealousy was upon her face. What was the matter with them? "She will stay with the magic woman for a few days. The woman says that she has brews that will ease her."

"Bah!" retorted Pomm, then flushed and pretended to be wiping gnats from her nose when she realized that, in her jealousy of the magic woman, she had unintentionally challenged a man.

"She is wise and beautiful," Karana breathed, as though he were making a litany to the spirits.

Torka's smile returned now that he understood. "I thought that Karana had no use for girls?"

"That is no girl! She is the most beautiful woman in the world!"

"She may well be that," conceded Torka, taking such pleasure in seeing the lovestruck look on the boy's face that he failed to note the expression of abject misery that transformed Lonit's features.

"Come! We hunt now!" Zinkh had his spears in hand and his fellow hunters at his back. "Look, even old Lorak walks out of camp with his spears—not that he can use them. Wait till he sees what Torka can do with his spear hurler, then he will know what magic truly is!"

They went out across the land like wolves, a great pack of howling men and youths, with the dogs running point as though they were directing the hunt. The old woolly rhino heard them long before its small, dull eyes saw them circling through the frost-toughened sedges of the bog in which it had been chomping berries—leaves, branches, and all. Its horned head went up; its ears swiveled; water and muck from the bog bottom dripped from its sloppy lips. Broken leaves dangled from its jaws, and the blue-black blood of its vegetarian feast stained its snout.

The first spear went wide, as did the second and the third; but each served to alert the animal to impending danger. Short-tempered and incautious, it huffed several times, adjusted its great, shaggy weight, and charged.

As panic-stricken men and youths went rushing past him toward the rhino, Torka held his position on a rise just beyond the bog, appalled and angered by the raucous, totally undisciplined, flagrantly careless manner of the hunt. Now, with one of his spears positioned in his spear hurler and the others easily accessible, aligned upright across his back in his spear carrier, he stood prepared to escape from the assault of the dangerous beast, which should have been stalked in silence. If the hunters had used the wind to mask their scent, they could easily have edged to within striking distance and dropped the monster while it was still wallowing within the bog.

But they were out for sport as well as for meat, and from the first it had been their intention to provoke the animal. Thus they should have expected its violent charge and its sideways, head-swinging attack, as Torka had. He warned Karana to stay back, to be ready to leap for his life.

The rhinoceros thundered past them in a blur, its horned head stabbing upward with such power that, had any of them failed to leap aside, they would have been impaled and thrown over the shaggy back of the animal and into the bog.

It stood facing them on open grassland now. Blowing enraged snorts of air, it pawed the earth, sending grass and soil flying. Led by Aar, the dogs circled it, barking, snapping, charging in and out in threatening forays. The rhino's small eyes, white with cataracts, strained to see its attackers through a fog of near blindness. It tossed its head, made high, whistling noises of threat as it trotted in circles, its tail flicking angrily. One of the older dogs, a member of Aar and Sister Dog's first litter, lunged just as the head of the rhinoceros swept down and sideways, slicing the air and the dog with its great horn. The dog flew through the air, yipping pathetically and raining blood before it disappeared into the bog scrub without a further sound.

Torka was angry. Beside him, still on high ground, Karana stood white-lipped and trembling, the butt end of his spear nocked into the barb of his spear hurler, the haft of the weapon poised across his shoulder as, like Torka, he wondered why Zinkh and the men of the Great Gathering were taking such obvious pleasure in risking themselves, and Torka's dogs, unnecessarily.

But the death of the dog had excited them, and they howled now in appreciation but disappointment over the rhinoceros's killing of the bold and fearless animal. Never had they seen dogs hunt with men as though they were of one pack; they had not believed that such an alliance was possible, in spite of what Zinkh had claimed. They were still howling as, with Aar ferociously leading them, the other dogs continued to menace the prey, confusing it, enraging it. With old Lorak in the lead the hunters howled, urging the brave dogs on as though they themselves were dogs, but with none of the canines' dignity. They stamped their feet, danced sideways and back and forth, mocking the great, harried rhino with chants of deprecation, threatening with their spears, then hurling them as one.

Only two of the projectiles struck and held, neither inflicting a mortal wound, for the rhino was encased in an armor of thick, matted brownish-gray hair over a tough, virtually impenetrable hide and insulating fat. With the spears protruding from its shoulder hump, it whirled and ran.

Lorak raised a feathered arm and shrieked his whooping cry. The others, enflamed, followed him and burst into a run, also screaming. Again they were wolves. But this time their run was short. The rhino had not gone very far before it wheeled and reversed the order of the chase.

Now, pursued by the pounding-footed, slobbering-lipped, shaggy mountain with death in its half-blind eyes, dogs and men raced toward the rise where Torka and Karana still stood.

Old Lorak had been in the lead, but now he was falling behind. Looking back over his shoulder proved a serious mistake, which caused him to lose ground, trip over his own feathered garments, and fall flat. As Torka and Karana stared, the old man bravely positioned himself, spear up, ready to impale the rhinoceros as it ground him into the earth.

Still on high ground, with their spear hurlers already positioned, Torka and Karana loosed their weapons simultaneously. Their spears arced over the running hunters. With the power of a grown man behind it, Torka's weapon struck first. Its pointed stone head tore through the skin and fat of the rhinoceros's shoulder, carrying the shaft through the beast's flesh as the projectile point buried itself in bone, then shattered. The animal screamed and nearly fell as it veered sharply, just as Karana's spear found its side, ripped through hair and hide to penetrate one of the animal's lungs. Choking on its own blood, the rhinoceros threw up its head, gasping for breath. In this moment Torka's second spear penetrated its breast to sever veins and arteries in a mortal wounding that struck cleanly into its heart.

While Zinkh jumped up and down with pride and all of the other hunters looked back in disbelief and awe, Lorak shamed himself by crying out with relief when the rhinoceros collapsed into a heap of bleeding meat that had come only breaths away from crushing him to death.

*   *   *

They stood in reverence of Torka and Karana—of their magic spears and the power that they exerted over their dogs. Having learned a bitter lesson in Supnah's band, Torka spoke no denial of the magic. Let the people of the Great Gathering think of him what they would; a man needed status when he walked among strangers.

They opened the belly and throat of the fallen rhinoceros. Torka and Karana were honored with the prime portions because they had made the kill, which not only had brought man meat to the people at the Great Gathering, but had saved the life of Lorak, supreme elder among magic men.

They lounged by the corpse, gorging themselves on hot, sweet blood, then the ultimate delicacies: the tongue, liver, heart, and contents of the intestines, which Torka and Karana graciously insisted upon sharing. They passed around the eyes and sucked the juices from them. No man complained when Torka and Karana offered generous portions to the dogs; they had more than earned it.

When they had eaten their fill, a call went out to the women, who came with their butchering tools, carrying babies in frames or walking with children beside them. Lonit basked with pride. This was the kill of the males of her fire.

She stood tall before them, surveying the size of the great and dangerous animal they had slain. She was happy that Iana had remained behind with Demmi and Summer Moon. Iana was not really Torka's woman, not in the full sense of the word. Nor was Aliga, she thought. Torka sometimes went to ease her loneliness within the night because it was a man's responsibility to keep his women content. But once Aliga was pregnant, Torka lay only with Lonit. She was his first and only woman again, and she was glad!

But her mood darkened as she thought of Aliga at Sondahr's fire. Torka had gone with her. He had admitted to Karana that he thought her to be the most beautiful woman in the world. Sondahr, with no man of her own, truly was worthy of Torka.

But if anyone could help Aliga, Sondahr could do it; her healing powers were all that the women had spoken of when the men had gone off to hunt. If Aliga gave birth to a son, Torka would never let her go. A woman's value was measured by her strength and her skills and, ultimately, by her ability to bring strong hunters into the world. And Lonit had borne only daughters.

Her shame deepened because her preoccupation had caused her to neglect her own responsibilities. Torka had called her to partake of the meat, so she must praise him with song, in the way of their people, and hope that the onlookers would not laugh.

But they did not laugh. They were quiet, entranced by the measured grace of her steps, the quiet cadence of her song, and her beauty. When at last she completed the required circuit of the fallen game and paused, eyes downcast, before her man and Karana, asking permission to butcher and eat their kill, everyone exhaled with approval. Her heart swelled with joy and relief to see that he was beaming with pride and love.

But then his eyes focused beyond her, and Karana also seemed transfixed. She turned to see Sondahr standing behind her.

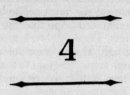

4

The meat of the woolly rhinoceros did not last long when shared by many. Lonit allowed the other women to assist in the butchering. They praised her for her generosity, and all but Sondahr helped to skin the animal, pack its meat, and carry the usable portions of its dismembered carcass back to camp. The women, headed by a particularly belligerent Pomm, drove Sondahr away, telling the magic woman that her powers were such that she would have her share and must not bloody her hands in the work. In the night of feasting that followed, all the meat was eaten, but the magic woman stayed with Aliga within her hut upon the Hill of Dreams and did not come to claim a portion of it.

In the morning one of the magic men brought word from the Hill of Dreams that the tattooed woman's fever had lessened and that, in the care of the mystical Sondahr, she was sleeping easily. Lonit asked if she might sit with the sister of her man's fire, but was told that only magic men, Sondahr, and those specifically invited by them might set foot upon the sacred hill.

Disappointed and trying hard not to be jealous of Sondahr, Lonit set to work with the other women. By the end of the day they had stretched the rhinoceros hide and secured it to a drying frame for curing. Its sinews were strung, its fat rendered, its bones cracked and scraped of precious marrow, and its skull added to those that lined the encircling wall of bones and tusks.

The beast's horn was set upright at the edge of Torka's camp circle. He and Karana initially had placed it next to the entrance to their pit hut but were soon forced to move it. The horn was reputed to have great magical powers, so every male ventured near to lay his hands reverently upon it. Since the men were forced to run a gauntlet between barking dogs to do so, Torka carried the horn well away from the fire and the dogs to assure quiet and make certain that no one was bitten. Nevertheless, Lorak, glowering, said that magic such as that within the horn had no place among the encampment of mere men.

By dusk the elders of the various bands were calling for a night of storytelling, games, and dancing to celebrate the hunt, but the supreme elder was still sulking. He kept to himself, expressing only surly resentment of those who had saved his life.

"Better to have let the great horned woolly one take the life spirit of the ungrateful old condor," hissed Zinkh, still holding a grudge against the supreme elder for the way Lorak had publicly insulted him.

Torka looked at the summit of the Hill of Dreams where Lorak brooded alone outside his feather-covered hut. He had unintentionally made an enemy of the supreme elder. For the sake of his women and children, it was not wise to displease Lorak's many friends among the magic men; theirs was the power behind those who were assembled at the Great Gathering. Besides, he felt sorry for old Lorak.

"It must be a terrible thing to lose one's pride," he told Zinkh. "Perhaps this man can find a way to give back to Lorak that which he and Karana have inadvertently taken."

So he took up the horn, and since all believed him to be a shaman, he had Karana follow him in unquestioning silence onto the Hill of Dreams. As several magic men appeared at the entryway to the house of bones, Torka respectfully placed the horn before the seated old man.

"Torka's spirit has walked his dreams," said Torka, searching for the right words, standing stiffly beside Karana in the overbearing way that he had seen magic men always stand when they wished to press a point in a manner that would allow no debate. "Torka's spirit has relived the hunt. Torka's spirit has understood that by the tradition of this man's people, the horn of the great woolly one must go to the one who risked his life so that others might make the kill."

Lorak frowned up at him, not understanding. From the house of bones the watching magic men murmured. Karana looked at Torka, confused by his words and his uncharacteristic behavior.

"It was bold and brave and beyond the ways of most men to fall deliberately before a charging rhinoceros so that the other members of a hunting party might escape death."

Lorak winced at Torka's statement, knowing it to be a lie and suspecting that Torka also knew it. Their eyes met and held. Why was this younger, physically stronger man deferring to one who, in a moment of terror, had screamed and fouled his garments like an infant?

Lorak growled resentfully. Lie or not, Torka's premise promised a path to heroism. He had only to assent to it, and he would be supreme magic man again. And Sondahr would respect his power once again. And he might finally find a way to seduce her into sharing his bed skins!

"Yes. It is so!" he snapped. "It took Torka long enough to see past his arrogance to the truth!"

They went down from the Hill of Dreams, with Karana looking back to where Sondahr stood at the crest of the hill, looking at him as no woman had ever looked at him before.

That night, when the games of evening were finished, Karana came away as a delighted and breathless victor from nearly every challenge that Torka forced him to accept from youths of his own age. Several of the combatants came to him and offered friendship.

"I am Yanehva, son of Cheanah. My brother Mano and I say that there is much we could show you in this camp. And with Tlap here, and also Ank, we could hunt in the days to come and show the men what we can do, eh? And now, if you want, we can show you another kind of game."

Karana was amazed. It had been many years since he had had friends his own age, so he did not know what to do except nod and follow happily as they led him off in a circuitous route in search of the huts of the prettiest and most well-endowed girls in the camp. Here they stalked in the firelit shadows, peeking through seams in pit-hut walls well-known to the brothers, winking and suppressing laughter at the sight of the women and girls as they dressed for the night's festivities. Karana enjoyed the company of the other youths, but though many of the girls were beautiful to behold, his mind and heart were filled with images of the proud and mysterious Sondahr. He could think of nothing else and soon wandered off, bored with the game and content to sit with Torka as he savored the camaraderie of other hunters.

Soon a great feast fire was blazing. Karana joined Torka and the others around a huge, stone-lined pit in which flames fed off turf and lichens and bones, crackling, popping, spitting sparks high into the stars. In the sky above the eastern horizon an aurora glowed like a shivering, oxbowed river of red and gold.

As was customary, the women and children sat together on one side of the circle, while the men and youths sat on the other. All listened as Lorak pointed to the sky and told wondrous stories of the great fish that swam in the sky rivers, of the stars that were their eggs, and of how, when clouds covered the sky and the rain fell, the stars fell to earth in the rain. This, he said, was how fish came to swim within the rivers of the earth so that men and women could catch and eat them.

"Fish!" exclaimed Zinkh with disgust when the story was done. "This man says it would be a fine good thing if the sky rained stars that were the eggs of man meat instead of woman meat! In this land there is lately too much fish and berries and birds."

"All food is spirit given!" countered Lorak. "All! We who gather here to await the coming of the great mammoths will eat only that meat if the choice is given. But the gifts of Mother Below are gifts, nonetheless; and while we wait for the coming of the great ones, fish are plentiful in the streams and rivers, and waterfowl are fat with summer's end, and berries are sweet for our children. We are of many bands in this camp. If woman meat is forbidden you, then refrain from partaking of it. When the hooves of the great herds move across the world, when the wind spirits howl in the distant canyons, when Thunder Speaker's roars split the sky, then all men know that Father Above is the force that puts life to man meat within the bellies of the mothers of the game!"

"Eh yah, hay!" The affirmation was spoken in unison from many youths.

Courteously, and with much pride in their style, men of many bands joined in the storytelling. They spoke of far lands and of different yet always similar ways of life. They boasted of adventures. They thrilled their listeners with tales of survival. The last man to speak enthralled them all with a story of how he had single-handedly killed a great short-faced bear and had eaten it himself, sharing none of it with his women because its belly had been so filled with just-eaten char that there had been enough of that to feed his women for weeks, while he alone savored the meat of the great bear.

"The red meat of the great horned one was the first fresh meat that many men in this camp have eaten in all too many days. The man Torka has brought luck with him to the Great Gathering," said one magic man, and all of the hunters who had seen his spear fly faster, farther, and harder than any other cheered him.

"Tell us of your band. How is it that Torka's people come to this camp speaking of a land rich in man meat when we have hunted the game trails of our fathers for an entire season with little to show?"

Torka spoke quietly, with no embellishment. None was necessary, for all men knew of the great mammoth Thunder Speaker. They trembled when he told them of how it had destroyed his band and forced him to wander the world with only an old man, a young woman, and a wild dog, until at last he had made his peace with the Destroyer and had come to name it Life Giver for leading him to a new life in a strange and forbidden land.

"Why should land rich with game be forbidden?" The question came from one of two disreputable-looking bandless hunters who hunkered close together. Between them, tethered with a thong collar, was a frail, femininely pretty, haggard-looking boy.

"And why has Torka left this land of good hunting to winter in a camp where neither mammoths nor any of the great herds have come?" pressed the second of the two hunters, drawing Torka back to the moment as he looked him straight in the eyes.

Torka's head went up defensively. He measured the dirty, grimy-faced man. The rudely prodding tone of the question had not startled and offended him. But among his people and all bands he had ever had contact with, it was forbidden to look directly into the eyes of another unless that person was kindred or lover, and thus a part of one's own life spirit. To do so was to invade the other person's soul through his eyes and open a vent by which the life spirit could escape and fall under the control of the invader. Perhaps the man was unaware that he was breaking an ancient taboo. Torka deliberately met his stare; to look away once eye contact was made would be an admission of weakness.

There was something of an overfed lynx about his features

as one of his hands played idly with the thong that held the boy captive beside him. The hunter flinched and looked away.

"The game has followed Torka to this camp!" declared Zinkh to the hunter. "Or did you and your boy-using brother not hunt with us and eat of the flesh of the great woolly rhinoceros?"

"We hunted. We ate. But the flesh of the horned one is gone, and you, Zinkh, are always the first to complain about eating woman meat in this camp. Mammoth meat is the best meat for us, but Tomo and Jub, we will eat anything and not complain. We do wonder why a man who says he will not hunt the mammoth has come to this camp of mammoth hunters, and why, if Torka has come from a hunting ground full of game, he does not tell us where it is, so that we may go there. We are not afraid to hunt alone. You—all of you here—would be amazed at the stories Tomo and Jub could tell of the things that we have killed and of the kinds of meat that we have eaten."

"It is a land forbidden to men," said Zinkh, bristling as he spoke in defense of Torka.

"Yet Torka went there. He has brought prime skins. He has—"

"Torka is a magic man! The spirits walk with him. He may go where he will go!"

Torka waved the pugnacious little Zinkh to silence, needing no advocate to speak for him. "This man followed his totem, Thunder Speaker, into the Corridor of Storms. Although there may be game, there are no people, and so a man who is without a band—even if he is a magic man—must live in constant fear of what must happen to his women and children if his life spirit should walk the wind. For this reason Torka has come back into the world of men."

"No man has ever returned from the Corridor of Storms to tell of it!" Lorak's tone was sharp.

"I tell of it," replied Torka evenly, momentarily regretting his kindness to the elder, which had been at his own expense. "Far to the east is an endless river of grass—the forbidden Corridor of Storms, a place of constant wind that speaks gently to a man in the time of light and savages him during the time of the long dark. No one could long survive the dry, freezing storms of terrible cold except in hidden, wind-protected valleys. In one such valley has Torka lived beside hot springs that feed pools of water that do not freeze, even in the darkest nights of winter, and to these pools game comes to—"

"Torka must also tell the people that it is a land where the mountains rain fire and the earth shakes, to demolish the camps of men!" Karana, heart pounding, was on his feet. He had been sent a sudden vision of the land that he had reluctantly left behind. The image was as red and hot as blood. It laked within his eyes, scalding them as he looked at Tomo and Jub. He knew for a certainty that if such men entered the Valley of Songs, they would desecrate it by hunting its creatures to extinction, including Life Giver himself. "It was a *bad* land, a land wisely forbidden to men by the spirits. That was why we left it!"

The intensity of Karana's words affected all who heard them, including the youth. He had not meant to shout or to shame Torka by his outburst, but he was certain that he had done both. His face was burning with emotion as a terrible restlessness took him, and he strode boldly out of the firelight, leaving Torka and Lonit staring after him, confused by his violent change of attitude, and everyone else gaping in amazement at his audacity.

Karana walked quickly. The darkness covered him. He was glad. Had it not, he knew that Pomm would have followed him, as she had taken it upon herself to follow him everywhere, backhanding away any young girl who even dared to come close. She shadowed him even when he went to the latrine, where, angry and frustrated, he made no attempt to hide his bodily functions from her. She watched him with moon-eyed adoration, and not even the strongest of his epithets had succeeded in driving her away.

He looked up now at the stars and the trembling, arching rivers of the aurora borealis. Somehow the light seemed to flow within him: He *felt* the colors, was warmed and strengthened by them as he picked his way through the dozing dogs. Aar looked up at him. Sister Dog did not move. She eyed him listlessly and exhaled softly; she had been moping ever since Torka had carried Aliga onto the Hill of Dreams and had commanded her to stay behind.

Karana bent and touched her head, communicating understanding. She whined softly, nuzzling his hand. He walked on, restless almost beyond bearing as he passed the capacious pit hut that he shared with Torka and his family. It had been his intention to enter and throw himself onto his sleeping skins; now he could not bring himself to go inside.

He turned and looked back to the communal fire. From where he stood, he could not see Torka, Lonit, or any of Zinkh's people. He found himself smiling a little as he was forced to admit that the funny little headman in his outrageous helmet with the dead fox hanging over the top of his brow was proving to be a loyal friend.

Then his smile vanished as he realized that Torka had been right: This was a good camp. It had been so long since he had been in the company of those of his own age that he had forgotten the enjoyment such associations could bring. His part in the killing of the rhinoceros had given him status not only among his peers but among everyone at the gathering. As much as he was loath to admit it, the prospect of wintering here no longer seemed repugnant—the thought of being anywhere near the magic woman Sondahr was enough to warm him and send his wits flying happily from his head.

Thoughts of her took the moment. He looked up along the smooth, sloping contours of the Hill of Dreams. Sondahr had not been at the communal fire. She must be there, in the hut that Torka had described to him, working her healing magic upon Aliga. It was dark upon the sacred hill. The bones of the council house shone dully in the soft pink light of the aurora. He shivered at the sight of it, recalling the vision that had prompted him to interrupt Torka at the communal fire.

Blood. Death. Desecration. These things filled his senses, then ebbed, leaving his mind almost painfully clear. Karana had felt so welcome here that despite the encampment's circling wall of bones and tusks and the council house of bones upon the Hill of Dreams, he had forgotten that these people were primarily mammoth hunters. Tomo and Jub had caused him to remember.

He looked again at the communal fire, which had ebbed into hot, glowing coals giving off smoke that smelled of burned bones and fat and of sods cut from the skin of the tundral earth. In their red, pulsing light, Karana could see that several middle-aged women had risen to dance for the assembly within the circle. He heard the flat, nasal, atonal resonance of their song. It had to do with the pride that women felt when their men killed mammoths, the joy they experienced when they were called to butcher mammoths, the pleasure they knew when working together at the stretching

and scraping of mammoth skins. It chafed some inner portion
of his consciousness that could not bear the sound of it.

Just sharing the mammoth hunters' encampment made him
a consenting party to their ways. And he had sworn before all
of the spirits of Creation and the great Life Giver himself that
he would never hunt the mammoth. *Never*. He felt suddenly
confined by his surroundings. He was desperate for the open
tundra, for the song of the free, unfettered wind.

With a grunt of determination, he took one of his spears
from where it stood upright against the pit hut next to Torka's
weapons and walked across the broad compound, past innumerable huts, shelters, and drying frames, until at last he
reached the break in the wall of mammoth bones through
which he had first entered the camp with Torka. He paused,
reached out, and lay an open palm against a great tusk.

"Mammoth spirit, know that Karana has not come to hunt
your kind. He has come with Torka's people to winter in this
camp with those who have not named you totem. But though
they may draw their strength from your spirit, Karana and
Torka will not wet our spears in your blood, nor eat of your
flesh, nor point the way to the river of grass or to the Valley
of Songs to which Life Giver has gone."

Beneath his palm the tusk seemed suddenly warm, as
though the spirit of the great mammoth had heard the promise of the youth.

Karana withdrew his hand, startled. For the first time he
noticed that Aar was at his side.

"Come, Brother Dog," he said softly, grateful for the
company of his faithful companion. "You and I will walk
alone a while. Karana's spirit feels small and confused in this
place of too many people."

Together they ran beneath the open sky and breathed in
the clean, cold, smokeless Arctic night air. The youth and the
dog paused atop a high mound of tundral earth and listened
to the singing of wolves, and Karana raised his arms, crying
aloud to the forces of Creation. The wind carried his voice to
the magic woman, unseen upon the hill.

"Great spirits, bring forth the game to this land. Bring
forth the bison and the caribou to die upon the spears of men
who hunger for the red meat of life! But great spirits of the
mammoth, hear Karana! Walk now away from this land. Do
not come to this place where death awaits you!"

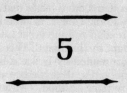

5

The next day the people at the Great Gathering slept long, and only the magic woman, standing as a silent, lonely sentinel upon the crest of the Hill of Dreams in the light of dawn, saw dust and circling birds upon the far western horizon.

Bison. The youth has called them! He has the power! Tomorrow we will hear them. Tomorrow most of the men will hunt. But the meat will not be mammoth meat, and neither they nor I shall be nourished by it.

She turned and went back into her hut. The tattooed woman was awake, sitting up, sipping at a warm broth of strongly steeped bearberry leaves and thick, oily marrow extracted from the bones of many animals—but not from the rhinoceros whose flesh she had not been allowed to butcher.

"The magic of Sondahr is great!" proclaimed Aliga, smiling, displaying her filed, tattooed teeth. "The woman of Torka feels stronger every day!"

The magic woman expressionlessly observed her patient. Untroubled rest and the rich broths had done Aliga much good, but her eyes were still yellow, and her fever, although under control, was still there. The slightest stress would set it free to burn wild once again.

"My baby sleeps, growing strong. It will be born soon, yes?"

Sondahr felt such overwhelming pity for the woman, it was difficult to remain aloof; but she had learned long ago that a betrayal of emotion was also a betrayal of power.

Frowning, she moved to sit beside the tattooed woman. "The youth, the one you call Karana. Tell me of him."

Aliga's smile disappeared. "There is nothing to tell! He is a rude boy with eyes that see too much for his own good! With luck he will find a woman in this camp and follow Torka's people no more!"

"As Torka's son is it not more likely that he will eventually bring the woman of his choice to walk with his father's people?"

Aliga rose to snap at the bait. "*This* woman will bear Torka's son! Karana is named by Torka as his own only out of kindness and blind affection. But the boy is son to the headman Supnah, and by right he should walk with his own true people. Do you know the band? They have a wondrous magic man among them—Navahk, the most beautiful man this woman has ever seen. I mean no offense, but in truth I had hoped that Navahk would be in this camp."

"No, Navahk and his people have not been to the Great Gathering in many years. And I am not offended, Aliga. I have never known a woman who was not drawn by the beauty of Navahk—including myself long ago, when he was not much more than a boy who looked so much like Karana that . . ." She paused. She had known the truth from the first moment that she saw him.

Aliga made a face of annoyance. "Karana thinks that he will be a magic man like his uncle someday! He goes off alone. He calls upon the spirits. He *sees* things, that one does. Things that no one but a true shaman has a right to see! You would do well to put him in his place, Magic Woman! For he will never be like Navahk!"

"No one in the world of men or spirits will ever be like Navahk," Sondahr replied guardedly, her eyes full of memories.

Aliga dared to reach out and touch the forearm of the older woman. "Sondahr's powers are great. If you called to him, if you put your summons upon the spirit winds, would Navahk come to this camp to help this woman's baby to be born?"

Sondahr rose. Her exquisite features hardened into reproach. "Navahk is a man whose magic is a thing of death, not of life. Be glad that he is not in this camp. Be glad that this woman will not summon him. I will summon a better man for you—*Torka*. He may take you back to your own pit hut now. I have done all that I can for you."

It seemed to Lonit that Torka was not ever going to come down from the Hill of Dreams. When he did, he carried Aliga in his arms and was quick to share with Lonit the information that the magic woman had given him about how the tattooed woman must be cared for.

"She must have rest and plenty of sleep," he explained, placing Aliga onto the piled sleeping skins that Lonit had arranged with great care so they would be ready for her return. Aliga settled herself without so much as a word of thanks, commenting huffily that the pallet of the magic woman had been thicker with heather and moss and therefore more comfortable, then added that Lonit must learn to make a better bed.

"This woman has always tried to do her best," Lonit countered. She was actually glad to have Aliga's waspish tongue stinging her again; she must be feeling better! "Aliga has never complained before."

"Aliga complains now," drawled the tattooed woman, folding her hands across the dress skins that were tautly stretched across her enormous belly.

"She must have this to drink with her food," Torka continued, handing Lonit a bladder flask of brew that Sondahr had given him.

She took it, lifted it, sniffed it, and blinked in surprise. "It is what this woman has been brewing for her all along! Marrow broth with bearberry leaves."

"Lonit just *thinks* that this is what it is," said Aliga haughtily. "Lonit's brews never helped this woman! But look, Aliga is much better now! Sondahr has mixed much magic into the medicine that she has made for me!"

The strangest expression crossed Torka's face. "Yes, much magic to have made Aliga feel so much stronger."

Lonit could not read his face. He seemed lost in his solicitude to Aliga, so much so that he did not notice when Sister Dog slunk in from outside. Eyeing Torka and Lonit warily, expecting to be commanded out at once, the dog made it to Aliga's side and hunkered low, extending her snout in wary greeting. Lonit scolded the animal and made to shoo her away, but the tattooed woman was actually glad to see the dog. She ruffled the grizzled fur of the animal's wolflike head with her fingers and asked Torka if the dog might stay.

Lonit was amazed. Aliga had never shown affection to the dogs; indeed, she usually kicked the pups and complained about the fact that Sister Dog had taken such a fancy to her. And the dogs were never allowed within the pit hut. Even during the coldest storms they were content to stay curled close to the lee walls, tucking noses beneath tails, their thick coats forming more than adequate insulation against the cold. Karana had begged Torka to allow them inside, and he had agreed once. The pups had come in to loose such pissing pandemonium that the entire hut had nearly collapsed, and the interior had never been completely cleansed of the strong odor of puppy urine. Since then it had been an unspoken law: No dogs were allowed within the pit hut.

So it was that Lonit was startled when she was reprimanded by Torka for trying to make Sister Dog remember her manners.

"If it would cheer Aliga, let the dog stay, Lonit. And stop arguing with her. She needs her strength."

Hurt and confused, she bowed her head and backed out of the hut. Iana sat outside with the baby, changing is swaddling moss. Summer Moon was sitting cross-legged before her, trying to untangle the mess that she had made out of an old fishing lure of musk-ox hair.

The encampment was athrob with morning activities. Everyone was up and about. Smokes rose from cooking fires, so thick that they stung Lonit's eyes—or were those tears that burned beneath her lids? She impatiently backhanded them away. Across the coals of her own meticulously made, nearly smokeless fire, a summer-fat ptarmigan was roasting to perfection, dripping pink juices that had the dogs up and at attention.

Karana sat close by. He had torn off one of the bird's legs and was gnawing on it as he made certain that the rest of the bird did not burn or fall prey to the salivating dogs.

Miserable, weighted by all of the old self-doubts that had plagued her since childhood, Lonit took up her bola and walked through the teeming camp, knowing that the men who looked at her as she passed must be pitying Torka for being burdened by such a worthless female. Several women said good morning. She answered and barely knew that she spoke at all. Perhaps along the shores of the tundral lake that lay south of the encampment she could snare a few waterfowl to add to her family's main meal; because of her generosity, much of the rhinoceros meat that otherwise would have been drying within the peripheries of Torka's camp circle was now in the bellies of strangers. Her man had given her permission to portion the butchered meat and share it, and as his first woman, she could have turned up her chin and said that until her own camp was fully stored, other women must be content to butcher the kills of their own men. But she knew that Torka wanted to make friends among the hunters. As she walked out of the encampment now, she nevertheless wondered if she had done the right thing.

The sky was free of clouds, and the sun was warm. The wind was so strong that biting flies were instantly carried away on a wing-shredding tide of air that allowed no safe landing or return.

Lonit walked across a russet-colored land and paused at the edge of sedge grasses that lay between her and the lake. The wind skimmed across the surface so that the lake seemed to be running like a river. Now, in that brief time of year when berries ripened and tubers were sweet and ready for picking, cranes were still standing stilt-legged in the shallows. Loons called, and Lonit saw the bobbing forms of myriad species of ducks and geese and the larger, more elegant swans.

Her bola was a compound sling composed of four long lengths of braided sinews drawn together at one end. The loose end of each sinew was weighted by shell-shaped stones of equal size—rare finds gleaned in the far, undulating land that had smelled strongly of salt. She could not know that the shell-shaped stones were not stones but fossil remnants of another age. Yet somehow she sensed magic in them and a strange gentling of her spirit whenever she handled them.

Now, moving boldly forward, she took the secured ends of the thongs in her right hand and the shell-weighted ends in the other. She drew the thongs taut as, whistling and hooting, she deliberately frightened the birds into flight.

The sky was filled with the sound and presence of wings. Had she possessed no skill at all, she still could have easily killed one of the hundreds of eider ducks. She flung the weighted ends of her bola up and out and sent the weapon whirling in a deadly spin. Encircling the body of the hapless bird and breaking its wings instantly, the bola rode the duck to earth, where Lonit easily retrieved it, broke its neck, and in seconds had the bola flying again. And again, until she had a dozen birds strung through their beaks upon a carrying thong. She paused, breathing hard, forced to admire her own skill. Not one bird aimed at had been missed or struck in a way that she had not intended. The fat, pink meat of many ducks would be sweet in the camp of Torka this night. They would feast. Later, the white feathers would make lovely tunic trimmings. The down would insulate the winter boots and mittens of her family. And surely, as Torka, Karana, Aliga, Iana, and the children wiped warm grease from their chins, they would praise Lonit's efforts on their behalf. In this she *was* worthy, and nothing would make her believe otherwise!

Feeling better, she seated herself amid the soft, feathery, virtually unbloodied mound of dead ducks, plucking at them idly with her fingertips. Their eyes were glazing, looking at her.

Woman meat.

Did the admonition come from the spirits of the slain waterfowl? She had forgotten to thank the ducks for the gift of their lives. Shame replaced pride. She thanked them now, wondering why she should believe that her man would admire her for bringing back to camp the kind of meat that every woman knew how to kill?

No woman is as good with a bola as Lonit. No woman dresses better skins or makes a better fire or devises more clever fishing lures or cooks a better meal or raises a more wind-resistant pit hut or loves her children or loves her man more than Lonit does.

She drew her knees up to her chin and wrapped her arms about them, waiting to feel guilty for agreeing with the voice that spoke within her. Strangely, she felt no guilt. Startled, she thought of all the years of childhood punishment and abuse that had cowed her and forced her to hone her skills so that, through their excellence, she who had been called ugly and unworthy would be useful enough to her people so that they would not abandon her to death.

For the first time in her life the memories made her angry instead of ashamed. The inner voice made her feel bold, heady, much as she had once felt within the Valley of Songs after drinking too much fermented blood and berry juice at a summer's end feast, when her life with Torka was everything that she had never dared to dream was possible for her.

The grasses broke the wind, and the warmth of the morning was making her sleepy. She yawned. Dreamily, with her chin on her knees and her head tilted to one side, she eyed the ducks thoughtfully.

"Tell me, was the aim of this woman not so true that you fell from the sky before you even knew that you were being hunted? Was the strength of her thrust not such that, when her bola struck you, you fell stunned to the earth in little pain? And was her hand not steady when she snapped your necks so quickly that death was yours before you knew fear of the ending of your life?"

She stared at the silent birds and knew that had they been alive and able to speak, they would have confirmed her confidence:

The woman who has killed us is a bold hunter. The woman who has killed us struck us down before we could fully react to danger. The woman whose bola brought us to the earth flung it with such accuracy and power that we never knew what felled us from the sky. The woman whose hands brought quick death to us was merciful.

"Yes, Lonit is merciful, and because she is such an excellent hunter, the meat of her ducks will be tender from their quick death, for which she thanks them." Another yawn stifled her words. She closed her eyes, drifted into sleep, and dreamed that she was a black swan such as one of the mated pair that she had seen upon the lake . . . flying away with Torka and her swan babies into the face of the rising sun, back into the Corridor of Storms where the Valley of Songs awaited her return and there were no people to disrupt her life or her love . . . forever.

"Where is Lonit?"

Torka's question caused Karana to put down the second leg of the ptarmigan. "She went off with her bola. Birding, I imagine."

"Alone?"

The youth shrugged and snapped an irritable answer. "How should I know? She is *your* woman, not mine!" He had been too busy staring off toward the Hill of Dreams, hoping to catch a glimpse of Sondahr; and he was still more than a little annoyed with Torka for not allowing him to accompany him to the magic woman's hut when he had been summoned there to retrieve Aliga. "Why do you look so worried? She always hunted alone in the Valley of Songs."

"Your memory does not serve you well, Karana, if you have forgotten that our pit traps and snares kept dangerous carnivores out of the valley. That is not the case here. And Zinkh says that the tracks of a leaping cat were seen not far from where we took the rhino."

*   *   *

It was neither scent nor sound that roused her from her dreams. It was the sensation of being watched and the sudden, unnatural quiet of the tundral world around her. No loons called. No ducks chortled. No geese or swans cackled or honked or whistled. There was only the sound of the waters of the lake rolling incessantly landward, lapping at the shore as the wind hissed benignly through the tall grasses and, far away, the sounds of the huge encampment droned like distant insects.

She awoke with a start. Something was lurking, poised to spring upon her from within the grasses to her left. Panic screamed at her to rise, to run, to flee from whatever the danger was, but the inner voice of boldness overrode it. She knew from Torka and Umak that panic was her worst enemy. Panic fed upon caution, and without caution, prey stood no chance against predator. It was not often that the caribou fawn, frozen in camouflaged terror amid the scrub, drew the eyes of lions, wolves, and bears; it was the frightened animal, young or old, weak or strong, that bolted from cover and inspired the hunter to take chase.

She barely breathed. Her heart was racing, and she could feel her blood pounding in her veins. Whatever was watching her might be doing only that. It might not be hungry. It might have fed upon other meat and was merely drawn by curiosity to see what sort of animal was dozing in the grasses with a pile of dead birds at its feet.

Slowly, invisible under the fall of her windblown hair, her eyelids opened as her fingers tensed around the thongs of her bola. A small spark of relief flared within her—at least she was not totally unarmed. A bola was not a spear, but the thongs were threaded through her fingers, the weighted tips dangling loose, and the weapon was ready to be thrown in a deadly arc if—when—the moment came.

Lonit's eyes focused on the grasses through the windblown stalks of gold and russet to a deeper gold that lay beyond, to meet the eyes of a great, fang-toothed, lion-sized leaping cat.

Panic threatened her again, but the inner voice counseled: *Do not run! To run is to die! You have seen the thing you fear. It is the thing that one does not see that one must fear. The woman is wise, while the great leaping cat is stupid. Be clever, Lonit! Be bold if you would live to see your man and your children again! Do what the great leaping cat will*

*not expect! Make it fear you! Do not let it make the first
move! What have you to lose? Only your life, and that may be
lost already!*

Without another moment of thought, Lonit leaped to her
feet, shrieking as ferociously as any lion. She lifted the thong
of ducks and, with all of her strength, threw them into the
grasses where the great cat lay waiting to pounce. And now,
bola swinging and whirring above her head, Lonit went crashing through the sedges, howling like a wolf with its blood up
for the chase.

Stunned by falling ducks and confused by the fearless
onslaught of the woman, when the bola was released and its
weighted thongs hit the cat squarely across its face, blinding
it in one eye and shattering its broad, flattened nose, the
animal jumped straight up in the air, screamed in terror,
turned, and ran for its life.

Led by Torka and Karana—with Aar and the dogs running
out ahead of them on Lonit's scream—Zinkh and a small
party of hunters stopped dead when they saw the golden
body of the huge cat leap from the grasses. As it shrieked, its
stabbing fangs flashed in the sunlight and its massively shoul-
dered torso twisted into a grotesque circle of pain. It seemed
to hang suspended for a second before it arched its body back
and around and disappeared into the grasses.

The dogs froze, awaiting Torka's command. On either side
of him Karana, Zinkh, and the others, eyes wide with disbelief,
stood with their spears poised. They had seen Lonit stand
bravely to some unseen danger and had heard her wolflike
howl. As they watched her throw her thong of ducks and hurl
herself and her bola at something within the sedges, they
realized that they were too far away to help her. Not even the
spear hurlers of Torka and Karana could have sent a thrust
the required distance. Besides, there had been nothing to
aim at until the powerful body of the great cat had jumped
straight up and then disappeared.

"Torka's woman fears *nothing!*" exclaimed Zinkh in profound admiration as the hunters stared in gape-jawed awe of
the woman's unprecedented behavior.

Torka was shaking with relief and pride. From where he
stood, Lonit's beauty and strength were at one with the wild,
golden land and the incomparable grace and beauty of the
black swans that had risen from the lake.

"We will go after that great cat, yes?" prodded Zinkh. "If the woman has wounded it, it will be doubly dangerous."

The suggestion was enthusiastically taken up by his bandsmen. They spoke of the threat that a large, injured carnivore would be to their women and children when they ventured from the encampment to fish and gather berries and roots.

Torka told them to venture on without him and insisted that Karana go along to command the dogs and to try to claim the first strike for himself. Torka watched the youth go off eagerly with the others, Aar loping at his side like a faithful shadow, as he had once run with old Umak.

They reached the lakeshore, and the dogs became invisible except for the indentations that they made in the sedges. He saw Lonit proudly stand to greet the hunters. She was as tall and beautiful as Sondahr, and he could tell from her stance that their words pleased her. Karana turned and pointed back, and he knew that she asked why he was not with them.

For a moment she stared across the distance that separated them; then, purposefully, with her head held high and a newfound pride in her step, she strode toward him.

Strength was returning to him. He began to walk slowly. The tide of relief that had swept through him when the cat had turned away from her had awakened him. If the cat had leaped upon her, she would be dead now, and for Torka life would be a burden to be endured for the sake of their children.

She was before him now, holding out her thong of ducks, her face radiant.

"This woman has driven off the great leaping cat!" she proclaimed, awaiting his approval. "Alone! With only her bola! The hunters of Zinkh were impressed! This did they say to Lonit: that she was bold and brave and beautiful, and in these things, a magic woman like Sondahr! Did Torka see how Lonit faced death boldly?"

"Torka saw." He could barely form the words. He wanted to draw her into his arms, to hold her close, to kiss her mouth, her nose, her eyes . . . to tell her that he did not need the words of other men to know that she was bold and brave and more beautiful to him than the strange and aloof Sondahr could ever be. He wanted to tell her that her love for him was the pride of his life.

But he had never been a man who could easily speak of his feelings. He felt ashamed for not having been able to help her, and shame became anger at himself, at the great cat, and at the woman who had put her life in jeopardy.

And so now he saw only the ducks. He glared at them. At feather-covered, stiffening flesh and beaks, and at webbed feet from which the juices of life had already faded. Suddenly he was furious. He struck the offending birds from her hand with such power that she spun around, crying out in dismay.

"Ducks!" he raged. "Lonit has risked her life for *ducks*? And for this taking of woman meat she is compared to Sondahr? Sondahr is wise! Sondahr is wary! Sondahr is watchful! Unlike Lonit, Sondahr would know better than to cause men to put their lives at risk so that she might return safely to her camp—from which this man gave her no permission to stray! For *ducks*!"

The cat died hard. Half-blind, fighting for breath through its mouth since its ruined nose would not serve it, it went down with Karana's spear through its lower side, just above the pelvis, in the soft flesh that covered its belly. The barbed, obsidian spearhead tore through flesh and went straight through the animal to bury itself in the permafrost, pinning the mortally wounded cat to the earth.

Zinkh and the other men cheered while the dogs barked and circled madly. Karana stepped back to allow the others a chance to wet their weapons, observing as they closed for the sport of a prolonged kill. The great cat flailed in agony, screaming in outrage as each man placed a spear for pleasure, until at last, with a final and unexpected burst of power, it pulled itself free of the earth.

It was on its feet now. Its body bristling with spears, it staggered in pathetic circles while Zinkh and his men stamped their feet and chanted at it.

"Leaping cat spirit come forth!"

"Come to the brave men who have killed you!"

"Come, spirit. Too long have you lived in the skin of the one who leaps!"

The right side of Karana's upper lip lifted into a sneer of contempt for the hunters. When the cat had been on the run, they had not been so quick to taunt or venture near it. It was the dogs that had run the injured beast to exhaustion, and it was his own spear, thrown from the spear hurler, that had struck the first blow. If Zinkh had not yipped with excitement at the moment of his weapon's release, it would have struck true and the great cat would be dead, its spirit free to roam the world of spirits, not suffering such a dishonoring as Zinkh and his men were torturing it with now.

Karana was sorry that he had not killed the cat. He had no taste for this kind of hunting. Zinkh stood ahead of the others, directly between Karana and the cat. His hat slipped into an odd, sideways angle as he jabbed with his spear, brazenly flaunting safety as he ventured to within what would have been easy range of the swiping paws of a healthy animal.

Karana saw no bravery in his action. The cat looked as though it were incapable of doing anything more than dropping dead. But suddenly, with lightning-fast motion, the cat pounced. Zinkh fell, with the cat on top of him, and the dogs on top of the cat. The hunters surged forward, but only Karana's position in the line of men allowed him to strike the mortal blow.

The cat went limp. Karana called off the dogs. A snarling Aar forced them to obey as the hunters approached and, cautious now, rolled the body of the cat off the headman. He had instinctively pulled himself into a fetal tuck when the beast had downed him. He lay unmoving, his clothes soaked in blood—his or the cat's, no one could say.

"This man . . . he is still alive, yes?" Zinkh did not sound certain.

No one could have been sure, except that common experience told them that dead men did not usually speak.

He began to uncurl slowly. With the exception of severely clawed garments and several bleeding lacerations that would need stitching where the cat's claws had penetrated the fabric, he appeared little the worse for his mauling. When Zinkh had gone into his tuck, the cat had sunk its fangs into his helmet, not his head. Now he sat up, looked at his hat, held it out, noted the punctures and the tears and the fact that what was left of the ornamental fox was conspicuously missing a head.

His eyes strayed to the dead cat. The spears of each hunter were clearly incised as to ownership; only Karana's were unmarked, and the one spear that protruded from the fatal heart wound was his. Zinkh looked at the youth, then at his mutilated hat, then back at the spear-riddled corpse.

"It is better the leaping cat eats fox instead of man, yes?" He set the ruined helmet purposefully back onto his head. "This hat has always been lucky for this man." He rose, walked stiffly to Karana, and, to the youth's astonishment, solemnly took the helmet from his head and placed it firmly onto Karana's. "Now, for son of Torka, this hat be lucky hat. Now does Zinkh give in gratitude this hat to one who saves his life! Now will Karana wear this hat . . . *always*."

So it was that when Karana walked back into the encampment of the Great Gathering, he wore the hat of Zinkh and the mutilated, spear-riddled skin of the leaping cat as he brought forth the fangs of the beast to a sad-eyed Lonit and was disappointed to find that there were no ducks for dinner.

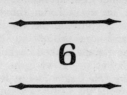

6

Wavelike vibrations trembled within the permafrost, caused by the great herd passing far to the west of the encampment. Grazing as it moved, it passed slowly, in numbers so vast that, although darkness and distance made it invisible, the thudding of countless hooves was a low, constant rumble.

Karana awoke. Staring into darkness, he lay unmoving, his senses taking measure of the night, knowing exactly what it was that had drawn him from his troubled dreams: dreams of wild horses running toward him across the starry sky . . . a pale stallion leading them, white mane flying, tail upturned and twitching upon the wind. The dream stallion tossed its head and tore open the skin of the sky with ripping teeth—fanged teeth, not the teeth of a horse at all, but the teeth of the great leaping cat that Karana had killed.

Dreams of falling stars and disembodied eyes watching him out of a bleeding sky . . . red dreams . . . of blood . . . of Navahk . . . coming toward him.

He shuddered, glad to wake from such nightmares. He lay very still, wondering if they were drawn from fear or premonition. He could not tell. Or perhaps he did not want to know. Either way, he was awake now. He willed the dreams out of his mind as he listened to the sound of the distant herd and realized that only last night he had called the game, and now it had come. It *had* come! The realization sent shivers along his arms.

Coincidence, he told himself, reasoning that the encampment of the Great Gathering lay upon the migration route of many game animals. Nevertheless, instinct told him that it was more than coincidence.

He closed his eyes. He saw the herd. Bison—not caribou or

mammoth or elk—but a teeming river of *bison*, which would take days to pass. And while it passed, the people of the encampment would hunt and hunt and hunt again. When the time of the long dark fell upon them, they would have meat and marrow, hide and horn, tallow and sinew to last them well into spring. They would have no need to seek the flesh of mammoths.

He had to be sure. He had to see with his own eyes if reality would mesh with what he saw within his vision. He rose from his sleeping skins, glad that he had slept beside Aar outside Torka's pit hut, as he often did on summer nights.

Fully dressed and still in his boots, he hushed the dogs and, with Aar treading quietly beside him, silently made his way across the encampment to the break in the wall of bones.

Above him the aurora was not nearly as bright as it had been the night before. The night was afire with stars, but already the first pale glow of dawn had turned the sky above the horizon to a thinner, softer darkness against which the distant mountains stood in black, impenetrable silhouette. A faint gauzing of dust sheened the air above them, and as the wind blew out of the west, it was strong with the stink of herd animals. But just what species of animal were they? Had his vision been correct?

"Bison."

The affirmation was not his. Sondahr stepped out of the shadows directly to his right. Her clean, mild, smoky scent had been masked by the overpowering stench of the wind. She was slightly taller than he. Even in the dark her beauty was staggering. Karana was startled to see her. Aar gave off a "woof" and then a low growl that somehow sounded more embarrassed than threatening.

The magic woman stood her ground, as though the dog were not there. "The encampment will awaken soon. I thought you would come long before now." Her statement was puzzling, her tone vaguely hinting of rebuke, as though he had disappointed her.

"How could you know that I would come at all?"

"I knew. As you knew the name of that which walks within the night."

"I did not speak to name it. *You* did."

"Yes. But last night, was it not *you* who raised your arms and implored the forces of Creation to hear your voice as you called the game to come to die upon the spears of men?"

He was appalled. "You could not have heard. I was too far away."

"Have you never heard without your ears, Karana? Have you never heard from within the core of yourself, understood things unspoken in the hearts and dreams of men?"

He blinked. She had trespassed into his soul, into that portion of himself that not even Torka could accept or understand, and she had understood. "It is so," he assented with wonder.

"Yes, I knew it the moment I saw you. You *are* his son, and yet, as I have watched you I have come to know that you are all that he could never be. The gift is yours. You will be a man of spirit as well as of flesh."

"He?"

"Your father."

Somehow he knew that she was not speaking of Torka.

Your father. You are what he could never be.

Was this, then, why the magic man had hated him?

"He is nothing to you, Karana. Flesh holds no lasting bond to the spirit. Put away the past unless it serves the present. Soon, when the dawn is fully ripe, you will see the bison summoned by your power as a gift from the forces of Creation. For now, since you have not yet come to trust your inner vision, breathe in the wind. Let *it* be your eyes. Let *it* serve your other senses." Her voice was no louder than a sigh. "The herd comes closer. Do you feel it? Do you hear it? Do you smell it?"

She was so close to him that her left arm brushed his as she turned slightly and stood poised within the night. Her head was raised. Her eyes were closed as, through her nostrils, mouth, and skin she drew in the smells of the wind and the night.

Karana looked up at her. The night did not exist for him. The wind did not blow around him. He was aware only of her. He smelled the exquisite, earthy essence of her body, her soft skin and hair and garments redolent of the smoky fires kindled with fragrant artemisias and dried, crushed tundral blossoms. He knew at last what it was to be totally enraptured by a woman. Although she was probably twice his age, she was the most perfectly beautiful creature he had ever seen; and she was beside him, seeing into his heart, talking to him, expecting an answer from him.

His mind was blank. He forced himself to speak, lowering

his voice, trying to sound manly and intelligent and fully in charge. To his dismay a boy's voice mumbled about the smell of grass and cud and urine. He was grateful to the fading darkness for concealing his blush as he cursed his ineptitude and wished that the tundra would open to swallow him whole, as it had once before within the Corridor of Storms; this time, he would not come out!

He thought he saw her stifle a smile. He knew only that she was looking at him now, her hand upon his forearm. His reaction to her touch was so intense that he nearly cried out. He would have run off like a frightened animal had her fingers not tightened upon his arm as she spoke with enthusiasm and the rising excitement of anticipation.

"Yes, you are right. Grass and cud, and a urine that smells so strong that it burns the eyes and can strip the hair from a hide at first contact! That *is* bison! Tell me now of caribou!"

He gulped. He forced himself to think. He spoke reluctantly, afraid that his voice would humiliate him again. This time it held steady, at a normal pitch. "Caribou reek of the moss and lichens that are its favorite browse."

"Yes! And at this time of year bull elk whistle and scream like women giving birth, while mammoths walk in the ever-present scent of spruce, and highland shadows seem to cling to their backs like mists that smell of fog and rain and rock gone rotten under ice. But you are a hunter. These things you have been *taught* to see. There is another seeing, and Sondahr tells you now that, had your eyes been bound and your nostrils, mouth, and ears packed with moss, you would have known that the herd that walks to the west of this camp is a herd of bison, not elk or caribou or mammoths. And this sense—this *Seeing*—is what brought you out of your dreams and led you to stand here in the dark to affirm to yourself that what you summoned from the world of spirits has indeed come to walk among the world of men!"

"I hoped that the game would come."

"There is no power in hope. Hope is nothing. Hope is as a man cowering beneath darkening clouds and saying that he hopes it will not snow, but if it does, he will deal with whatever comes! Does the hopeful man want it to snow or not? If not, why does he not clearly say so! As Karana clearly *asked* the game to come. With your arms raised and your voice a command, you made the spirits listen as you commanded the forces of Creation to bring forth bison or caribou but *not* mammoths."

"Mammoth is forbidden meat to my people."

"Not to mine!"

He was startled by the sudden angry intensity of her tone. It vanished as quickly as it had flared.

"You have much to learn, Karana, of your gift and the power of Seeing. You will be a great spirit master someday. This woman will teach you all she knows. It is what I do best, for the spirits have named me Teacher. I have lived among many bands, but I am at this camp because my power comes to me through the flesh and blood of the great mammoths. That is why tonight, while the others feast upon the meat of the bison that you have called to die, you and I must stand together and call upon the forces of Creation to inspire the spirits of another kind of game to come forth."

"Mammoth?"

Despite his overwhelming attraction to her, he felt like a guileless animal that has been suddenly maneuvered toward a pit trap. But he had seen the overlay of branches in time and now veered to escape. "You are a magic woman, Sondahr. If you and your people hunger for the meat of the great tuskers, *you* call them forth! Your powers are greater than mine!"

"I am a teacher, Karana, and a healer, but because I am a woman, denied the use of a spear, so, too, am I denied access to the power of calling. Through me the forces of Creation work for the good of all, but they will not respond to my command. That is a gift given only to spirit masters, only to hunters, only to men."

"Then you must seek another man to call the mammoths, Sondahr. Lorak, perhaps."

"Lorak is a man of flesh, not of spirit. Few indeed are the true callers, Karana. So few that in my lifetime I have known but a handful, and all were weak, all put flesh above spirit." She paused. "You might be a true spirit master . . . if you let me teach you."

"I will not call forth mammoths to die upon the spears of men, Sondahr. Not even for you."

"Bison!"

It was Lorak who gave the cry from the Hill of Dreams as several of the younger magic men, hunters now, hurried out of the house of bones and, still pulling on their outer clothes, poured down from the hill to join with various bands, eager, after their predawn chanting, for the excitement of the chase and kill.

In the thin light of the rapidly growing morning, the encampment burst to life as people clambered out of their huts. Men gathered their spears, and whole families rushed past the wall of bones to observe the passage of the bison.

The herd was still several miles away and would probably not come much closer. Nevertheless, the sound of it filled the sky, and the weight of its passing shook the earth. As far as the eye could see, it was not so much a grouping of animals as a vast, surging wall of life that obliterated the horizon. Little children were held high by their mothers and fathers to view the distant parade as their parents named the beasts and spoke of past hunts.

With Summer Moon riding excitedly on his shoulders, Torka joined them. At his command, Lonit followed, withdrawn and obedient, as she had been ever since the incident with the great cat, as though she were waiting for him to forgive her for her carelessness with her own life. But he would not do that, ever. Surely she must have known how much she meant to him when he had drawn her to him in the night and had made love to her, wordlessly lest he disturb the others; yet she had seemed sad and listless. No doubt the confrontation with the beast had exhausted her. No doubt she would think twice before going off to hunt alone again. He nodded, satisfied; if she had learned that lesson, then to the end of his days he would thank the spirit of the great cat whenever he saw its fangs dangling from Karana's neck.

Karana. The boy had not been in his sleeping skins when he had gone to wake him. Where was he? As Torka made his way through the crowd, he saw him slipping back into camp from beyond the wall of bones with Aar at his side and Sondahr following.

"That's an interesting twosome," he said to Lonit, startled and curious.

She made no reply, but Pomm did. The fat woman had fallen into step behind him, along with others of Zinkh's band.

"That one is old enough to be his mother!" Pomm glowered when they passed her. Her mumbles of frustration were intended for herself, but Torka heard every word. "What does he see in her? Everyone knows she is too bold for her own good! She has used her magic on him, just as she uses it on all of the magic men, who should make her behave as a proper female. It would be like Sondahr to take a better woman's man! Karana is mine! Zinkh has said so! The youth may not have seen my fine points yet, but he will if Sondahr stands away and minds her place! Bah! Her magic's no good. Can't people see that? Torka's new baby should be born by now. This woman told Lonit to change the sick woman's name and drive the bad spirit off in search of it. But does anyone listen to Pomm? No!"

The men who intended to hunt gathered before the wall of bones for a meeting that would set their strategy. All wanted Torka, with his magic spear thrower, to lead them, and his dogs to run point for them, as they had when they`had successfully taken the rhinoceros.

It was to be a team effort, yet to Torka's surprise, fewer than a third of the able hunters had the desire to go out after any other meat except mammoth, and Lorak enthusiastically supported their reticence.

"Most men in this camp are mammoth hunters," he explained with a condescension designed to imply that a man who hunted any other kind of animal degraded himself.

"You hunted rhinoceros quickly enough," reminded Karana, who had joined the hunters after retrieving his spears.

The supreme elder's head went up defensively. "Rhinoceros is rhinoceros! Like mammoth, it has great spirit, great power!" He paused, allowing the words to settle, then gestured widely with a benign equanimity that was canceled by his scowl. "This man would keep no other from hunting when there is meat on the hoof waiting to be taken. Torka has said that mammoth is his totem. He cannot hunt it or eat of its meat. So go, all of you who are caribou people and bison people and eaters of anything that walks. You have not come to this camp to hunt mammoth. You have come here in days of lean hunting to seek shelter during the coming winter. So go, those of you who would follow Torka, those of you who have need of magic spears and dogs to help you make your kills. Strike the bison! Kill the bison! It *is* man meat . . . more or less. But it is *not* mammoth!"

Once again Torka regretted having gone out of his way to restore the old man's pride. Lorak's reasoning was dangerous, but too many thought he could do no wrong. "This man intends no disrespect, but what if the mammoths do *not* come?"

The question brought the old man and the mammoth hunters to absolute attention. "The mammoths have *always* come! Then Lorak and those who are mammoth hunters will take meat. Until then we will fast. Our sacrifice will call the spirits of the great tusked ones to us."

Several men scowled at Torka. Others laughed. A few youths elbowed each other and shook their heads.

Karana stiffened resentfully as Lorak's frown expanded into an expression of contempt. "Since time beyond beginning, men have come to this camp to hunt mammoths and to feast upon their flesh throughout the long dark winter. Since I was an infant sucking the milk of life from my mother's breasts, I have known the taste of mammoth, for her milk was strong with it, and its meat was all we ate when we wintered in this camp to which the mammoths have come *always*."

Always. The word troubled Torka as he tried to conceptualize it. The mountains, the sky, the mile-high glacial lobes that extruded from the passes onto the broad, rolling skin of the tundra—these things were always. And yet he had seen the mountains fall and the glaciers collapse and the sky rain fire. Uneasily his eyes scanned the thousands upon thousands of bones and tusks that comprised the long, encircling windbreak walling the encampment. Was it possible that so many mammoths had ever lived? Even the majority of the pit huts and the council house of this encampment were built of mammoth bones. Could it be that these mammoth hunters had killed all of the world's mammoths with the exception of Life Giver and those that walked within the Corridor of Storms? Could it be that the great beasts that were always a part of the seasonal migration of animals would never again set their shadows upon the earth because of wasteful hunting practices of generations of mammoth hunters? Could the consistent hunting of one species annihilate another?

The premise was shattering. Torka was stunned by the thought that a time might come when hunters might be forced to become grazers because they had hunted to extinction all but themselves.

No! It could not be! He had only to look at the vast, black river of bison to know that there were not enough hunters in all the bands in the world to deplete the great herds of grazing animals. Men were few. Grazing animals were many. They would feed man—always!

Yet the mammoths were late this year. And in their place had come bison. To watch them walk away while men capable of hunting stood by seemed to Torka to be an offense to the spirits of life. He felt a need to speak.

"Among the people of Torka it is said that when the spirits of the game come forth to die upon the spears of men, they must be honored, they must be hunted, unless the camps of men are already full of meat and any further kills would be wasted. Among my people caribou is to our hunters what mammoth is to the men of this camp. Of its meat and skins and sinew and antler were our lives made. The caribou, upon which my people had *always* depended, failed to return along the migration route they had *always* taken, because one winter the storms of the time of the long dark refused to end and snow blocked the passes. More than half of Torka's people starved to death that winter.

"And so Torka says now to Lorak that he and his mammoth hunters must do as the custom of their people commands. But since the mammoths have not returned, Torka would lead as many hunters as would follow him in pursuit of bison. The days of light will soon be ending, and the time of the long dark will follow. In this camp are many men, many women, and many children. But where is the meat that will feed them if the mammoths do not come? There, to the west, is meat. It may not be mammoth, but in these times when mountains walk, when winter snow closes the passes and does not melt in spring, and when game must find new ways of migration to calving and wintering grounds, Torka remembers that it was said by the father of his father that in new times men must find new ways . . . or die."

They approached the herd at a trot, running into the wind so that the beasts would catch no scent of them. They could see individual animals now, no longer a black blur of noise. Their shaggy, fat-rich humps rose an average of six or seven feet above their hooves, and their horns were enormous, horizontal projections that spanned outward on each side of their skulls, narrowing into deadly, forward-curving tips.

The grasses concealed the movement of the hunters. The land conspired with them in their hunting plan. Torka soon understood why this area had been chosen for the Great

Gathering year after year. Not only was it along the major easterly winter migration route of mammoths and other big game, but to the north and south of the nearby lake it was cut by long, deep, natural gullies into which panicked animals could be driven by experienced hunters. And this they were.

The herd grazed, ambling mindlessly along in broken segments of hundreds to thousands of animals. With Karana and Aar directing the movement of the other dogs, the animals hunkered low and twitched with restrained excitement as the hunters slowed their steps. In groups of fifteen to twenty men and youths, they advanced slowly on a group of several hundred animals. The grasses provided ample cover. At a shout from Torka, they burst forward into a mad run, closing on the startled animals, leaving them only one route of escape as spears rained down.

Panicked, the bison grouped into a protective mass and stampeded in the only direction available to them—toward the lake, directly into the waiting gullies. A few of the younger, lighter, and more agile of the animals managed to leap across and run to safety. Others fell, stumbling headfirst into deep, narrow defiles from which they could not extricate themselves. Other animals fell on top of them, crushing them, suffocating them as still others charged across the ravine, over a bridge now made of dying bison.

And then the herd was gone, rumbling off across the edge of the world, while Torka, Karana, and the others shouted praises to the life spirits of the dead animals. They killed those that were still alive, driving their spearheads deep into quivering, bawling flesh. The dogs barked and pranced around, snapping at any hapless beast that seemed even half-capable of dragging itself out of the pit.

Now that the excitement and pleasure of the hunt was over, the work began. It took four or five men to heft a single two-thousand-pound bison out of the ravine for butchering. This done, one man twisted its head around by the horns while another slit its throat with a stone splaying dagger, then reached up and under its jaw to sever its tongue, jerking it loose. He sliced it into portions, and each man hunkered down to indulge himself in this tenderest and tastiest meat.

They ate in silence, nodding and smiling at one another with satisfaction. When all had eaten their fill, they shared the delicacy of the tongue meat with the dogs, then rose and rolled the carcass of the tongueless bison over, four men holding it so that one might open the hump. The knife wielder cut out wedges of bloody, fatty meat, and again they ate and smiled, glad that they were men who did not choose to limit their diet to only one kind of animal. This had been a good day to hunt. Thirteen bison lay waiting to be butchered along the rim of the ravine. Over one hundred more still lay within the pit.

"Even if the mammoths do not come, there will be enough meat to feed the entire encampment throughout the winter," said Torka.

"The mammoths will come," assured one of Zinkh's men. "Truly it was said that they have *always* come. Perhaps tomorrow, yes?"

Torka nodded. "Perhaps. But in the meantime this man will eat bison and be glad for the gift of life that the spirits have given him today."

7

The butchering went on for days. Still the mammoth did not come. But the bison killers were not concerned—they would have meat to see them through the time of the long dark, and the thick, shaggy hides of the slain bison would make warm robes and sleeping skins for them and their women and children. While those mammoth hunters who had refused to participate in the hunt continued to pursue their day-to-day activities, the bison hunters set up a temporary butchering camp under Torka's direction on the killing site.

Their women and older children had come out from the great camp to begin the enormous task of butchering so many animals. They dismembered the carcasses and set to the arduous work of fleshing the skins and staking them out in the wind to dry and cure, according to the various methods of their bands and the different uses to which they would be put. But first they had praised the hunters and delighted in their good fortune as they were allowed to feast upon leftover tongue, intestines, and blood meats before setting prime haunch and hump steaks to roast over spits of bone.

By nightfall the exhausted women slept together with their children, apart from their men but close to their work. And the next day Torka, Zinkh, Karana, and several others went back to the main camp and told all who were interested that if they would come out and help with the preparation of the meat, they and their families would be welcome to their fair share of it, for there was more than enough for all.

A few came. Many, noting Lorak's scowl of disapproval, did not.

That night in the butchering camp, while exhausted women again slept close to their work, bison hunters and mammoth hunters ate together. The smell of the roasting meat and dripping fat drew wolves, wild dogs, and other larger, more dangerous carnivores close to the butchering site, but sentries, along with Aar and his pack, kept watch. No one ventured far from the camp, not even to relieve himself, for in the night, eyes glowed from every tundral rise and the surrounding grasses, and the wind carried the scents of many animals.

But not of mammoth.

Lonit slept deeply but fitfully, too bone weary even to remove the thick pads of rhinoceros skin that she wore to protect her palms from being worn raw or nicked by her razor-sharp obsidian skinning dagger. She dreamed tortured dreams in which Torka turned his back upon her and walked off toward the Valley of Songs with Sondahr at his side. She awoke, her heart aching and her mind a roiling river of confused emotion.

Suddenly fiercely annoyed with herself, she sat up and stared across the moonlit butchering camp to the Hill of Dreams. The council house of bones gleamed white, and she could just make out the white-tipped teratorn feathers that covered Lorak's hut; they made it look as though it had been encrusted with ice. Smoke issued through the vent hole. Lorak must be within, doing whatever magic men did in such high and mysterious places while, on the crest of the hill, the figure of a woman stood against the sky, arms raised, head back, as though opening herself to the forces of Creation.

Sondahr.

Lonit almost spoke the other woman's name aloud with resentment. Every night, while the majority of the women fell exhausted into sleep, Sondahr stood upon the Hill of Dreams, making her songs and chants to call forth the mammoths. It seemed blasphemous to Lonit, who had suffered near starvation many times, for anyone to so prefer the meat of one species of animal to the exclusion of another.

Nearby a little girl tossed in her sleep and whimpered that her hands hurt. Her mother, who had made a new skinning pad for her, whispered softly to her, telling her to go back to sleep, that in time her blisters would heal and become calluses, a mark of pride she could show to prove to any man that she was a hard worker and would make a worthy mate.

Lonit sighed, missing her children. She longed for the day

when Summer Moon would be old enough to join her in her work and not remain always at Iana's calm, ever-doting side. Shadows skimmed across her thoughts. The children adored Iana; did they love their mother less because by necessity she hunted as a man beside their father in the Valley of Songs, spear and hurler in hand, her bola bound around her brow, the shell-weighted ends dangling behind? She had been not only a mother to her children, but a provider of man meat as well.

Lonit frowned. She had seen the hands of Sondahr. They had no blisters, no calluses. That woman did not hunt. That woman did not butcher or flesh or work skins or make garments for the many men who stared at her with open adoration. Other women's men hunted for her and brought meat to her fire. They considered themselves honored by her smile and blessed by her invocations to the spirits on their behalf.

And yet Aliga's baby did not come forth. And yet the mammoths did not come.

Lonit smiled. Why should she sit here in the night, full of self-doubt?

Lonit can hunt as well as any man. Lonit can butcher and flesh and cook and sew, and Lonit has stood alone against a great leaping cat! Lonit drove it off with only a bola and a thongful of ducks! Sondahr would not have been so brave!

Yet Torka has said that Sondahr is wise. Sondahr is wary. Torka has said these words to Lonit's face. And Sondahr is so beautiful that she does not have to be brave! What man would not desire to possess and protect such a woman . . . even if she is useless.

She lay back, feeling miserable. She pulled her sleeping skin over her head, wanting to feel bold again, recalling that in this camp, as in the camp of Supnah, many men had looked at her, including the disreputable twosome that held the little boy captive by the thonged collar. She had not seen them in the camp for many days and often wondered what had happened—not to them but to the unfortunate child who suffered at their hands. They had come close to her once, when Torka was off with some of Zinkh's hunters, and made lewd comments, suggesting that any time she grew tired of living with a man who walked with dogs, they would show her what they could do for such a beauty as she.

After she had threatened to call Torka if they did not go away, they slunk off like a pair of dirty foxes, leaving her

appalled by their outrageous behavior toward another man's
woman, yet strangely pleased by their flattery. After nearly a
lifetime of thinking herself ugly, it was now always gratifying
to know that among all but her own people, she was considered beautiful. Even funny little Zinkh had said so, and his
hunters had echoed him. And far away, long ago, another
man had looked at her . . . a man more beautiful than the
moon . . . a magic man whom every woman wanted. . . .
Navahk.

At last the butchering was done. But still the mammoths
had not come.

Using the thigh and rib bones of their kills, they fashioned
crude sledges upon which they piled their meat on neatly
stretched skins, which they then folded into packets so that
they could more easily drag their bounty back into the camp.

As the hunters trudged toward the wall of bones, the
people of Zinkh's band watched in amazement as Torka,
Lonit, and Karana not only devised sledges for themselves
but also for their dogs. When at last they stood ready, their
own bodies were burdened by less than half the load of the
others.

"Could other men do the same with other dogs, or would
they need a magic power such as Torka's?" The question
came from Simu, one of Zinkh's young bandsmen.

Zinkh, whose minor wounds had been stitched and were
healing nicely, had come out to keep company with the men
and women of his band. Now that he was feeling more or less
well and strong again, he wanted to do his share in helping to
carry the bison meat back to the encampment. He was not
in a good mood. His lacerations were tight and itching, and
during the last few days he had begun to chafe at the sight of
Torka leading his hunters. It seemed that no one asked him
anything unless Torka was unavailable. He was also insulted
by the fact that Karana was not wearing his good-luck helmet.
The youth had assured him that he had left it on his bed skins
within the main encampment lest it be damaged in the hunt,
but Zinkh was not happy with the reply, any more than he
liked Simu's query.

So he snapped emphatically, as nastily as a dog irritated by
blackflies, "What kind of man be you to question the magic
powers of Torka? It is enough that he and his spirit dogs walk
with you in one band! He will not share his magic! You will

not ask him again! You are Zinkh's band. Always for us carrying sledges has been a good way. Why now, suddenly, is it not good enough for you and your woman? Does Simu think he is better than the rest of Zinkh's people? Maybe he would make his own band with Torka as leader and forget that Zinkh has been his headman and leader and friend, yes?"

Standing beside Eneela, his pretty and very pregnant young woman, Simu sucked in his breath with shame. As he looked down at his feet, unable to look at his woman or at any of his people, his face congested with resentment of his unwarranted humiliation.

Torka was astounded by Zinkh's unexpected display of animosity. He had not failed to note the sting in the little man's voice when he had snarled his name.

He was aware of Karana watching him with a bemused expression upon his handsome young face and was suddenly struck so sharply by a memory, it was as though the boy had flung it into his head like an invisible spear.

Torka is not like other men. Torka cannot live within a band, he must lead it. And so other men will always try to bring Torka down or drive him out from among them.

Karana had spoken those words on the day they had left the Valley of Songs. They had rankled him then; they rankled him now. Once again Karana seemed to be right. Torka found himself virtual headman of Zinkh's people, and now Zinkh, who had been so eager to yield his rank, coveted it and resented Torka for having accepted it from him in the first place. Torka snorted as he realized that he had not even set foot within the encampment of the Great Gathering before he had inadvertently roused hostility and jealousy in old Lorak, who seemed determined to lock horns with him. Surely he meant no challenge to the supreme elder. Yet he *had* challenged him over his decision to refrain from hunting when so much meat was at hand.

Nevertheless, his course was set. For the sake of his women and children, he would not be intimidated by either man. To be the only adult man in a band composed of women and children compromised the lives of his loved ones.

He eyed Zinkh and saw for the first time that he was a small man, in ways that had nothing to do with his minimal stature. Torka knew he must give Zinkh back his sense of importance, or for all that the man feared his powers, Torka would have an enemy in him.

"Zinkh is headman of this band, and Torka walks beside him at his sufferance," he declared, taking that chin-out, arms crossed over chest position that magic men always assumed. "But it is good that Simu asks. Zinkh has taken Torka into his band as though he were a brother. Perhaps it is time that Torka behaves as a brother and makes Zinkh and his hunters magic men at Torka's side?"

And so it was that in the days that followed, Torka began to teach Zinkh and Simu and the hunters of his new band the way to use a spear hurler and the way to gentle a dog so that it would respond to commands. He was a patient teacher. The men were eager pupils, and since the use of the spear hurler was an exacting and difficult discipline, it was easy for them to believe that only through his magic were they able to learn . . . that the gift of the knowledge and skill that he gave to them was special and only for them. Zinkh was given back his pride, and his hunters strutted more boldly than any others and kept the secrets that Torka gave to them, lest other men learn them and thus become their equals.

And still the mammoths did not come.

The women gathered berries. The children's faces, hands, and tunics turned red-purple with juice. With several hunters to guard them, they sloshed through the boglands around the lake, waded across a cool, clear freshet, and headed out of surrounding willow scrub upward toward a thick expanse of berry shrubs, which grew on a slight rise amid a thin stand of birch trees. They formed a small, white-barked, stunted forest, with broad areas of sunny patches between their meager trunks.

With Summer Moon holding her hand, Lonit paused and looked back toward the stream, noting the way it tumbled easily from the heights, emptying into the lake within a small, stony-bottomed, shallow cove, which would serve as a wonderful catch basin for fish if a stone weir were built across it.

"What see you there?" asked one of the other women, wondering why she had fallen behind.

Enthusiasm filled her as, beaming with memories of the days when she had devised the weir within the Valley of Songs and had caught her first captive grayling, she told that woman and several others what they could accomplish with minimal effort if they all worked together. "There would be fish in the pool always. We would need only to come with our tridents."

"We are not fish eaters in this camp. Except in the worst of starving times, our men will not eat of such woman meat."

"Fish is good!" piped Summer Moon, frowning, not liking the disdainful tone with which her mother had been addressed.

Lonit could have kissed Summer Moon for her loyalty. She would, later. Now her fingers curled about her daughter's pudgy little hand, communicating her desire that the child should be still. Summer Moon obeyed but continued to pout as Lonit quietly replied that she had been taught as a child that she must eat whatever food was put before her, not only by her own parents, but by Father Above and by Mother Below. "All meat gives life from life, and all food is spirit given," she said.

A broad-bottomed, flat-faced matron named Oga turned up her bridgeless nose with a snort of reproof. "The man of *this* woman is a mammoth hunter, not an eater of bison or of things with scales or feathers!"

"Then you must be growing hungry, Oga," Lonit responded coolly. "For this woman has seen no mammoth anywhere near this camp."

"Come! We are one band in this camp until the time of the long dark is over," Pomm cut in. "We women have enough work to do without arguing about whose ways are the best."

They went on, with snow geese scattering out of the bushes before them, tails up, honking hysterically as they ran from cover to cover. The great white geese were flightless now, bound to the earth by the seasonal molt that made them easy targets. Crying aloud with delight, the women momentarily forgot about berry picking and turned to goose killing instead, striking the hapless birds with stones that they carried in pouches at their belts. Feathers flew like snow in a blizzard. But only a handful of women seemed to be killing for meat; the rest left their prey where it fell, having merely enjoyed the sport.

When Lonit refrained from joining in, Oga looked at her with satisfaction. "You see, we have no need to learn to use the weapon of Lonit. The sling with many arms takes too much time to master. In this camp if we hunger for goose, we eat it now, not in the season when the birds can fly away from our stones."

"But there is so much meat in the encampment now.

There is no need for you to hunt the white geese," Lonit pointed out.

"Not all of us are bison eaters!" Oga snorted with derision.

"But most of you are leaving the birds that you kill!"

"What do a few birds matter? Soon the sky will be filled with so many birds that anyone who makes the mistake of looking up will be sorry! Those of us who will eat their flesh will take the fattest geese and leave the rest with thanks to their spirits for allowing us to perfect our stone-throwing aim."

"But there might well come a time when you will hunger for the meat that you have thrown away. The birds could be smoked and dried and—"

"Look who would tell us about bird hunting! Just because your man walks with dogs and teaches the men of Zinkh to throw their spears farther than our men can, that does not mean you know everything! Why do you have to make a special weapon to hurt birds, one that nobody but you can use?"

"I would gladly teach you."

Oga snickered. "For what purpose? All the women here know that when the berries are ripe, the white geese lose the big feathers that allow them to fly. Why waste time hunting birds before then? And not one of us would go out from camp alone and make our men come after us!"

She walked with them, trying not to be angry as they left the dead geese where they lay and set to picking berries in earnest. She blamed her irritability on exhaustion; it had only been a week since she had returned from the butchering camp. Even her hands were still sore. She reminded herself that these were women of the open tundra. They would never believe her if she told them that in a far and forbidden land that their men feared, she had hunted as a man beside Torka and Karana, using a spear and spear hurler as effectively as any male. If they knew that, her companions would surely shun her as one who had offended the spirits of Creation.

A dark thought crossed her mind. Perhaps she had? Perhaps that was why the land had shaken and the Mountain That Smokes had rained fire from the sky. But no, it could not be! While working at the butchering, other women had spoken of how the earth had shaken this part of the world and how a great cloud of smoke and ash had drifted across the sky from the east, pouring down dirty rain for many days. They

had wondered among themselves if this was the reason that
the mammoths had not come. She had kept her thoughts on
the subject to herself. If Torka had heard of it, she did not
know; he was so busy with Zinkh and the other hunters that
he hardly spoke to her these days.

She sighed, longing for him and for the love that they had
shared in that far, sweet land. Perhaps it was best not to
think of it. It only made her unhappy. As she filled her skin
basket, eating her fill of berries as she walked, she smiled
down at Summer Moon, who strode happily in her shadow
with her own little basket, scrupulously plucking her own
berry harvest.

Pomm caught up with her. "Do not worry about the other
women. They be not magic women, like Pomm and Lonit!
They all have noses stuck up like Sondahr. Bah! Women they
be jealous that you have fine man like Torka. Girls they
jealous that Pomm has fine young man like Karana."

Lonit felt sorry for the ungainly old woman. She still honestly believed that Karana, given time, would see her in the
same light that she saw him.

"Where is that Karana? He is never around when Pomm
looks for him."

"He will not be found picking berries and braining geese
with a bunch of women," Lonit answered while she thought:
*Nor will he ever be where you can find him, poor woman.
Unless you catch him by surprise . . . and Karana is not one
to be caught—unless he wishes it.*

Pomm stuffed a fistful of berries into her mouth and chomped
noisily until juices appeared at the corners of her lips. She
backhanded them away with a fierce look of determination in
her little eyes. "Tonight Lorak has called a great meeting of
all men and women. Tonight, while children sleep, at the
plaku dance, this woman will dance naked for Karana. He
will see what he is missing and come hard and hungry to—"

"*Plaku?*" If another earthquake had moved the ground
beneath Lonit's feet, she could not have been more shaken.
Not even the thought of fat old Pomm dancing naked in the
firelight could obliterate the sick, sinking feeling that had
suddenly overwhelmed her.

"Lonit knows the *plaku* dance, yes?"

"Lonit knows it."

"What is a *plaku* dance?" asked Summer Moon, her wide

eyes, so like her mother's, growing heavy lidded with drowsiness in the warmth of the morning sun.

"It is a dance to call the spirits of the great mammoths to this camp before those who have chosen to fast become so weak-kneed that they cannot hunt, let alone dance." Pomm answered for Lonit, enthusiastically smacking her lips and sucking the last traces of juice from them. "When you are a big girl, someday at some camp you will dance the *plaku* for the men of your band—for the man that you like best. He will come happy to your fire, and the spirits of Creation shall grow strong because of the dance you will do together."

"Will you dance for Father, Mother?"

"No! Never!" Again the fat woman answered before Lonit could speak. "On the night of the *plaku* dance, a woman may not dance for her own man. She must choose another for that one night."

Summer Moon looked very serious. "Father will not like that."

Perhaps he will not care. Lonit very nearly said the words aloud, but once again Pomm went on euphorically about how the women would wear paint upon their bodies and masks of feathers over their faces. "It is a much long time since a *plaku* was danced, at the last Great Gathering. Surely now that Lorak has called for a *plaku*, the mammoths will come! It will be a good thing! Pomm will look her best for Karana! He will see what he has been avoiding and be sorry, this woman can tell you that. Yes!"

Lonit took her daughter's hand and turned away. "Come, my little one. We have more than enough berries. This woman no longer feels like picking, and it is time for your nap."

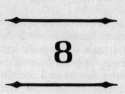

8

As preparations for the *plaku* began, Karaña stood back, observing with dismay. He had witnessed the ceremonial dance once before, years ago, when the cave that he had shared with Torka, Lonit, and Umak high upon the flanks of the distant Mountain of Power had been taken over by the despicable headman Galeena and his band of filthy, murderous usurpers. Only a boy then, he had hidden in the shadowy recesses of the cave, watching as men and women joined in a firelit orgy of drinking and dancing. Torka had been forced to participate while a pregnant Lonit had turned away in shame for them both.

Now Karana was suddenly aware of Pomm looking at him lasciviously from her fire circle. He winced. He had told her a thousand times that he was not yet of an age when he felt ready to take on the responsibilities of a woman! How could the old hag be so insistent? Had she no pride? Her behavior was ludicrous! It was degrading! But it was also apparent that as long as Pomm deluded herself into thinking she was a young and attractive woman, she would behave like one. Behind her back, however, men rolled their eyes and women younger than Pomm who were sagging, graying, and toothless shook their heads at her. But the worst part for him was that while Pomm persisted in her aggressive pursuit, the eyes of many young girls were on him as they giggled conspiratorially with their mothers, aunts, and grandmothers.

They were giggling now, and blushing. And tittering together as girls had a tendency to do when they whispered secrets to one another. It suddenly occurred to him that he was the object of their secrets. Flustered by their unwelcome attention, he wondered if they knew that he was still a virgin.

And then, suddenly, it struck him: Tonight the men and women of this encampment would dance the *plaku*, and he was a man.

Over and over he had insisted upon that fact to Torka, claiming that he was no longer a boy to be bullied or a child to be coddled, but a man fit to make decisions and mature enough to live by them. But was he man enough to dance at a *plaku* and be initiated into sexual activity with every man, woman, and peeking child at the Great Gathering looking on?

No!

For this he would choose his own time, his own place, and most assuredly his own partner. If he stayed for the *plaku*, he would have Pomm; she would make certain of it. The thought was too much to bear.

Several of the youths with whom he had hunted and engaged in contests and friendly bouts of wrestling sauntered by to make lewd, lustful boasts about the coming events.

"Come, join us. It is traditional for the men to build the great *plaku* fire while the women—except those who are pregnant—prepare themselves to pleasure us . . . and the spirits of Creation."

"Which one do you want to dance for you, eh, Karana? That one there, or the little plump one sitting with her skinny sister? All will dance except the ones who are in their time of blood or who have not yet bled."

"Girls! Babies!" scoffed the first youth. "They may have holes in the soles of their boots, but they can't compare to their mothers when it comes to dancing under a man."

"Holes in their boots?" Karana queried.

They laughed. They made crude, unmistakable signs with their hands to indicate that their statement alluded to the first piercing of a female by a male.

He blushed at his naiveté. There was not a youth standing around him who was more than a year his senior, yet it was clear that not one of them was inexperienced when it came to joining with the opposite gender. It was also clear from their friendly, taunting winks that they all now knew that he had yet to lie with a female.

"Come," they urged. "There are a mammoth's weight in bones to gather for the burning!"

He did not move. He watched them leap and dance off, flirting with the watching girls, who flirted back. He told them that he would be along as soon as he fed the dogs; but the dogs had already been fed and were dozing in the sun. Torka was off with the men of Zinkh's band, and Lonit was inside the pit hut with Iana, Aliga, and the children—resting, no doubt, for the activities of the night to come.

He went in. He told them that he was tired and lay on his bed skins. It was quiet. The children were sleeping. He waited tensely until, at last, shadows grew long and he crept out of the pit hut, wrapping himself in them and in his traveling robe, taking up his spears and making his way through the camp, avoiding all fire circles where he knew that Pomm or girls would be watching for him.

Just beyond the peripheries of the wall of bones, he broke into a run, heading for the tundral rise where he had made his invocation to the spirits of Creation, calling to the game while asking the mammoths to stay away. The air was clear of smoke this far from the camp, and the soaring vault of the sky swept all apprehension from his soul. He breathed freely at last, with infinite relief. Somehow, as always seemed to happen, he looked down to see that Aar was with him.

"We made it, Brother Dog!" He sighed, then ruffled the fur on the dog's shoulders as he hunkered down. Alone with his faithful companion, Karana was profoundly happy. Content with his solitude, he stood and raised his arms, threw back his head, drew in the scents of the wild land, and heard the voices of the spirits whispering all around him in the wind.

Upon the Hill of Dreams Sondahr's brow furrowed thoughtfully as she watched the large, wolflike dog follow the solitary figure at a lope across the tundra until the hunter paused on a distant tundral rise and lifted his arms to the infinite.

Behind her, heavy smoke was rising from the council house, and Lorak, on his way to join the other magic men within that structure, saw her and paused.

"Sondahr, will you dance tonight?"

His high, whining voice offended her. It was predacious, yet she did not move. She was conserving her strength; days of fasting were having their effect. She felt light-headed, yet more in control of her body and aware of her senses than usual. Sound, light, texture—everything seemed brighter, louder, more intense. Fasting was not alien to her, so she knew that if she did not eat soon, the brightness would fade, sound would grow dull, textures would seem flat, and what

little power was left to her would become as ashes in a
wind-scoured pit.

"Sondahr, do you hear Lorak speak to you? Will you dance
for the spirits to bring forth the great mammoths for the good
of the gathering? Will you dance tonight? And for whom?"

She heard the hope in his voice and despised him for it.
He had wanted her for years but had never had the courage
to confront her openly with his lust—no doubt because he
feared that it might make him only a man and not a shaman
in her eyes. No doubt he wanted her to believe that if he truly
desired her, he could enchant her into a reciprocal emotion
even if it were totally against her weaker woman's will. Her
mouth moved with displeasure. Lorak was a miserable old
hawk who imagined that he might dare to fly with eagles.

"Sondahr will dance," she replied obliquely.

"For . . ."

"One whom the spirits have chosen." She did not move.
She felt him waiting for a more descriptive answer. She
remained in silence, and when at last he turned away in
frustration, she smiled.

Night came slowly to those who had gathered eagerly
around the great communal fire circle that the men had
made. They had come early to assure themselves a good spot
for viewing. In the background, out of the direct light of the
sacred fire, a grouping assembled to watch: pregnant women,
women in their time of blood, the elderly, and even Aliga,
who insisted that she be allowed to observe because of the
healing powers that everyone knew emanated from the flames
of a *plaku* fire. Torka carried her. Leaving the children in
Iana's care, Lonit followed with furs for the sick woman to lie
upon. She was pleased when everyone fussed over Aliga and
expressed gladness to see her feeling well enough to attend
the night's festivities.

"The magic healing powers of Sondahr are great!" she told
them. "Soon this woman will bear her child. Soon she will be
completely well again! Next time there is *plaku* at the Great
Gathering, this woman will dance, and you will have the
pleasure of seeing this tattooed woman all over!"

Everyone laughed, and Aliga settled contentedly into her
furs, contemplating the future with happiness.

Torka made no comment. The moon had shown its horns
eleven times since Aliga had first danced in happiness over

her pregnancy. Too long . . . much too long. And though she claimed that the child moved, he had watched her in the night, focusing on the mound of her belly, watching for ripples of life that never came.

One of the nearby crones startled him by winking at him. "This woman has heard much woman talk. Many will dance before Torka this night. Tonight we will all see what Torka's magic can or *cannot* do! Best rest, man of Lonit! You would not shame your woman by not being able to rise to them all! And talk is that Sondahr will dance this night. Rare it is for that one to choose a man. Perhaps this night it will be Torka, and there will be great magic between you, eh?"

The old woman was trying to embarrass Torka, but he was not a man to be embarrassed easily, and he was not embarrassed now. He was annoyed. The old woman's words had sent Lonit hurrying back to their shared fire circle. He was irritated over the fact that his woman would have to dance before another man and actually grew angry when he thought of her lying with anyone else but him. He had bad memories of the last *plaku* he had been forced to attend, and if there was a way of avoiding this one without offending the elders of the encampment, he would do so. He had said as much to Lorak, but the supreme elder had pointed a horny finger at him and made it quite clear that he must participate or take his women and children and leave the encampment. With the time of long dark coming on, he had no choice but to stay and join in the cursed ceremonies. Surely Lonit must know that he wanted no part of them—not for himself and most certainly not for her.

His eyes followed her as she disappeared between several pit huts en route to their own shelter. How tall and graceful and beautiful she was! Sondahr might match her, but only that, no more; it was the magic woman's arrogant, almost masculine bearing that drew the eyes of all men to her—to the strong, confident line of her shoulders, to the careless way she walked and stood so that her breasts seemed always to be moving restlessly beneath her downy tunic.

Most of the men within the encampment resented the way she intruded into the council of elders at will, as though she were not a female at all but a man deserving of every privilege and courtesy accorded to their superior gender. A member of no band but welcomed by all who knew of her powers, it was said that she moved at whim from tribe to tribe,

teaching and healing. Her presence was tolerated with a
combination of awe and distress, for although she blithely
ignored every rule that applied to others of her sex, her
well-proven gifts of Seeing and healing were too valuable to
disdain. Truly, it was said, Sondahr was a magic woman of
great power. It was wise to fear her. And both men and
women did; but Torka knew that there was probably not a
man in the encampment who would not have liked to put her
in her place, to take her down and ride her to submission.

He drew a breath. He had to admit that that would be an
interesting endeavor; yet when she had called him to walk
with her onto the Hill of Dreams, when he had seen her with
Aliga, he had seen another side of the woman—a gentleness
. . . a sadness . . . a loneliness—and he knew that if the
choice were hers, she would relinquish her powers, for what
seemed a gift to others was a curse to one who was, because
of that gift, forever set outside the circle of friendship and
easy companionship. For all of her beauty and haughtiness,
Sondahr was one of the loneliest, saddest individuals that
Torka had ever known. He thought of her wintering alone in
her permanent hut of tusks and mammoth bones upon the
Hill of Dreams.

"Go, Torka. Cleanse yourself now. The sun has set, and the
plaku shall soon begin."

It was Aliga who prodded him. He was glad to go from her,
and from the others. He ignored their snickering and further
comments as he followed Lonit, eager to talk to her now, to
tell her that perhaps there was a way for her not to join in the
dancing. She had only to declare that she was in her time of
blood and she would be excused, allowed to sit out the
ceremony with others who were similarly afflicted. He reached
his pit hut and called to her to come out to him. She obeyed,
her eyes red, as though she had been crying.

"You need not dance," he said, and told her what was on
his mind.

"It would be a lie. The spirits of the night would know.
They would be offended. Besides, the other women would
remember that I have only recently shared the hut of blood
with them. They would know that it was much too soon for
me." She paused, her mood suddenly lightened. *He does not
want me to dance! He does care!* For the first time in days
she smiled and tried to devise a plan that would accommodate their purpose. "But sometimes the time of blood is a

thing of whim. Lonit could say that it is so with me, and perhaps the old women would not seek to check the truth of my words."

"But if they did?"

"It would not be a good thing. They would be angry."

His face worked with frustration. "And then, if their precious mammoths do not come, they will lay the blame upon you, for having offended the spirits." He shook his head. "Who knows what would happen then? Lorak is not exactly in love with Torka or his band. No, it is not worth the risk—not for the sake of my pride."

Her smile faded. He had not said "my love." He had said "my pride." Her heart sank. She was one of his women, a possession; and Torka always looked out for his possessions. "You will dance . . . with Sondahr?"

"I *must* dance. Lorak has told me that if I do not, it is finished for us here."

"We have much meat and many hides. With the dogs to hunt as men beside us and Karana to help . . . We have been alone before."

His voice was sharp. "This man will not live with that fear again, Lonit."

She hung her head. "This woman was not afraid."

"And what of Aliga or Iana and the children? They are happy in this camp. They are safe in this camp. Even Karana has stopped his endless complaining!" He wanted to draw her close and hold her, to kiss her, to speak assurances of the love and pride that filled his heart whenever he looked at her. But surely she already knew this. And among their people it had always been considered unmanly to speak of such things to a woman. So he put his hand beneath her chin and turned her face up to his. "We have survived the humiliation of the *plaku* before. We will survive it again for the sake of our children. We will dance. We *must* dance, and tomorrow nothing that has happened tonight will matter . . . except that we will have assured the future."

"Help!"

Coming from Pomm, it was a thoroughly uncharacteristic word. Lonit looked up from where she sat dejectedly outside her pit hut, to see the fat woman gesturing pathetically through the deepening shadows of evening from her own little pit hut.

"Come, Lonit, yes? Help make Pomm beautiful for the *plaku*?"

It was not the sort of request she could easily refuse, even though no amount of help could achieve what Pomm requested. That would require the forces of Creation.

She rose, still in her berry-stained picking apron, and entered Pomm's pit hut.

Stark naked, looking very much like a wide, soft, fleshy mushroom that has forgotten to stop growing after a bounteous rain, Pomm sat cross-legged upon a neatly stacked pile of furs with a bladder flask in her lap. "Come, good friend of Pomm. We will drink together before we prepare ourselves for the *plaku*."

Lonit knelt across from her, accepted the flask, and took a sip. Not much liquid passed her tongue into her throat, but it was enough to make her gag and choke. "What is *this*?" she sputtered, wide-eyed.

"Just a few berries, roots, blood, and herbs from last year's camp. It is good, yes?"

Lonit had had fermented berry juice before, but nothing that came close to the fiery sweetness of Pomm's drink. "It *is* good," she agreed, sipping again, carefully. "But it is also very strong."

"Without heat, what good is the flame, yes? Drink! It will make Lonit dance better at the *plaku*."

"Lonit does not want to dance at the *plaku*."

"Lonit must dance!"

"Yes, Lonit must dance." She took another sip. It was sweet and it was fire, but now that she was used to it, it no longer burned. She drank deeply.

Pomm reached out and took the flask from her. "Drink it quick like that, and you will not dance at all. You will sleep . . . for days! And when you wake, sorry will you be!"

"No," responded Lonit, suddenly angry and frustrated. "I would not be sorry! I would be glad."

Pomm sipped and shook her head sadly. "Strange it is that the woman of Torka is sad to be a part of the *plaku*. Many men are no doubt hoping that she will dance for them, and here sits Pomm—*fat* Pomm . . . *old* Pomm—wanting so badly to dance, but only for one man. For Karana, and because he knows this, he has run away."

"Karana is only a boy, Pomm."

"To one who had been as a mother and sister to him, yes. But trust this woman to tell you that to the eyes of any other woman than Lonit, he is a man."

"A very *young* man, then."

"That is the best kind."

They sipped in silence for a while, slowly but steadily. Lonit had never seen Pomm in such abject misery. It was as though she had suddenly looked into clear ice and, seeing her own reflection for the first time, knew at last what time and the forces of Creation had made her: an old, ugly woman, whom no youth in his right mind would lie with. Lonit felt great pity for her and wished to lessen her pain.

"Truly, Pomm, he *is* only a youth. A woman of your . . . uh . . . maturity would be better served by a more experienced man."

"A more experienced man will turn his back on this woman at a *plaku* unless he is drunk on his own woman's berry juice. And then he would be no good to anyone at the *plaku*."

Once before, within the Valley of Songs, Lonit had sipped too much of her own fermented berry brew and grown slightly giddy on it; but never before in her life had she been fully intoxicated. She was intoxicated now. The liquor was so sweet and flavorful that it was difficult to stop sipping it. It tingled in her blood and put a strange edge to her mood and tongue. She found herself speaking more freely, although her words sounded a bit slow and slurred. For a few moments a delicious sleepiness swept through her, then passed, leaving her blinking and suddenly feeling bold and angry.

"I do not like this *plaku*! I do not want to dance or lie with any man but my man!" Her thoughts drifted through a warm haze, and from somewhere within that haze the form of a man in white took shape to name her Liar. She had not invited Navahk into her thoughts. He made her feel guilty. She did not want to feel guilty. With a blink she banished him. Torka took his place. Torka, the one man she had ever truly loved or desired. Torka! He was the best man of all. And he was her man. Possessiveness ignited anger within her.

"If any woman, especially Sondahr, dances for Torka, I will . . ." She paused. What would she do? She was Lonit. Sondahr was Sondahr, and a magic woman. But she was not afraid of her. She felt very brave, very much in control. "Sondahr will see what this woman will do! Do you know, Pomm, that

Lonit can throw a spear as far as any man and use a spear hurler? Yes! It is so! Lonit has hunted beside Torka and taken much game! Man meat too! Not just fish and fowl, scales and feathers! And Lonit would wager that Sondahr could not say that!"

Pomm belched, sighed, and belched again. Then she daintily lifted a fat little finger to cover her mouth as it puckered into a thoughtful knot. "Sondahr should not know of this, I think. Or Lorak, either, or any of the magic men. Truly . . . Lonit has used a spear?"

"Truly so, against wolves and bear and all kinds of man meat. And maybe now against Sondahr if she tries to take my Torka from me!"

"Sondahr . . ." The fat woman's thoughts slid into oblivion for a moment, then returned blearily to Lonit. "Pomm will tell Lonit that the magic woman is not prettier than Torka's woman. Same height, same body shape—slim, but not skinny—breasts big, but not too big . . . men like that. Naked with your faces behind a feather mask and a few ashes streaked in your hair, no one could tell the difference."

The words were almost sobering to Lonit. "Sondahr could tell the difference."

"But she will be naked too. Her face will be hidden behind a feather mask." Pomm shrugged, took her turn at sipping from the flask, and followed a long swallow with a loud burp. "Pomm says that men at this *plaku* would very happy be if two Sondahrs danced at their fire. Then Torka's woman could dance before her own man, and no one would know—maybe not even Torka—and if she danced better than Sondahr, he would turn his back upon the magic woman and take Lonit. It would be a big joke on everyone, yes? And only the spirits would know."

"It is not a good thing to make jokes on the spirits."

Pomm's little eyes narrowed into slits of resentment. "Maybe not, but look here at young Pomm trapped in the flesh of an old woman. The spirits make jokes on me! They make jokes on all of us in time. But come now, the night will soon be upon us, and the men will light the *plaku* fire. We must be ready to dance. Help me to be beautiful, Lonit. Help me to be young and unashamed for this one night."

Night. Stars. Fire. And heat.
The world burned. Torka burned—with frustration at hav-

ing to endure the night, and with a basic, sensual anticipation of it. No man, no matter how he might claim to be averse to the ceremony, could long remain cool and aloof on the night of a *plaku*. They had laid out the great ceremonial fire and cleared a broad circle around it for the dancers and viewers; this done, men and women began to gather and jostle for the best places, until Lorak called the hunters to join with the magic men in the council house of bones.

Inside, within the overcrowded gloom, a fire burned somewhere beneath the floor of mammoth bone. Smoke and steam issued upward through the planking. It was hot . . . close . . . humid. The smoke was so thick, the hunters could barely see as they stripped naked and sat in silence, sweating out the impurities of their spirits, which had accumulated since the last such gathering, exfoliating their bodies with rough, pungent stalks of wormwood, drinking deeply from a flask of ceremonial liquor that they passed round and round. Somewhere along the way someone must have refilled it or substituted another when it went dry, for magically it was always nearly full when it reached Torka. The drink was good, intoxicating, as thick and sweet as blood sucked hot from a recent kill. He drank deeply and passed the flask once, twice, until soon he lost count as the magic men, led by Lorak, chanted to the spirits of Creation and asked that the mammoths come forth to die upon the spears of the assembled hunters.

Torka sat amid the throng, drinking with them, a part of their ceremony but still feeling very much the outsider. He alone had no wish to kill mammoths. It seemed to him that in a camp full of meat, the hunters should be praising the spirits of Creation in thanksgiving, not begging for more. Nevertheless, he understood the reasoning behind their need, even if he did not agree with it. He looked for Karana but could not see him. He worried a little; Lorak would be very angry if he discovered that anyone who sheltered within the Great Gathering of mammoth hunters saw fit to flaunt their traditions.

The chanting of the men droned on. Even Zinkh and his hunters sang as if their lives depended upon the flesh of the great mammoths, not like those whose bellies were full of bison meat. Torka listened. All sang the song, the same prayer, intoned in countless dialects. Somehow they blended into one, as soothing to his ears as the soft summer run of a river—one body fed by many tributaries, gathering its life from the substance of many.

He listened, closing his eyes, letting the mood wash over him. It was good to be a man among men again, a part of a whole—no longer alone, vulnerable, his every hour weighted by the responsibility he had taken upon himself for the lives of his women and children. If his spirit were to fly from his body this very moment, they would be safe, members of Zinkh's band, and through generations of his children yet to be born, his spirit and his name would live forever.

Suddenly the chanting stopped. Lorak spoke so sharply that Torka looked up, startled, to see the supreme elder, nude and scrawny under a cape of shaggy mammoth hide, strutting and posturing violently as he invoked the spirits with raucous and almost angry intensity. He sounded like a teratorn squawking in pain after a spear had been thrust through its breast. After a moment it occurred to Torka that Lorak was imitating the movement and trumpetings of a bull mammoth . . . not very well, but he was trying, and everyone else seemed very taken with his performance. They began to sing again, and clap, inspiring the old man to an even louder and more aggressive display. Even Torka had to admit that it was a valiant effort, until Lorak whirled and pointed a finger directly at him.

"Torka does not sing!"

"Torka is new to this camp. He does not know the song."

"Perhaps he makes another song—a silent song—one that will drive the great tusked ones *away* from this camp!"

The accusation did not surprise Torka. Although he knew that Lorak was wrong, the old man was justified in his suspicion. "The supreme elder is right. This man will not hunt the mammoth. But he would do nothing to keep others from the hunt. He will join in the *plaku* ceremonies that take place in the hope of awakening the spirits to the needs of the people at the Great Gathering. Torka honors the mammoth hunters among you and is grateful to those who have taken him into their winter camp and offered his women and children a place of refuge."

Lorak growled, shaking his head. "It is not enough. Torka will sing with us. He will call the mammoth to this camp, or Torka will take his women and children and dogs and leave this camp forever!"

And so he sang with them, no longer an outsider except in

the sharp, hot fires of Lorak's eyes, which continued to burn him until they walked from the council house and were sobered by the cold sting of the night wind as they walked together to the great fire circle. The *plaku* dance began. His mind thick with drink, it did not seem important at the time. Calling mammoths was not the same as killing them. Life Giver was far away, in another world. And it was good to feel one with a group again. A member of a band again.

The fire burned high. It was comprised of bones and turf, grass and fat and secret offerings from many a man's and woman's pouch of little talismans gleaned over many years and upon many a past hunt. These were sacrifices to the fire, gifts to the life spirits of the great mammoths so that they would see the flames, feel the heat, and know that the people at the Great Gathering were summoning them to come and give them life.

The men made music on bone flutes and hide drums. They clapped their hands, and the women danced naked in the dark, circling before them, their hair loose, their faces hidden behind elaborate masks of feathers, their bodies adorned with anklets, necklaces, and bracelets of stone, feathers, bones, teeth, and claws. Their flesh was burnished in lines and dots, and swirling patterns made from the juices of the berries they had picked earlier in the day. And fat Pomm was conspicuous— not because she was old and ugly, but because of the long, white, lovely strands of goose feathers that cascaded from the topknot of her tightly plaited hair, disguising her girth and floating down about her aged form like downy mists, actually making her appear to float over the ground with the grace and confidence of a young girl.

Their circle widened, closed, and widened again. And all the while they moved, circling, sliding their bare feet sensuously along the earth, their backs to their men, arms raised to the spirits, drawing down the forces of Creation into themselves.

Sondahr danced with them. She was taller than the rest, more lean and supple than the others. Voices called out to her:

"Sondahr . . . Sondahr . . . dance for me . . . for me . . ."

There was not a man there who did not lust for her. Including Torka. But she circled with the others, passing the salivating Lorak and a slack-jawed Zinkh. Torka thought that she was the most beautiful woman he had ever seen as she moved slowly past him, half shadow, half flame. Her contours were so similar to Lonit's that, along with his passion, jealousy flamed and he found himself looking for his woman in the line of sinuously moving dancers. For whom was she dancing? What man would dare to lie with his woman this night? He could not see her. She had disguised herself well. Or perhaps she had refused to participate, after all?

The line stopped. The women turned as one. Sondahr stood before him, her face hidden behind a mask of owl feathers, her long gray forelock festooned with a roping of white feathers and tiny, vaguely familiar shells. The dance began again. This time the women remained in one place, moving for one man alone. Torka caught his breath, enflamed by fire, smoke, and drink. Sondahr danced for him. She performed the same movements as the others, a dance of pure sexual provocation. Yet hers was magic. There was a bold, almost angry assertiveness to her motions. With her long arms still raised, knees bent, limbs splayed, she rocked from heel to toe and back again, her hips rolling, inviting, her breasts swaying, nipples circled boldly with paint, like eyes watching him, waiting for him as his eyes looked back. Firelight glowed gold and red between her parted thighs, defining the curves of her hips and sides and soft, entwining arms. He saw that along the pale, velvety skin of one of her forearms, meticulously painted patterns failed to cover a series of impressive scars that looked as though they might have been made by the slashing teeth of a large carnivore. A wolf perhaps. Or—

His mood shattered. Wolf scars on her inner forearm? Lonit had such scars! Scars inflicted long ago when she had risked her life to stand with him and Umak against a marauding pack of hunger-maddened animals that had nearly killed them all. Incredulous, he squinted through fire and smoke and shadows to see not Sondahr but Lonit—*his* woman—dancing as he had never seen her dance before, moving as he had never seen her move, with every man in the band looking at her . . . wanting her . . . certain that she was Sondahr, Sondahr the beautiful, Sondahr the wise. But not half as wise as his own woman, and surely not half as beautiful, from behind her owllike mask of feathers. He saw her eyes, Lonit's unmistakably beautiful eyes, no longer as wide and soft and vulnerable as an antelope's but as hot with drink and firelight as his own—bold eyes, risking everything so that

he would not be forced to lie with another man, so that he
might not lie with another woman. Tonight she was Sondahr
. . for him . . . only for him.

And as he leaped to his feet, inspired by the bravery and
daring of her ruse, he danced with her, matching her move
or move, and could have thrown back his head and howled
her name like a wolf baying to the full, brazen face of the
rising moon; he was that filled with pride and love for her.
But to speak her name, to acknowledge her identity would
betray them to others who were near, choosing partners now,
dancing, taking them down in savage, drunken ruttings all
round the fire circle. No man was allowed to mate with his
own woman on the night of a *plaku*. But he was Torka,
grandson of Umak, and he knew that in new times men must
dare new ways.

He pulled Lonit to him. Lustfully, his hands slipping from
her shoulders, cupping her breasts, then easing downward
round her supple waist, he drew her down . . . down . . .
kissing her . . . whispering his love to her so that, if anyone
should overhear, only she would know that he knew the
dangerous secret that they shared.

"*Sondahr* . . ." He spoke the other woman's name, know-
ing that she knew that he meant Lonit, only Lonit, for
Torka the first woman, the last woman. "Always and forever,
Sondahr . . ."

Drumbeat throbbed across the tundra. In the darkness,
beneath the rising moon, Karana felt it beating . . . pulsing in
his heart and mind and loins. He could see the fire clearly, a
red aurora leaping into the sky, illuminating the wall of bones
and the Hill of Dreams and the tiny fingers that danced
round it, circling, merging, falling away into the firelit
shadows.

He did not know just when Sondahr joined him. Suddenly
he was there, standing between him and the fire glow, a tall
form wrapped in a robe of feathers with a white circlet of
bown upon her brow.

"Karana." She spoke his name in a whisper as soft and as
warm as the wind.

He caught his breath, startled. Beside him Aar lay his head
down upon his paws and made a low huffing exhalation that
bunded very much like self-recrimination. Once again the

magic woman had come upon him unaware; the animal sense
no threat in her, except to his self-respect.

She stood very still, unfolding her cloak as though it we
not a single garment but a pair of wondrous wings. The win
took them and blew them back.

Karana gasped. Beneath the winged robe Sondahr w
naked. She did not move. She might have been a woma
carved of bone. In the pale glow of the moon she was th
white, that smooth. Then the wind touched her and sh
trembled, and the youth knew the softness of her form wi
his eyes. He took in every curve, every line. He could n
look away.

She knelt. Her hands reached for his, drew them to he
breasts, filled them with her breasts. She sighed, arched he
back, and tilted her head, revealing her throat to him, yiel
ing all to him.

He burned as though the fire upon the distant plain ha
somehow come to flame within his flesh. Eyes, mouth, hear
lungs, loins—all burned, especially his hands. A *boy's* hand
so full of woman that he was afraid to move them. If only l
knew what to do with them! He could have cried at h
ineptitude.

She straightened and drew back, smiling softly, unde
standing. The time was not right. She drew her robe aroun
her and moved to sit beside him, close but granting hi
space—room to breathe, room to cool as the wind rose. A
the moments passed, neither youth nor woman spoke. The
needed no words. They were attuned to each other, to th
land, and to the black, star-filled enormity of the sky. Slowl
within the caul of the wind, beneath the silent sentinel of th
moon, their hands reached, touched, held. They were on
with the night. Theirs was a joining more profound than
physical mating; their souls were one as, from across th
tundra, dire wolves howled, and far across the world a high
thin cry ululated across the night, like that of a lost chil
mourning for a parent it knows will never come.

Torka awoke with a start.

Lonit lay sound asleep, curled in the fold of his arm
Shivering, his head pounding, he listened to the lonely how
ing in the distant ranges. No wolf or dog that he had eve
heard had sung a song like that. It was almost human, a
though a young girl moaned from across the miles.

Images flared, misted, tangled in memories of the distant past. *Wind spirit.*

He had heard its voice before. In the depth of the winter dark, from a hundred unnamed and all-but-forgotten camps, he had listened to its kind howling in the night. Beneath the light of auroras long faded from his memory, he had heard it cry as he had hunted as a boy with his grandfather. As they had hunkered together in the endless winter days of impossible cold, Umak had pointed to the glittering vapor that hung above the earth. Not unlike smoke from invisible campfires, it sparkled white, blue, red, and gold, in the way stars shimmered on clear nights.

Umak had told him that this was the mist that killed, for it was so dangerously cold that if a man or boy inhaled carelessly, it would cut his lungs and he would die. As patient as the night, Umak instructed Torka how to breathe through the cold-filtering guard hairs on his ruff and told his grandson how in such cold as this, the stars above froze and shattered and fell to hover low in particles so small that they formed the mist that kills—star mist, he called it—and only spirit masters could tell that it was a thing of the sky and not of the land. In his dark curly winter robe of bison hide, the spirit master had told Torka to observe the star mist closely, and if the stars allowed, he would hear them calling to the wind to blow them back into the sky where they belonged.

"And so it is that hunters must be wise and wary, for if the wind comes and they are caught within the mist of stars, then they shall be blown away into the sky, never to walk in the world of men again."

The boy had been frightened and fascinated all at once. In his hooded, multilayered garments of caribou hide, with his hands stuffed into thickly furred mittens padded with swan's down, his face buried deep within the extension of his wolf-tail ruff, he had listened, thinking that it would be a wonderful thing to hear the stars speak. But the wind never came, and he never heard the voices of the stars in the strange, glittering mists that hovered above the earth in times of severe and protracted cold.

But he *had* heard the voices of wind spirits. With Umak at his side he had looked through the star mist toward the clouds that wreathed the higher, night-veiled ranges, and he had heard the lonely keening of the creatures of the wind.

Umak had told him that men did not hunt within the mountains, for the high country was the realm of the wind spirits.

"Since time beyond beginning it has been so."

Torka's fingers moved to press his eyes. It was as though Umak were with him now, speaking to him, and he was a boy again, listening eagerly as his grandfather lowered his voice and reverently explained that wind spirits were neither man nor beast but things of mist and power. They caused avalanches to thunder from the heights and captured men not only to feed upon their flesh but to mate with them and hold them captive, to suck the blood from them until they were dry and wasted like fragments of old skins blowing on the wind.

The words of the old man faded.

The howling stopped. He closed his eyes and slept, to dream of the past, of Umak, of a great white bear with his grandfather's spear in its belly. Of childhood. Of his people. Of laughter and of all the good things that could never be again.

When he woke, it was not yet dawn. Lonit was still curled against him within the fold of his arm. The *plaku* fire was dead, and the dancers of the night before were asleep in snoring little heaps and piles of tangled limbs and arms. Memories of the past night drifted through his head. The ache was still there. He regretted drinking so heartily of the liquor that had been passed around in the council house. He wondered if Lonit had partaken of a similar brew. Perhaps this was what had enabled her to overcome her shyness among strangers. He stroked her shoulder. She shivered.

Suddenly he realized that if others awoke to find them in each other's arms, her masquerade would be discovered and her deception and flaunting of tradition of the *plaku* would endanger them both.

"Come . . ." he whispered, lifting her as he rose and began to carry her away from the fire circle.

She awoke and wrapped her arms tightly about his neck, nestling close.

Her warmth stirred him. He quickened his pace, stepping over sleeping bodies until he was well out of the area of celebration and halfway to his own pit hut. He was smiling as he spoke to her, softly, in the tone of a passionate and loving conspirator. "Torka is proud that 'Sondahr' had chosen him.

Torka desires no other woman. Always and forever he would have 'Sondahr.' "

She moved so quickly that she cut off his words. Exhaling a little cry, she twisted from his grasp, leaped to her feet, and ran off into the dawn.

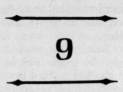

9

The next day it rained, but no one cared except the dogs. They remained outside, tucking noses beneath tails against the weather while the people were content to remain inside their huts, nursing the headaches and nausea that invariably followed a *plaku*. It would be several days before anyone felt strong and rested again.

Within Torka's pit hut, while Summer Moon listened wide-eyed with wonder, Aliga babbled constantly about the *plaku* and could not refrain from informing Lonit that her eyes had not missed the fact that Lonit had somehow avoided attending the sacred dance.

"This woman was there," replied Lonit dully, her eyes on her sewing, her fingers tightening noticeably on her bone needle—so much so that she cracked it and, despite the protection of her leather thimble, pricked herself.

"Do not worry. We are sisters. This woman will keep your secret." Aliga smiled and turned from Lonit to display her pointed, tattooed teeth for Torka as he came in from the rain. "It is a true thing that no woman of Torka would want to dance before other men." She smiled at him. "Of all the women at the Great Gathering, Sondahr chose you, and this woman saw how beautiful you were together!"

He stood looking down, trying to win Lonit's glance but failing as a startled Karana looked up from his sleeping skins, where he lounged moon-eyed and quietly daydreaming. "Sondahr danced for Torka? But that is impossible! She was with me."

Aliga laughed. She was growing weary and beginning to feel vaguely ill again, but the youth's statement brought welcome amusement to her. "Go back to your dreams, little boy! What would the magic woman want with you and your pretentions? She would see right through you and name you for the arrogant, foul little wind that you are!"

Karana sat straight up. "I tell you, she was with me."

Lonit felt sick. Her eyes met Torka's for the first time since she had run off after hearing him proclaim his love to Sondahr. Now he would know the truth. Now he would be angry for the deception that she had worked upon him. He would be ashamed for the words that he had spoken to Sondahr, realizing that he had been speaking to Lonit all along. His eyes met hers. Her heart nearly broke. There was no shame in them—only an expanding anger as he looked at Karana with absolute warning.

"All saw it!" Aliga persisted. "At the *plaku*, Sondahr danced for Torka. At the *plaku*, for the good of the Great Gathering, to entice the spirits into watching and hearing the need of the mammoth hunters, Torka called forth the mammoths and joined with Sondahr and—"

"*Torka* called the spirits of the mammoths to come forth to die?" Karana was incredulous.

"Torka called them forth. Torka will *not* kill them!"

"In the end it is the same thing!" The youth's head swung slowly from side to side in disbelief. "Torka would not do that any more than he would lie with Sondahr. And she was with me. Torka could not—"

Torka's face flushed with defensive frustration. "Karana cannot say what this man would or would not do to protect his band! With the magic men in the council house of bones, my choice was to call forth the mammoths with the others or be driven from the encampment. So it was done for the good of all of us. And for the good of all of us, the entire gathering saw Torka dance and lie with Sondahr! Karana will not challenge that fact again!" he shouted, not daring to speak the truth to Karana lest Aliga, Iana, or the children inadvertently reveal it to others. When they were alone, he would explain it to him.

"Karana must be wary of his words and his actions," he advised, hoping that Karana would understand and, for once, be as perceptive with people as he was with game and the vagaries of the weather.

The youth glared back at him. "Karana will not sit here and be shouted at and called a liar by a—a—mammoth hunter! Unlike Torka, I have not forgotten that I am alive only because Life Giver chose to give me my life instead of my death. The great mammoths are totem to me, and I will not live with one who would call his totem forth to die!"

"It is a bad sign, this rain."

Lorak's voice cut sharply through the gloom of the council house. Several elders winced. The shamans sat cross-legged on the uncomfortable bone floor, nursing the aftereffects of the previous night with sips drawn from the same brew that had made them ill in the first place.

"It always rains this time of year," reminded one of the bleary-eyed men.

"Not after a *plaku!*" Lorak glowered. "Who among you remembers it ever raining after a *plaku!*"

"After days of fasting, followed by a *plaku*, Lorak, there are not many who will remember much of anything."

One of the older men nodded and smiled euphorically. "I remember. . . . I lay with a good woman last night. Fat she was under many feathers, and not young, I think. She danced for many men before I grabbed her. Her elbows were horny, even with all that fat, but she could not have enough of the meat that I gave her and said that it *was* mammoth! An older man weak from want of mammoth meat needs a woman who can make comparisons like that. But she was gone when I awoke. *Phssht!* Like a dream. A good, fat dream. I wonder who she was."

"Forget women! Forget meat! Unless it is the coming of the flesh of the great mammoths to this camp!" Lorak shouted, enraged. "Know only that the spirits rain upon the earth of this camp. The signs are bad, all bad."

"Perhaps not," suggested the man who had just spoken with such pleasure of his union with the feathered fat woman. "Perhaps the spirits give us other sign—bison. Perhaps the mammoths will not come, as Man Who Walks With Dogs has said? Perhaps the spirits have sent us other meat and would have us eat of—"

"Never! We are mammoth eaters. Our fathers and their fathers for untold generations have hunted only that meat and praised only that great spirit. Of its bones is this encampment made, of its flesh is our flesh made. To forget this is to forget life! Is this what befalls us when we are generous in lean times and allow caribou eaters and bison eaters to winter among us? They are not our kind! Their spirits are not our spirits! The game that they kill cannot feed us! Man Who Walks With Dogs cannot nourish us—not with his flying spears or hunting beasts or bison meat, which offends the spirits with its stench! If the mammoths do not come, Lorak says now that it is because Man Who Walks With Dogs has driven them away—as he and his people should be driven away."

Red-eyed men looked at their supreme elder and wondered how, after days of fasting and a night of *plaku* celebrations, he could still seem as restless and full of angry energy as a man half his years. Then they remembered that when Sondahr had chosen not to dance before him, when she had lain with the Man Who Walks With Dogs, they had seen the jealousy in Lorak's eyes as, growling, he had turned away and stalked off into the night, to spend it alone within his hut upon the Hill of Dreams.

"It is also an insult to the spirits to accuse a man behind his back because you are offended by the actions of another whom you believe favors Torka above you."

All eyes flew to Sondahr as she drew back the heavy door skin of mammoth hide. She stood fully clothed in the arching entryway, then advanced boldly into their midst to stand before Lorak.

Shocked, the supreme elder stuttered, "No woman may enter here!"

"I, Sondahr, have entered."

"You, Sondahr, may *un*enter! No man wants you here!"

"Do they not?"

Her question was so sweetly baited that the others hung their heads lest, in their weariness, they laugh at Lorak and risk rousing not only his rage, but the further marauding of their hangovers.

"Torka is a good man, Lorak," the magic woman said coolly. "He is a strong hunter who sacrifices his own desires for love of his women and children . . . and son. He has shared all that he has with us, and still, although you know that mammoths are his totem, you forced him to join with you to call them forth to die. But this he did, and not easily, lest your threat against his family be carried out."

Lorak's head flew up so fast and hard that for a moment, it seemed it would leave his neck. His eyes bulged. "How can you know these things that your eyes have not beheld?"

"I am Sondahr. I am a shaman. I know."

"Because *he* has told you!" His features twisted with malevolence. "Torka betrays this council! And no woman can be a shaman!"

She measured him as though he were worthy of nothing more than her contempt. "If you would accuse such a proud and honorable hunter as Torka, you owe it to him, and to the honor of the spirits of this encampment, to speak your accusations to his face."

"Lorak owes Torka nothing! Torka owes everything to Lorak! His place in this camp, Lorak has allowed! His permission to hunt the meat of his own choice, Lorak had allowed! Allowance to bring within the great wall of bones meat from species other than the great mammoth spirit sanctified here, Lorak has allowed!"

"And in the long dark days of winter, the meat that Lorak had so wisely suffered Torka to bring into this camp will feed the people who have gathered to hunt mammoths that do not come."

He glared at her, measuring her as she measured him, and then he smiled a grotesque parody of mirth at her expense. "You may speak for Man Who Walks With Dogs, Sondahr, but you cannot heal his woman or bring forth her baby. Your powers are weakened because you, like us, are a mammoth eater. You fast even as Lorak fasts. Whatever powers you say you possess are drawn from the flesh and blood of the beasts whom Man Who Walks With Dogs has sworn that he will not kill. Will he kill them for you, Sondahr? Or will he stand by and watch you die—for without the flesh of the great tusked ones, Sondahr is nothing. *Less* than a woman."

The assembled elders saw her eyes go blank. The words of the supreme elder had struck her deeply.

Her beautiful head rose. Her face remained impassive. "Lorak's powers grow as weak as Sondahr's if he imagines that it is Torka who keeps the mammoths from this camp," she said.

"Then who? *What*?" screeched the old man, so vexed that he nearly came at her with his fists.

"I am Teacher. I am Healer. I am Seer. But as Lorak has said, I am also a woman, and it is true I hunger for the flesh of that which nourishes. Without it, all that I am *is* lessened. But even with it, Lorak has made it quite clear that Sondahr must not offend the masculine spirits of this council by suggesting that she might possibly know what Lorak, the su-

preme elder, does not." This said, she turned and strode
regally from the shadowed space and into the falling rain.

In the rain, under a leaden sky, Karana walked with Aar
across the land, and as the distance slipped away he wished
that he had not been so impetuous. He had stalked out of the
encampment without his rain gear. Beneath his boots the
tundra was soggy as he sloshed along, thinking that soon his
feet would be quite wet while his waterproof leggings and
overboots sat warm and dry beside his bed furs within the pit
hut, not far from the fine new raincoat of oiled bison intestines that Lonit had sewn for him. That had a hood, which
could be pulled snug about the face with a sinew tie, and an
effective water baffle, which projected well outward over the
eyes and sent rainwater funneling off his head without spattering into his face.

But there was no use lamenting now. At least he had his
spear, and although his clothes would soon be soaked, the
rain was not unduly cold. He would be uncomfortable, but he
would not freeze.

He looked up. Water sloshed into his eyes and sheeted off
his face. He grimaced at the rain, at the sky, at himself, and
at Torka, for having been the cause of the anger that had
driven him to leave the warm, dry pit hut without thinking
about where he was going or what he was going to do when
he got there.

Aar looked up at him, blinking against the rain, his mouth
straining back into that stressed smile that dogs displayed
when they were confused and nervous. Woofing softly, Aar
circled, pointing the way back toward the encampment.

Karana felt the blue eyes of the animal censuring him when
he did not move. He looked down and shook his head. "I am
sorry, Brother Dog. I will not go back yet—not until I think
things out. Lay the blame on Torka for your soggy coat.
Would you ask Karana to stand back in silence when Torka is
wrong? Who else will speak the truth to him? Not that he
listens. He will always look upon me as a boy, no matter what
I do or say."

The dog's eyes were steady in its sodden, black-masked
face as it cocked its head, trying to understand the words of
the youth.

Again Karana shook his head, sending rainwater flying. His
mood was no better than when he had left the encampment.

He walked on, full of anger, pounding across the land, complaining aloud, imploring the spirits of the great mammoths to hear him, to heed him, to ignore the chanting and dancing of Torka, to stay away from the camp of the Great Gathering where men were waiting to kill them.

The tundra was sodden and treacherous beneath his feet as he walked on, lost in thought, paying no heed to the fact that he had blundered into an area of tussocks. Each mound of grass was a wide, spongy island of new growth sprouting from a near knee-high clump of accumulated years of now-dead growth. To move through this pyramidal forest of grass required either hopping from tussock top to tussock top or finding surer, albeit soggier footing between the clumps. Because his mind was on his argument with Torka, Karana did neither. Instead he slogged blindly forward until he tripped and went down hard onto his face and belly. He felt the uneven, mounding surface of the tussocks against his chest and gut and thigh, and heard his spear snap beneath him. He was certain that its obsidian head had slit through his clothes to pierce his shoulder—not because of the pain, which was minimal, but simply because he knew that in his carelessness he deserved no better luck.

Cursing, he levered up and shook himself like a wet dog; pain flared, so intense that he fell again and lay still until it passed. With caution now he rose to his knees, knelt back, stared a moment at his broken spear, then examined his injury. His clothes had blunted what might have been a major wound; as it was, with clenched teeth and fixed will, he drew two inches of spearhead from the flesh of his left shoulder and, gasping, nearly fainted as blood spurted along with pain.

Then the pain ebbed; the flow of blood did not. He sat still, gathering his thoughts. He packed the wound as best he could with grass and mud and watched the blood continue to ooze through, making a mockery of his efforts, informing him in its own hot, red terms that he must get back to the encampment and have someone knowledgeable tend him.

Lonit! Her adept and gentle fingers would have it stanched and stitched in no time. He felt better just thinking of her. But if he returned to the pit hut, he would have to face Torka and endure another tongue-lashing. This one he would deserve, but he was in no mood for it. Until Torka was willing to listen to reason concerning his compromising attitude toward the mammoth hunters, Karana would not listen to any criticism from him.

Aar whined and hunkered close.

Karana lay one hand on the dog's shoulder while the other pressed his wound, trying in vain to slow the loss of blood. He began to worry. He had come so far from the encampment. He felt weak, but from the bleeding or from fear, he could not tell. The wound was starting to ache cruelly now. He must get help. But could he make it back to camp? And if he could and did not go promptly to Torka's pit hut, old Pomm was bound to see him and pounce upon him. After that, no other healer in the encampment would be able to come near him, unless . . .

His thoughts drifted. He felt less weak. Shakily he got to his feet and began to walk. "Come, Brother Dog. We will go home now . . . to Sondahr."

She was standing in the rain outside the wall of bones, as though she knew that he would come and would need her. She was strong for a woman, and he was glad to have her arm about him and her shoulder to lean on, because he could barely walk as she guided him around the peripheries of the wall and into the encampment through a narrow break in a piling of great, weatherworn tusks.

"It would not be good for either of us if any of the elders should see me with you now," she explained.

He did not understand or care. With Aar following, she led him upward along the back of the Hill of Dreams and into her hut before anyone saw them.

He was weak and shaking with cold as she guided him through shadows. The dog watched protectively as she helped him to strip out of his clothes. She gentled him onto a fur-covered pallet and covered him with soft, combed pelts beneath which he shook himself warm, watching as she exposed the wound to her scrutiny and then, still without a word, brought a bone bowl of water and began to cleanse it with the ends of her hair.

"This will need fire now," she said at last.

He stared at her, wondering if any flame could burn as hot as he now burned at the sight of her . . . even now, in his pain and weakness. And then, suddenly, he knew that the answer was yes as, with tongs of fire-hardened antler, she

pressed a burning coal to his wound and he half leaped
through the roof of her hut in agony.

Then he fell back and knew nothing at all for hours.

When at last he awoke, Aar was sleeping peacefully in the
shadows. Days or weeks could have passed and Karana would
not have known or cared, for he awoke with Sondahr naked
beside him beneath the bed furs, touching him as no woman
had ever touched him, guiding him to touch her as he had
not even dared to dream that he might ever touch a woman.
Trembling with pleasure, he knew that he must be dreaming
and gave himself fully to the dream . . . and to the woman.

His wound ached dully, but his dream balanced above
him, murmured above him, pressed so lightly that he barely
had to move at all as he was enveloped in moist warmth,
throbbing, moving, dancing—yes, it was a dance—and when
it was complete he awoke and stared into the face of Sondahr
and knew that it had been no dream.

"Again . . ." she whispered.

And although his wound brought pain, somehow it en-
hanced the pleasure that was now real to him, alive to him, as
Sondahr arched back, still joined to him, moving and leading,
then being led as Karana's world caught fire. His hands
gripped her, moved her, and he was a man with her, taking
her as he would, slowly, surely, plunging and withdrawing
and then plunging again, ascending to heights of passion that
carried them both away until at last they lay exhausted and
fulfilled within each other's arms.

Karana slept again and dreamed of mammoths being driven
across the tundra by a pale, savage stallion whose hooves cut
the earth and made it bleed.

"Navahk!" he cried, and within his dream he leaped upon
the stallion's back and called to the mammoths to follow, to
come forth to die upon the spears of the hunters of the Great
Gathering. "No!" He awoke with a start.

Sondahr knelt before him, offering a horn of liquid. "A bad
dream? I have them often. Here. Drink. This will ease you
and give you strength."

He complied. He drained the horn of its watery brew that
tasted of blood and the sap of spruce bark. "Mammoth blood!"
He spat out what was left in his mouth and threw the horn
away. "Have you given the blood of my totem to me to
drink?"

"Yes. Old and dried and cherished from last year's hunt. And now it flows within you, a part of you, and in your dreams you have called the great tusked ones forth to die."

He was so angry that he could barely see. "This is what you intended all along! Yes, of course! I should have known better than to trust you!"

Her hand rose to touch the packing that she had placed into his wound. It was oozing again. He did not care. He slapped her hand away.

"Do not be angry with me for tricking you, Karana. But your powers are greater than you know. I have seen this. The mammoths *must* come, Karana, for truly Lorak is right. Although this camp may be stocked with other meat, it will not nourish my people. They will die without the flesh of the mammoth, as I die now—slowly, day by day."

"Meat is meat! Flesh is flesh!"

"Then you should have no repugnance at consuming the flesh or blood of that which you claim is forbidden to you."

He covered his ears and shook his head in furious negations of her claim.

She persisted, pulling at his hands. "If the mammoths do not come, Torka and his people—*you*, Karana—will be driven from this camp. And Aliga will die the sooner."

The threats rattled him, but he would not allow her to have the satisfaction of seeing it. "Lorak will not know unless you tell him," he snapped, and almost added that he did not care about Aliga; yet that was not true. He did not like her, but he wished her no ill. And what he saw in Sondahr's eyes now was so sobering that it cooled his anger.

"There is no child in her belly?"

"No."

"And you could not heal her?"

"I could not even if I had the powers of all Creation. But in this camp, with the company and gossip of other women, the tattooed woman will not die alone or afraid. By the power that names you shaman and allows you to see into my thoughts, you know I would never betray you to Lorak. Yet I swear to you now, Karana, that with mammoth blood to strengthen me, I can heal others and will teach you to form your powers into such spears of insight that such as Lorak will be rendered into melted fat that will burn transparently before all, thus depriving them of the authority they have no right to possess! You are a seer, Karana, but you have not yet learned to focus your sight any more than you can control your temper. And until you do, you will be as a man in fog, sensing but never quite knowing what danger lies ahead. But it will be all right now: The mammoths will come; you have called them. And in time you will forgive Sondahr for her trickery."

"They will *not* come! What is said from dreams is not heeded by the spirits!"

"We shall see. . . ."

He glared at her. Throwing the bed furs aside, he swung his legs off the end of the sleeping platform and demanded his clothes. She brought them to him and would have helped him to dress, but he backhanded her away and did not thank her even when he noted that she had tended them with great care, so they were neither stained by blood nor stiffened by water.

He dressed quickly but not easily or without rousing pain from his injury. She stood in silence, watching and waiting. He swept by her without a word and, pulling the shaggy door skin aside, bent and strode impatiently out of the hut into the clear light of early morning.

From the smell of the cold air, several days had passed since the last rain. The sky was clear, cloudless. He walked boldly to the crest of the Hill of Dreams, ignoring the hateful stare of Lorak and the envious glances of several magic men who were lounging before the entrance to the council house. He looked beyond the encampment to a world gone red and gold and umber with the full fiery splendor of autumn . . . and saw with a start what no one else had yet seen: A large band was approaching from the west, led by the unmistakable staff-carrying figure of a magic man dressed all in white, except for a robe of gray and the head of some huge and misshapen beast upon his head.

"Navahk . . ." He exhaled the name. He remembered his dream and knew that the mammoths would not be far behind.

PART V

SPIRIT KILLER

1

For endless days it seemed, the child had followed the beast as he led his kind across the world—hunting, camping, then moving on eventually to hunt and encamp again. As his kind moved from one place of shelter to another, the beast would always pause and look back, making certain that the child was following, and would leave meat when he could not come away from his kind to deliver it himself. And when he did come, he stayed longer and longer each time, making sounds and offering no threat—only food, only sustenance. In the dark he would hunker low and purr like a great white lion, his eyes fixed, pupils huge, and garments as pale as ice glittering beneath the stars.

The child would look at him and think about how one day she would leap out of the shadows of the shrubs in which she always hid herself, and the man would be her meat. And she would dance in his skin, as he had danced in the skin of her mother. Soon now, very soon.

When she looked at her body, she saw her mother gradually taking form before her very eyes. She sensed that her kind must grow much faster than the little ones of the beasts, for she had watched them walking close to their mothers, perceptibly no larger now than when the beast in white had first led them off across the world. They were very small. Sometimes they would fall behind the other beasts, and the child would observe them and measure the many heartbeats that passed before their mothers would come shouting after them. It would be easy to leap at them, to drag them off and eat them. But the child was well fed. It was the beast in white that she wanted.

She mewed in sudden confusion. When she ate him, his

meat would soon be gone and she would have nothing left to
hate. And when she danced in his skin, he would be a limp,
lifeless, silent thing that did not purr and speak and, through
his presence, take away the loneliness for just a little while.
And once he was eaten, who would leave meat for her?

The wind of fear ran within the child again. The beast had
always left meat for her. Always . . . but no more. Not since
he had led his kind into their new country of broad outwash
streams and distant hills that sometimes glowed blue upon
the horizon. Not since he had begun to follow the huge
tusked creatures that the child recognized but had no desire
to eat because memories recalled their bitter and unpleasant
taste. She hoped that the beast would hunt other meat, but if
he did, the child never tasted it. He and his kind pursued the
tusked ones but made no move to raise their flying sticks
against them. They seemed to be driving them instead, shouting, keeping them moving away from water courses and the
forested hills toward which they seemed to want to go.

And all the time they drove the tusked ones, the beast did
not look back to see if the child was following, nor did he
leave meat for her or come to purr to her in the night.

And now the child was hungry and afraid. The tusked ones
had been driven into a dead-end canyon. The beasts had dug
a long hole in the earth and made piles of sticks and bones
and grass, and in the night light leaped and danced from
those piles and the child heard the tusked ones bellow with
fear.

That night the beast again brought no meat to the child,
and the next dawn, when light seeped into the world through
the hole in the sky, the child had awakened to discover that
the beast in white was gone, and most of his kind with him.
Only a few still sat with their flying sticks before the smoking,
stinking piles of light behind which the tusked ones still
bellowed.

In panic the child followed the beast. For a day she walked,
and for another, resting only in the deepest dark, and even
though she cried for him to bring her meat, he did not come.

And now, at last, the child had found him. She stood upon
a tundra rise and looked at the great camp toward which the
beast was leading his followers. Bones surrounded the camp.
Dogs ran out of it. And many beasts came forward with flying
sticks to greet the beast in white. Together they walked
toward the circle of bones over which the air was filled with

smoke, as though the tundra burned beneath it from a summer grass fire.

The child's belly lurched with hunger, and fear kept her in her hiding place. But it was rage and hatred that made her scream.

Once again, as he had not done since the first day the child saw him, the beast walked in the skin of her mother.

"Mammoths! The new band speaks of mammoths not two days' walk to the west!"

The words moved through the Great Gathering like slingshot stones rebounding off canyon walls as Zinkh came running into camp shrieking the news.

Sitting with Pomm inside her little hut, Lonit winced as though one of the stones had struck her.

Pomm saw her reaction. "You will have to go out now. The men will hunt. The women will be called to butcher. Your man will want you."

"Torka will never hunt mammoths."

The fat woman scrutinized Lonit and shook her head. "You cannot hide here with Pomm forever. Does Lonit not miss her children?"

Lonit flushed. "Iana cares for them while I am away and . . . I have not been hiding. Torka agreed that this woman should come and stay with Pomm until Pomm felt better."

"Pomm will never feel better," stated the fat woman, pouting like a spoiled child. "Not as long as Karana stays on the Hill of Dreams with Sondahr."

"He is hurt. She is a healer."

"Bah! This woman knows what kind of healing she does! And I can imagine how Karana rises to the treatment! Pomm is shamed before all! Zinkh gives me to Karana. A fine and valuable gift! Why will Karana not see this?"

"I have said it before, Pomm," Lonit replied with elaborate patience, "he is very young. Sometimes, as with the very old, the young do not see things clearly. And in the light of Sondahr, I wonder if all men are not blind."

"Bah! Together Karana and Pomm could make best ever magic in all the world! Not like with Sondahr. What kind of magic woman be she if she cannot even make one small baby come out to be born?"

Lonit sighed. "She is beautiful. . . ."

"Bah! On the night of the *plaku*, Pomm was beautiful. In

all her feathers she danced before many, but Karana was not
there to see. That is bad, very bad—an insult to the spirits,
an insult to Pomm. That was why the old man grabbed
me—the little one with skinny knees. What could Pomm do,
yes? It was a *plaku*, yes? He did not seem so old in the dark.
Pomm could imagine that he was a boy, young like Karana.
We were very drunk, both Lonit and Pomm, yes?"

"Yes, very drunk," Lonit assented quietly, regretfully. Nearly
three days had passed since she had come to nurse Pomm
through an after-*plaku* illness that seemed to be plaguing all
the participants in the form of lingering headaches and stomach distress. She herself had not been an exception. Nor had
Torka. She believed that the sickness must have had something to do with the magic of the night—a reaction to such
close contact with the spirits of Creation or to overindulgence
in the celebratory brew. Regardless of the cause, when word
had reached her that Pomm was feeling so ill that she refused
to leave her hut, Lonit found the excuse she needed to avoid
facing Torka. She was afraid she might shame herself by
weeping or losing her temper. Either would be unforgivable;
she was Torka's woman, the mother of his children, and she
owed him her loyalty, her dignity, and her best efforts in all
things. He had always been good and caring toward her.

"Is bad woman, this Sondahr," Pomm hissed, "to take
Karana from Pomm. And it is bad for Karana to take her to be
his woman, when Zinkh gave me to be his first!"

The words drew Lonit from her reverie. Karana was like a
younger brother to her. It always set her on edge to hear him
criticized. When word had reached Torka's pit hut that he
was on the Hill of Dreams recuperating from a minor injury,
in the care of the magic woman, she had been relieved to
know where he was and that he was not seriously hurt. Torka
had been so distraught that he stalked onto the Hill of Dreams
to see for himself the extent of the youth's injuries.

When Torka had come down from the hut of the magic
woman, he had smiled, nodding to himself as he explained
that Karana was sleeping and, with Sondahr's special care,
would soon be "a new man." Seeing secrets dancing in his
eyes, Lonit's emotions had eddied like whirlwinds. Her face
had flamed with jealous anger, and she had nearly wept with
grief, certain that he knew all too well of the special sort of
care that such women as Sondahr could give. It was then,

unable to face him, that she asked to sit with the ailing Pomm.

Now, in the warm, daylit shadows of the little hut, a cool wind slapped at the door skin, which was held open by a loop of thong. Pomm's hut was cleaner than most, but since she lived in it alone and carried its bone framework and skin walls from camp to camp upon her own back, it was also by necessity smaller than most. It smelled of oil and rancid fat, of leather and old furs and stored meat that might have been cured more carefully. But the air from outside was tangy with autumn, and Lonit found it soothing. It helped to clear her head of memories and longings that she knew could never be assuaged unless Torka came to her and told her with his own lips that her fears were in vain.

She sighed disconsolately. She felt no anger, no grief—only sadness—and was strangely composed and strengthened by her thoughts. She could face Torka and whatever came now. Torka had been her first man, and no matter what the future brought, she would have memories that few women could share and all women would envy. That would be enough, always and forever. They would be everything.

"Lonit! Have you heard a word that Pomm has said?"

"Yes, I have heard."

"The spirits should make Sondahr pay for her kind of magic. Together we could call the spirits. This woman knows the words. Lonit and Pomm could make Sondahr sorry that she had shamed us by taking our men!" Her small eyes glinted. "Lonit doubts Pomm's magic! Yes! It is so because of Sondahr! Because of Karana! He shamed Pomm from the first. He makes this woman feel old! Fat! Ugly! Lonit must warn Karana. He listens to you. Tell him to remember that Pomm is his woman and that if she tells Lorak that he was not at the *plaku*, it could be bad for him! Bad for all of Torka's people!" Pomm glowered at her across the soapstone lamp.

Lonit was startled, not only because of Pomm's unexpected threat but because the fat woman seemed to have no memory of assisting Lonit to disguise herself as Sondahr. Lonit frowned. Where was the sad, endearing woman who had touchingly lamented the passing of her youth and beauty? Watching Pomm now, Lonit saw her petulance, her anger toward Karana, and her blind jealousy of Sondahr. She hoped that she had not revealed too much of herself to the woman while intoxicated. Pomm would make a nasty and vindictive enemy.

The sounds of the encampment intruded into the little hut. The shouting, chattering, and laughter increased as Zinkh stuck his head inside.

"Come, Pomm. Strangers come! Very great, proud band!" Excitement shone on his face. "You, Lonit! You come too! Everybody come! Tomorrow we hunt the mammoth! Great spirit master, Navahk, he will lead us to the kill!"

He stood boldly to Navahk as he came forward at the head of Supnah's band. Torka knew immediately that Supnah was dead, because along with the skin-beribboned staff of bone that proclaimed the magic man's rank, Navahk wore his brother's taloned collar and headman's circlet of feathers. But the circlet did not crown his brow; it adorned the skull of the thing in whose skin he walked.

Torka was not the only man to stand in repulsed amazement at the sight of the pelt. He stood near Simu, in line with Zinkh and an assembly of hunters from several bands. Ahead, Lorak and the magic men were posturing so the newcomers would not mistake their importance. Nevertheless, Navahk shone among them, more handsome than Torka remembered as, in his fringed garments of white, he smiled within the shadows created by the massive head of the beast balanced atop his own.

Torka stared at it as those around him whispered and frowned, asking one another what sort of animal it was—or if it *was* an animal at all.

In life it would have been the size of a small bear, yet it was more narrow across the back and midrib than a bear. Its pelt was gray, wolflike—a summer pelt, thin, with sparse underfur and long, darker guard hairs. If it had a tail, it had been removed, as had its rear paws. Its forelimbs were draped forward and attached to the arms of the magic man, its paws overlying his own hands.

Torka took a second look and recoiled. They were not paws; they were hands—broad, hairy, and huge despite the withering effects of desiccation. Four furred fingers and an elongated, opposing thumb hung stiffly down—long, wide fingers that must have been graceful in life, inordinately powerful and dangerous because, instead of flattened nails, they had claws.

But it was not the hands of the thing that held Torka's glance and hardened his gut with revulsion. It was its skull, balanced atop Navahk's own head. Still attached to the hide, its lower jaw had been cut away. Its cranium was covered not so much with fur as with thick, stringy, humanlike hair that fell around pointed furred ears, which were lobed like a man's. Its hairless snout was bearlike, yet impossibly, it had the nostrils of a man, soft fleshed and very wide, turned back in a hideous face. Heavy brow ridges encircled eye sockets in which the eyeballs had shriveled and sunken beneath lids that had dried and darkened to the texture of leather. At either side of the temples the bone structure of the upper jaw was massive, leonine, clearly designed for breaking and crushing bone, but nonetheless the face of the thing was disturbingly like that of a human being.

Its desiccated skin twisted as though in agony, its lips turned up against fleshless gums to reveal teeth that also looked human, except that they were oversized. Any man who had ever been pursued by wolves would have envied the stabbing teeth, for with such canines, he could have turned and faced his predators on equal terms. And beneath the hideous, half-human face of the beast, Navahk was smiling at Torka, his small, white, unusually serrated teeth glinting like those of a predacious animal.

"We meet again." There was no welcome in the words, only challenge: low, resonant, like a deep growl emanating from the throat of a lion poised to pounce.

Lorak looked back, his expression showing resentment of the newcomer's recognition of Torka. "Spirit Killer knows Man Who Walks With Dogs?"

"Spirit Killer?"

Navahk's smile broadened with smug satisfaction at Torka's query. "Navahk walks in the skin of the wanawut. It is a great pride and power for my people. Torka must remember the wanawut—the wind spirit that my brother did not fear because he had never seen it? Look upon it now—as Supnah looked upon it in the moments before it killed him and fed upon his flesh. Now the life spirits of my brother and of the wanawut are one with Navahk, for I have eaten the flesh of the thing that ate of Supnah. I have partaken of the heart of the wanawut, and because of this power, I drive the mammoth before me as a gift to the hunters of this band!"

Zinkh nodded with ecstatic affirmation. "Two days to the

west he says, for a band walking. Less than a day for running hunters!"

Torka was aware of the tension of the men who stood with him and of the whispering that moved through the people of the Great Gathering like a tremulous wind. Never had any of them looked upon the actual body of a wind spirit, of the wanawut. They must be thinking that a man who could kill a spirit must be more than a man, more than a shaman. Torka frowned. He knew Navahk well enough to think that there was not a word to describe what he was, unless it was *manipulator*.

He looked past Lorak, past Navahk, to the familiar faces of the people of Supnah's band. They looked well fed but drawn with tension. He saw Grek. There was a good man. *He* should have been headman in Supnah's place. He would have led his people well, with wisdom, not guile and deceit. Their eyes met and held. Grek's head went up. He looked older than his years until, holding Torka's glance with what could only be described as ferocious relief, he smiled and suddenly looked almost young again.

Mahnie stood between Grek and Wallah and peered through the gaps between elbows and sides in the wall of hunters. Her eyes widened at the sight of so many magic men in one place, and at ferocious-looking old Lorak in his feathers, and beyond him at Torka. It was good to see Torka! When he had first walked into Supnah's band—had it been more than three long years ago?—in his black-maned lion skins, with his bludgeon and spears and tall, beautiful, antelope-eyed woman, Mahnie had thought that he was the most wonderful-looking man she had ever seen. Much better than Navahk, who had cruel eyes and the perpetual smile of a bird of prey; it bent his mouth but never touched his eyes. Even before he had killed Pet, Mahnie had seen no beauty in him. But she had seen at once that Torka was kind, and although he had not smiled easily, his eyes were clear and unguarded, and he had always had a caring or amusing word for children. He had been a man to put all men of her band to shame. Except Grek, of course.

She looked up along her father's back, frowning a little at the half-dozen crooked strands of gray in his hair. Grek was growing old! The other day, when Navahk had forced them to travel instead of allowing them to rest at the head of the canyon where the men had driven the family of mammoths into the bog, she had overheard her mother say sharply to Naiapi that Navahk should heed the advice of Grek, who made no secret of the fact that he did not care whether they wintered alone or at the Great Gathering, as long as they settled into a good camp. There, after winter supplies were prepared, women could rest after their arduous and seemingly endless trek, and their children could play the games that little ones needed to play if they were to grow strong and straight. Mahnie had pretended to be asleep in her bedroll, worrying that Grek had challenged the magic man again by asking why they must go on to the Great Gathering to summon other men to hunt meat that could easily be taken by their own hunters.

Naiapi had looked down her nose at Wallah and replied that Navahk knew what he was doing and that no man had a right to question him—especially Grek, who was obviously complaining because he was growing old and tired and incapable of keeping up with younger men.

Wallah had grown purple in the face but had managed to reply calmly that Grek was the most experienced hunter in the band and that any hunter who was still strong and agile after over thirty risings of the starving moon was a man to whom others should listen.

Over thirty years! Mahnie could not imagine anyone being so old until she saw the ruin that time and weather had worked upon Lorak's craggy face. Would Grek look like that someday? Would Torka? And—her heart beat a little faster—would Karana? Would he be here, with Torka in this great camp?

When he had run away from Supnah's band, everyone said that such a young boy had virtually no chance of catching up with the Man Who Walked With Dogs. But Mahnie knew that with the great dog Aar at his side, he would do it. He was the most arrogant, willful, and accomplished boy she had ever known, as well as the handsomest. Yes. Easily that. So handsome that sometimes it hurt just to look at him. When he had walked near her, she stared and stammered and could not even bring herself to speak his name, except on the night that he had run off alone into the darkness; fearing that he would become food for stalkers of the night, she had cried out to him. He had not listened. She had run to Torka to tell him in what direction Karana had gone, but Torka had already taken off after him with Supnah. She had wept, wishing that she were old enough and brave enough to go after him herself.

The band was beginning to move forward again. Wallah took Mahnie's hand to be sure that she would stay near, but the girl waved the gesture away. She was nearly twelve, too old for holding hands with her mother, although she had yet to shed a woman's blood. She was in no hurry for that. Just thinking about the ritual of first blood made her palms cold and her mouth dry, and although Wallah was full of assurances, her mother's eyes grew haunted when she spoke of her little girl growing up, and Mahnie knew that they both were seeing the same ghosts.

She looked up at her father now and could see just enough of the side of his face to know that he was smiling. Oh, it had been such a long time since Grek had done that!

She walked through scattered groups and individuals with Wallah and Grek, past the many pit huts and shelters of the various bands, toward the Hill of Dreams—and stopped dead in her tracks. Someone bumped into her, impatiently spoke her name, and told her to move on.

She did not turn to see who it was, nor did she move. She stared ahead to where the hill rose smoothly out of the pall of smoke that lay across the encampment. She saw the enormity of the council house of bones and the odd little shelters of the magic men, but these things were only background to a somehow large and infinitely more entrancing image: Karana.

He stood motionless upon the hill, intently watching the approach of the newcomers, of the magic men, and of Navahk. As in the past, the great, black-masked, blue-eyed dog Aar stood at his side. The dog was exactly as Mahnie remembered him, but Karana was not: He was a young man now, tall and strong and so handsome that she caught her breath not only at the perfection of his face and form, but at the startling resemblance that he bore to Navahk, who was staring back at him while standing stock still beside Lorak at the head of the congregation of magic men. His face was so contorted with loathing that, although his smile was fixed beneath the hideous skull that shadowed it, there was no mistaking the expression of murderous hatred.

Mahnie shivered with apprehension as she looked from Navahk to Karana and back to Navahk. Dark inferences of things best kept unknown and unspoken disturbed her. What could lie between two people that could cause such enmity? And how could Karana look so much like a man who was not his father?

Wallah tugged at her sleeve. "Come, my girl. Stop gaping. We must move on to our campsite."

She looked up at her mother, her face aglow. "Do you see him? There! Upon the hill, it is Karana! I told you he would be all right! I told you he was alive!"

"I see him," Wallah replied, so eager to be free of her pack frame that she was barely seeing anything at all. She told Mahnie to follow before they lost sight of Grek, who was walking on ahead with the other hunters of their band.

Mahnie sighed. Her own weariness suddenly struck her, but not so intensely that she could not turn back for one last look to make certain that Karana was still there and that her eyes had not been tricking her.

They had not. He was still there. But he was no longer alone. Mahnie's heart sank. A beautiful woman in a robe of feathers, with a crown of white down upon her head, had come to stand just behind him. Karana gave no visible acknowledgment of her presence, but from the way the dog moved to nuzzle her hand, Mahnie knew more than she wanted to know. Turning on her heels, she followed her mother, wishing miserably that she had not turned back for that last, painful look.

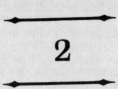

2

"Torka will hunt!" Lorak's command was as sharp as a well-placed spear.

Torka turned. He had intended to leave the other men to their hunting plans and return to his own fire, where he hoped to find that Lonit had returned from tending Pomm. The supreme elder's shout caused him to stop and look back.

Navahk stood beside Lorak, in front of the other magic men and hunters. "As this man recalls, Torka does not hunt the mammoth," he said with false affability.

"And since when does Navahk hunt at all?" retorted Torka with no attempt at affability.

"Torka would be surprised at what Navahk had stalked and killed since he left the band of my people."

Torka measured him coldly. "Nothing you could do would surprise me, Navahk."

Lorak's face collapsed about his nose, as it always did when he frowned. "Torka will make ready to hunt. This man Navahk, he speaks of many mammoths mired in a bog, driven there by his hunters as a gift for the people of this camp!"

"Navahk and his hunters are generous. Why have they not killed these mammoths for themselves?"

Navahk's eyes narrowed at Torka's question, but his smile never quavered. "We are few compared to the many who will winter at the Great Gathering. In lean times like these, we thought it would be a good thing to share this kill with those people who look only to the spirits of the big tuskers for sustenance."

His words were so well received that the din of appreciation did not quiet for several minutes. Lorak waved his people to stillness. "It is a good thing! Thanks to the spirits and to Navahk, at last we will hunt!" His eyes fixed Torka. "And *all* will be mammoth hunters in this camp. Not to hunt when the mammoths await our spears would be to offend their spirits. So Torka will join in this hunt, or he and his people will winter in a camp of their own, far from this place."

"Torka's 'people'?" pressed Navahk, his smile benign, his eyes malicious. "You were one man, a child, and three women when last I saw you, and only one of those women was worth keeping—the tall one with the eyes of an antelope and the grace of a swan. And I see you have brought one of my band along with you. Or has Karana somehow managed to stumble onto this place on his own?"

Navahk's reference to Lonit caused jealousy to erupt within Torka. Memories flared along with anger. *This man has shamed me. This man has tried to take my woman. If he tries again, that smile will not be long upon his face, nor will any woman want to look at him when Torka has given to him what he deserves.* Deliberately avoiding the mention of Lonit's name, he replied with open disdain: "Karana is called Lion Killer in this camp. This he has done, and in this killing he has saved the life of a man. He has hunted the great horned rhinoceros. He has shown that he has the gift of healing. Karana left his people of his own accord. He has come to the Great Gathering at Torka's side, and Torka is proud to call him son, since the members of Navahk's band, at Navahk's urging, abandoned him to die."

The tension between Torka and Navahk was palpable. Everyone felt it. The two men measured one another. Lorak measured them both, then looked toward the Hill of Dreams, where Karana was still standing with Sondahr at his side. The old man's jealousy was overwhelmed by his impatience. Although strong, dangerous winds of hostility were blowing between Torka and Navahk, Navahk spoke of hunting mammoths, and Lorak had been fasting for far too long.

"Enough talk! There will be time for that later! Now, come! It is time to hunt!"

When the hunters reached the mammoths, they were greeted by Navahk's watchman. As night slowly fed upon the last light of day, they ate traveling rations together, resting before the trench that Navahk's people had dug across the narrow neck of the canyon lest any of the animals struggle free from the bog and attempt an escape. Navahk's hunters related how Grek had led them to the bog; along with Stam and Rhik, he recalled killing an entrapped mammoth there many years before. It was spruce country, so the mammoths had turned toward it almost gratefully. With Navahk in the lead, the hunters had driven the creatures into the dead-end canyon, setting fire to the dry summer grasses that surrounded the lake. This forced the animals into the water, where their great bodies sunk to the knees in the treacherous, quicksandlike loess that lay below. Hurriedly, the men had felled young trees, stripped them of leaves and branches, and carved them into stakes sharp enough to keep even mammoths at bay; if the tuskers tried to cross the trench, the stakes would allow them no footing.

From where they sat at the peripheries of the large group of hunters, Torka and Karana could see the mired animals—several cows and calves ranging from yearlings to adolescents. Their low, weary moans told the hunters that there was little fight left in them. One of the older cows was already dead. She had lost her balance, the hunters said, and had fallen onto her side. Using their trunks and tusks, the other mammoths had tried to help her up; nevertheless, unable to right herself in the deep ooze of the lake bottom, she had soon succumbed to exhaustion and drowned. Now her calf leaned against her enormous exposed side, shoulder deep in the muck, its head down, its trunk moving listlessly.

Lounging and speaking in the slow, mellow tones that tired men on the verge of sleep will use, the hunters droned on about meat and hides and killing, while the magic men sang softly to the spirits of the night, asking that tomorrow's hunt be all that their people desired.

Torka and Karana listened in silence. Then the youth spoke, his voice low and urgent.

"I have come because Torka has asked it. But Karana will not wet his spear in the blood of his totem."

Torka nodded. "I have told Lorak that we would hunt. I have not told him that we would kill."

"Is consenting to an act of killing truly different from taking part in the act itself?"

Not for the first time, Torka was taken aback by the youth's wisdom. The question stung him because he knew the answer as well as he knew that he had never been a man to hold patience with expedience. Nevertheless, Lorak's threat weighed heavy on him. He repeated it to the youth, only to have Karana shake his head. He seemed older since he had come down from the Hill of Dreams, somber and more reflective. He sat with his back to the magic men.

Since returning from Sondahr's hut, he had avoided Navahk completely, refusing even to speak his name. Now he gestured toward him with a snap of his head. "Do you really think it matters to Lorak whether you kill mammoths or not? He only threatens you to prove his authority over you. He has disliked you from the first because you see through the thin mists of his magic. And now *he* is here, just as I warned before we left the Valley of Songs. I have seen him in my dreams a thousand times since we turned our backs upon the land to which Life Giver led us. With Navahk in this camp, it will be as before: Navahk will turn the others against you. You will see. Already he has Lorak on his side."

That night the wanawut howled in the nearby hills, and men awoke to listen to her cries while Navahk stood motionless with Lorak, beneath stars veiled by thin bands of ice crystals. As magic men of lesser status circled and chanted, Navahk and the old man raised their voices as one, asking the forces of Creation to grant the hunters a clear dawn that would give birth to a good day to hunt.

And it was so. The killing began at dawn—an orgy of killing led by Navahk and Lorak. With the hunters whooping and yipping at their heels, they swarmed into the canyon, scrambling for footing on high ground that allowed them to rain spears down into the trapped mammoths. The lake turned red with blood, and the frenzied screams of dying animals filled the world. On that day Torka lost much of his reputation as a magic man, for Navahk and his hunters used spear hurlers that he had taught them to make. And since he had also instructed them in their use, their skill was great, but not so great as Navahk's, who boldly claimed the invention as his own.

"Come, Lorak says you must join with us. You must not stand back from the kill!" Stam cried to Karana, gesturing Torka and him forward.

Karana had never liked Stam. He was a dull, indecisive hunter who had always deferred to the magic man, carrying his pack and sharing the best portions of his kills with him.

Karana glowered, pointing at Stam's spear hurler, which the bandy-legged man held balanced over his shoulder. "It was Torka who taught you to use that."

Stam looked at Torka with wide-eyed innocence. "Was it?"

"It was." Torka's tone was as cold as his rising anger was hot.

Stam shrugged. "Navahk says not. Stam does not argue with Spirit Killer!"

Torka clenched his teeth. His hand tightened about the grip of his own spear hurler as Stam turned and ran into the canyon where Navahk could be seen climbing a high promontory that jutted out of the canyon wall. It was a gray, lichen-scarred slab upon which the agile, graceful magic man found solid footing from which to lever back and make his throws. Below him most of the hapless mammoths were already dead or dying, their bodies riddled with the spears of the hunters who stood in howling, arm-waving ranks along the shore of the lake. Torka saw Zinkh and his men among them and wondered where their undying loyalty to him and dislike of mammoth meat had flown.

Beside him Karana pointed, drawing Torka's glance away from the hunters and back to where, bellowing pitifully in the mud-thickened lake of blood, the little calf that had moved so listlessly beside the body of its dead mother the night before now slipped beneath the water. Only the bubbles of its dying breaths and the spears embedded in its side were visible.

With a shudder of empathy, Torka allowed his anger to surface. The body of the little animal was lost now, its meat irretrievable, and, hence, its death useless and an affront to the spirits. At his side he heard Karana exhale a hiss of contempt and knew that the youth shared his thoughts and feelings. He put his free hand upon Karana's shoulder, wishing to communicate his sadness and discontent with the killing. He was startled when the youth shook himself free, turned violently, and glared at him with his teeth bared and his tear-filled eyes wide with rage.

"Karana will not stand and watch this!" he shouted. "Karana has *not* called the mammoths! No matter what Sondahr may believe, Karana has not called his totems to *this*!" He was sobbing like a child. "If I truly possessed the power of calling, as Sondahr believes, know that I would call Life Giver from across the far land, upon the back of the winds. I would call him and name him Destroyer and command him to kill them all. *All!*"

He wheeled and fled from the scene, back toward the encampment, as a defiant shout from Navahk caused Torka to turn back toward the lake just in time to see the magic man, his last spear spent, hurl himself into space. Torka stared, only half believing his eyes as, with arms out, Navahk appeared to fly to a perfect landing upon the back of the largest of the cows. Riddled with spears, with blood pumping from her wounds, the animal was weak and near death, but she still had enough life left in her to try to rid herself of the weight of one of her killers. Her eyes rolled madly as she trumpeted in outrage. Tossing her massive head, she gored the sky with curling, twelve-foot-long tusks, and as Navahk withdrew one of his weapons and with triumphant cries of pleasure drove it deep again and again, the cow, enraged by pain, managed to pull a single forelimb free of the muck that imprisoned her and, with all of her failing strength, reared up—but then, still screaming, finding no footing in the bog, fell sideways.

Navahk leaped straight into the air like a great, white bloodstained lion. He roared and laughed with delight as he landed once again, this time on the heaving side of the beast. The cow lay nearly immobile now, her great, domed head straining to remain above water. Failing, her trunk twisted upward for air as her head went under. And Navahk, mad with the joy, stabbed his spear deep into the shoulder of the mammoth, withdrew his butchering blade, and bending, set himself to flaying open her hide, to eating of her flesh while she jerked and spasmed in agony beneath him.

Torka could not have said just when he entered the canyon and, in an explosion of rage and hatred, ascended the promontory. He only knew that suddenly he was standing above the lake, breathless from his run and climb, watching as his spear went flying, falling, its broad, lanceolate, deadly sharp head burying itself in the flesh of the helpless mammoth, striking deep, striking true—killing instantly, and mercifully ending her agony.

And only the depth of his love for Lonit and his children prevented Torka from hurling one more spear . . . into the throat of Navahk.

*   *   *

"Lonit . . ."

She turned, startled by the sound of her name, and was more startled to see who had spoken it.

Sondahr stood at the entryway to her pit hut. "Come out," she beckoned swiftly. "This woman would speak to the woman of Torka."

Within the shadows behind Lonit, Aliga stirred on her pallet. She was sitting upright, her tattooed face all but invisible except for the yellowish whites of her eyes. "Torka has three women," she said belligerently. "Lonit is only one of them."

Sondahr's features remained expressionless. "Lonit is Torka's *first* woman. My words are for her alone."

Lonit's heart sank. *She has come to tell me that she wants my man. She has come to win my understanding. Look at her, standing with the sun behind her. Could any woman compare with her beauty? Is there a man alive who would not want her as his own?*

"Feather woman . . . pretty . . ." piped Summer Moon, pointing to the crowns of swan's down that circled Sondahr's brow. The little girl sat between Lonit and Iana, playing with a buckskin doll that Lonit had made for her and with a blunt, baby-sized needle with which Lonit was teaching her the basics of sewing by allowing her to mend a rip in the waistband of the doll's feather skirt.

The little girl held up the doll and dimpled as she waved it at Sondahr. "This girl's doll wears feathers too! Like feather woman! Do you make magic?"

Sondahr smiled tenderly at the child. "There are many kinds of magic, little one. I do what I can to help others, that is all."

Aliga snorted. "It has not been much, not for me! But now that Navahk is here, we will all see what a *true* magic worker can do! In the end, it takes a man to make real magic." With the mention of Navahk's name, Aliga's features changed, her voice softened, and she fairly glowed with anticipation. "He is like no other man. He will make my child come forth. You will see. When the hunters return, when the women have done with the butchering, and all gather together at the feast fire, you will see what Navahk can do."

"Lonit, come. This woman *must* speak with you now."

Lonit winced against Sondahr's command and knew that she was behaving like a child. She could not put off the inevitable. With a sigh of acquiescence she rose and went out into the light of the ebbing day, following Sondahr through the camp, onto the Hill of Dreams, and into her hut.

A tallow lamp burned in the center of the little shelter. It smelled of old fat scented by oils pounded from the leaves of artemisias. Inhibited by the confines of the unfamiliar interior, and intimidated by the presence of the magic woman, when Sondahr bade Lonit to be seated, she obeyed, albeit hesitantly. She was almost painfully aware of her surroundings. Mammoth bones. Mammoth teeth. Mammoth tusks. Mammoth hide and hair and—

"You are a stupid, foolish woman." Sondahr's accusation was spoken evenly, directly, without malice. She had seated herself opposite Lonit, on an identical raised platform. Its base was the grinding tooth of a mammoth. Its seat was softened by moss and lichen-stuffed cushions of mammoth hide, overlaid by shaggy skins that had been brushed to a sheen no mammoth had ever known in life.

Lonit was so taken aback by Sondahr's words that she stared, unable to think of a reply—perhaps because she half agreed with them.

"You fear losing your man to me?"

Again the directness of the magic woman was unsettling. Lonit felt ashamed but could not quite understand why. "I . . ."

Sondahr's left eyebrow arched toward her hairline. "You *should* be ashamed," she said, in the same disconcerting way of reading thoughts that Karana had. "Do you truly believe that Torka thinks that he danced with me instead of you on the night of the *plaku*? Can you imagine that he is such a fool that he could not tell us apart because of a few feathers and strokes of paint? Believe me, Lonit, when Sondahr dances for a man, he knows with whom he lies, and any woman who cannot say the same for herself is indeed unworthy of any man at all!"

Lonit stared, aghast.

"*Are* you unworthy of Torka, Lonit?"

Her mind was swimming. "I—I— He is so fine a man, and I am . . . am . . ."

Sondahr's head went up. "You are young, woman of Torka. You are beautiful. You look strong, and your skills are many for one who is blind, and deaf, and very, *very* dumb. If you believe yourself unworthy, you will be."

Lonit blinked. She was suddenly angry. "You have no right to speak so to me!"

Again Sondahr's left eyebrow arched. "You have given me the right, through your silence and your stupidity and your misdirected jealousy."

"I—I—"

"Stop stammering. If you want to keep your man, you must learn to be bold, to fight for him against anyone or anything that threatens him."

Now it was Lonit's brow that arched. Her fingers curled against her palms so tightly that her knuckles went white. "What does Sondahr know of fighting? Lonit *has* fought for Torka! Against wolves, storms, and the forces of Creation that nearly took his life spirit after he dared to stand against Thunder Speaker. Lonit has fought for Torka until her body bled, and she would fight again—to the death, if the spirits would ask it of me! But Lonit is only a woman. Lonit has no rank! No authority! No power! Lonit cannot fight against you, a magic woman! If Torka chooses Sondahr over Lonit, that is his right. Lonit cannot—"

"—be as blind as she seems!" Sondahr's beautiful head swung slowly from side to side. Her features relaxed. She sighed, rose, crossed to Lonit's pallet, and sat beside her. "Lonit, this woman does not want your man, and even if she did, his heart is yours. His spirit is one with yours. Never has Sondahr seen a man so loving of one woman. Can it be that Lonit truly does not see or understand this?"

Lonit's anger shriveled. Again she felt ashamed and confused. "But I have seen him look at you. He has been with you alone in this place of magic."

"Yes, Torka *has* been with Sondahr, but only to ask for healing for the tattooed woman—nothing more. Yes, he *has* looked at Sondahr as a man looks at the beauty of the first dawn of spring or the great herds of caribou when they move across the world in the last red glow of sunset, to winter in the face of the rising sun. He has looked and has looked away, knowing that he has seen a rare beauty but nothing more than that, nothing that he would reach to keep and hold." Sadness moved upon the magic woman's face, and with it came regret, then acceptance as a small, bitter smile lifted the corners of her mouth. "All men look at Sondahr. It has always been so. And Sondahr has lain with many men, although she assures Lonit that Torka has not been one of

them. Not that she has not envied Lonit, for Torka is the best
of men. But Sondahr will never have a man of her own.
Sondahr is Teacher. Sondahr is Seer. Sondahr is Healer.
Sondahr is all that the forces of Creation have conspired to
make her, and so she has no band of her own. All men fear
her as much as they desire her, and many resent her for her
gift, so that she has wandered among the people of the
tundra, until now, at last, she dwells alone in a house of
bones and grows old, childless, sharing her gift with the
young, like Karana, who show promise as shamans. Sondahr
had hoped that someday one of them would truly have the
power to take the gift from her so that she might at last be
'only' a woman, content to walk beside one man, with children sucking the sweet milk of life from her breasts. Sondahr
has lived long and has learned that the gift of love between
man and woman is the greatest magic—the only true and lasting
magic—a magic that Sondahr has never known. It is a rare
gift, great enough to create life, to gentle the days and bring
joy to all the nights that otherwise must be endured alone."

Lonit was deeply moved. "It might yet be for you."

"No," said Sondahr, "it is ending for me now. I have seen
it in the mists. There will be few tomorrows for Sondahr, and
so I have called Lonit here to warn her."

"Of what?"

"Of her own stupidity! Lonit must stop doubting herself!
Lonit must stop hiding in the shadows. Lonit must stand tall
and confident beside her man and know that there is no other
woman in the world for him." She paused, and her eyes
narrowed speculatively. "Can Lonit say the same now that
Navahk walks within this camp?"

Lonit gasped. Sobered, amazed, and ashamed, she hung
her head, not wanting Sondahr to see the truth in her eyes.
Once again the magic woman had seen into her thoughts.
Once again she had spoken words drawn from her own heart,
and those words frightened her, because Sondahr spoke them
with such intense urgency that Lonit knew they would forever be seared into her soul.

"Look at me." Sondahr's hand reached to lay long, gentle
fingers beneath Lonit's chin and turn her face up. "You must
heed me, Lonit, daughter of Kiuk, child of a people who are
no more. Look not to Navahk. His beauty is deceptive. He is
a man of flesh, not of spirit. He is a magic man, not a shaman.
Navahk walks in the skin of wanawut, but look beneath the

skin of that beast, for the man who has slain it is infinitely more dangerous. I know—I have seen into his soul and have turned away, as you must turn away, or he will devour you as he has devoured his brother and will devour Karana if he can. And when he has sucked your spirit dry of life, he will throw you away to walk upon the wind forever, and he will smile and grow stronger by your death.

"Heed me now, Lonit, for in the days to come you must be a guide to Karana. He is wise and his gift is great, but he is as wild as a north wind and his moods are as dangerous. He has much to learn, but I cannot teach him. He might have been the one for me, but time will not allow it. He is of the world to come, and Sondahr is of the past. Lonit is the future. Lonit must be strong—for Torka, for Karana, and for the children of Man Who Walks With Dogs. Lonit must become all that Sondahr would have been in a new world, beneath a new sky, beneath a new sun. First woman to first man. Mother. Sister. Friend. A new Creation."

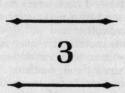

3

Torka jogged alone across the land. He did not know when the day ended. He did not know when the night began. He knew only that he trailed Karana and that it was good to run alone, away from the scene of the mammoth killing—one man carrying one spear and trying to forget that the other lay embedded in the body of his totem.

Yet he was unable to forget. And this, too, was good, for the memory was cleansing, clarifying, and it enabled him to look back over his past to see the fault in it.

To have led his little band out of the lonely country in the hope that they might seek shelter within a larger band, that had been a good thing; but to compromise all that he believed in, all that he held sacred, that was an offense to the spirits of Creation, an offense to the great mammoth Thunder Speaker . . . Life Giver . . . who had brought him and his people into a new and better world. And an offense to himself.

The terrain, open grassland devoid of tussocks, allowed a good pace. In the thin, fading light of dusk, he saw Karana trotting ahead of him. The youth had made no attempt to conceal his trail. As Karana ran, his legs cut deep depressions through the grasses, which made Torka's way easier.

He lengthened his stride. Soon they were running together, side by side. Neither spoke. They ran until the dark came down and they could run no farther.

They rested together, ignoring hunger, watching the night thicken and the stars prick its surface like embers from a crackling fire. Far off across the tundra the sounds of the still-distant Great Gathering reached them: The women were singing, the elders beating drums. The single lonely whistle of a flute rode across the night. In the opposite direction, from the dark, tangled foothills in which the mammoths had been entrapped and killed, the voices of hunters rose in a song of their own—a praise song, a song of life for men, a song of death for mammoths.

The darkness seemed suddenly heavy, palpable, as though some great, black creature were moving invisibly across the sky, pressing down upon them, watching them from above. Torka looked up, half expecting to see ghostly cloud shapes above him in the dark. But the sky was clear; the feeling of heaviness and foreboding was within himself. He looked at Karana, wondering if he had also felt a presence within the night. But the youth stared off, his handsome features set as he balanced himself beside Torka, forearms resting lightly across his thighs, his spears held loosely in one hand, buttocks tucked to heels, weight held forward, balanced upon the balls of his feet. They had both assumed this half crouch, half squat. It was a comfortable position in which to rest and doze; if danger threatened, it would allow instant action as their limbs uncoiled and they sprinted forward.

Moments passed. Torka listened to the distant singing and became aware of smaller sounds as well—little sounds, stirrings and scurryings, soft, silken whisperings in the grasses as creatures all around slipped between them unseen. His hand tightened around the haft of his spear. His eyes scanned the benighted land, then moved to rest upon the youth. But he found a man instead—a man who so resembled Navahk that Torka actually winced. Again the night felt heavy. He wished to lighten it.

"So. Once again Torka pursues Karana and finds him alone within the dark. You are still easy to track."

"Only because I hoped that you would follow." Karana's lips tensed visibly against his teeth as his head turned slightly. There was weariness and sadness within his eyes. "Either your step has slowed with the years, Torka, or you did not leave the killing site at once. I see but one spear in your hand. Did you hunt? Did you take the life of that which is totem to us? Did you wet your spear in the blood of mammoth?" Karana's questions were soft, tentatively spoken, as though he were not certain of wanting answers.

"I killed. And in the killing, deprived Navahk of *his* kill. Before, he was not a friend. Now, he is an enemy."

"He has *always* been your enemy, Torka. And mine. Until he is dead, it will be so." The youth's expression changed from weariness to absolute intensity. "I have listened to the wind, Torka, and now you must listen to me. I have let the wind pour through my spirit as a river pours across a rocky river bottom, and I have drunk deeply of the wind—the *spirit* wind—and it has told Karana that he and Torka cannot share the same world with Navahk."

"I do not know of another."

"Think back. The answer will come to you. You have warned me not to speak the words again. I will honor your wish and my promise. But I will not stay in the encampment of the Great Gathering. I will take Aar and go from the world of men. It is not a good world."

Torka nodded, taking measure of the youth and of the validity of his words. "To live among others is demanding; compromises must be made. Perhaps I have made more than I should have, but we live among many diverse peoples in this camp."

"And when the headman is wrong? Must all follow him then?"

"If others see no cause to challenge, yes."

"Because it has always been so from time beyond beginning?"

Karana had thrown his own oft-asked question back in his face. It was an answer that was not an answer, yet he could think of no better one. "Someone must lead," he said at last. "And the old ways are proven ways."

"If Torka believed that, he would never have made a spear hurler or created a new type of spearhead. If all men believed that, then things would always stay the same, never getting better, never getting worse, but always staying the same. And from what Karana's eyes have seen, nothing in the world stays the same forever: Rivers that are frozen solid in the dark times melt and flow in the days of sun and sometimes rise to flood their banks and cut new courses. The earth moves. The white mountains walk. Peaks of stone give birth to clouds that rain fire. As old Umak taught me, in new times men must learn new ways or die. In this camp, if the mammoths had not come, Lorak would have kept his people fasting and praying until they starved to death, even though there was bison meat for the taking. And in order to be accepted by the people of this camp, Torka has become another man entirely!"

"No, Karana. But I am not headman here except within my own pit hut. As you have yet to learn, when a man is responsible for the lives of his women and children, he has more than his own pride to care for. This has been a good camp for us. The men in this part of the world are good men. Their fellowship has been welcome. They have named you Lion Killer, and you have become a man among them. Many a young girl looks at you with hopeful eyes. Many a grown man envies what is between you and Sondahr. Many a youth names you friend. Would you not miss these things, Karana, if you were alone, one man in a world without people, with only the wind to speak to your spirit? All of your decisions are easy because you have only your own life to care for."

"You will stay, then?"

"Until the time of the long dark has come and gone, yes. I will not put my family at risk by a confrontation with Navahk."

"He has shamed you. In Supnah's camp, and now at the Great Gathering. He will try to take Lonit from you. He has forced you to take the life of your totem. He is—"

"—a man who will not shame me again. I do not fear him or his magic."

Karana was silent. Then: "It is because of me that he hates you." The words were very soft.

"No. He and I see each other for what we are. He hates me because he knows that I see through him—not because I saved the life of one small boy whose life he threw away upon the wind."

"He wanted me dead. He still wants it. My presence reminds others that he is not infallible. He hates me for that."

"Then, by all means, you must run off alone and give him what he wants!"

"I am *his* son." The admission came as though from an open wound.

Torka nodded. Yes. Somehow he had known it all along, yet his head moved in slow negation. "No," he said. "I have made you mine."

Karana's love for Torka was so great at this moment that it nearly choked him. Nevertheless, words could not undo the truth. "You are the father of my heart, but I *have* called the game and I *have* called the mammoths to die upon the spears of men. And if the spirits have turned against us, it is because of me, because I am of *his* blood, because I share *his* powers and do not know how to use them!"

Again Torka nodded, only this time he smiled and swung

an arm around Karana's shoulders, drawing him close. "Then you must learn, Lion Killer. For the good of us all, you *must* learn. As you have said, in new times men must learn new ways. You are a man now. It is time to stop running. It is time to face Navahk. Like it or not, we must share the world with him."

They returned to the main encampment. By dawn they were within the wall of bones and tusks, with the dogs yapping and crowding around to offer greetings and complaints about having been left behind when there was hunting to be done. The old and sickly and the women and children gathered to hear of the killing of the mammoths. Torka eloquently told them what they wanted to hear and kept his opinions to himself. These were mammoth eaters, and so he told them of the killing site, the courage of the men facing certain danger, the way they readied themselves for the kill, how their spears flew to take their prey, and of the size of the mammoths that lay dead in the lake, awaiting the skilled hands of the women who would now go out to butcher them and honor their life spirits by turning them into meat and hides and useful tools for the people.

The people cheered while Torka tried not to think of the piteous sight of the little calf slipping beneath the surface of the water, its body riddled with spears, its last little bleats of life rising unheard except for the bloodied bubbles that told of its death, as a snarling Navahk crouched upon the body of the dying cow and grew strong upon the pleasure that he took in the agony of her death.

Karana turned away, wanting no part of their adulation.

"Karana! Your woman Pomm, she has been proudly waiting!"

He rolled his eyes with exasperation as Pomm elbowed her way tenaciously through the throng like a small, fat, hornless rhino charging through the crowd. But this rhinoceros had ribbons of white goose feathers streaming from the top of her head. He could not remember ever having seen a more ludicrous sight as, before he could backhand her away, her strong, fat fingers latched onto his arm at his elbow and she pressed close to him, fawning like a young girl.

"Pomm has prepared a soft pallet for the returning hunter!" she simpered. "Within Pomm's hut sweet balls of fat and berries await the returning hunter to restore strength to one who has—"

"I have *not* hunted. Karana's spears have *not* tasted the blood of mammoths, nor will he eat of their meat with Pomm or with anyone else! Leave me alone, woman! Let go of my sleeve and find a man your own age to fuss over!"

With Aar at his side he twisted violently to the left, freeing himself of Pomm's grasp to leave her standing ashamed and bewildered with a handful of his torn, stone-beaded fringes laced through her fingers.

Her face turned as red as if he had scorched her. "Sorry will you be, son of Man Who Walks With Dogs! Pomm does not forget or forgive those who spurn her magic! And Zinkh will make you pay for refusing to wear his hat and for turning your back upon his one great wonderful gift to you of me!"

He heard her shriek after him, but in the noisy crowd it was easy to ignore words that he had no wish to hear. A few elderly men teased him as he passed, and one of them, a skinny fellow, asked if he might have what the young hunter obviously did not desire.

"Take her and know that Karana will forever thank the spirits for your favor to me!" he snapped, and heard the happy hoot of the man and the laughter of others as he strode off across the camp, past Grek's family, and a small, pretty young girl who resembled their daughter, Mahnie. She was staring at him with the expression of one who longs to speak to another yet cannot quite find the right words. Yes. It *was* Mahnie. She still had the look of a cloth doll in her lightweight buckskin tunic and trousers, with her thick black hair loose and shining about her shoulders. So she was still a girl; the women of his band wore their hair plaited and piled into topknots upon their heads as a sign of maturity.

Wallah nodded to him as he passed, and he felt obliged to nod back; he had always liked Grek and his woman. Wallah was brusque and outspoken, but as kind and steady as her man. Beside her Naiapi stood watching him in silence. She was still a handsome woman, and from the imperious set of her chin and mouth, she was still as hard and unforgiving as he remembered her. From the corner of his eye he looked for Pet. Now *she* was a girl who must have grown into a beautiful woman by now; but if she had come across the land with Navahk and his people, he saw no sign of her.

The girl Mahnie finally found her tongue and called after him softly as he walked by her.

"Karana . . ." she stammered. "I knew you would still be alive. I am glad to find you in this camp."

He said nothing to her. Her words annoyed him, for although she was glad, he was not. He wished he were away from here, back within the Valley of Songs, hunting antelope within the river of grass, in the forbidden land where men did not hunt mammoths and where Torka deferred to nothing but the spirits and the weather and the land.

Lonit stood with Sondahr upon the Hill of Dreams. With a gesture of infinite grace the magic woman summoned Torka. Puzzled to see his woman with Sondahr, he left the elderly and the children. He assumed that the women needed his assistance to prepare for the trek to the butchering site.

"I must join the others on their trek. They will need me to invoke the spirits on their behalf," Sondahr said when Torka had joined her and Lonit on the high ground of the shamans. "Torka and Lonit, you will stay here in my absence. It will be good for you to talk alone, without anyone to distract you." Granting him no time to reply, she moved past him, her leather cloak flowing behind her, her head high.

Torka felt a sudden sense of foreboding. "Has Aliga died? Are the children all right?"

"They are all well, even Aliga. Since Navahk has come to his camp, she feels so much stronger. She is awake all the time and preening like a young girl. That is why Sondahr has asked you to come here . . . so that we might— So that I might—" She was looking down, breathing shallowly, fighting for every word.

His puzzlement grew. He reached out and turned her face up to his. "What are you trying to say?"

Her face was ashen. "Only that Sondahr has made me see that I have been a foolish woman. I have seen things that have not existed . . . and refused to see that which is true and real."

He shook his head. "I do not know what you are talking about."

She bit her lip and shook her head defiantly, as though she dared some inner part of herself to try to stop her from saying: "In this camp or any other, in the land of mammoth eaters or in the Corridor of Storms, in this world or the next, whatever Torka does, Lonit will accept without question. And wherever Torka goes, Lonit will be at Torka's side. And when Torka's spirit walks the wind, Lonit's spirit will walk with Torka, always and forever—*if* this is what Torka wants."

"*If?*" Her proclamation was so unexpected that he was struck dumb by it. She was staring at him boldly, with her beautiful head held high and her eyes steady, yet there were tears in her eyes and she trembled. Suddenly he understood, drew her close, and held her tightly as he realized that it was he who had been the fool. How could he not have realized how deeply she had misunderstood him and how desperately she needed assurance of his love?

"Forgive me," he said, kissing her gently and closing her eyes with his lips. Breathing the breath of his life into her nostrils and mouth until, at last, he felt her body meld to his, then lifting her into his arms, he carried her into the hut of Sondahr high on the Hill of Dreams.

The tallow lamp still burned. The room was aglow with sunrise and shadows. He lay Lonit onto a sleeping pallet, and casting his spear aside, he undressed and lay down beside her. "Torka would never want your death, Only Woman In The World. *Never.* For you are that to me—the only woman I will ever love or desire. And someday, if the spirits grant that we grow old together—so old that our own spirits yearn to be released from our bodies to seek life and youth anew—then we shall walk the wind together, one and unafraid. But now we are young, and Torka has only one request of Lonit. I ask only for her love, one with mine, always and forever."

With a sob she threw her arms about him and held him as though she feared that the forces of Creation would sweep down and rip him from her life.

Afterward, as they lay naked within the hut of Sondahr upon the Hill of Dreams, entwined from their lovemaking, Lonit slept and murmured against troubled dreams while Torka held her close, watching the shadows change as the sun claimed the height of noon, then began to ease slowly across the sky on its inexorable passage toward dusk and dark. He slept, and awoke, and stared at the room in which he lay: mammoth tusks above him. Mammoth hide and bones and hair all around and beneath him.

Visions of the hunt filled him, choking him—memories of the baby mammoth, of the screams of the entrapped dying animals, of Navahk's savage and sadistic butchery of a living animal, and of his own killing of that animal.

You have killed that which is totem to you!

He sat up, so filled with distress that he could barely breathe. The warm, fragrant confines of the little hut were suddenly suffocating.

Lonit stirred sleepily beside him, reached for him. "What is it?"

He took her hands, drew her up, kissed her, and said imperatively: "We must go from this hut. It is not good for us to be here. And no matter what may be said to you by others, you will not join the other women at the killing site."

She blinked, startled and alarmed by his intensity. "I will do whatever Torka tells me to do."

He kissed her quickly. "Dress then. Go back to our own hut and our children."

But Torka did not join her. He dressed, took up his spear, and stalked across the encampment, through the opening in the wall of bones, and did not stop walking until he had reached the shores of the nearby lake. Fully clothed, spear in hand, he plunged into the shallows, seeking to cleanse himself and his weapon and garments of mammoth blood. But although he swam and splashed until he was exhausted, it was not enough; he felt unclean, as though the blood of his killing would never be washed away.

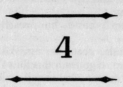

4

For all that day and into the night, the shamans sang magic songs and danced magic dances while the women who had come to assist the hunters with the butchering worked side by side with their men atop the bodies of the fallen mammoths. The women had spoken not a word to Sondahr on the long trek out from the encampment to the killing sight, unless they had a special "spirit request," and when they arrived, they refused to allow her to assist them at their work. She stood at the edge of the lake of death, appraising the slaughter scene; then she ascended the promontory from which Navahk and Torka had made their kills.

The sky clouded, and a thin, sleeting rain began to fall. Nevertheless Sondahr stood unmoving upon the promontory, her arms extended and head back, chanting praise to the spirits of the slain beasts until her voice was gone. And still she stood silently invoking the mammoth spirits to grant their strength and wisdom to the women of the Great Gathering, until at last the day thickened into dusk. Exhausted and shivering against the cold, she climbed down from the stony heights to be confronted by Lorak, who held a steaming cup made of hollowed tusk out to her.

"To Sondahr, who speaks to the spirits for the females of the assembled bands, Lorak offers the blood of that which is sacred to us: the blood of life, of strength, of power. Of the great, tusked ones. Of mammoth . . . at last!"

She took the cup. She drank deeply, gratefully.

Everyone saw the old man's eyes shine and his organ rise with lust beneath his bloodied, loose-fitting tunic, straining the skins as he took back the tusk. "Too long have we fasted, Sondahr. Too long have you stood alone in the icy rain.

Come! Rest, eat. There is much man meat at the place where Lorak has spread his sleeping skins."

Navahk had come to stand beside him. The eyes of Sondahr moved slowly, from Lorak to Navahk, where they measured, then dismissed the man. They moved back to Lorak. If she noticed the expression that her dismissal has caused to move upon Navahk's face, she gave no sign of it. Making no comment to either man, she turned and walked to the closest of one of several small, communal fires that the women had made and shielded from the rain with broad tarpaulins of staked hide. Without a word to anyone, she bent, took a slender bone of spitted meat from where it roasted upright over the flames, rose, and strode into the thickening shadows of dusk, where she seated herself and began to eat alone, shivering within her sodden robe of feathers.

From where Mahnie sat beside Wallah, she could see the magic woman clearly and thought how beautiful Sondahr was, even when she was wet. A pang of jealousy stabbed her as she recalled the way the woman had come to stand at Karana's side on the Hill of Dreams. Rumors about them had been the talk of the women and girls as they had hurried to prepare for the trek to the butchering camp; and on the long walk across the tundra, everyone seemed to avoid Sondahr. Mahnie had not failed to notice the glaring, murderous looks that Naiapi was giving the magic woman, and she had asked Wallah why everyone seemed so hostile toward Sondahr. Her mother answered in a hushed voice that because everyone feared the powers of the great Sondahr, no one really knew quite how to address or approach her. She had been Navahk's teacher and lover, long ago, when he had been little more than a child. Supnah had worn her feather, sign of a great favor. One could not blame Naiapi for resenting her. And mere females could not assume friendship with such a legendary seeress and healer. Sondahr was one who called the spirits. Sondahr was one apart.

Mahnie frowned. It was true that she did not like the magic woman; after all, she *had* seen Sondahr with Karana upon the Hill of Dreams. But Sondahr had spent an entire day standing in an icy rain while she invoked the forces of Creation on behalf of the females of the various bands, and it did not seem right that not one of them had so much as offered the magic woman a dry skin in which to shiver herself warm. With a little sigh of resolve, Mahnie reached for her traveling bag and began to rummage through it for the extra, lightweight cloak that she had brought along in case the nights at the killing site turned unduly cold.

Wallah stayed her hand. "What are you doing?" she whispered, her voice barely audible, her expression strained with disbelief and fear.

"Getting my cloak for the magic woman."

"Stay out of this!"

Again Mahnie frowned. She had not thought it possible for someone to whisper and shout at the same time, but Wallah had done just that. Why? What danger could threaten her in a butchering camp? The prey was slain. The people were tired and well fed and looking forward to a good night's sleep before trekking back to the main camp under their heavy load.

Mahnie felt a poke at her side and saw her mother indicate with a snap of her head that she should direct her attention elsewhere.

Bewildered, Mahnie followed her mother's glance to where the magic men had gathered behind Lorak. The supreme elder's face had grown purple. It was as engorged with anger as his penis had been with man-need only moments before. But now his organ was deflated, and his only visible erection—other than the sizable protuberance of his nose—was the twisted, bony finger he was pointing at the magic woman.

"Beware, Sondahr. That which is female is of Mother Below, that which is male is of Father Above, and what is below can easily be crushed by the powers above. Lightning rends earth, remember that!"

She looked at him, observed that his "power" had wilted, and nodded. "Where is your bolt, Lorak? And if you rend Sondahr, who then will speak to the spirits for the women of this camp? Who will share woman wisdom with them, deliver their babies, and call forth the pain and fever spirits from their little ones, if not Sondahr?"

Suddenly, from all around, birds flew skyward, shrieking, wheeling, and forming winged clouds that shadowed the dying day. And from beneath clumps of grass and burrows in the earth, rodents scurried and ran in frenzied circles.

Everyone was standing, staring, waiting for the earth to move. Far away to the east a terrible roaring rent the sky. No one could have said exactly where it had come from, except that it came from the forbidden land where the world ended, somewhere beyond the Corridor of Storms.

And then the earth did shake. It rolled once, like a single wave surging across the surface of a wind-tossed lake. It lifted them and dropped them, so gently that no one was knocked from his feet before the wind reached them, a wind that stank of sulfur and smoke and the innards of a distant mountain that rained fire. They could feel its heat. They could smell its breath. And they were afraid.

Even when the wind had passed and the world was still again, they stood in stunned silence, listening and waiting for the end of the world.

The world did not end. It grew quiet instead—so quiet that the lack of sound pressed against their ears. Where had the birds flown? Only moments before, the sky had been filled with them. Where had the little ground-dwelling animals scampered off to? It was as though they had disappeared. Even the ever-present wind, which moved across the sky as blood flowed in the veins of men—constantly until death— had stopped. They held their breath, lest breathing offend the spirits as they watched the sky and listened for the pulse of the earth, wondering if Mother Below and Father Above had died.

But clouds moved across the sky, and rain continued to fall. Black rain. Their eyes turned up. Their faces were darkened by it. Father Above made the rain. It was his tears—or his urine, depending upon the mood of the diviners of such things. It must be very bad for them if Father Above wept black tears or voided black urine.

Slowly, like a lioness coming up out of sleep, Mother Below stretched and moved . . . not enough to shake the earth, but enough to cause the skin of the permafrost to tremble, enough to cause the surface of the lake to stir. Then she was still again, and from deep within the flesh of the world, a sigh was heard, as though Mother Below were yawning and returning to sleep—for now.

No one moved. No one spoke or looked at anyone else. The lake sloshed back and forth, slopping softly against the dismembered carcasses of the mammoths that lay stripped to the bone within it. Creatures began to scuttle and make welcome little sounds from the grasses and shrubs, assuring the people that the order of their world slowly was returning.

But then Navahk leaned close to Lorak and, smiling at Sondahr, whispered slowly, almost sensually to the old man.

Lorak bristled like a spear-stung teratorn as he once again pointed a finger at Sondahr. This time he did not threaten; he accused. "Yes! Navahk is right! The mammoths have returned, but the signs and omens are bad! Mother Below and Father Above have spoken together! This is a rare thing! Sondahr has offended them by defying Lorak and taking sides against this man and with the people of Man Who Walks With Dogs. With Torka and Lion Killer—who has run from this killing site—Sondahr has called down the dark spirits of Creation in the form of trembling earth and stinking wind and clouds that bleed black rain."

A trip that had taken only a day now required twice that and more when the meat was being transported. And all the long way, the black rain fell, and Grek mumbled and ground his teeth until Wallah warned him to stop lest his molars split and he would be unable to chew that which he carried.

"The wanawut cried in the hills last night . . . close, very close. Did you hear it?"

"I heard," she replied in the resentful tone of one who does not appreciate having her memory jogged. They were bent nearly double under the weight of their pack frames, and between them they dragged a meat- and skin-laden sledge. Leaning into her own load, her head pressing outward against her brow band, Wallah stared straight ahead and plodded onward, her mouth set and scowling.

The sodden tundra made travel slow and difficult. At dusk, while a few solitary hunters went on ahead, others encamped again, although they were only a few miles from the main gathering. The rain continued. Mahnie was glad that Grek had chosen to rest, eat, and sleep before going on.

The magic men walked on, led by Navahk, with Stam, Zinkh, and several other hunters as protective spearmen. Sondahr had left long before. No one had seen her go. Mahnie thought about her as she watched the magic men disappear into the rainy distance. She felt better when she could see them no longer. She was tired; more so now that her pack frame was off and her body could relax.

Wallah and the other women were too tired to bother with fire making, and since none of their men wanted to wait for food, they quickly put up individual family shelters that shielded them from the direct fall of the misty rain. Clustered close beneath the support poles of bones, they ate raw strips of mammoth meat, wrapped in packets of intestine, which they had carried under their pack frames. The meat had been tenderized and "cooked" by the heat and motion of their bodies as they had moved and chafed against their heavy loads.

Mahnie did not like the taste of the strong and fibrous meat. She looked up at her parents. Neither of them seemed to be eating with much enjoyment.

"They say that the man Torka has brought much bison meat into the camp of the Great Gathering. When we return to the main camp, perhaps he might share some with us," said Grek thoughtfully.

Mahnie felt instantly revived. "Do you think he would? Could we ask him?"

From where she sat next to Wallah, Naiapi nastily mimicked Mahnie. " 'Do you think he would? Could we ask him?' " Naiapi sneered. "We know who you *really* want to ask! The youth! The one called Karana!"

Mahnie's face flamed. How she loathed Naiapi! How she regretted the day that Navahk had given the woman to Grek. She was mean and vindictive and made Mahnie feel unhappy in her own family circle.

"He looks so much like Navahk," Wallah remarked with distaste, ignoring her daughter's hurt and lovesick expression. "And they say that he has refused to hunt the mammoth. Also do they say that Man Who Walks With Dogs is not in favor with the elders of this camp. This woman has seen the other hunters look at Grek with admiration and respect. Let us keep it that way. The winter will be long. Perhaps it would be best, Mahnie, if your eyes found some other young man to look at."

"And what if she does not!" snapped Grek, seeing his daughter's horrified expression and coming to her defense. "Karana is strong! They call him Lion Killer in this camp. He wears the fangs of the great leaping cat around his neck. They say that he has hunted rhino, and he has saved the life of the supreme elder himself! Mahnie would be no daughter of mine if she did *not* look at such a youth with interest."

"He will not look at *her*." Naiapi smiled like a well-fed wolverine, practically licking her chops as she added with cloying sweetness and highly arching brows, "He would not even talk to her when she spoke to him. All the young girls talk about him. They say that he already has a woman, a magic woman from the band of Zinkh. Pomm. The old fat one he shouted at in front of everyone when he returned from the hunt. She boasts about him constantly, and he openly shames her by calling her old and coupling with Sondahr."

Wallah saw the heartsick look on Mahnie's face and grew angry with Naiapi. It did not take much for her to turn against the nastiness of the other woman. "Grek is right. Karana is strong. Karana is bold. It is good for a young man to have his first experience with older women before he at last chooses the woman to keep a fire. You should know, Naiapi: You have been trying to teach Navahk more than a few things ever since Supnah took you to be his woman. With memories of Sondahr as his teacher, it is no wonder that he has never desired you and has given you away to Grek, who does not want you either!"

"Navahk *does* want me! He *does* desire me! He has said so! Only for the sake of his powers has he put me aside and sacrificed himself by allowing me to come to Grek's miserable, grieving fire." Naiapi was so insulted and upset that she nearly snapped to her feet and brought the entire little lean-to down upon them, but Grek took hold of her wrist and yanked her down.

"Enough!" he warned sharply. "What has been done has been done. What will be will be. No one at this fire can truly know Navahk's heart. Naiapi has been put into the light of this man's fire, and as long as she is here, she had best remember her place, because this man still grieves over one whom Navahk killed unnecessarily. In the coming days of the long dark, if indeed this fire is miserable and wanting, Naiapi will be the first to leave it so others will not starve for her sake." He let the threat settle, then turned to Mahnie: "Your mother is right. A man must know many women in his life. If he is lucky, he will find one good woman to warm him in the night and keep his fire and cook his meat as—"

Naiapi hissed like a jealous, threatened goose, lowering her head, spitting at Mahnie with her eyes. "You would like to cook Karana's meat, eh?"

Her double meaning did not pass Grek, who nearly struck her. "Watch your tongue, Naiapi. This man might yet cut it from your mouth and make you eat it!"

Silence settled, along with the threat. The sounds of the

temporary night camp were all around them: man talk, woman chatter, yawns, sighs, snores. The sound of the mistlike rain falling ever so softly upon the hide tarpaulins of many small lean-tos.

Dusk had yielded to dark as Grek and his women had talked. The night was young, the rolling contours of the barren land silhouetted against it. Mahnie had no appetite. She gave the last of her mammoth meat to Wallah, who grimaced as she ate it. Mahnie smiled. She loved Wallah. She snuggled down between her and Grek, closing her eyes, pretending that Naiapi was not with them tonight, not a part of their family at all. Perhaps Navahk would take her back one day. She would ask the spirits for that. And for Karana.

She slept without dreams of spirits or handsome youths to disturb her.

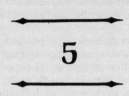

5

The rain stopped. Low clouds veneered the night. A day had passed since the last of the hunters had returned from the killing site. Despite the huge communal fire of bones and turf that had been built within the center of the great encampment, the air was cold and damp. Smells of roasting meat and fat steamed and dripped, but the enormous blaze reeked of the sulfurous ash that had fallen with the rain. Accompanied by a beating drum, Lorak, Sondahr, Navahk, and the rest of the magic men, all in ceremonial attire, came down from the Hill of Dreams to join the assembled people. The climax to a night of feasting was about to commence. The shouting stopped, and the storytelling was about to begin.

Sondahr, regal and beautiful—albeit very pale in her shaggy, mammoth-hide dress, feather robe, and circlet of down—took her place amid the magic men. Navahk, in the skin of the wanawut, stood behind her.

Sondahr stared straight ahead as the women of the various headmen hurried forward to bring bone plates piled high with meat and fat to her and the others of her rank. Her mouth was dry and her skin hot. She had been chilled by the rain during her invocations at the scene of the kill, and fasting had weakened her. She licked her hips. She could not remember ever having been made ill by an extended exposure to the weather, but she was a mammoth eater, and it had been too long since she had tasted of the flesh that gave her strength and power. The blood and meat that she tasted at the killing site had restored much of her flagging strength. Her vision was returning, along with a sharpened insight.

Lonit was not with the others who came forward; no doubt Torka had not allowed her to take part in the butchering, and what Lonit had not prepared with her own hands, she could not bring as an offering to the shamans. Sondahr hoped that there would be no trouble over it; yet she *knew* there would be. Lorak was too envious of Karana to overlook the slightest infraction on his part or on the part of his people.

Her attention was drawn to the generous offerings of two women who brought meat to her from the fire of a man they called Grek. She had noticed him on the hunt and remembered him instantly. A member of Navahk's band, he was past his prime, yet he was as strong and steady as he had been as a youth, and was an exceptionally good man with a spear.

The first woman came very close, as though she feared being overheard as she whispered a request that was not unusual. "For Mahnie, daughter of Grek, Wallah asks Sondahr to speak to the spirits that bring a woman's first blood, so that Wallah's child may become a woman in this good camp, with Sondahr to share the secrets of woman wisdom with her and oversee the ritual of first blood."

"Sondahr would be honored," she replied.

The other woman took the place of the first and spoke her request softly but forthrightly. "Across the world of men, Sondahr's name is known. Praise the spirits in the name of Naiapi, Magic Woman, so that she might come to share the meat and keep the fire of the man she would have."

The woman named Wallah looked at Naiapi with an expression of disgust. Sondahr accepted the offering but not as graciously as she had accepted the generously piled plates of others. There was something about Naiapi that put her on guard as the eyes of the woman strayed past her to Navahk, who stood at her back. Women always looked at Navahk, but she could not blame them, even though now, in the skin of the wanawut, he wore upon his back the physical manifestation of his inner ugliness for all to see.

She had told him that just before leaving the Hill of Dreams to join the others at the feast fire. He had come alone from the council house of bones to block her exit from her own hut. . . .

The moon had stood behind his back, cauled within the clouds, shadowing him, making the moment as cold as the eyes of the man who stood before her.

"We meet again, Sondahr," he had said. "Only this time it is Navahk who walks into *your* world. This time it is Navahk who will be Sondahr's teacher. Behold. Navahk is headman of his band, and shaman. Navahk will be supreme elder of the Great Gathering soon. Yes, perhaps Navahk will yet wear the feather of Sondahr, for while Sondahr wastes her time with one who is nothing—*nothing*—Navahk will make her see that he is all that she believed he could *never* be."

"No, Navahk," she had told him quietly. "You may lead your people, but you are not headman—not by right. A headman leads his band for the good of all, not only to serve his own needs. And you will never be a shaman. Never. You are a magic man, a man of the smokes, a trickster and a liar. A manipulator and, yes, a man who has taken the life of others. You are everything that I knew you *must* be. You will never wear the feather of Sondahr. . . ."

The memory was one she would like to forget, but the presence of the man was still a shadow over her. She could see his face reflected in the eyes of the woman who called herself Naiapi as she set the woman's offering with the others before her. When she straightened, she felt restless and irritable. The brew of willow leaves and mammoth's blood that she had made for herself earlier in the day had yet to lessen her fever. She wished that the night were over so she could retire to the privacy of her hut and rest, as any other woman would be able to do if she felt weak with illness. But she was not any other woman. She was Sondahr. And the night was young.

"Look at me when you speak to me, Naiapi, woman of Grek. Sondahr's power lies only in Seeing and in her knowledge of the ways of healing. Sondahr will praise the spirits in Naiapi's name, but in truth, Naiapi must know that they have already smiled upon her if Naiapi is the woman of Grek."

But Naiapi would not look at her. She ducked away and, with Wallah, joined the others at the women's side of her circle.

Sitting with the other women, with a restless Summer Moon on her lap, Lonit thought that the giving of meat to the magic men and to Sondahr was going to last forever. It seemed that nearly everyone had special requests for those men and the one woman who they believed could commune with the spirits on their behalf.

As the last man and woman returned to the main body of the assemblage, Lonit was shocked to see a thoroughly intoxicated Pomm, still in her flowing headdress of feathers, teetering on her feet. She brought no gift of meat to the magic woman as she paused before her and announced belligerently: "Sondahr is magic woman, but so, too, is Pomm of Zinkh's band magic woman. Pomm should not sit with other women. Pomm will take her place here. She is not like other women who come and go as their men say. Pomm will not be given away to old men by young boys! Pomm will sit here with magic-making people!" And this she did, huffing as she seated herself so abruptly that it appeared as though someone had knocked her down. Her legs folded under her, her arms crossed, and her enormous belly, hips, and bottom expanded around her. "Who will say no to Pomm?"

Lonit saw Lorak's face collapse about his nose in shock as he wheeled and pointed at Zinkh. "This woman is of your band?"

Zinkh wilted under his censorious glare. He nodded. Words refused to leave his mouth.

"She is a magic woman?" Lorak demanded an answer.

Pomm responded before Zinkh could find his tongue. "No woman in the world be such a wonderful magic woman as Pomm! If the sick woman of Torka be left to me, long ago would she be better, and the baby in belly would be in belly no more, but would be loud and noisy and making good, stinking baby messes in its swaddling moss!"

Lonit stared, aghast, knowing that the fat woman had been sipping at her berry brew again. As on the night of the *plaku*, it had loosened her tongue. But this time it had not weakened her self-confidence, and now Pomm's arrogance had put her life in jeopardy. All around her, eyes had gone suddenly wide. Mouths gaped. A murmuring went through the assembly. Lonit wished that Torka had not insisted that she attend the celebrations of the mammoth eaters. She felt frustrated by her inability to help Pomm, and worse than that, it was all she could do to keep her eyes averted from Navahk.

Navahk. There he stood, behind Sondahr, as though deliberately overshadowing her. Lonit felt sick. Even in the hideous skin of the wind spirit, he set her heart racing—a heart sworn to Torka, to the one man whom she would ever love

. . . but not the only man she desired. Shame filled her. All that she feared was coming true. If her eyes met Navahk's, if he came to her and held out his hand to her . . .

She looked at Pomm again, and her heart went out to the fat woman. To love and not to be loved in return—who else could understand the pain that Pomm was enduring if not Lonit? If only Karana had not insulted her! There he sat, glowering beside Torka. He must know that his thoughtless dismissal of her was the talk of the encampment. He had actually given her away to another man! In front of others he had made it clear that he was glad to be rid of her. Surely the youth had not meant to hurt her, only to put her in her place; he was too immature to understand that this was the one place that Pomm could never bear to be.

To Lonit's left, Wallah shook her head as a flustered Zinkh rose and stepped forward to stand directly before Lorak and admit that, among his people, Pomm *was* considered a magic woman.

"It has been so for a long time, yes. Pomm will be first always to tell everyone that she knows everything! Especially when she has been sucking at a bladder of her special berry juice . . . and this she does much too often these days—but it is very good juice, yes!" He tittered, cocking his head to one side in obsequious deference to the supreme elder. "Perhaps if Pomm she gives her bladder flask of juice to Lorak, he would drink and know that it has made a usually pretty good woman silly enough to assume that she might join those upon the Hill of Dreams and—"

Pomm cut him off with a wave of her hand and a snowstorm of goose feathers. "Silly? Bah! If one magic woman sits among men, so, too, will Pomm sit. Sondahr, you move over now and make room for Pomm. This woman will be afraid no more of you!"

Lonit could not believe her eyes as the fat woman forcibly unseated Sondahr with a wide sideways swing of her hip. Rather than be knocked off the piled skins that had been arranged for the magic men and magic woman, Sondahr rose just as Zinkh and a skinny, terribly flustered little elder hurried forward. Magic men stepped aside to make way for them. They gripped Pomm by her elbows, hoping to carry the offending fat woman away. They might as well have tried to heft a mammoth. Grunting, they staggered against the weight of her rigid form as she told them, through gritted

teeth, that if they did not put her down at once, later in the
night they would find their crotches as flat as a woman's.

It was Navahk who laughed and broke the stunned silence
of the onlookers. "Wait. Perhaps Lorak will agree when Navahk
says that any woman brave enough to seek so blatantly her
place among the shamans must indeed be worthy of her own
recommendation?"

From where Lonit sat, Pomm looked more surprised than
anyone else. She blinked and pursed her tiny lips, looking at
Navahk suspiciously out of bleary, drink-reddened little eyes.

He smiled back at her, so sweetly that she sagged, overwhelmed by his beauty.

Lorak's face was still a bundle of wrinkles. He made an
effort to focus on Navahk as that magic man's words brought a
smile to his time-ruined mouth and a terrible feeling of dread
to Lonit.

"Perhaps it *is* time that Sondahr was not the only woman to
dwell upon the Hill of Dreams," suggested Navahk. "Perhaps
this—Pomm is it?—*is* more worthy of a place among us.
Later, when Lorak has told us the mighty tales of his people,
when the feasting is over and the last song of the hunters has
been sung, we will see who should be magic woman among
the mammoth hunters: Sondahr, Pomm, or perhaps neither
of them?"

Torka observed as Lorak, no longer dressed in bird skins
but clad entirely in shaggy mammoth hide, lifted his drum
and struck it hard with the time-smoothed beater of thong-
wrapped tusk.

"Now is the time for story chanting! Now is the time to
sing the songs of mammoths and mammoth eaters! Now is the
time to remember the way of our people, to ask the angry
spirits to look past those who have offended them in this
camp, and to remember always those among us who have
praised them!" Again he struck the drum.

Torka flinched. He sat between Karana and Grek, cross-
legged with the other hunters on the men's side of the circle.
The incident with old Pomm had been unsettling. And now
the supreme elder stared at him, and it was as though the
strike of the tusk had been not against the drum but against
Torka. His head went up defensively.

Lorak's drum was very large, round, and flat. Its inflexible
frame of bone had been softened with water, then bent into a

hoop nearly as broad as Pomm's midsection. Held upright before the fire in the old man's hand, its tough skin was nearly transparent. Lorak was obviously feeling strong after hours of gorging himself upon mammoth meat within the council house. When he struck the drum again, he hit it so hard, it seemed that the blunted tip of the time-yellowed tusk would pierce the skin. It did not, but Lorak's eyes pierced Torka, then moved to where Karana sat beside him and pierced the young man as well.

The youth glowered as Lorak whirled away around the feast fire. "I told you that I should have stayed away," he hissed out of the side of his mouth to Torka.

Torka whispered back, "You were commanded to attend. If you had refused, there would have been trouble."

"There is trouble anyway, and there will be more before this night is done."

"Maybe. Maybe not."

"Hrrmph!" exhaled Karana with disgust, as though he and not Torka were the adult attempting to reason with a stubborn youth.

Lorak was dancing vigorously now, striking the beater against the drum skin repeatedly, rousing a loud, flat vibration that resonated across the minds of all of the magic men and the assembled people. They watched in anticipation as he danced on one foot, then on the other. He intended grace, but what he achieved was the hopping movements of an inebriated, flightless bird trying to leap over hot coals. The men of the assembly clapped their hands against their thighs and exhaled loud, guttural shouts that matched the cadence of the drum.

From where he sat, Torka had an excellent view of the section reserved for the magic men. In the hideous skin of the wanawut, Navahk was easy to recognize. Torka saw him smile. It was an illusory expression, a mere tightening of his jawline. Torka knew that there was contempt in Navahk's eyes for what he must surely perceive as the pathetic performance of the old man. Long ago, in the firelight of Supnah's fire, Torka had seen Navahk dance. He doubted if any magic man or shaman could equal that display.

The old man strutted before them, beating the drum, his voice as harsh and atonal as the "music" that he made. He chanted praises to the life spirits of the mammoths that had died in the bog. He told the story of how his people had become mammoth hunters, how they had been favored above all men by the forces of Creation when Father Above personally spoke to their forefathers and told them the secret route along which the mammoths traveled to their far and forbidden winter grazing grounds within the face of the rising sun. He told of the construction of the wall of bones in the time beyond beginning, when men first hunted mammoths together and joined at the Great Gathering along the migration route. He told how the herds walked across the world in the last of the days of light and vanished into the sun itself, disappearing over the edge of the world into a land where no men might follow.

Torka frowned. He had followed the game over the edge of the world and had returned to tell of it. Lorak knew this. Was the supreme elder hoping to instigate him by deliberately calling him a liar? Beside him Karana drew in a low breath as though about to speak. A well-placed elbow told him to keep silent as Lorak's tale continued.

The supreme elder looked at Torka as he spoke of how only fearful men chose to hunt bison and caribou, moose and elk, camel, yak, and musk oxen. Torka and Karana were not the only men to scowl as he turned to his own hunters and proclaimed that only the bravest men chose to hunt mammoths. The hunters who found themselves in this category—and they were the majority by far—nodded vigorously, pleased at the expense of others as Lorak sonorously chanted on about the many ways men found to kill the great mammoths: of bog traps and blinds and ravines staked with sharpened bones onto which panicked beasts were driven. He told how his people often drove the mammoths ahead of lightning-sparked fires. His face shone as he told of how the summer tundra sometimes burned at the command of Father Above and how the great tusked ones screamed and ran before the flames, only to be killed by men.

"Gifts are they to men from Father Above, from male to male, not from Mother Below to females, who feed only when their men say 'Eat!' " He hurled the words as an accusation against Sondahr, and nearly everyone gasped in surprise at his obvious hostility toward her as he beat his drum in her direction, waiting for her to rise to his baiting.

She refused to oblige him.

He made a rude noise and danced on. His chant began to ramble as he spoke of his youth. He named the names of hunters long dead. He spoke the names of the more memorable mammoths that he and they had killed in days so lost in the past that only he was left alive to remember; but all men knew the names.

He spoke until his tales were finished, and this was for a very long time. And all the while, the people ate, and the smell of roasting meat and dripping fat and sulfur filled the night, and the magic men from the various bands responded by adding to the litany of names of mammoths to be remembered: Big One Tusk. Charger Who Is Unafraid of Men. Bald Tail. Two-Calf Maker. Mud Roller. Bull Who Walks With Females. Curl Tooth.

Thunder Speaker.

Torka's head went up. Although he had not partaken of either meat, fat, or the rich drink made of blood and water and a mash of fermented berries, Lorak had demanded that he and his people join the others at the feast that the mammoth hunters had so long awaited. Torka had not demurred; this was their camp, and he and his people were guests. They would keep their own traditions; but they would not demean the customs of others.

He could see Lonit, Iana, and the children sitting together at the women's side of the fire circle, refusing meat but singing with the others when it was their turn to chant. Lonit looked strained. Summer Moon seemed to be having a wonderful time, clapping her little hands and captivated by Lorak's tales of adventure and daring. Even Iana seemed to be entertained and actually smiled, albeit wanly, when Wallah and her daughter, Mahnie, now and then spoke to her. The woman of Grek had brought a gift for Summer Moon, a little doll of buckskin. Torka could just see that it had real hair, probably snipped from the ends of Wallah's braids, a face of stone beads, and a dress pieced of remnant fur. Torka had not missed Lonit's pleased expression or the way his little girl had embraced the doll when Lonit allowed her to accept it. It sat on his daughter's plump little lap, as Demmi sat upon Iana's.

And now he was suddenly distracted by the moon-eyed way that Wallah's daughter was staring across the fire circle at Karana.

Karana spoke loudly, startling him, not in the tone of a boy but of a man who is not afraid to challenge other men.

"Thunder Speaker lives. No man in this camp has killed that mammoth. And any man who says otherwise is a liar!"

*   *   *

He felt the eyes of several youths upon him: Mano, Yanehva, Tlap, and Ank. He was no longer a child; he was a man who had been accepted by other men, who hunted with them and brought meat into their camp—not mammoth, perhaps, but meat nonetheless, and he had helped to save the life of Zinkh and also of the supreme elder. This gave him the right to speak his opinion to the others.

"The great one walks far away, in a land beyond the far mountains, within the Corridor of Storms. Karana knows this. Karana has dared to touch the twisted tusks that have killed lesser and greater men than he. Karana has breathed its breath into his nostrils; Karana has looked into its eyes and has not been afraid. In the firelight of this night, Karana listens to other men talk of their brave deeds and the mammoths they have killed, but what man—other than Torka and Karana—has dared to venture into that forbidden country to hunt in that game-rich land beneath the living shadow of Thunder Speaker, the great mammoth called Life Giver by the people of Man Who Walks With Dogs?"

He was suddenly and painfully aware of how cold the night wind had become. It was almost as cold as the resentful eyes of the people of the Great Gathering. From his position in the men's side of the circle, he could see across the fire to where Lonit, clearly distressed, sat with Grek's women. Mahnie, the young daughter of Grek and Wallah, looked as though she were about to cry. Beside her, Wallah's lower jaw hung open in surprise, and Naiapi's chin was turned so high that she stared at him as though from a height.

Beside him Torka reached to touch him imperatively with a warning hand. He ignored it; in truth, he barely felt it. His eyes had moved to Pomm and Sondahr and the magic men. Sondahr's exquisite face was immobile in the firelight, but from the arch of her brows he knew that she was troubled. Just to her right, in his hideous skin, Navahk was leering at him, smiling like a great, raptorial bird, its eyes wide and unblinking, its mouth twisted cruelly as it fixes its gaze upon small, land-bound prey that it is about to tear to pieces.

"No man has claimed to kill the great mammoth that you say is totem to you," Navahk pointed out as he slowly came through the ranks of the other magic men to stand beside Lorak, who was sagging with weariness. "We have sung praises to its power—the power of bone and muscle and tusk, and the power that brave men reach to own when they set themselves to kill the great mammoths. But where is the spear that Karana has reddened in their blood? Has Karana, who boasts of such mighty and fearless deeds in a far land that no man here has ever seen, sought such power?"

Lorak made a low grumble of approval and nodded his head in vigorous agreement. "Karana has *not* killed. Karana has put himself outside the circle of the people. And yet we allow him in. The wise Navahk has suggested to Lorak within the council house that Karana, with Sondahr and Torka and the People Who Walk With Dogs, has called down dark spirits in the form of birds that rise to cover the sun and trembling earth. Perhaps from the first, Man Who Walks With Dogs and his son, Karana, have brought bad luck into this camp?"

"Bad luck?" Karana nearly choked on his anger. "Until Torka came to the Great Gathering, you and your people were going hungry! And until Navahk came, you had nothing but good to say of Man Who Walks With Dogs and his magic spear hurlers, which he used to bring meat into your camp— even if you were too stubborn to eat it!"

"Bison is not meat! Mammoth is meat!" Lorak roared, shocked by the youth's willingness to challenge him in front of the entire assembly. "Navahk brought the mammoths to the camp of the mammoth eaters! Navahk! Spirit Killer! Man who walks not with dogs but in the skin of the wanawut! *Navahk* is magic man! *Navahk* will stand beside Lorak as his brother shaman! Torka is nothing in this camp. His magic is as weak as—that of a woman who claims to be a shaman but cannot bring a baby to be born out of its mother!"

"A baby!" Sondahr's voice was cool, but the fever in her eyes was not. "At the births of how many children has this woman assisted? Speak, women of the Great Gathering! You and you and, yes, you! Over how many years has Sondahr brought life out of your bellies!"

"Too many years." Pomm was not about to be left out of this chance at Sondahr. Her little eyes were on Karana, but her words were aimed at the magic woman like invisible little spears tipped with venom. "Sondahr grows old! Her magic grows weak, not like the magic of Pomm! Let this magic woman of Zinkh's band put her wisdom to work on the baby in the belly of Torka's woman, and out it will come quick, yes!"

"Torka's woman?" Navahk's query was as thick and sweet as the brew of half-clotted mammoth's blood that he had been drinking. He looked to Torka, then to Lonit. Hunger for her rearranged his features, and when she looked away as though in fear of him, his smile widened.

Karana knew what was in Navahk's heart and hated him.

Sondahr spoke. "It is Aliga who lies within the shelter of Torka, unable to be free of her child, not Lonit." Her brows came together. The corners of her mouth moved with disdain. "Where is your Sight, 'Shaman'? If it is as clear as Lorak seems to think it is, then show him! Show us all! Bring forth the woman Aliga into the fire circle. Let the great Navahk heal her and bring forth her child! Let him prove his magic and send away the bad luck that he believes Torka and Karana have brought with them to this camp!"

The sounds of the encampment were very loud now. Drum beating. Ferocious chanting. Aar began to salivate with the need to lunge and kill.

"Here, come, dogs. Stam and Het, we bring you meat. Yes, that is good. Come, eat! All of you! You, too, Brother Dog—Aar. Is that not what the whelp Karana calls you?" It was the one called Stam who cajoled. "Come, eat from the hand of Stam and die. It is not a good thing for dogs to live in the camps of men, and, once again, Navahk has need of the guts and liver and heart of one of you."

Not one of the pups barked. Stam tossed the meat, and they fell upon it. All except Aar. He was standing now, head out, tail tucked, ears back. The hair on his back and shoulders was raised. He could not understand the words of the man, but instinct told him that the meat was bad and that his pups would die if they ate it.

"Beware of the big dog, Stam. I don't like the look in his eyes."

Het was gripping his spear nervously as Stam crouched, holding a thick, gristly hunk of raw meat to Aar. "What's the matter, Het? You still believe the dogs are magic?"

"They are not like other dogs."

Stam snorted derisively. "They're dogs, all right—just dogs, no more, no less. And soon they'll all be dead dogs. Look at them gorging themselves on the meat. Stupid beasts. When they start yelping, drive your spear as fast and true as you can. We don't want to damage the pelts. Navahk said we could have them when the excitement dies down. Your women will like that. They're prime pelts. And if anyone comes near, remember the dogs attacked us."

"I don't like it. . . ."

"You will when Navahk rewards you with his spirit powers. You'll hunt as never before."

"But if Man Who Walks With Dogs finds out that Navahk has sent us here to—"

"Stop being such an old woman. After tonight no one will listen to him. If I know Navahk, Torka will soon be as dead as his dogs!"

The words of the men were low, like insects droning on a warm, muggy summer day. The dog scented the apprehension of Het and perceived the threat in Stam as the man balanced himself on his heels and gestured the dog forward with his free hand. "Look at all of your fine, big children, Aar. You have been busy since we last camped together. Have you missed the pup I took from you then? No matter. Soon you will have no pups at all. Come. Eat from the hand of Stam, and then you will never have to eat again."

Somehow Aar understood the intent of the man. He growled and showed his teeth, warning the man back. But Stam kept smirking, reaching out with the meat, flapping it, waving it in Aar's face.

"Come . . ."

To his shock and terror, Aar obliged him. The great dog leaped forward with such force that the stake to which he was tethered tore loose from the permafrost as he hurled himself straight up and out, knocking the man completely off balance. With one bold, tearing thrust, Aar turned his head sideways and ripped out Stam's throat . . . but never saw the brutal sideward swing of Het's spear that sent him hurtling into oblivion.

Het was trembling. Stam was dead. He was still twitching, but he was dead. How could he be otherwise? The man lay in a pool of so much blood that, had it not been for the hideous, gaping wound where his throat had been, anyone looking at him might have assumed that he had drowned in his own life fluids.

Het was shaking violently now as the dogs started to show signs of pain—all except the big dog that Stam had called

Aar. It lay so still that Het was certain that his blow had killed it. He was glad for that. Stam had been wrong about it. Only a dog with magical powers could have pulled free of its stake and killed a man so effortlessly—as Het now killed the others, one by one. The kills were easy, although the dogs made more noise than he would have preferred. They cowered or lunged at him, according to their natures, but the stakes that held their tethers kept them from escaping his intentions for them. His spearhead bit deep again and again, and soon fourteen dogs lay dead and silent, and he was thinking that now he would have all of the pelts for himself. Prime pelts. His women would be pleased.

He stood a moment, drawing his splaying knife, walking from one dog to another, cutting the tethers that had held them fast, so that those who discovered the animals would believe that he had been forced to kill them when they had broken loose and attacked him.

The job done, he thought about which dog he would gut. The big dog, he thought, the one called Aar. It would have the largest heart, with the most power in it, and Navahk had said that he needed a large organ, the larger the better. But as Het looked at the motionless form of Aar, he hesitated. The dog was dead, but it still frightened him; he did not have the courage to disturb its spirit, else it come back to haunt him. So he turned to the largest of the other dogs, a big male that resembled its sire. He drew a length of thong and an oiled intestine from where he had folded them over his belt. He knelt and set to his purpose, working quickly to slit the underside of the dog from throat to crotch, to open the muscle tissue just below the rib cavity, to reach into the animal's breast to free the heart and—

A great, snarling weight struck him from behind. He was too stunned to cry out. In the darkness, with the stench of hot blood in his nostrils, Het knew that it was the magic dog Aar that had leaped upon him.

But the dog, weakened and disoriented by his earlier blow to its head, tore into his shoulder, not his neck. Fighting for his life, Het lunged forward with Aar riding his back. In desperation he grasped for his spear, which lay just out of reach, next to the dog he had been butchering. Gasping, sobbing, he stretched his body out . . . out . . . feeling the teeth of the dog tearing flesh. With all of his strength, Het's fingertips grasped the butt end of the spear and levered it toward him. It took every ounce of his strength and will to twist his body hard to the right, rolling the dog off, allowing him to jam the butt end of the spear into the animal's side. He heard it woof with pain as it went down. Or was that his own exhalation of pain? He was not sure; he would never be sure. He only knew that the dog lay unmoving in the dark. The magic dog, the dog that would not die . . . but it was dead now, its eyes glazing and its tongue lolling and blood darkening the gray fur at the back of its ear.

The sounds of the feast fire reached him, moved him to action. Fighting against pain, he rose and tore the heart from the other animal.

Navahk was waiting.

The dogs had been making great commotion as, at Navahk's command, a small group of women hurried to Torka's pit hut to fetch the woman Aliga. No one was concerned—the dogs often barked and made a nuisance of themselves over trespassing rodents that wandered into the encampment. But Torka's pit hut was far from the central fire, and the noise of the increasingly inebriated celebrants was so loud that the noise of the dogs was barely noticeable.

Aliga's voice was very weak. "Why do you take me from my sleep?"

Lonit felt great concern for her and a terrible trepidation. What if Navahk actually could heal her and bring her baby forth after Sondahr had failed? That would be good for Aliga, but not good for Sondahr or anyone else of Torka's band, for if Navahk eclipsed the legendary Sondahr, he would hold great power.

"I am not feeling at all well today," she protested. She had been prostrate all day and had barely opened her eyes when the women had hefted her in her sleeping skins and carried her out into the night. The dogs were all quiet now. "Oh, it is night. There is a fire. A feast fire? What do you celebrate?"

"Surely you must remember, Aliga," Lonit reminded gently. "I have told you. The men have hunted mammoths, and they celebrate the kill! Sondahr will be strong now. She has eaten the flesh of the animal that gives her great healing powers. Think of it! Soon you will be well!"

The women who had accompanied Lonit to Torka's hut to bring Aliga into the gathering exchanged knowing looks. They walked on either side of the woman's reclined form, supporting her weight by holding tight the broad bison-skin mattress upon which she had taken what seemed to be permanent residence.

"Sondahr has challenged Navahk to heal you," informed Wallah.

Oga sighed and patted Aliga upon the shoulder. "Imagine it! Most magic men will not consent to touch a woman. But Navahk will touch Aliga and make chants and magic and dances! Oh, I would almost be willing to be sick if I could have that man tend me!"

"*Navahk*? Has asked to heal *me*?" Aliga's eyes blinked and actually cleared. "Then I am healed already, for his are the greatest powers of all!"

"He is only a man," Lonit said quietly.

"He is a magic man!" snapped Oga.

"Since he has walked within the skin of the wanawut, he has great powers," said Wallah, frowning meditatively, as though trying to decide if she should say more.

"He is the most beautiful man in all the world," sighed Aliga euphorically, too weary to make any attempt to hide her infatuation. "If Navahk says that he can heal me, then it will be so. I know it. I feel it."

It was growing very cold as Aliga was placed on a raised dais of piled furs laid over the grinding teeth of mammoths. Women added fresh kindling to the ceremonial fire: dried mosses and grasses, lichens and sods cut and cherished until they were crisp and ripe for burning, bones gleaned from meals and scraped free of marrow, dung gathered upon the open tundra as the people followed the herd animals from hunting camp to hunting camp, and stones to absorb the heat of the fire and radiate it back to the people long after the flames had died.

But now the flames leaped high.

Navahk stood at the periphery of the circle, head high, arms folded across his chest, the arms of the wanawut moving slightly in the rising wind as though the skin of the beast still possessed a life of its own. From the shadows behind him a haggard, blood-spattered Het came close, making certain no one saw him. He whispered something. Navahk's head rose a little higher; other than this he did not move. A small, intestine-wrapped package was passed from the hunter to the magic man, then Het slipped back into the shadows as though he had never been there at all.

For Torka it was like being trapped within a nightmare that propelled him backward into time, as if three years had not passed and he was back within Supnah's band again, before the feast fire, watching Navahk dance.

The only things that were different were the skin that the magic man wore upon his back, the taloned necklace of feathers that had once been Supnah's, and the desiccated head balanced atop his own as he whirled and postured in ever-diminishing circles around the pallet of the sick woman.

"In the beginning, when the land was one land, when the People were one people . . ."

The words and the cadence were the same, flowing into the night, into the cold, growing wind that had trespassed through the wall of bones to lick the perimeters of the communal fire.

"Before Father Above made the darkness that ate the sun, before Mother Below gave birth to the ice spirits that grew to cover the mountains, the wanawut was born to hunt the children of First Man and First Woman—to follow them as they followed the great herds, to feed upon the People even as the People fed upon the meat and blood of mammoth and caribou and bison. For this alone was wanawut born: to teach the People the meaning of the word *fear*." He stopped and flung up his arms, and with the arms of the beast laced to his own sleeves, it seemed as though two pairs of hands rose in adoration of the night. "But I, Navahk, have eaten *its* heart and drunk of *its* blood. I, Navahk, have *killed* the wanawut! Behold . . . I wear its skin and know fear of no man, of no spirit, and so I call upon Father Above and Mother Below to witness this dance, to hear the song of Spirit Killer, who alone is worthy to demand that they bring forth the child of the woman known as Aliga!"

Torka sat straight and unmoving in his black-maned, tawny outercoat of lion skin, his face impassive, his heart pounding. The man *was* a magic man. The *man* was an enchanter. The people sat spellbound around him as he danced close to the flames, gesturing, circling, and the flames leaping high, as though at his command.

Torka looked at the magic woman. She sat unmoving, reserved, and calm, her face devoid of expression, her hands folded gracefully in her lap. His eyes moved to Karana. He was sitting rigidly, as though carved of stone. Only his eyes moved, watching, hating, resenting, seeing ugliness where others saw only beauty.

The firelight colored Navahk red and black as he danced in the skin of the wanawut. A man of two dimensions . . . or not a man at all? Perhaps something in between: half human and half animal, half beauty and half ugliness, half light, half shadow . . .

Torka leaned forward. The man had *become* the wanawut by embodying the fears of men, of all that was wild and threatening and savage in the world. It was as though the wanawut itself stood before them—fanged, powerful, the undisputed master of the night. He danced as gracefully as a hawk, with wings spread wide upon the wind, soaring, then plunging, mimicking the piercing, stabbing moment of a kill. He sang the high, wild, wordless song of wolves and wild dogs, of stallions driving mares before them upon the vast, open grasslands of the summer tundra. He raced, he reared, he vaulted. Then he hunched into a bestial crouch, rocked on his heels and wailed and hissed, then leaped and prowled, no longer flesh but spirit, no longer man but beast. He was the thing whose skin he wore. He was the wanawut. He was fear.

Torka was enthralled but not beguiled as Navahk paused before him and raised the skin-beribboned staff of office with which he had been dancing. It, too, was a thing out of memory, and as he had done on that night so long ago in Supnah's camp, Navahk raised the fire-hardened thigh bone of a camel atop which was affixed the horned, oiled skull of an antelope. He shook the staff viciously, and all the claws and talons and beaks sewn onto the streaming ribbons of skin rattled and clicked.

"Does Torka not fear the wanawut now that he sees its spirit dancing within the skin of Navahk?"

Torka did not move. The question, like the dance and the song and the chanting, was of the past, as was his reply. "Torka is wary of all things he does not understand."

The magic man glared at him rapaciously. "Not wary enough." He sighed the words as, beneath the fanged skull of the wanawut, he smiled, showing his white, serrated teeth as an animal does when it warns another that it is ready to attack. Then, suddenly, he leaped straight into the air and turned, dancing again, chanting again, this time without words. The sounds he made were the wanawut's. The hands of the beast dangled over his own hands. He circled the fire once, twice. On the third time he stopped before Aliga's pallet, swooping down upon her with arms outstretched.

She screamed.

He straightened, threw back his arms, holding up a clotted mass of fatty, bloody tissue for all to see.

A startled gasp of incredulity rose from the mouths of everyone at the assembly except Torka, Karana, and Sondahr. Several little children began to cry. Summer Moon buried her head in Lonit's lap.

In a feigned trance, Navahk whirled and wheeled away from the staring Aliga, arms still upright, tissue dripping blood. "Behold the spirit of the woman Aliga's pain!"

On her pallet Aliga wept with joy and covered her face with her hands. "I am healed!" she cried. "I am well and without pain at last! Soon my baby will be born and—"

"No!" Navahk screamed the word. Again he leaped straight into the air, twisting violently so that when he landed, he stood on both feet, poised before a gaping, awestruck Lorak, who sat with the other equally hang-jawed magic men.

Never had any of them seen a performance to equal the magnificent display of sorcery that Navahk, Spirit Killer, had just completed. From beneath the skull of the beast, his magnificent face shone with sweat. His eyes pierced them until they were forced to turn away lest he suck the life spirits from their bodies and draw what little power they had into himself.

His smile broadened. His teeth glistened. "No baby will come forth out of that woman . . . not as long as Torka is allowed to live in this camp . . . not as long as the youth Karana continues to offend the spirits." A laugh bubbled at the back of his throat. He held it captive, then threw back his head and howled like a beast at the gathering storm clouds.

From beyond the wall of bones, from somewhere within the nearby grass-choked lakeshore, a terrible howl answered that of the magic man. It was like the high shriek of a woman in pain; and yet no woman had ever made a cry like that, for it was the cry of a beast . . . the cry of a wanawut.

For an instant Navahk stiffened. Torka felt Karana's hand reach to close upon his forearm. The youth had seen it too: The magic man was afraid.

But only for an instant. He immediately threw back his arms again. "Do you hear? The wanawut answers the call of the man! It is close! It comes at my command! It is hungry now. It feeds from my hand. It will feed upon the people of this camp, one by one, unless Torka and Karana leave this camp—alone."

"No!" Now it was Sondahr who nearly screamed the word. She was on her feet, shadowing a bewildered Pomm. "Your guile and trickery have not fooled this woman!"

"Guile? Trickery?" He hurled the bloodied mass of flesh at her feet. "Here is the substance of my claims! Where is yours, woman? I have driven the pain of Aliga out of her body and into my own hands! What have you done for her? What have you done for anyone in this camp except to keep the mammoths away? It is Sondahr who has practiced guile and trickery, welcoming within your bed skins a youth who has been bad luck in every camp that has been foolish enough to take him in!"

Torka rose. The wind was cold, but somehow the night was hot. The light that burns behind a man's eyes when death is near was blinding him. He started to speak, but again, from beyond the wall of bones, the cry of the wanawut pierced the night. Beside him Karana was on his feet, and from where he stood before the other magic men, Navahk turned and malevolently pointed with his skull-topped staff.

"If the skies are to clear and the mammoths are to continue to come to the people of the Great Gathering for future generations, Karana and Torka must go from this camp. If they will not go, they must be driven. If they will not be driven, they must be killed. The wanawut cries for their flesh. Across the long distances it has followed the people of Navahk because it has known that this man would lead it to them."

Torka was shaking with suppressed rage. His right hand flexed, longing for a spear. "By the forces of Creation, Navahk, I will not stand here and listen to this!"

"No, you will not! Het. Mond. Stam. Take him!"

Torka felt shadows moving at his back and turned, eyeing the men away with deadly intent.

"Stam is dead. He cannot answer the summons of Navahk!" Het's proclamation stunned the assembly as he came forward through the shadows where he had been skulking, parting his way through the throng, his garments torn and bloodied as he waded through the men's side of the circle to stand beside Navahk. "Because of Torka and Karana, Stam's throat has been torn by an unprovoked attack! The dog that usually walks at the side of Lion Killer tore out his throat. I, Het, could not save Stam, but bravely did this man kill the dogs when they broke loose from their tethers to attack me."

"Liar!" The accusation was hurled across the night at Stam by Karana.

Torka was as stunned as the youth. The dogs dead? All of them? Aar too? Surely it could not be!

Het glanced nervously at Navahk, was bolstered by an encouraging smile from the magic man, then gulped audibly before saying in a voice that sounded well rehearsed, "Has Navahk not said that it is not good for men and beasts to walk together? Has Navahk not said that it is not good for Man Who Walks With Dogs and Lion Killer to share this camp? Yes! It was their presence here that has kept the mammoths away from this camp. And this night Stam is dead because the spirits frown on all men who walk within the shadow of Man Who Walks With Dogs!"

Torka's rage broke loose within him. "I'll give you a shadow to walk within!" He would have gone for the man's throat, but he was suddenly grabbed from behind by Mond and another man.

"Let him go!" Karana leaped to his defense, only to find his own arms pinioned behind his back. He fought, twisting and snarling at Navahk and glaring at Het with loathing. "That skinny little vole could not have killed my brothers!"

"Brothers?" Navahk turned his question with sweet malevolence. "You see? Out of the boy's own mouth he admits that he runs with dogs—with wild beasts—and names them kindred. How can Lorak have allowed such men as these to take shelter among the people of this Great Gathering? Navahk says now to Lorak that he must let beasts live with beasts, not with men! Send Karana and Torka from this camp! Their presence among us offends the spirits. Father Above and Mother Below will not smile upon this encampment as long as such violators of tradition are allowed to live within it!"

Torka strained against those who held him as, at the women's side of the circle, Lonit snapped to her feet. Never had she looked so bold and beautiful and recklessly defiant. "Navahk is a liar! It is he who wants Torka and Karana out of this camp, not the spirits! He has wanted them dead before. He—"

"Silence, woman!" Navahk's command cut the night like a blade.

"This woman will *not* be silent! This woman will—"

Her words were cut short as Oga took a step forward and slapped her so hard that she nearly fell. All of Oga's long but ill-contained jealousy of Lonit flared to disfigure her face with hatred. "No woman speaks so to a magic man! Many a woman in this camp will be glad to see Lonit go with Torka and Karana! This camp will be well rid of the People Who Walk With Dogs!"

Torka's anger was blinding as, to no avail, he twisted violently to be free of those who held him. A knee drove hard into his groin as, beside him, Karana bucked and lunged helplessly against those who bent his arms up across his back.

"And we will be glad to be free of the fools who dwell within this camp!" retorted the youth.

Sondahr's voice was low with warning as she said, "Beware of what you do in the name of the forces of Creation, Navahk. Father Above and Mother Below may be listening and may not approve of what you do in their name."

Torka saw Navahk's eyes narrow as they fixed her with cold and venomous resentment. Then, slowly, the magic man's gaze moved from Sondahr to Lonit and then to Torka. His smile changed, broadened, to become thoughtful and so full of virulent malice that Torka recoiled, somehow knowing what his words would be.

Navahk's head swung in slow negation. "I am Navahk, Spirit Killer. I walk in the skin of the wanawut, and I bring forth the living flesh of pain from those who believe in me. In my dream times I leave my body to walk the wind from this world of men and into the world of spirits. Mother Below and Father Above speak through my mouth, and so I, Navahk, speak without fear in their name: Torka and Karana must go from the Great Gathering. But the woman of Torka, she is for Navahk! Since time beyond beginning her spirit has belonged to this man. Torka has stolen her from me."

Torka's anger was so great that he could not speak. He hurled himself at Navahk with such force that he broke the hold of those who tried to keep him in his place. He was across the center of the great circle, with several men at his back, and he would have been at the magic man's throat had they not tackled him and brought him down, flailing into the fire. He rolled savagely to be free of the flames and the heat,

kicking out at those who grappled with him until the butt end
of a spear found the side of his brow and the world exploded
into light and pain and he fell alone into darkness.

"Torka!" Lonit shrieked the name of her beloved and,
hefting little Summer Moon in her arms, ran toward her
man, telling Iana to follow with the baby. Lorak had begun to
beat upon his drum again, ferociously. She looked toward the
old shaman but could not see him or Sondahr or any of the
magic men. A crowd of women had gathered around her,
shouting, punching, and shoving with unrestrained hostility
as she tried to sweep past them. Summer Moon began to
scream in terror. Confusion and rage swarmed within Lonit
as she tried to understand what she had done to make them
all so angry. Only moments ago most would have smiled at
her, and many of them would have named her friend.

But that was before Navahk had claimed her for himself.
Navahk! So many of them wanted him. Even in the hideous
skin of the wanawut, he was more handsome than she remembered, but there was no doubt in her mind that she hated
him now. Men were chanting, making new sounds inspired
by Navahk's exhortations to drive Torka and Karana from the
encampment. No matter what he said, she would *not* stay
with him. Just let him try to stop her from going with Torka!

But many men surrounded Torka and Karana, and she
could not see them. Panic filled her. Someone had carried
Aliga off into the crowd, and she could not see Iana or
Demmi when she turned back to see if they were following.

Oga was behind her, with several others whose faces were
contorted with grim little smiles and leers of hatred. Suddenly, accosted by a sharp, painful push to her shoulder, she
was stopped in her tracks by Naiapi.

The woman's face was engorged with jealous loathing.
"Navahk has told me to escort you to his hut on the Hill of
Dreams."

"You go!" Lonit hissed hotly, her shoulder stinging from
contact with the heel of the woman's hand. "You've always
wanted him, even when Supnah was alive!"

Naiapi's features tightened, and her head went up. Then,
as Oga pushed Lonit, distracting her so that she could not
duck away in time, Naiapi's hand came out and slapped Lonit
hard across the face. "If I had my way, there would not be
enough left of you for *any* man to desire!"

Lonit reeled, staggered by the blow. Her face stung and her ears rang as several women maliciously echoed Naiapi's sentiment. Several more shoved her from behind. She nearly fell. Summer Moon was gasping and wailing hysterically in her arms as blood spurted from her nose and ran warmly in her mouth.

Then, to one side, the woman Wallah spoke up for her. "Leave her alone! Can't you see you're terrifying her child?"

Lonit would have thanked her, but Wallah was shouted down and shoved away, with her frightened little daughter, Mahnie, holding onto her arm.

"What do we care for the child of Man Who Walks With Dogs? No doubt she's as unlucky as her parents. We ought to do ourselves a favor and smash her little head in!" snapped Oga, grabbing for the little one, who shrieked and wrapped her arms about Lonit's neck.

Lonit screamed in outrage as her child was ripped from her arms by Oga and Naiapi. She managed to land a solid kick into Oga's belly and to rake her fingernails deeply into Naiapi's cheeks. She knew that she drew blood. The woman screamed in anger, and both Naiapi and Oga retaliated by kicking Lonit so hard across the shins that she nearly fainted. She did not see an enraged and protective Wallah pounce upon Oga and wrest the little girl from her grasping arms, nor did she hear Mahnie cry out with despair as several women backhanded Wallah out of the way and descended upon Lonit to pummel her with blows, knock her down, and kick her brutally.

Lonit curled into a protective tuck, wrapping her arms about her head, wondering why Sondahr did not come to help her. She wanted to scream curses at those who were abusing her, but she could barely breathe. The booted toes of one woman after another found her side and legs and arms.

"Stop! He'll be angry if we kill her." It was Oga's voice, pinched with frustration. "Don't, Naiapi. If you ruin her face, he'll set the forces of Creation upon us to blight us all!"

The kicking stopped.

Lonit felt herself being lifted and carried. She heard Wallah imperatively calling for Mahnie above the din of the encampment.

And then she felt and heard nothing.

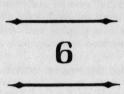

6

Torka awoke in a haze, surrounded by a whirlwind of shouting, angry men who were dragging him across the tundra holding torches high to light their way.

Stunned and disoriented, he did not know where he was. Then he heard Karana curse and, through a pounding headache, saw the youth being driven forward, his brow bloodied, his lips drawn back, his arms bound behind his back.

"What—?" He paused; his mouth hurt so badly that he reached to touch his lips, only to find that his own hands were tethered at the wrist behind his back. He explored his mouth with his tongue. His lower lip was split and swollen. His mouth tasted of blood.

Someone pushed him forward hard. He nearly fell, but strong hands hefted him from behind and shoved him on. When he hesitated, a hand closed on his right wrist and jerked his arms up across his back, half breaking his right arm.

He gasped and blundered on. Although the torches lighted the way, he could not see where they were headed; too many men crowded ahead of him and on all sides, moving at a rapid pace. His breath came hard from bruised lungs. He looked up, his vision clearing. Above him the torches bobbed up and down with the movements of the men. Fashioned in a hurry from the long leg bones of bison, they were sloppily packed wads of oil-soaked grass and moss bound to the tips of the femurs with thong. They stank, and their light was hot and tremulous. Fragments of burning grass broke off in the wind and rained cinders down upon those who carried them and upon Torka, burning his skin where his loosened hair did not cover his scalp and battered face. When he shook them away, pain broke loose behind his eyes, so intense that it nearly dropped him.

Still dazed, in confusion and pain, he felt himself supported and pummeled and heard himself mocked as he caught a glimpse of Zinkh's face in the firelit crowd to his left. The little man looked lost. Simu and Cheanah were at Zinkh's back. Torka looked at them imploringly for answers, for help. They both looked back, grim and angry—at him or at his tormentors, he could not tell, but neither man moved to aid him. They slowed their steps and fell back into the crowd. In a moment Torka could not see them anymore. He looked back, straining to be free of those who held him, panic and anger rising in him as he recalled the feast fire—Navahk's dance, and his words.

The wanawut will feed upon the people of this camp unless Torka and Karana leave—alone. The woman of Torka, she is for Navahk!

"Lonit!" he screamed. The thought of her and his children with Navahk infuriated him. He fought madly against those who held him. Bending, bucking, oblivious to his pain, he used his head and shoulders to gouge his way to freedom, ramming forward, kicking sideways at shins and knees, which buckled under his onslaught. He heard the startled grunts of pain from those who stood in the way of his fury until the butt end of a spear jabbed him so hard in the spine that he stumbled, and his head swimming, he cried out in agony and rage as he was caught beneath the armpits by two men who closed ranks on either side of him.

"There's no use fighting," sneered one, striking Torka across the face. "You will pay for what your dogs have done. The magic man was right about you and your son. Bringers of bad luck, that's what you are. We should have known it from the start!"

The man was not well-known to Torka; he could not recall his name or his band. Nevertheless he was one of those who had left the encampment to hunt bison with him. He was a man who had shared meat and danger with him, and one whom Torka had assumed to be a friend.

Beside him Karana was also unsuccessfully twisting violently to be free of the two who held him. The youth was sobbing, but not with despair. He was half choking upon his own rage. "The dogs have done nothing but tear out the throat of Stam. He must have fed them poisoned meat! I saw the dogs in the torchlight as they dragged us out of the encampment. All bloated and dead. At least one of them gutted. And Aar, our brother, with them! Navahk must have—" One of the two who held him drove a fist hard into his face. His head went limp for a moment, then rose as he was carried forward, his mouth swelling, his nose gushing blood.

Anger struck Torka harder than the butt of the spear had done. He could not help Karana. He could not help Lonit or himself. He felt as though he were caught in the turbulent rapids of a river at spring flood. Aar dead? It could not be. Yet it *must* be, or Karana would not have said it. The thought of the bold, brave dog lying lifeless was numbing. His step lagged. His head was pounding again mercilessly. He was certain that he was going to be sick.

The butt of the spear found the small of his back again.

"Hurry on. We don't want to be out of the encampment once the torches have all been burned out!"

Again someone clouted him from behind, and for a span of time that could have been moments or hours, he ceased to exist except in his dreams . . . dreams of fire and pain and blood.

The dog whined softly. The rest were still—one gutted, the others stiffening in the twisted, unnatural positions created by terrible paroxysms of pain. All had been pierced at least once by a spear.

Mahnie crept from dog to dog in the freezing dark. She touched each animal on the side, pressing for the feeblest tremor of heartbeat. There were none, except within the great dog Aar.

Mahnie crouched before him. He did not look great now. He alone among the dogs had not been pierced. She could find no wound except a bloody gash below his right ear, where someone had struck what he had intended to be a killing blow. But the blow had struck low, hard enough to open his flesh, but stunning instead of killing. The dog looked dazed, vulnerable, confused, and in pain . . . as Karana and Torka had looked after they had been beaten and carried from the encampment and into the night.

Her heart was pounding. She felt weak with fear for them and yet very angry—angry enough to have defied Wallah by refusing to help the other women carry Lonit to Navahk's hut or to go with her mother when Pomm had called several women to Sondahr's shelter upon the Hill of Dreams when the magic woman had suddenly taken ill. Instead Mahnie had followed Grek and the other men and youths. Hiding within the shadows, she had watched them sweep Torka and Karana along with them in a great avalanche of shouting and cursing and—yes, laughter! Some of them had actually laughed! Only hours ago they had numbered themselves among the friends of Torka and Karana. Now they were like wolves and wild dogs, turning on those among them who were chosen by the master of the pack to be expelled. She was heartsick as she recalled how the men had turned on Torka and Karana when Navahk had declared what their fate must be.

As they had channeled through the wall of bones, Grek had seen her and warned her back. She had no choice but to obey as, sobbing over Karana's fate—a fate that forever ended her dream of someday being his woman—she had hurried back to the dogs, hoping against hope that some might still be alive. They were Karana's brothers, these dogs! Especially the big animal with the black fur around its pale blue eyes, making it seem as though he were wearing a mask. How she had loved watching Karana and Torka hunt with their dogs in the days when they had traveled with her band. The animals came at their command and worked with them to drive the game as though they did indeed possess the spirits of men instead of beasts.

Kneeling beside the prone, erratically breathing form of Aar, Mahnie sighed restlessly, then rose to examine the tethers. All had been cut. Sister Dog had dragged herself to die by her mate. A question formed; she pursued it. Bending over the dog that had been gutted, she found the answer and caught her breath. The heart was missing! Might a heart not have been the bloody mass of tissue that Navahk had thrown at Sondahr's feet, declaring that it was the flesh of the pain he had drawn from the woman Aliga? And years ago, when Navahk had drawn the pain from the poor old woman Hetchem, was a pup of the great dog and its mate not missing soon after? Mahnie blanched, realizing that all the times in the intervening years when Navahk had drawn the visible substance of pain from those who were ill, it was always after a hunt, when there was fresh gut and blood meat at hand.

Yes! And so it was tonight! A trick, not magic! A trick worked at Navahk's command by Stam and Het at the expense of Karana's dogs! Kill the dogs by poison. Gut one.

*Take the heart to Navahk. Spear the rest and claim that they
attacked viciously and without provocation. Then lay the
blame on Torka to affirm Navahk's claims against him. But
the dogs had turned, Stam was killed, and in the end Navahk's
lies against Torka and Karana were better served by Stam's
death than by his life!*

She felt sick. Who would believe her?

Sondahr. Yes. The magic woman might listen. She had
accused Navahk of practicing guile and deception. But she had
taken ill so suddenly, and Naiapi was among the women who
were with her on the Hill of Dreams. Mahnie had seen
Naiapi's treatment of Lonit and the way she looked at Navahk
with longing. Mahnie would not ask Sondahr questions about
Stam and Het before Naiapi, lest she use them against her
with Navahk.

The dog stirred beneath her hand, whined softly, and lifted
his head to lick her fingers as though in gratitude for her
solicitude. "Stam should not have come hunting you, Brother
Dog. Karana said that you were not like other animals. Stam
should have listened. He has killed your band, but he has not
killed you. Now he is dead. Tomorrow his body will be put
out to look upon the sky forever, and Mahnie is glad."

Within the hut of Sondahr, Wallah crumbled dried willow
leaves between her palms. She let them sift through her
fingers into the waiting cup that she held steady between her
knees. The cup belonged to the magic woman and was made
of the hollowed tip of a mammoth tusk. The little fragments
of faded leaves filtered down through a steaming brew of
watered mammoth blood: blood for the giving of strength,
willow for the killing of pain.

But this would be the second cup, and Sondahr was not
stronger. If anything the crippling pain that had come upon
her so suddenly at the climax to the events at the fire feast
seemed to be growing worse.

Wallah was sorry that she had been drawn by Pomm's
command onto the Hill of Dreams with the other women,
and sorrier still that Sondahr had selected her. She did not
want to be here. She knew the basic way to alleviate minor
pain, to stitch wounds, to salve burns, and to lessen fever;
any woman worth a man's keeping knew them. But she was
no healer, not in the true sense of the word. There was no
magic in her skills.

The confines of the overcrowded room were stifling. Wallah felt trapped, even though she sat apart from the other women, listening to their singing and spirit calling as her carefully heated brew cooled in its ivory serving cup. She thought about her daughter and wished that she had immediately gone after Mahnie when the impetuous girl had run off, deliberately ignoring Pomm's command to stay. Where was the child now? Her limbs twitched to be up and after her. She would be in serious trouble if, as Wallah feared, she had dared to follow the men out of the encampment.

But when Sondahr had put the cup into her hands and had specifically requested that she prepare the brew of healing while Pomm led the other women in the traditional chants designed to drive away pain, how could Wallah refuse? She had told the magic woman that she was no healer, but Sondahr would have no other, even when Naiapi offered to ready the cup instead.

"Have you not done enough already for Sondahr, Naiapi, woman of Grek?"

Although the crowded interior was lighted by only a single oil lamp, Wallah had seen Naiapi flush, and as she had stammered that she did not know what Sondahr meant, her handsome features had twisted with an expression that had filled Wallah with suspicion.

As the last of the brittle willow leaf fragments settled into the cooling brew within the cup, the eyes of Wallah, first woman of Grek, found Naiapi in the gloom. She was sitting with the others now, in a circle around the raised sleeping platform where Sondahr lay thrashing. Wallah frowned. Naiapi was smiling a tight, smug little expression of contentment inspired by Sondahr's ever-increasing pain.

The first woman of Grek rose, suddenly sick and wary and uncomprehending of the befuddling and savage events of this night. She wished the sun would rise so she could look out upon a new day that mocked all that had transpired! Mahnie would be back where she belonged; Sondahr would be well; Torka and Karana would be asleep with their women and children within their pit hut. And Navahk would have vanished into yesterday, along with the smokes of last night's feast fire—and Grek would be headman in his place!

She sighed. Such things could not be. Life moved forward, never back. And the cup was growing much too cool within her palms. Sondahr had need of more of the strengthening, painkilling brew of blood and willow. Now.

The magic woman cried out against her pain.

"Drink this," soothed Wallah. "It will ease your pain."

The magic woman sat up, eagerly grasping Wallah's hands, drawing them close as she drank greedily from the cup. Wallah tipped it, assisting her, heartsick as she saw the agony in the woman's eyes and felt the clammy texture of her fevered skin.

Sondahr shuddered, and although the cup was drained, she continued to hold Wallah's hands. "This pain will not end until my life has ended with it, for I have eaten death. Is it not so, Naiapi?"

Wallah saw the smile slip from Naiapi's mouth.

"You should not have challenged Navahk, Sondahr," Naiapi replied with a scowl of vindictive wrath. "If death eats at your gut, it is your own doing. You have invited the punishment of one whose magic is much greater than your own. You were once his teacher, his lover. But Navahk loves Naiapi now. He cares not for Sondahr. Before the sun rises, Navahk will teach *you* that *no one* has power over him—not you, not Lorak, and certainly not Torka or Karana, for Navahk is more than a man. His will shall triumph, and your spirit will walk the wind forever, along with the people of Man Who Walks With Dogs!"

Wallah was so stunned by the wide-eyed, slavering madness that distorted Naiapi's face that she did not hear Pomm's sigh of distress.

But there was no missing Pomm's hissing admonition to Sondahr: "What has happened to Karana is the fault of Sondahr—all of it! He wanted you instead of Pomm because of your black powers of enchantment. If he and his people have fallen out of favor in this camp, if they have become bringers of bad luck, if Karana dies instead of lives to pleasure this woman, it is the fault of Sondahr . . . all of it, the fault of Sondahr!"

The room was hot from the combined body heat of the crowded women, but Wallah went cold as the smile that had vanished from Naiapi's mouth now reappeared upon Sondahr's lips. The magic woman's eyes moved to Pomm. "Woman Who Knows Everything . . . when Sondahr is no more, when you dwell as a woman alone upon the Hill of Dreams, upon whom shall you heap your blame and excuses for failure when all of the bands of the Great Gathering see what you can and cannot do?" A wave of pain stopped her words. She went rigid, and her hands closed so tightly about Wallah's that Wallah winced and gasped in pain.

"Go!" Sondahr issued the command through clenched teeth. "Go, all of you, and leave me with this woman Pomm, who brags before all that she can fill the space of my shadow! Go!"

Still holding the cup, Wallah got to her feet and, with the others, backed out of the hut in silence. She was the last to leave. As she bent and stepped backward through the entryway, she put the cup down upon the floor skin of mammoth hide just as a thoroughly flustered Pomm rose to stand angrily before Sondahr.

"I am Pomm! I *am* magic woman! My powers *are* great! But woman am I, and before the powers of Navahk, not even Mother Below could—"

"You are where you have chosen to be. You have dared to boast before all that your powers are greater than the powers of Sondahr, so offer no more excuses to me, fat woman! Cast off your feathers and heal me—if you can!"

Torka stared up through thinning, pain-filled shadows. A wall of hostile faces glared down at him, the features red and black in the torchlight. He saw Grek, grim, scowling, his thoughts impossible to read. When their eyes met, the older hunter exhaled through his teeth and turned away, to be absorbed by the darkness of the heavily clouded night. Dimly— from somewhere beyond the edge of the world, it seemed— Torka heard the lapping of water and the hiss of the wind. The wind was cold, well below freezing, but Torka was in so much pain that his shivering brought flames of heat rippling through him.

Lorak stood over him imperiously. The slag heap of his time-ruined, raptorial face twisted with pleasure as he poked Torka with his feathered staff and watched the younger man flinch from pain.

"Now does Lorak speak these words to Torka!" He shouted so that all of those who stood behind him might hear and be impressed. "Lorak says, go from this land—you *and* Karana— and return to the far and forbidden land out of which you have come. Look no more to the country of the mammoth hunters, for if you return to this land or to the encampment of the Great Gathering, you will die as your dogs have died—but not before you see the deaths of your women and children."

From deep within some inner well of reserve, Torka glowered contemptuously up at the old man. "Lorak does *not* speak . . . Torka hears his voice, but it is only a puny echo of Navahk's voice. Where is Spirit Killer? Has he decided to step aside for a little while in order to allow Lorak a continuing delusion of authority?"

"Navahk is with Torka's woman." Lorak's reply was sinuous with hatred, a sharpened awl probing for pain he knew must come. "But she is Navahk's woman now, isn't she? And she must be mated with him by now. In the light of Navahk's fire she will forget that she ever had another man."

"She will remember. And Torka will come back for his Lonit . . . for all his women and his children, and when he does, Navahk had best look to his throat. For like Aar, who has ripped the throat of Stam, Torka will rip the throat of Navahk wide, and when he is done and Navahk's spirit has bled out of his body, Lorak had best look to his own neck, because as long as Torka lives, you will not be safe in your bed skins, old man!"

The old man's booted foot swung out fast and hard, striking Torka in the belly. The second kick cracked two ribs. "Then this 'old man' will see to it that Torka will not live long enough to carry out his threat!" His promise was a curse. "Let the mammoth hunters see what Man Who Walks With Dogs can do without his dogs, without his spears, without his flying sticks. He and his son are alone upon the tundra, alone in the night and the coming storm, alone with the wanawut— with their hands tied behind their backs!"

The vibrations of Aar's low growling awoke Mahnie. Startled, she opened her eyes to find herself slumped against Aar, her arms embracing him. His fur was soft and silken against her face. His body was warm against her own.

With a start she looked up, surprised that she had been asleep. It was snowing hard now, and the wind was whistling. A good distance away men and youths were filing back into the encampment. Led by Lorak, they walked as though in need of rest and broke ranks the moment they came through the wall of bones, scattering to their individual campsites. She watched them, stroking the dog, whispering into his fur to shush him until all the men and youths had gone and she was alone in the snowy dark with the dog. Suddenly Grek was standing close, hesitant to come too close to the animal.

"Come away, girl," he whispered imperatively. "Only the forces of Creation know how the others passed by without seeing you! Come quickly, before the bad luck of Man Who Walks With Dogs contaminates you too!"

"Are he and Karana—" She dared not complete the question lest speaking of their deaths make them a reality.

"No. And they may yet survive. I fell behind the others coming back in the dark, slipped back to cut the thongs that bound Torka and Karana, and left them with a spear and dagger and my wind coat and surplice."

Her eyes widened. Could he have done such a wonderful thing? Her ever-cautious father? Yes! It must be so! He was without those warm layers of clothing!

"Hurry now before someone guesses what I've been up to!"

She jumped up, ran to him, and would have thrown her arms around his neck to kiss him, but he waved her display of affection away just as frantic Wallah appeared out of the dark to cry out with relief at the sight of her daughter.

"I have been searching for you everywhere!" She was so distraught, she did not notice the absence of her man's outer clothes. "I should have known!"

"No time for that now!" Grek silenced her as he took Mahnie firmly by the hand and began to pull her in the direction of their own fire circle.

She balked. For the first time Mahnie felt how cold the wind had grown. Snow stung against her cheeks and caused her eyes to tear as she looked up at her father. "But Karana's brother Aar lives. They'll kill him if they find him and—"

"He is but a dog, girl! Forget him!" Grek jerked her onward angrily.

Wallah walked beside her, bending close. "Bad spirits walk this night for all of us, Daughter! The wanawut has been heard close by, much too close to this encampment! And Sondahr lies in terrible pain. The woman Pomm, who calls herself a healer, is unable to help her, nor have any of the magic men been able to drive her pain away. Some say that it looks as though she will be dead by dawn. . . . Naiapi says that it is Navahk's magic—punishment for Sondahr's daring to challenge his powers. And Navahk, he has gone to his hut to take Torka's woman while her little daughters weep and cannot be consoled!"

*   *   *

Through a veil of formless dreams and shadows, Lonit slowly became aware of pain and darkness, and of sweet, liquid fire burning at the back of her throat. She swallowed. The fire entered her, expanding deliciously within her body, warming and soothing her pain. She sighed and drifted in darkness, unable or unwilling to rise through it.

Someone was holding her, soothing her with gentle strokings . . . someone . . .

Torka! Her lids flickered. Shadows seeped into her eyes. Black on deeper black. An arching vault of night curved above her, defining the confines of a space without moons or stars . . . the interior of a pit hut. There was danger here. But unable to understand what its nature was, she closed her eyes and lay motionless and hurting upon soft, enveloping furs that covered her, warmed her, allowed her to drift in and out of unconsciousness, mixing with the warmth of the intoxication that had entered through her lips.

She could hear the wind now, long and strong. It was hissing beyond the pit hut, prowling in the darkness—dangerous, fanged, a watching, waiting wind with the cold compassionlessness of a beast. The danger lay there, in the eyes of the beast. She shivered. Even that slight movement roused pain, and she moaned softly. Someone whispered her name, and his voice was the voice of the wind.

"Drink now again. This will take away your pain," the wind urged.

A flask was pressed gently to her lips. She drank greedily of the sweet, painkilling fire that lay within. It was good, so good. Her eyelids flickered. In the darkness a shadow sat beside her, bent over her, stroking her, soothing her with low, sinuous exhalations of her name. The shadow of a man. A man who was not Torka.

"Navahk?" Panic and recollection exploded within her with white-hot intensity, sending her mind swimming back down through darkness, away from a stark reality that she could not bear to face. Not yet. No. Not yet.

She willed herself into oblivion, away from her pain. She swam downward through the core of herself, deeper and deeper, through layers of her life. But pain was there also—in childhood days and nights of brutalization at the hands of her father and his women, in a girlhood of hopelessness and endless abuse, until at last, within the darkness, she walked alone across a storm-driven world with Umak and Torka, in the wake of a killer mammoth that had made her Only Woman In The World. She raced across the broad, golden river of grass, hunting at Torka's side, laughing and loving and living with him and their children within the Valley of Songs, boldly lying naked with him beneath the benevolent eye of the watching sun and the towering blue shadows of the Mountains That Walk.

Lonit sighed, content within the caul of her dreams. Within her body the world was blue, expanding, as soft and warm as the sweet summer skies of the forbidden country. An equally warm, soft wind was blowing moistly against her face, downward over her throat and breasts and belly, licking tentatively between her bruised and slightly parted thighs. Again she sighed, relaxing in the arms of her man, opening herself to the trespass of the sweet and gentle wind that, as though by magic, transposed pain to pleasure. It entered her, probed languorously until her loins caught fire, then withdrew as the hands of Torka began to salve her body with some sort of balm that was fire and ice against her skin. As he followed the course of the wind, she trembled and reached to draw the heat of his naked body closer to hers.

"Torka . . ." She whispered his name with longing, and as she flung her arms about his neck and arched to accept him, his entry startled her from her dreams. He stabbed deep, deliberately rousing pain.

Stunned, she opened her eyes. She felt hot and disoriented, as she had felt after drinking too much of Pomm's mind-numbing berry brew. Her mind was a blank, which was slowly filling with confusion. Her arms and back and limbs ached from the beating, and even in the darkly shadowed interior of the pit hut, with dreams and reality still half-fused, she knew that the man who was joined to her, poised over her, and balanced upon his splayed hands was not Torka.

"Forget him." Navahk's voice was that of the slow, warm wind that moved upon and within her body. "Do not speak his name in longing when you lie with me. I have wanted you, Lonit, across great distances, across the long seasons, and there have not been many women whom Navahk has desired. But Lonit has been one of them. *Beautiful* Lonit, move now for Navahk, as I have dreamed of you moving beneath me."

He gave her no chance to reply. He bent his head and kissed her slowly. He probed hungrily with his tongue.

The kiss put the fire into her loins again, but she was free of her dreams now. She bit him fiercely.

He knelt back and pulled out of her, backhanding his mouth, observing his blood and smiling as though he enjoyed the pain.

"This woman is Torka's always and forever!" She spat the words at him.

His smile lengthened across his face. Even in the dark she could see his teeth, small and white and serrated, like the teeth of a hunting animal. "We will see," he intoned, and bent to her breasts.

She tried to twist away from him, but a bare, hard knee rammed between her closing thighs, forcefully holding them open as his hands clasped her wrists and held her fast to the bed furs as he slowly suckled her breasts, drawing throbbing fire upward from her loins. She sobbed, enraged by her own body's betrayal. His tongue was tracing a line of moist fire downward from her breasts, across her belly, to become a probe as it entered her. She gasped, desperately wanting to flail free of him, yet he *was* a magic man. He had broken her will to resist him. She yielded, opened herself to him as he moved to mount her, penetrating deep, moving with slow, controlled, and rhythmic thrusts. She heard him exhale through his teeth with excitement and triumph as he felt the change in her.

She hated him—but no more than she wanted him now.

Until, from beyond the little pit hut and the darkness that encapsulated it, the cry of Sondahr rent the night. It was a high, wild cry, like that of an animal at the moment of its death, and as it faded, it formed into words that struck Lonit to the heart.

"Woman of Torka . . . re . . . mem . . . ber me. . . ."

Lonit went cold.

Navahk stiffened. He raised his head, listening, waiting. His face contorted with hatred, and when the cry did not sound again, he sighed with infinite satisfaction and pleasure. "Sondahr is dead."

"No," she said coldly to Navahk. "Sondahr is *not* dead. Her spirit will live within this woman forever."

"That will not be long if you do not dance for me."

"I will *not* dance for you."

"You will, or I shall find my pleasure in your death, and your children will die as surely as Torka."

"I am his woman, always and forever. When he dies, my spirit will die with him. And you will kill my children whether I dance for you or not—I see it in your eyes, as I have seen through your 'magic' into your spirit, Navahk. You are ugly and twisted and more repulsive to me than the skin of the wanawut in whose skin you dance."

Her words enraged him. He forced entry, brutally, jamming himself deep, watching her, waiting for her to cry out in pain or fear. She did neither. She lay passively beneath him, daring to look directly into his eyes as he moved on her—not as a man but an animal, riding her as a stallion rides a mare, gripping, pumping in hard thrusts. But unlike the wild, savage stallions of the open steppes, his release did not come quickly. He worked at her hard, deliberately hurting her, purposely prolonging what he knew she loathed him for, and all the while she smiled her contempt at him, until, at the moment of climax, she laughed, ruining his release. He roared with anger and struck her so hard across the face that he rendered her unconscious.

And still he rode her, a limp and useless doll, but it was no good for him. His power over her lay in her fear of him, and Lonit did not fear him anymore.

Unless . . .

He smiled again. With Torka gone, her children were alone with a mute woman and a dying one. He rose and reached for his clothes. He would make Lonit fear him yet!

Grek lay close to Wallah, shivering himself warm, bundling together with his woman as the two of them drifted into troubled sleep. Mahnie watched them from her own sleeping skins, adoring them both, so proud of Grek that tears of love welled beneath her lids when she thought of leaving him.

But she must leave. Her time of blood was at hand. There was no use denying it; she had seen the signs. Her eyes scanned the shadows, moved to the closed door skin, half expecting Naiapi to come in from the rising storm. Where was she? Not that the girl cared; she was glad Naiapi was not in the hut. What Mahnie intended needed privacy and secrecy, even from Grek and Wallah and especially from Naiapi.

In stealth, moving as silently as a night creature that fears itself watched by predators, she moved from her own bed skins to rummage through Wallah's personal supplies of soft, absorbent hare skins. Her mother had prepared extras, anticipating the day when Mahnie would need them. She kept them in a special sack made from the skin of a female mountain sheep. Now the girl took half of them and, scooting back to her sleeping place, donned one where need demanded and placed the others on her top bed fur.

Kneeling back on her heels, she peered through the darkness at the closed door skin. It was moving in and out, straining the thong ties that held it in place. For a moment she feared that Naiapi was about to come barging in, but it was only the rising wind pressing against the hide flap. Mahnie breathed a sigh of relief. Naiapi was not coming. Wherever she was, she would probably not return until well after dawn. By then Mahnie would be gone.

Hurrying now but working in absolute silence, she began to assemble her belongings: sewing supplies, her all-important awl, her bone needles in their carrying cylinder made of the hollow shaft of a feather, a new roll of freshly prepared sinew, her knife and scrapers and pounders and—still biting her lip— Wallah's bow drill and most of her emergency supplies of moss wicks and dried grass for kindling. She would need these things more than her mother would. Wallah would have time to gather more grass and make new wicks, as well as a new bow drill; Mahnie would not. She would have two broken, beaten men to care for, and with a storm coming on, fire would mean the difference between life and death—fire and warm clothes.

Grek had left his surplice and wind coat of opaque, meticulously stitched and oiled antelope intestines with the injured men, but Karana and Torka would need warmer clothes than that, and winter boots if the weather turned cold. From the howl of the wind outside the pit hut, it sounded as though the weather was already turning. If they were as badly beaten as Grek said, they would not be able to hunt. If they could not hunt, they would have to rely upon her to provide meat. Her skills and gender would bring only small animals to their fire; and from small animals there would not be enough hides out of which to make decent clothes. Again she bit her lip, momentarily paralyzed with indecision. If Karana and Torka were to live—and they *must* live if *she* were to have any chance of survival—then the time for indecisiveness was over. She moved quickly and quietly, and in a moment Grek's new winter boots, as well as his old ones, were on her bed fur and she was rationalizing her theft to herself. If Wallah could make new wicks and a new bow drill, she could make new boots.

Mahnie nodded. Yes. It must be so.

She took food now from the shadowed niche where Wallah kept her cooking supplies and extra stores: dried meat, wedges of fat, and a few cakes of berry mash and tubers. Not much, but enough to last through the storm until she could brain a few ptarmigan with well-placed stones or could catch a few fish. Fish! She had almost forgotten her lures and hooks and nets. She had spent hours tying those nets, knotting every sinew filament.

She reached under her bed skins where they lay stretched flat and pulled them out . . . along with her little doll.

Memories flashed, and tears welled. The time that Wallah had spent making dolls for her and the other little girls of the band! Hours and hours of cutting and sewing and piecing. Dolls for Ketti, dolls for Pet!

Oh, Pet. How this girl misses you! Oh, Wallah, you will never know how sorry this girl is to leave her mother!

With yet another sigh, she took the doll and the net and placed them onto the bed fur along with her assembled things. Hastily and with deft hands, she rolled her bed furs into a carrying pack, then took up her winter coat from where it lay next to her sleeping place, put it on, checked to make certain that her gloves were still folded within the storm flap, jammed her feet into her winter boots, picked up her pack, and slipped out, letting in as little cold air as possible.

Snow continued to fall. Although the encampment was hushed with sleep and whiteness, there was an underlying tension about the place. She sensed that many would be plagued by troubled dreams this night. Her eyes strayed toward the Hill of Dreams. It was shrouded in clouds of wind-driven snow. A figure emerged from one of the huts.

Her belly tightened.

"Navahk . . ." She whispered his name as an invocation. *Keep him there. Away from me.* She thought of Lonit, Torka's woman, and she wondered if she was still alive. She wondered if Torka and Karana would be willing to turn their backs upon her and her children. It did not matter. If they were still alive, she would walk with them, regardless of what they decided to do. She picked up her pack frame of caribou

antler from where it rested with those of Grek, Wallah, and
Naiapi against the leeward wall of the hut. She slung it on,
hefted her pack, secured it, and hurried on, surprised that
the weight of the pack was much less than she had imagined.

Her step was light, as quick as a vole darting across open
land where owls and hawks were known to fly. She took the
shortest route to the opening in the wall of bones, then
paused. The snowfall was so heavy. The wind was so strong.
She knew she must hurry. Yet she turned back, sought out
the place where the dogs lay dead, white now, their fur thick
with snow. By morning they would be buried, frozen stiff—
even the great dog Aar. She went to him, bent, and brushed
the snow away with her palm, pressing lightly, surprised to
feel the animal's heart beating strongly. The dog raised its
head, weakly licked her bare hand, and whimpered softly.

Carefully, still a little afraid of him, she nudged him gently,
hoping that he would rise and follow her. He seemed to
understand what she was trying to do, but try as he might, he
could not do more than lift his head.

But though Mahnie was small and burdened with a pack
frame, she knew she could not abandon the dog. She stole a
sledge, used to haul meat, from where it leaned against
Torka's pit hut, and hefted the dog onto it. "Come, Brother
Dog," she said, dragging the wounded animal out of the
encampment and into the snow-driven night. "This girl goes
to Karana, and he would not want me to leave you behind."

"Navahk . . ."

He stopped and turned, annoyed to have been called from
his purpose. Naiapi stood behind him in the wind-whipped
snow. Her voice had struck him with an imperative ring. He
waited as she walked to him from the crest of the Hill of
Dreams. She strode proudly, wrapped against the weather in
a heavy shawl of mammoth hair. It was deep red and shaggy
beneath a quickly thickening coat of snow that would soon
make its color and texture invisible. "I come from the house
of the magic woman Sondahr. She is dead."

His brows met over the bridge of his nose. "Sondahr does
not concern me now," he said, making no attempt to conceal
his irritation. He would have continued on his way down
from the hill to the fire circle of Torka's family, but her hand
shot out and grasped his wrist.

"Navahk did not come to tend Sondahr when he heard her screams."

He jerked his arm free. "No."

"It was not wise of her to challenge you."

There was an odd, anxious tone to her voice that set him on edge. "Get out of my way, Naiapi."

"Lorak is very angry. He curses your name. But do not be concerned. I will kill him, as I have killed Sondahr. For you. To make her pay. No one may insult Navahk and not suffer Naiapi's ire."

He froze, startled. "You . . . killed Sondahr?"

"With this!" she boasted, holding out her palm so that he might see the tiny skewers of bone that had been soaked in water until they were pliable, then bent into tight circles and allowed to dry. "I put them in her meat, just so, so they would not take long to open, like this." Her hand closed into a fist, then opened sharply. "Her belly was pierced in many places. Her pain was great. She asked to die. Pomm is magic woman in this camp now, at Sondahr's request. And also at Sondahr's request, it was Pomm who took her life, quickly, as though she could not wait to do it, with a blade carved of mammoth tusk provided by Sondahr herself. But it is Naiapi who killed her, in the way my father taught me long ago to kill wolves and leaping cats so that their skins may be taken whole and without blemish. The woman of Torka would not do this for you. She could not please you as Naiapi would if—"

He heard the longing in her voice. "She pleases me," he interrupted coldly, and smiled when he saw the misery in her eyes. "And soon she will please me more."

Iana sat in Torka's pit hut with Summer Moon in her arms. The baby, Demmi, suckled fretfully at her breast. It had taken her hours to quiet Summer Moon, and even then Iana had been unable to lull her to sleep until she had allowed the child to hold Lonit's bola. Iana's own thoughts had been so troubled that she had lain awake, her mind drifting, as it so often did, through broken fragments of the past, lingering over memories of her murdered husband and children, remembering all the gentleness and kindness that she had found in Torka's camp.

The happenings at the feast fire had so shocked and appalled her, she had willed herself not to see them, not to

acknowledge them as reality. Torka and Karana had not been
beaten and driven from the camp. No. They were only hunting and would come back soon, as would Lonit. They would
come back and, if the day were warm and the wind strong
enough to keep the blackflies from settling, she would take
the children out into the sun, and together with Torka, Lonit,
and Karana, she would bathe with them in the sweet waters
of the warm springs and—

Who was the man standing in the entrance to the pit hut?
He had drawn the door skin aside as though it were his right
to do so. Snow and wind blew in as he stood in the opening.
She could see the light of dawn behind him. It was snowing
outside. Where was the sun? The wind was very strong, but
even if it were not, blackflies would not be pests in the snow,
and the springs were warm, so warm. . . .

Confused, she closed her eyes. Behind her Aliga stirred
upon her own pallet and moaned softly as she readjusted her
weight beneath her sleeping furs.

"I have come for one of the children, woman. Which one
you yield is up to you," informed the intruder.

Iana did not like the sound of his voice. It purred deep at
the back of his throat, like a lion threatening. She drew the
children closer. She remembered him now. She feared him
now.

He was advancing toward her, smiling, showing sharp white,
pointed teeth. What did he want with her children? Iana
looked into his eyes and knew the answer.

She sat up, pulling Summer Moon up with her, drawing
the bed skins around them both. The child made soft noises
in her sleep. And suddenly, for the first time in many years,
Iana's thoughts focused with exquisite and brutal clarity. She
knew exactly where she was and what had happened to set
her alone in the pit hut with Aliga and the children. The man
who was coming toward her had ordered the banishment of
Torka and Karana, and what must surely be their deaths. He
had taken Lonit to be his woman, but not before he had
allowed the other women to abuse her and had caused the
children to scream.

Her arms tightened protectively around Summer Moon and
Demmi. She would not allow him to make her babies scream
again. He would have to kill her first. But if she died, she
would never see the little ones again, unless he killed them,
too, and their tiny spirits followed her to walk the wind forever.

"No!" her statement was emphatic. It had been so long since she had spoken except to croon or whisper soft words and baby stories to the children, that her voice sounded as though it had come from the throat of a stranger. And in a way it had, for the sad, dull, vacant look was gone from Iana's eyes.

"You will not hurt my children . . . not as long as I live," she warned him.

"Then you will not live long, Madwoman," he promised.

Shame filled her. Is this what he thought of her—what they *all* must think of her—that she was mad? Mindless? Is this what she had been all of these long years—useless except as a dull-eyed caretaker for another woman's babies, and in the end not even good for that because when danger threatened, she retreated into herself, aware of nothing but her desperate need to avoid confrontation with the realities of her life?

In the darkness Navahk failed to see the change in her. He dared to come closer, snarling at her, wanting her to see the intent in his eyes to maim or murder the children, taking pleasure in her fear.

But she was not afraid. She moved so quickly that he had only a second to react as she leaned back and with a grace, power, and dexterity that she had forgotten she possessed, gripped the braided leather thong in her right hand. As she had seen Lonit do a thousand times, she gathered the ends of the four long, shell-weighted thongs in the other, stressed the cords taut, then swung them high. She whirled the bola until the thongs sang and whirred, and the shells flew round and round as she released them in a deadly, spiraling arc.

Navahk jumped to evade the weapon but not fast enough. He went down flat on his face, unconscious before he could utter a cry, with one shell embedded in his eye, the thongs of the bola looped about his neck, his right eardrum bleeding.

Grek awoke to the sound of wind and the sting of snow hitting the exterior walls of his pit hut. He could not hear anyone stirring within the encampment. He sensed the rising dawn but lay still for a moment, knowing that people would be staying within their shelters today, sleeping off the results of the previous night's drink and talking low about the happenings at the feast fire. The memories disturbed him. Not even the good feeling of Wallah lying warm against him could soften his misgivings.

Carefully, not wishing to disturb his woman, he rose and reached for his winter boots. They were gone—both pair. Startled, he squinted into the shadows, noted that Naiapi was not there, and knew that Mahnie was gone before he saw that her bed furs were missing. He cursed quietly; he knew where the girl had gone—and with his winter clothes!

Wallah stirred. "What is it?"

He told her.

She looked around, her mind groping against panic. "Naiapi did not come home last night. Many of the women spent the night with Sondahr, chanting with Pomm to strengthen her healing powers. Even some of the girls were invited to go. Mahnie must have followed Naiapi onto the Hill of Dreams after we were asleep. You know how curious and willful the girl is, and—"

"You know better than that. Mahnie wouldn't follow Naiapi anywhere. She's gone off after Karana. Name me Fool for telling the child where the others had left him! But why would she take such a risk, and in weather like this? I know she's moon-eyed for the youth, but he's so much older and has never said more than 'go away' to the child in all the years of my remembering!"

Wallah was sick with apprehension. She noticed her misarranged belongings. Insight struck her deeply as she saw the opened flap of the sheepskin sack in which she kept the supplies of skins that every woman kept for her bleeding times. She folded her sleeping furs aside and went to check the sack. It was as she expected. "She is no longer a child."

He growled, understanding and yet not understanding at all. "Only a child would do such a foolish thing in this weather!"

Wallah looked at him. "This is a bad camp."

Grek nodded a silent assent as he pulled on his summer boots and both his lightweight summer tunics, grumbling with annoyance because Mahnie had taken his favorite winter coat as well.

He had just stepped from his pit hut when he saw Lonit stumbling down from the Hill of Dreams. He could barely discern her form. The wind was blowing hard, driving snow in thick, oblique sheets of white. If it snowed any harder, he would be unable to find the lake, much less follow his daughter. Her tracks must have been buried long before now. He turned, took up two of his spears, and would have jogged on toward the break in the wall of bones and out across the stormy tundra in pursuit of his child had Lonit not staggered and fallen.

As she got to her feet, the heavy drape of dark fur in which she had been wrapped against the cold fell away. She seemed not to notice as, with her black hair whipping in the wind, she staggered on, naked, hurrying toward her pit hut, an unlighted torch held as a weapon in her hand, her steps betraying her pain and the urgency of her errand. Grek squinted in amazement.

He was no magic man, but he knew that something was wrong. Why was Navahk not pursuing the naked woman? And why was she carrying the torch as though she intended to kill somebody with it? Grek was a big man, and his stride was long if not graceful. Instinct set him to the chase, but although Lonit was running stiff with cold, half stumbling toward her destination, she was nearly to her pit hut before he caught up with her.

"Woman of Torka, what—"

She wheeled, straining against the broad, strong hand that curled around her upper arm. "Navahk is going to kill my children! He is—"

He was shocked to see her swollen mouth, blackened eye, and bloodied nose. And he had not known that a female could be so strong, for before her statement was complete, she had broken away from him and entered the hut.

Grek would have pulled her back by her hair, but his ungloved fingers were stiff with cold, and the long strands slipped through them before he could manage a grip. Then the anger was back. What was he doing? If Navahk was going to kill the children of Torka, was Grek going to stand back and once again allow the magic man his way? Would he stop the mother and thus sanction the murder? No! With his spears at ready, he entered the hut, ready to kill the man who had plagued him for so long.

But Navahk lay sprawled and bleeding from a head wound that had stained the clean expanse of furs that covered the hide floor of Torka's domain. The thongs of Lonit's bola were wound about his head. Blood and eye fluid darkened the fine pelage of the furs, and dark veins of blood ran from his ear.

Lonit stopped abruptly in front of Grek. He nearly knocked her down trying to arrest his own forward momentum. No lamp or fire burned to light the deeply shadowed interior, but Grek and Lonit clearly saw the prone and motionless figure of the magic man, with the madwoman, Iana, sitting before him with Lonit's children in her arms.

"Iana?"

Grek heard Lonit's tremulous, whispering query, and to his amazement, the madwoman smiled. Even in the dark he could see the change in her. She sat erect. Her eyes were bright, her face radiant.

"He came to kill our babies. This woman could not let him do that. Iana hopes that Lonit will not be angry that Iana used her bola and set its spirit free to hunt . . . a different kind of bird."

"Is he . . . dead?" breathed Grek.

Lonit did not hear him. She stepped around the motionless Navahk and, with a sob, embraced Iana and her children.

"Oh, Iana, if Navahk has brought your spirit to live again within your heart, to speak again as a woman to another woman, then in his life he has done at least one good thing!"

"I will kill him now and have done with it," said Grek.

Lonit whirled, her battered face intense. "One man may not take the life spirit of another! That is the way of Navahk, not of Torka's people!"

"I am not of Torka's people. And if that man awakes with a memory of what has happened here, not one of Torka's people will be left alive." He saw fear in the women's eyes and in the face of the child whose name was Summer Moon. Then, as clearly as if the wind had just blown the sky free of storm, he saw the way that he must follow. He actually smiled, he liked the route so much. "All right. So be it, then. Let him lie. Dress yourself and your children, women of Torka. Gather up your warmest furs and whatever you must carry from this camp to maintain another—but nothing too heavy, nothing that will slow our steps. We will go from this place together. Grek will see you safely to your man and to the boy Karana. They were alive when I left them. If we hurry, you and I—with Wallah and Mahnie—we will see to it that they stay alive. This man will be of Torka's band. Together we will go far from this camp, and let others follow the way of Navahk and live with fear forever!"

PART VI

THE
CORRIDOR
OF STORMS

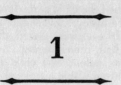

1

The child hunched within the tall, sheltering grasses of the lakeshore. Its fur was thick now, its undercoat so downy that the wind could not have penetrated it, even if the child had risen and walked out into the savage beat of the rising storm.

The world beyond the grasses was white: white sky, white land. But within the windbreak of the grasses the world was still gold and russet with the bent, dry stalks of autumn, although upon the ground little frozen rivers of granulated snow intruded here and there wherever the breath of the wind managed to find a break in the grass.

The long, clawed index finger of the child disturbed the delicate, lacelike patterns of the fine, dry snow as it remembered another snowfall, another nest of grass, within a distant willow grove where Mother Killer had first come to leave it meat. That all seemed so long ago, so far away.

Frowning, the child stared at the unconscious young beast it had dragged to shelter within the grasses. It leaned close to his face, sniffed at his nostrils.

Yes. Like the other larger, older beast it had left undisturbed by the lakeshore, he was still breathing. The child's head cocked to one side. Its finger slowly traced the hideous, bloodied features of the creature. He looked so much like Mother Killer, yet the child perceived that he was different. He had the face of youth, not of maturity. His body, when erect, would be taller, more muscular. The tattered, bloodied skins that covered the beast were not white, but his face was somehow the same face as Mother Killer. So the child had dragged him off, to kill him . . . to feed upon him . . . to tear off his underskin and dance within it.

The child was not particularly hungry, however, and this

wounded, murmuring beast was not Mother Killer. More-
over, there was something disturbingly familiar about him,
something that robbed the child of its desire to kill him. Now
and again he opened his eyes and stared up sightlessly out of
troubled dreams. His eyes were glazed, dull, and unfocused.
The child watched him, remembering. . . .

Only a few hours before, the child had been eating a
still-twitching ptarmigan within a grove of stunted trees, close
to the massive circle of piled bones in which the beasts
encamped. It had been spitting feathers and sucking blood,
scenting the dangerous smell of the beasts' fire. Its broad,
infinitely sensitive nostrils had picked up vague inferences of
the smell of Mother Killer, but there were other odors, foul
and repugnant, of Man and the dried skins of dead animals,
of cooked meat and congealed blood, of burned fat and ashes,
and overriding all, the smell of the accumulation of mammoth
bones and tusks, ancient and new. It was a place that reeked
of death.

The child had listened to their strange bangings and clap-
pings and whistlings, and to the even stranger howling of
their voices. A little while later, with all but the head and
feet of the ptarmigan consumed, the child left its hiding place
to follow a firelit procession of beasts who seemed to be
driving Mother Killer before them.

As the child had trailed them, its fears of the beasts had
been confirmed: The one it had thought to be Mother Killer
and another taller, older beast that covered itself in the
maned skin of a lion were beaten, pummeled, shouted at,
and forced to their knees. The child had smelled their blood
and their anger and their fear as it saw the ugliest beast that
it had ever seen posture over them in the feathers of a bird,
then kick them until they collapsed into two silent, bloodied
heaps. Terrified of being discovered, the child had remained
hidden until the last of the beasts had walked away, leaving a
sharp man stone and flying stick behind. If they savaged one
another, what would they do to one who was not of their own
kind?

So the child had stayed under cover of the grasses for a
long time, recalling the death of its mother, longing for her as
it remembered what it had seen the beasts do to the great
tusked ones that had been driven into the bog of the distant
lake within the far hills. The beasts, especially Mother Killer,
had killed not only for meat, but for the obvious pleasure

hey took in the killing. Later the child had fed upon the
ones and remnant flesh of the mammoths that the beasts
iad not carried away, sating itself before leaving the killing
ite to pursue Mother Killer, certain that Mother Killer had
ntentionally left enough meat on the dismembered bones of
he dead mammoths for it to feed upon.

Its strength restored by meat and blood, the child had
noved quickly in the depth of night, to shelter within the
rasses and scrub growth that surrounded the lakeshore where
t hunkered now. It had rested and slept, dreaming of far
ands where it had once lived with those of its own kind,
arried in the arms of its mother beneath the vast black skin
f the night. Although it was a mere babe at that time, the
hild clearly recalled seeing soft, frightened eyes staring up
ut of the shadowed shrubbery, eyes filled with starlight,
fire with wonder . . .

. . . exactly like the eyes of the beast staring up at it now.

Eyes that were clear of dreams, eyes that focused upon the
ace of the child and filled with terror.

It smelled the rank, sudden rush of the beast's fear. As it
rimaced in revulsion, its broad, nearly seamless lips pulled
ack, revealing broad teeth and massive, stabbing canines.

The beast's face twisted in horror. His mouth pulled back,
howing his own small, even, useless teeth as he bolted
pright, screaming: *"Torka!"*

Startled by the strange, unexpected cry of panic, the child
imped aside as the beast ran past, frantically elbowing its
ay through the grasses and into the snow-driven world
eyond.

Karana ran straight into Mahnie. Looking back over his
houlder, he did not see the girl plodding toward the lake,
undering now and then where the snow was forming drifts
n the lee side of the tussocks. He went down on top of her,
nd neither knew which was the more startled as they looked
nto one another's eyes.

It was Aar's yip that broke the silence. Karana knelt back,
rimacing against the excruciating pain of his bruises, then
orgetting all about them as he saw Brother Dog lying on the
ledge.

"He is all that is left of your pack of dog brothers, I am
fraid," said Mahnie, sitting up, watching as Karana em-

braced the dog, earnestly checking the extent of its injuries as
the animal whimpered happily and licked his face and hands
with joyous recognition. "He will be better now, being with
you. He was the only one not speared by Het."

"You dragged him by yourself? All the long way from the
camp? A little girl like you?"

"If I had not taken him from the camp, someone was sure
to kill him once they saw that he was still alive. And I am not
so little. I am a woman."

She did not look like a woman as she sat there in the wind
and falling snow, amid the spilled contents of her pack,
looking much fatter than he remembered her, as though she
had dressed herself in every garment that she owned.

"I knew you would be alive, Karana. I was sure of it. It was
Grek who left you his spear and knife. And I have brought
food and boots and warm clothes and—"

That explained her extraordinary plumpness! She *was* wearing her entire wardrobe, and some of her father's too! He
recognized Grek's winter parka and his boots where they lay
upon the snow beside her. Then his mind went blank.

"Spear? Knife?" He felt suddenly sick. What was he doing
here in the snow with Mahnie and Aar when Torka lay back
along the shore? Had he truly seen the wanawut, or had he
been dreaming? He had to be certain.

She saw the expression on his battered face and was struck
with foreboding. "Where is Torka?" Her voice was tremulous. "Does he live? "

"I don't know!" His reply was a cry ripped from his heart.
"Stay here with the dog. Keep a weapon handy. And do not
go near the lake or the grasses until I call."

With a skinning knife hastily given to him by a wide-eyed
Mahnie, he ignored his injuries to race through wind and
snow, not slowing his steps until he entered the grasses and
areas of shrub along the shore. The way was clear to him; led
by Lorak, the men of the Great Gathering had flattened a
broad pathway to where he and Torka had been beaten and
left to die.

And there, before the motionless body of Torka, Karana
collapsed onto his knees. The bold, brave hunter who had
named him son lay with his back to him. He was so still.
There was no sign of breath in him. He saw the knife that
Grek had left. Mahnie must have been mistaken about his

aving a spear. Grek . . . kind, steady, trustworthy Grek. If
nly *he* had been named headman instead of Navahk, Torka
vould be alive and—

Suddenly Karana knew that Mahnie had not been mistaken
bout the spear, because the point of it was leveled at his
hroat as, in one whirling motion, Torka had rolled away and
round and up on one knee, holding the weapon out and
eady. His face was horribly swollen and bloodied, and he
vas snarling until he saw who it was who had come up
ehind him. Lowering the spear, he shrugged apologetically
nd winced with pain.

"I thought you might be Navahk, coming out to make sure
is work had been done properly by Lorak and the others."

Karana nearly collapsed with relief. "I thought you were
ead. I thought the wanawut had killed you."

"The wanawut? We've faced worse terrors than that, you
nd I."

"It was here, in the grasses of the lakeshore, in the snow
nd the wind. I saw it."

Torka nodded. "And in the night, in the light of blazing
orches, I saw it too—in the eyes of Navahk."

"My father . . ." Karana bowed his head and spoke the
cknowledgment with infinite despair.

"No, my son, the night and the fire and the distances we
ave walked together have made *us* one—two men, one
eart, one spirit. Navahk has neither. He is father of no one
ut himself."

The youth did not understand and said so.

Torka climbed slowly to his feet now, leaning on the spear
s though it were a crutch, one hand open against his torso,
entling the pain of two cracked ribs. He looked at Karana's
leeding, swollen face. "You look terrible."

"So do you."

"We are alive."

Karana's expression contorted with loathing. "Navahk will
ot be able to say the same for long."

"It would not be a good thing for a son to kill his natural
ther, Karana."

"You have said it, not I. Karana is son of *Torka*. And
gether, for the sake of Lonit, Iana, and the children, we
ill make the magic man pay with his life for what he has
one."

"That will not be necessary!" Grek said with an authority that surprised them.

Torka and Karana stared as the others came through the grasses. They had run all the way, abandoning their packs when Mahnie told them of how Karana had run off in search of Torka.

"Lonit, Iana, and the children are here!" It was Iana who spoke, breathless from her run. Demmi peeked over her shoulder from out of her furry-hooded back sling.

Torka stared at her, disbelieving and delighted. The woman positively glowed with pride in her newfound tongue and assertiveness.

Wallah held Summer Moon, who cried out her father's name and reached out to him with little mittened hands, but it was Lonit who ran to Torka. They stood together in each other's arms for a long time, and no one spoke. Wallah sniffled sentimental tears as Torka touched his beloved's bruised face, and she touched his.

"Always and forever?" he whispered.

"Always and forever!" she affirmed.

The backs of his fingers lingered over her swollen, darkening eye. "Navahk has done this to you?"

She saw the murderous hatred in his eyes and felt fear for him and for them all. "It does not matter. It is the past. Navahk is there, behind us. Lonit is here, with Torka. Surely you are not thinking of going back?"

He looked back across the snow-driven land, squinting against the wind, his mouth set, his eyes hard.

"You are one man, Torka. Navahk is the manipulator of many," reminded Iana. "And whenever this woman remembers Navahk, she will thank him for forcing this woman to find her voice and clear her eyes to look upon the world as it is without fear."

Grek grunted to himself and shook his head. "We must always fear the world, woman. But not so much that it makes us cower before those fears. And so this man says now to Torka that he will not take his women back into a camp where Navahk dwells. That man is worse than the beast in whose skin he walks, and we have no need of such as those who follow him. We are a band as we stand. Look: I see three hunters here: Grek, Karana, and Torka. Even though your woman Aliga was too ill to travel and refused even when this man offered to put her on a sledge and carry her, we never theless have the hands and backs of three strong women to help carry loads and butcher meat and—"

"Four women," injected Mahnie shyly.

"I knew it!" Wallah moved to her daughter and hugged her hard. "Sondahr's powers *were* great! My hopes were answered through her magic! Poor woman. To die such a death, to suffer so after doing only good for others all of her days!"

Mahnie saw the look of grief that swept over Karana's face. Her joy in the moment was gone.

"Sondahr . . . dead? How?"

Wallah's sadness and regret showed in her expression. "Naiapi said that it was Navahk's enchantment on her for daring to challenge him. But Sondahr's symptoms were those of a poisoning, and I wouldn't doubt for a moment that Naiapi was responsible. She took such time preparing the meat that she brought to the magic woman and wouldn't let me help with it or see what she was doing."

Lonit was cold despite the warmth of her traveling clothes. *Sondahr, I will remember you always.* She looked from Karana's tortured face to Torka's embittered one. *He will go back. He will seek vengeance against Navahk. And he will die. Unless I stop him now.* "Sondahr foresaw her own death," she told him, and in the telling, spoke firmly and loudly so that all might know her heart. "She foresaw what would happen on the night of feast fire and told this woman that when it happened, Lonit must go forward with her people, beneath a new sky and a new sun. We cannot go back, Torka. And why should we? Grek is right: Let those who choose to walk with Spirit Killer walk with him. When this storm is over, we must go forward into the face of the rising sun, with Torka as our headman and Grek his strong and steady right arm. Karana will be our spirit master, for like Sondahr, the gift of Seeing is his. His warnings have all come to pass. The world to the west is not a world for us."

Torka was amazed by her bold assurance. It was as though Sondahr had spoken through her mouth. Her face was as battered as his and Karana's, but as he looked at her now, he knew that she would never seem more beautiful to him. He actually smiled as he nodded his agreement, looking northwestward, back toward the encampment of the Great Gathering, into the wind and the still-rising storm.

"Woman of Torka," he said, "you speak with the wisdom of Sondahr. But we will *not* linger in this land until the storm is over. We are all weary, but there is no safe resting place for us in the country of the mammoth eaters. We will walk eastward now, into the storm. It will cover our tracks as we return to the forbidden country, back to the Corridor of Storms, where the Valley of Songs awaits us. And Torka will say this once to Karana before all, so that his son will know that Torka is a man who knows how to admit when he has been wrong. This *has* been a bad camp for us, and Karana *has* been right about the magic man. He *is* bad. Perhaps someday someone will kill him. But it will *not* be one of us."

Lonit embraced him.

But, to Torka's surprise, Karana was not pleased by his long-owed admission. A black, unforgiving hatred had congealed within the youth's eyes.

"Navahk is not a man," said Karana. "He is a spirit—a dark and crooked spirit—and not one of us will live in peace, here or in the far country, as long as he is left alive."

The wind rose sharply and blew the words away, but not before they were heard by all. Torka felt the wind of warning rise within him. Once again Karana had broken the ancient taboo by speaking Navahk's name and, in his hatred, thereby imputing terrifying powers to it.

Navahk, magic man, spirit killer, and now, thanks to Karana, a crooked spirit—half flesh, half phantom, a creature more malevolent than the man himself, more powerful and dangerous than the wanawut, more savage and less forgiving than the most brutal storm—would follow. Only Father Above and Mother Below could stop him now.

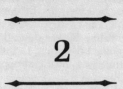

2

"Lie still, Spirit Killer. Lie still and it will soon be as well with you as Pomm can make it."

The trembling voice of the fat woman brought Navahk to his senses. He sat upright, momentarily disoriented. Where was he? Where had the night gone? In the dull, vague luminescence of a full-blown snowstorm he heard a high, shrieking wind batter the exterior walls of a pit hut that was not his own. Another wind shrieked within his right ear, scratching like a captive animal trying to claw its way through bone and flesh. The entire right side of his face was an agony.

He stared at the feathered fat woman, wondering why she was looking at him with such revulsion and . . . pity? In all of his life no one had ever looked at him with pity! He was Navahk! His physical perfection was legendary. He could feel that his face was thick with caked blood, but if this fat old bag was a healer, she should be used to that. He would have frowned, but it hurt too much; and then, suddenly, he realized that he was in Torka's pit hut and looking at the woman out of only one eye—his left eye. The other was— He reached to touch it with questing fingers and sucked in a gasp of incredulity and horror. The socket was concave—a well of pain, of congealed blood and fluid, with one of the shells of Lonit's bola still buried within the collapsed and ruined eyeball. He needed no one to tell him that the weapon had done its worst. He would be half-blind and half-deaf from this day on.

"Here . . . from her own hut in the camp of Zinkh, Pomm has brought a good drink that will make the pain less when the shell is withdrawn from the eye and—"

He backhanded the bladder flask from her with such power

that she was knocked off balance and the container went flying, splattering dark, sweet liquor all over Aliga, who lay on her side upon her bed furs, her tattooed head propped on her bent arm.

"Where is the woman who has done this to me?" Navahk raged, on his feet now and ripping the offending shell from his face, the resulting pain nearly dropping him where he stood.

Pomm had landed on her side and was now huffing against the strain of her own weight, unable to speak as her palms pushed against the floor skin in a vain attempt at leverage. Thus it was Aliga who answered.

"Iana has run away into the storm with Grek and Lonit and the children of Torka. But this woman has stayed. Even when her child comes forth, she will always stay at the side of the one who has healed her."

He stood as still as though carved of stone; her obvious adoration of him was not appreciated. "Lonit has run away?"

"Many hours ago," Pomm affirmed belligerently, not at all happy with the rough and undeserved treatment she had suffered at his hands. She was sitting upright now, rearranging her bedraggled feathers, still trying to catch her breath. The morning was not yet over, and already the day was growing bleaker by the moment; if events did not start righting themselves soon, the coming night would be as disconcertingly troublesome as the one before it. Karana was gone from her life. She had failed to heal Sondahr. Although she was glad about this—for now she was magic woman in Sondahr's place—she had truly done her best for the magic woman, not out of compassion for Sondahr but in consideration for her own reputation.

"Navahk must forget Lonit," Aliga urged softly, jarring the fat woman's thoughts out of reverie.

Pomm's little mouth twitched. She sat with her back to the loosely secured door skin, and a cold wind was seeping into the pit hut. She shivered as she looked from Aliga to Navahk. The tattooed woman was trying to ease Navahk's mood. He stood like a spear poised in an invisible hand, and it would not take much to send him flying into rage again.

In the strangely diffused storm light, Aliga was still looking at him with adoration, seeing past his ruined eye and bloodied face to the man whom she had long dreamed of having at her side. "Lonit will never look upon another man but Torka.

Everyone knows that. She will be loyal until she dies, even as Aliga will be to Navahk, the finest and handsomest man of all. I knew you would heal me. Time and again I told Torka that it would be so. And when this woman's baby is born, she will name its spirit in honor of someone of Navahk's line, someone whose life spirit now walks the wind, someone whom you have loved and would have at your side again—perhaps Supnah, if it is a boy." She paused, shrinking back, sensing something within him that had heretofore eluded her— something sinister and threatening.

"Would another of Torka's women dare to mock Navahk?" Through rage and pain and torment at his disfigurement, he saw Aliga as Torka's woman—like Iana, who had maimed him; like Lonit, who had spurned him.

From where she sat petulantly upon the floor skins, Pomm saw the change in Navahk and instinctively scooted back when he looked at her, until her body was against the door skin. The wind that blew beyond the hut was cold, but somehow the confines of the shelter had grown much colder.

"Gone for hours, you say? And you lay here like a great, swollen tundral sod and sent no one after her? You let me lie unconscious in my own blood and pain while Lonit escaped me?"

Aliga was frightened. Suddenly Navahk's transcendent beauty was bleeding from his face, transforming him. A bloody-eyed monster was glaring down at her, loathing and blaming her for letting Lonit escape. As though she could have stopped her!

She stared at him, trying not to cower as she saw his hands working the blood-blackened thong of the bola that he had ripped from his eye. The sharp-tipped, shell-weighted end dangled from his hand, its lovely, elongated configurations hidden beneath dark gore and fragments of tissue.

"I did try to wake you, Navahk," she told him, wondering for the first time if she had made the right choice by electing to stay. Grek had offered to carry her, and Lonit had implored her to come, warning her of Navahk. But she had not listened. She was so near to giving birth. So near. The child that she had so long despaired of ever bearing could not be risked—not when Navahk had sworn at the feast fire that it *would* be born as soon as the forces that impelled it to remain within its mother's womb were banished from the encampment. His words had struck her to her heart, but because the need to bear this child was greater than all other needs, more important than anything or anyone, she had rationalized his demands. Torka and Karana had behaved in an unprecedented manner, as had Lonit. They had brought their punishment upon their own heads. And she truly believed that Navahk's magic had healed her, although in the ensuing hours the weakness had returned, along with the deep, nagging pain in the small of her back. But she was convinced that when he was himself again, he would work the magic again, she would be well, and her baby would be born. Yes! And surely Navahk's anger would disappear when he understood why she had not sent anyone after Lonit and Grek.

"This woman *did* call out to others to bring help for you," she assured him, wishing that the strained, bestial look would leave his face, that his hands would stop stressing the thong. "And so Pomm is here to heal you . . . to . . . to . . . but surely Navahk must understand that not even a magic woman such as Pomm would dare to wake the great spirit killer! And Lonit is the sister of Aliga's heart, and Torka was my man. If they must die, that is the will of the elders and Lorak and the forces of Creation. But Aliga thought that it would do no harm to allow my sister time to run away into the storm. What does the great Navahk care for a handful of women and children, an aging hunter, and two men who seem to make trouble everywhere they go? It was Lorak who drove them into the storm. He will die soon, then Navahk will become supreme elder of the Great Gathering! Torka, Lonit, Grek, Iana, Wallah, Karana, and the children are nothing in the shadow of the great Navahk! So Aliga thought that it was best if Navahk rested and regained his strength for what is to come—and for the child that Aliga will offer to him as his own."

"*Child?*" He smiled. "Would the woman of Torka like to see her *child*?"

When Pomm saw his smile, she was stunned by terror and could not move.

Nor could Aliga escape him as he fell upon her, using the shell that had struck out his eye to rip open her belly as his free hand quested deep and pulled out a handful of truth—a hideous mass of formless, malodorous, and malignant tissue.

"Here is your child, woman of Torka. Look upon your child. Suckle it as you die! As Lonit's children will die. As all those who walk with Torka will die for what they have done to me!"

Pomm backed out of the pit hut on all fours. It had been years since she had moved so quickly or had snapped to her feet without conscious effort or had accelerated her girth into an actual run. It did her no good; Navahk was after her, a lion pouncing upon an aging, hornless rhino. She went down with a gasp and stared blindly into wind and snow as he dragged her back into Torka's pit hut by one of her ankles. She screamed for help; but the wind carried her voice away into the storm, and no one heard her. She screamed as he closed the door skin behind her. Sprawled on her belly, she was unable to right herself until he jerked her upright by one of her stubby arms, half-dislocating it as he did so.

"Do not dare run from me!"

Her chin wobbled in terror. Her bright little eyes bulged as she saw the lifeless form of Aliga sprawled upon her bloodstained bed furs, her throat as well as her belly cut.

"Do not look so appalled, fat woman! Was it not your knife that opened the veins of Sondahr and hastened the departure of her life spirit so that your flat little feet might tread in the tracks that she had made in the hearts of men?"

"At her request was the cutting done! And with her own knife and—"

"Stop squealing! Are you not what you have lusted to be—magic woman of the Great Gathering?"

She blinked, confused, frightened, anticipating where his words were leading. "For h-how long?" she whimpered.

"That is up to you. Help me to eclipse Lorak, and you will live. But run away from me with a loose tongue and an accusing voice, and I will turn you out from this camp and slaver your naked flesh with blood after I have bound you fast by your own innards to a tree. Then the carnivores will come to devour you. This I swear by the forces of Creation."

She could not still the hammering of her heart, and that frightened her almost as much as the man who loomed over her, for it leaped and fell wildly within her breast, leaving her dizzy and breathless.

He crouched before her, smiling. One hand lay over his ruined eye. The other found her face. His index finger traced her brow slowly, sensuously. "What Pomm has witnessed has

not been the work of Navahk. You must tell the people that
the wanawut killed the tattooed woman, and it will kill all
who oppose Navahk in the days to follow."

Her heartbeat quieted. With his one hand held over his
mutilated eye, and the other fingering her features as a lover
might, his beauty was as before—perfection, a maturer Karana,
so intense and compelling that she found herself a captive of
his one dark eye, nodding mutely as his smile deepened.

"Yes, Pomm, we know what you desire, do we not? Perhaps I can give it to you. Or perhaps, when I find Karana, I
will make a present of him to you upon the Hill of Dreams.
His body yours to command. You would like that, would you
not?"

"I would have these things . . . and more."

He heard the pitiful desperation in her voice and knew that
he had not misread her; she wanted him. "Pomm *will* have
more," he purred, thinking of the pleasure that wringing her
neck would give him. "But first Pomm must speak for Navahk
and affirm all that he will say to the assembled bands from
the Hill of Dreams."

Slowly her hand rose to his, pressed softly, questingly.
"Your eye . . . does it bring much pain?"

"I feed on pain, woman. It gives me strength. As meat
nourishes other men, so does pain nourish me." He moved
his hand from beneath hers and rose. The words had been
easy to say, but the wound was stressing him. There were
poultices in his hut that would ease his pain, but only a little.
The wound must be cleansed, but he would allow no one to
tend him, lest someone bear witness to any sign of weakness.
He must have time alone.

He stood above Pomm, fighting back the impulse to kick
her. "I will go to the Hill of Dreams to commune with the
forces of Creation. Stay here with the corpse of the tattooed
woman. When the day yields to dusk, you must burst from
the hut crying to all that the wanawut has slain the tattooed
woman."

She looked uncertain. "But how will they believe that this
woman Pomm has escaped unharmed?"

"Tell them that by Navahk's power were you spared . . .
that the beast comes and goes at my command. And when you
have said this, I will affirm before all that because of your
magic ways with the soothing of my injury, no harm could

possibly come to you from the wanawut unless—or *until* I say so."

"Get in out of the storm, woman. What are you still doing huddled here upon the Hill of Dreams? This is no place for you!"

Naiapi looked up through blowing snow to see the fur-blanketed figure of Lorak standing over her—a dark blur, like a mud stain on snow. Disappointment flooded her; she had been waiting for Navahk for hours. "To whose hut should this woman go, then? I am the woman of Grek. My man has abandoned me and taken with him everything but this bed-roll and my few belongings. I am shamed before all. No man of my band will take me in. So I wait here for Navahk, headman of my people and brother to one who was my first man. Navahk will tell me what to do. And he has said that I would be his woman someday."

She looked so lost, so cold sitting there in the snow in her shaggy robe. Sondahr's robe? He could not be sure—there was too much snow on it. Her face was handsome, well defined even through the gauze of snow. Beneath the shaggy, frozen robe, her body would be handsome too; he had no doubt of that if Navahk had spoken for her.

Lorak's face collapsed about his nose. He was annoyed with Navahk. He was happy to think of him minus an eye. That would ruin his looks and wilt his arrogance! The man had virtually taken over at the feast-fire celebrations before Lorak realized what he was doing. True enough, he had been delighted to drive Torka and his undisciplined whelp from the encampment, but Lorak had wanted to instigate the action. He had not liked the way Navahk had willed evil spirits into Sondahr without his approval. Now the magic woman was dead, and Navahk had enjoyed Torka's antelope-eyed woman. But Lorak would never have the pleasure of easing his lust upon Sondahr—a lust that Navahk must have sated years before.

Frustration and jealousy pricked the old man. He would fix Navahk and teach him not to trifle with his elders. He put out his hand to Naiapi. "So Navahk has spoken for you. Well, he is a one-eyed man who will be long recuperating under the care of Pomm. Lorak is supreme elder in this encampment, and Lorak now speaks for Naiapi. Come, woman. Grek has abandoned you, and the storm grows worse. This man has no woman to warm his bed skins. I would wager you know a few tricks to warm a hungry old man, eh?"

She accepted his hand with only momentary hesitation. "I know many tricks, Lorak, especially if you are truly hungry. Many would be amazed at the magic that Naiapi has been able to work with meat."

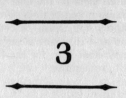

3

They went out across the land together. Although they heard the howling of wolves and the wanawut, they did not look back. Falling snow covered their tracks. Torka, Karana, and Lonit were battered and bruised, but they walked boldly, with Grek, Iana, Wallah, Mahnie, and the children following.

They dragged two sledges now: Aar rode upon the one that Mahnie had taken, along with her well-chosen supplies; the other, quickly constructed of caribou antlers by Grek before he had left to join Torka and Karana, had two mammoth-rib runners. These would double as roof supports when they encamped. In the cold, driving wind, Grek had iced them with his own urine so that they would glide atop the snow as the group fled across the land.

Grek marveled at the luck that had intensified the storm and kept the people of the Great Gathering inside their pit huts, then at his own good fortune, having such a one as Wallah for his woman. He looked back at her now as she trudged with head bent forward against her brow band. She had not hesitated for a moment when he had whispered his intentions of following Torka; she wanted to leave the encampment as much as he did, not only to find Mahnie but to be away from what she believed to be a place of very bad spirits.

With Iana and Lonit at her side working hurriedly and efficiently, she had broken down their pit hut in record time. In silence the women had prepared carrying packs and stacked upon the sledge the remaining rib bones, hide coverings, dried meat, packets of fat, and the few belongings that Lonit had brought from Torka's pit hut—including his spears, bludgeon, and spear hurler—plus all those things of Grek's that would mean life to them on the long trek.

At last they were committed to their course. As he walked beside Torka into the rising storm, wolves howling in the distance and the wanawut shrieking closer at his back, Grek walked confidently, without fear, for the first time in more years than he cared to remember.

The child watched them go.

Through cold, white wind and snow, the eyes of the child saw them—warm, brown, furs, and flesh.

The child's wide, splayed nostrils quivered. These were the sweet smells of life—creatures moving in unison. A pack. Young. Old. Many equaling one. One stronger because of many. Many stronger because there was one among them who was not afraid to lead.

The child shivered and tasted bitterness at the back of its throat. Loneliness always tasted bitter. Loneliness was a muddy color in the child's mind, blue around the edges, like a bruise that would not heal, cold at the thick, dark center that fell away to nothing—empty, like the eyes of Mother Killer.

Mother!

Leaning forward, staring through the ice-rimed, wind-broken grasses, the child mewed softly. The beasts were well away now. The one who looked like Mother Killer walked with them. But he was not Mother Killer. He was Star Eyes, a gentle beast—a memory from long ago. The child thought of Mother and pack, of times long gone by, of warm arms and soothing sounds, of breast milk as warm and sweet as blood.

Its mewing increased. The air was cold here by the lake in the white world, with the wind whipping at the child's fur and no hole in the sky to send sweet warmth to the earth below, and no Mother—or even Mother Killer—to offer comfort in the storm.

The child took a step forward through the grasses, heard ice crack along the stems and smelled the slightly acrid, dusty scent of the dried stalks. It wanted to go forward, to follow the beasts into the storm, but only moments ago it had heard Mother Killer howling with pain from within the circle of piled bones. He was hurt. Perhaps he would never bring meat again. Perhaps his breath would leave his body, and one of his own kind would gut him and skin him and dance in his flesh, as he had danced in the flesh of Mother.

A cramp bit deep within the child's belly. It hunkered down, still mewing to itself, confused by its own pain and the smell of its own blood. A massive, hirsute hand moved to explore the source of the scent. The child fingered warm redness against its inner thighs. The blood was scabbing there, encrusting within the thick, gray, downy fur. The child uttered a series of low, confused little hoots. Mother had bled, too, and not just at the time she had ceased to breathe. Mother howled and mewed at these times of occasional blood, as the child howled and mewed now.

Confused by the blood that came from no wound, the child ran its bloodied hand back and forth across the snow-carpeted floor of grass. It cried out. Something sharp had sliced its finger. The child sucked at it, tasting and smelling wound blood now. The cut was small but deep. The child kept on sucking, easing pain as it flailed its free fist angrily into the snow. Something hard bruised the heel of its hand.

Curious, the child huffed and circled, still crouching, bending close, blowing snow away, extending the index finger of its uncut hand to touch the offending object, shaped like an elongated willow leaf.

The child recognized it at once. The object was the lanceolate, meticulously carved dagger of obsidian, left behind, along with a flying stick, by one of the beasts that had come out from the piled bones carrying fire. Evidently when the child had dragged Star Eyes, the wounded beast that looked like Mother Killer, into the circle of grass, the oddly shaped stone must have been dragged along with him, tangled in the fringes of his garments. The child carefully lifted the stone, smelled it, and licked it. There was no doubt that it was a thing of earth formed by the hands of man to a new purpose.

The child cocked its head. It lay the edge of the dagger alongside its wound, measuring, defining the dagger's potential, understanding just how and by what its hand had been cut.

It grunted now in satisfaction, gripping the sinew-wrapped end of the dagger, remembering another such man stone . . . buried in the breast of its mother.

Torka led his people on through a world where sky and land were one, where snow and wind were the one wailing reality. At last he was forced to stop lest he become guilty of leading them in circles.

They erected a crude shelter against the storm, a mere lean-to that broke the back of the wind and allowed them to sleep huddled together until, at last, the wind veered and dropped. Torka awoke, with Lonit still dreaming in the curl of one arm and Summer Moon asleep in the other. Iana was a Demmi-protecting mound with a fur-clad arm and mittened hand. He could hear the pull of Grek's breathing, the light exhalations and inhalations of Mahnie, and the rather profound snores of Wallah.

He saw Karana standing alone in the white, silent world. Snow was still falling. Aar was at his side. Relief flooded Torka. The animal would live! He had feared that it would not.

Wincing against the pain of his tightly bound ribs and many bruises and moving carefully so that he would not awaken the others, Torka climbed to his feet and went out to Karana.

The youth did not acknowledge his presence. Torka put up his hood and adjusted his ruff so that snow did not fall into his face. For a long while he and Karana stood in silence.

"They will follow. If they find us—"

"They will not." Torka interrupted Karana before, once again, he inadvertently gave voice to words that might cause terrible things to happen.

Ahead of them, through the snow mist, the faintest diffusion of golden light glowed far to the east.

"The sun rises," Karana observed.

Torka nodded. "I will tell the others. We must go on."

All that day the snow fell. The voice of the wanawut was heard, and the wind blew in intermittent, vicious squalls into which no man at the Great Gathering wished to venture.

Within the council house of bones, the supreme elder was not feeling well. He looked gray and pinched and made no attempt to hide the fact that his belly ached. He adamantly refused Navahk's request to lead hunters in pursuit of the woman who had maimed him.

"The people of Man Who Walks With Dogs must be dead by now," Lorak wheezed. "Forget them. The wanawut has invaded this encampment to take the life of one who dwelled among us. The bodies of Stam and Aliga and Sondahr have been put to look upon the sky forever. Now wolves and lions prowl close to the walls. Bad spirits walk the world, Navahk.

Lorak says that it is good that the people remain within the wall of bones."

All the hunters and elders who had gathered to counsel within the great, smoke-filled room murmured in agreement.

From beneath the skin of the wanawut Navahk fixed the supreme elder contemptuously with his one good eye; the other was hidden beneath a wide band of white caribou skin cut from the inside seam of his surplice. His head ached. His ruined eye was a bottomless pit of pain; but he had rested and cleansed the wound and packed it with painkilling poultices of fat saturated with willow oil, and he was in control of it now.

He was surprised when the old man was not visibly intimidated by his glare. Anger and frustration showed on Navahk's face because he had been certain that the credulous elder and equally gullible magic men and hunters would have been his to command once Pomm screeched her story about the attack of the wanawut. But although they had been sobered, they had not been without questions, and he was in no mood to hear them. "Unlike Lorak, Navahk does not walk with fear. This man has brought mammoths to the hunters of this camp. This man walks in the skin of the wanawut. It will hurt no man who hunts with me."

From where he sat among the men of his own band, a scowling, thoughtful Zinkh spoke out: "Zinkh says that if Navahk wishes to hunt the eye-taking woman, that right be his right, yes! But with Navahk has come more than mammoths. With Navahk has come the thing we fear—the wind spirit wanawut. This man Zinkh does not hunt in the land of wind spirits. And this man Zinkh does not hunt women. If, as Navahk says, Lonit struck out his eye in order to escape, this man says that perhaps the spirits have punished her already. The storm is bad. The cold is worse. Lonit is only a woman, and Torka must be dead by now. A female must always do as she is told, so for her disobedience the spirits will punish Torka's woman. If Lonit was willing to risk walking the wind to be with her man, this man would not risk his life in the storm to stop her. And the man Grek has but one aging female and one girl child. What loss to his band is such a hunter?"

"Bravely and generously spoken. I wonder if Zinkh would be so forgiving if it was his eye that had been taken." Navahk's one eye narrowed. They had all accepted the lie that Lonit

had maimed him. They had all been outraged by Grek's
unprecedented behavior. But Navahk had been unable to
infect them with his own need for vengeance. Zinkh was a
particular annoyance to him, in the elaborate, grotesquely
moldering headdress crowned by a mutilated, headless fox.
Beside him several hunters, both young and old, looked at
Navahk out of fixed and wary eyes. Zinkh's band was small,
but his men were loyal to their headman. Not one had
participated in the violence against Torka and Karana with
any enthusiasm. They had hung back, hesitating when Lorak
had commanded them to follow him into the night by torchlight. Alone of all of the hunters, the banishment and beat-
ings had set Zinkh's men on edge.

"Zinkh grows bold since he has reclaimed the 'lucky' headdress that Karana spurned and left behind in Torka's pit hut!"
Lorak had only impatience and disdain for the little headman.

Navahk was pleased.

Zinkh glowered petulantly at the supreme elder. "Perhaps
Karana's luck would not have run out if he still wore it!"

"And perhaps Zinkh has other reasons for fearing to venture from this camp?" Navahk accused, sensing that the man
was strengthening Lorak's position and weakening his own.

"No man hunts in weather like this!" Zinkh responded
hotly.

Navahk's eye never blinked; his smile never wavered. "The
storm will not last forever."

"Storm or no storm, it is no good thing for men to hunt
women or take the lives of other men as though they be
game. Zinkh says enough has been done to the people of Man
Who Walks With Dogs. Let the storm spirits, not men,
decide whether to take them to walk the wind forever."

"Navahk has been told that Zinkh walked into the Great
Gathering with Torka," said the magic man. "Perhaps there is
a bond between you? When Torka was put out of this camp,
should Zinkh have been put out of it as well?"

Zinkh wilted visibly, but beside him the young hunter
Simu snapped angrily to his feet, having had enough of
insults and threats to his headman. "Navahk is not supreme
elder of this encampment! Navahk is not even an elder. This
man does not know Navahk from past camps! Navahk dances
an impressive dance and chants an impressive chant. Navahk's
band has driven mammoths before it, but trouble has walked
into the Great Gathering at Navahk's side! People have died

since Navahk has come to dwell among us! By what right does he challenge Lorak and threaten the headman of my band, who is known to all assembled here as a brave hunter and one who has brought harm to no man or woman in his lifetime!"

Navahk's head went up. Pain flared within his ruined eye—caused by Iana in defense of Torka's children, intensified by Lonit's shaming of him. He snarled at the bold and impetuous young hunter who had dared to challenge him. "By the right of the wanawut does Navahk speak! Be cautious when you address me, Simu, for your woman is great with child, and the wanawut prowls the storm, with its belly full of the unborn child of Aliga. Perhaps the wanawut feels a growing hunger for more of the same kind of meat."

Simu, his face ashen, seated himself as though he had been knocked down. There was not a man in the room who did not suffer an identical reaction.

For a moment Navahk wondered if he had gone too far, but fear had always been his ally. Men who feared could be led. And he could not expect to kill Karana and Torka's people alone.

He smiled at Simu kindly, benevolently, as a loving brother. "Only Navahk can keep the wanawut beyond the walls of this camp, and only Navahk understands that as long as a single member of Torka's band remains alive, the wanawut will hunger for human flesh. This man shares the heart and soul of the wanawut. The spirit of the wanawut bleeds as this man has bled. It is filled with pain as this man is filled with pain. It hungers to destroy the source of the pain . . . in blood. Will Simu and the brave hunters of the Great Gathering not be willing to cut boldly from the hide of the world those whose lives enrage the wanawut and endanger their loved ones . . . their women . . . their unborn sons?"

Lorak frowned, sensing deception. One of his old gnarled hands was pressed wide against his gut. "If the wanawut would feed upon blood, let it ride the back of the storm to seek out the ones who have maimed you, for it will find none of them here."

Navahk's smile was radiant. From the moment that he had entered the encampment, he had wished that Lorak would sicken and die. The old fool was apparently so sick that he was distracted and weary and anxious to return to his bed skins, where Naiapi awaited him. Navahk could smell the strong, rich smells of roasting meat emanating deliciously from the supreme elder's private shelter. Navahk was not surprised that now that Sondahr was dead, the old man had taken a woman to ease his days and pleasure him in the night; nor was he particularly surprised to find that he had chosen Naiapi. She was still a handsome woman, and she had a fawning, sexually avaricious way that would be appreciated by an old man whose male pride needed oiling.

He would oil that pride now. "If the wanawut goes with the storm spirits when they leave the sky, Navahk will speak no more of this."

The storm cleared slowly from the east, but for two long days and nights, as Torka and his people traveled under clear, albeit cold and windy skies, they looked back into the western world of men and saw snow-clouds still bulked upon the horizon. The storm lingered there, howling and striking the land with gale-force winds. In spite of their injuries and stiffness, Torka urged the others on, grateful to the weather, for he doubted that any men would leave a safe encampment in such a storm.

"Navahk would travel in any weather," Karana said. "In spite of the storm, his eyes will see the route."

"He has one eye now," reminded Iana.

"But Navahk has an inner eye lighting the way for his other senses. Sondahr called it the gift of Seeing, although his sight is not as clear as hers or mine." Karana paused, not wanting to sound like a braggart, but the Seeing gift *was* his; there was no use denying it. "But he can see into the hearts of men and know their thoughts, anticipate their actions, and more importantly, their *re*actions. With this gift he can twist their wills to serve his own. Mark me well: Navahk is not a man to forgive or forget. As soon as the storm is over, he *will* follow. And he will not come alone."

"This woman is not afraid!" insisted Iana, and with her head held high, she smiled a strong little smile because she knew that her boast was the truth. "Good spirits guided the stone of Lonit's bola, and their strength was in this woman's arm."

"I am afraid of him," Mahnie confessed, refusing to speak Navahk's name as she knelt beside Aar, checking the wound on the side of the dog's head. Karana had sutured it. It was clean and scabbed, and in the severe cold there was little chance of infection. Still, the girl was concerned, and only after looking close and flicking away a fragment of dried suture did she turn her face to the others. "My father has taught me that fear is a good thing. It gives strength and makes us alert for danger. Never will this girl—uh, woman—slow her step when she thinks that there is even the smallest chance that Spirit Killer might be following!"

She rose then, and Karana saw that Aar nuzzled her mittened hand as he stood ready to proceed at her side. The dog had walked since the end of their first day of traveling. At night he whimpered and circled a long time before settling down, posting himself to look back along the route, as though expecting Sister Dog and the pups to be following. He howled often, seemingly without reason, but the girl had told Karana that she was certain that he was calling to his lost family, hoping they would hear and follow. Karana knew that she was right, and as they walked together, he could understand why Aar had taken a strong liking to the daughter of Grek. She was a pretty, strong-willed little thing, but he wished that she would stop looking at him every time she declared her womanhood. He had no doubt about her word; if she said that she was a woman, it must be so. But after Sondahr, whose loveliness and womanliness no other woman could equal, Mahnie would always seem a child to him.

"We will go on, then, if Torka and Grek agree?" Wallah sighed, weary but ready to continue.

"Torka leads, Grek follows," assured Grek, helping Wallah to her feet. "And if Torka should grow weary, he has only to point the way and Grek will lead. Together with Karana we will make a strong band in the new and game-rich country!"

"It is far, this forbidden land." Wallah sighed again, adjusting her brow band so that it would not cut so deeply into her forehead.

"It is far," conceded Torka, wishing that he could tell the sturdy, patient, and almost uncomplaining woman otherwise. "We must reach it before the time of the long dark. Otherwise I fear that we will be forced to encamp within the Corridor of Storms itself."

"Is it as savage a land as they say?" pressed Grek, worry thickening his features a little; like Iana, he, too, had been reborn and would not allow fear to cripple him.

Torka nodded. "It is a land of endless wind and cruel winters. There is little snow, but the cold is so bitter that the skin of Mother Below freezes solid to its heart and the stars crack into uncountable pieces as they fall to cloud the earth with a killing mist no men may dare to breathe lest they die. But to this man the far and forbidden land seems no more savage than the land of men to the west, and within the corridor there is a valley that will protect us. By its warm pools we will encamp, feeding on the caches of food that we left behind. Game is plentiful and will feed us through the dark days that will soon be upon us. If the forces of Creation allow it, life will be good for us there."

"Then let us get on with our journey," encouraged Grek, "for by Mother Below and Father Above, life here is not!"

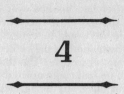

4

It snowed for three more days in the country of the mammoth eaters. The wind blew hard from the high barrens of the polar north, so the snow could not settle. It blew southward in a howling white tide, across the Arctic Ocean and over the rolling, tundral steppeland, which was an exposed seabed that stretched for thousands of miles to the shrunken shores of a vast ocean that would someday be misnamed Pacific.

On the fourth day Navahk awoke to silence within the encircling wall of the encampment of the Great Gathering. He lay awake for a long time, waiting to hear the sound of snow stinging the walls of his pit hut. But there was only silence. In the pale light of dawn he dressed and went out.

Snow was still falling, but thinly now, straight to the ground—soft and so fine that it made no sound falling upon the land and huts and face of the magic man as he looked up. It would not last. He closed his eye and let it melt upon his lid. His *one* lid. He scowled and wiped the moisture away. He would need to see clearly now, before the others awoke.

Now that the blizzard had abated, there was something he must do. For two long days the voice of the wanawut had not been heard. The people of the many bands rejoiced, and Lorak, sick though he was, had continued to tell them that the beast had gone off into the storm in pursuit of Torka and his band. Safe and warm within their shelters, their bellies full of mammoth meat and their women hot and willing against them beneath their sleeping furs, the hunters had no desire to abandon their leisure to pursue the people of Man Who Walks With Dogs, no matter what one of his women had done to Navahk. Things were good in the camp. No one had died since Torka had been driven out. True, Lorak was not well; but he was old, and old men were often sickly.

Navahk's scowl stretched his lips over his teeth until the tips of his canines showed. If it *had* followed to prey upon Torka and his people, he would be denied the pleasure of his vengeance against them—unless they killed it, destroying the magnificence of its power forever. The thought appalled him almost as much as if he had contemplated his own death. He wanted the wanawut alive. Its living close to him, feeding from his hand, looking at him out of its strange, wondrously beautiful eyes excited and strengthened him. But what if it had died? The storm had been so vicious and unrelenting. Twice he had secretly risked venturing out to the lake to leave meat for the beast, but he had seen no sign of it in the raging wind and blinding snow. On his second trip the meat he had left was still where he had placed it, untouched and frozen. But then, that was not the only meat that had been brought out into the storm from the encampment. Bodies had been put to look upon the sky forever. The wanawut might be feeding off them.

He knew he must find it and make it howl again. Or, if it was dead or gone from this country, he must howl in its place, to terrify the people and convince them to follow his will—and he must do it soon, for each day spent in camp put Torka and his people farther away. If they reached the Corridor of Storms, it would take the forces of Creation to convince any of the mammoth hunters to follow them into that forbidden land.

The child saw him coming through the white, silent mists of snow. She ran from him. In her panic she clutched the willow-leaf-shaped man stone to her breast as she fled back to her nest near the lakeshore, leaving the corpses where they lay, one half-eaten now, their flesh hard, their faces covered with grass.

The child did not like their ugly, staring faces, their beast eyes blank and glazed in death. She had covered them with grass lest she be revolted as she ate. And yet as she had hunkered over the bodies, delighted to discover the usefulness of the man stone in cutting away the freezing flesh beneath layers of skins and furs, she was nevertheless disturbed by the vague similarities between the beasts and her own kind: The shape of their torsos and their arms and limbs were weak and tendonous, yet they were somehow the same. And one had breasts not unlike her own. The child could not bring herself to eat that one, although she had sucked the blood; curious, she suckled the breasts for milk and was disappointed—but not surprised—when she found none.

Man meat was the best meat. Mother had taught her that. But the bodies were stiff with cold, and the flavor of the one she ate of was gone now that she had sucked the blood from it. The blood tasted identical to the blood that she had sucked from her own body whenever she cut herself. And there was something in the shape of the skull. So fragile! Such delicate eye sockets and weak, narrow snout. Such tiny, useless teeth.

When the other beasts had carried them out from the wall of bones and left them to lie upon the earth, the child had watched the bodies for a long time before daring to venture near. At last hunger made her bold. Despite the cold and snow, the stink of death was bad in one of them. The child had dragged it away from the other two and had not eaten of its black-swirled flesh. When wolves and a lioness had come near, the child had let them have that corpse; it had been nearly dry of blood anyway.

But the wolves and lioness had wanted no part of such foul meat, and the child had fought them for possession of the other two, marveling how lions and wolves seemed so much smaller and more timid to her now. One lunge and stabbing feint had driven back all but a single wolf, and that animal had been dispatched with a single blow of the child's fist. The other wolves had run away then. The lioness had dragged off the wolf, preferring its meat to that of the stinking corpse. And until now no predators had come to bother the child again.

She exhaled low, quick grunts of frustration as she ran, looking back over her shoulder at the figure slowly advancing through the falling snow. A beast. The one in white? Mother Killer? She could not tell. She only knew that an inner sense warned her to run. She had eaten of the flesh of man, and man would be angry.

Navahk pursued the creature through the grasses until he reached the place where the beast had been feeding. He slowed his step and saw what was left of Stam. There was no sign of Aliga. He was unconcerned and untouched by what he saw; he had seen kills before, what was left of game when large carnivores had been driven off after feeding awhile.

Then, for one sharp, stabbing instant, Navahk looked upon the body of Sondahr. The imperious, magnificent Sondahr. He stared down at the dead woman as he toed away the mounded stack of snow-covered grass that covered her face.

He gasped in horror as he took an inadvertent step back. Sondahr's face was intact. Iced and colorless, it appeared to float like a flawless moon on the black sea of her hair. Her eyes were wide and staring—*seeing* him. Her mouth was slightly open, upcurled—*smiling* at him, as though her spirit remained alive within the shell of her unmarred and exquisite skull . . . to name him trickster and man of flesh, not of spirit . . . to mock him and name him unworthy of her love or affection, even *now*, when she was a corpse and he was a living man.

With a brutal kick that half decapitated her, he wheeled and continued his pursuit of the beast, glad that it had not desecrated Sondahr's body and yet hating it for that . . . loathing it for that . . . wanting to kill it for allowing Sondahr to remain so beautiful, someone who had never been, could never be his.

Breathless with fear and from the exertion of her run, the child hurled herself into the high sheltering grasses within which she had made her nest. Snow was barely falling, and it was quiet within the windbreak. The child crouched silently, listening to the pounding of her heart and the rasp of her breath as she wrapped her long, hairy arms across her chest, rocking herself, shivering so violently against her fear that the man stone sliced into her palm. Instinctively knowing that she was being hunted, she made no sound against the pain as, with a purely reflexive outward flick of her fingers, she released the dagger and raised her hand to suck her wound.

The child listened. The man was close. She could hear his steps—slow, cautious, and measured, like a great white lion stalking game in the protective undercover of thick brush. The child could see him now. It *was* Mother Killer. The child relaxed. All in white, he was not wearing her mother's skin. Even one eye was banded in white, and as he moved forward, the child could see that snowflakes starred his night-black hair. Although he carried a flying stick and walked in the way of an animal that is wary and watchful and afraid, the child sensed no threat in him until he paused and parted the grasses with the sharp, stone-headed tip of his stick.

The child looked into his face and was terrified of the savagery that she saw there. Leering, showing his teeth, his black eye was full of something that the child had never seen before—something dangerous, as dark and treacherous as a pitch pool. It was more than the focused, direct expression an animal shows when it is about to leap to the kill. This was an expression unique to the emotions of the beast man: It was a look of cruelty and hatred, and the child was wise to fear it.

She was not quick enough to escape the forward thrust of the spear that struck out and pressed against her thigh, not piercing her flesh but pinning her to the nest.

The child screamed in outrage, confusion, and terror, a roaring scream that usually sent predators fleeing for their lives, a scream that rent the still air of morning as only the scream of the wanawut could do.

But the scream did not frighten the beast in white. The scream made Mother Killer smile.

Navahk froze, feeling the power of the beast through the spear in his hands. The fire-hardened bone shaft was close to snapping, but the creature held position and did not fully stress the spear. It could have leaped at him. But it did not, nor did it try to run. He was speaking to it now, whispering, his eyes devouring not only its power, which could have been hurled against him if it chose, but encompassing an even more amazing and intriguing truth.

He had been close to the beast before, but never *this* close. Always shrubs or grasses stood between them, revealing only suggestions of its hairy form. Now Navahk saw it clearly for the first time.

It was hideous and loathsome, half human, half animal, and completely female.

She had matured at an astounding rate. He could see her breasts and smell her sex. And slowly, as he met the wide, lustrous gray eyes of the thing, he realized with growing wonder that she feared him as much, if not more, than he feared her.

"*Wah nah wut* . . ." he whispered, moving the spear relaxing its pressure on her thigh, slowly withdrawing the shaft.

The creature blinked. She looked to the spear, then to the

man. Her grotesque head tilted to one side. *"Wah . . . nah?"* She copied his sound, questioning with it.

Navahk felt smug and victorious over the stupid thing. *"Wah nah?"* he echoed, his eyes moving over the animal, taking in the incredible power of her musculature, the size of her hands and arms and massive jaws, her bent and foreshortened lower limbs, and the hairy, barrel-chested torso out of which two bare, fully human breasts flared tender and pale like the budding breasts of a nubile young girl. He was stirred by them. Carefully, slowly, his free hand reached forward; his single fingertip traced a large taut nipple that crested and hardened at his touch.

He laughed, at once amused and disgusted but more deeply stirred than ever before. He resented his reaction; it revolted him. This thing was not a woman, not a girl. She was not even human! This beast nourished herself on the blood of man. Sondahr's blood had been sucked dry by the creature; Sondahr's blood gave her strength.

"Sondahr!" His exhalation of the dead woman's name surprised him. He had not intended to speak, and certainly not with such longing.

The beast frowned. Her head tilted in the opposite direction. "Suh . . . dahh . . ."

Navahk was stunned. The beast had done more than imitate his voice. She had captured the tone of desire that had seemed to bleed from his spirit when he had spoken. The tone had created a response in the animal. Again she cocked her head, looking at him, studying him with her impossibly human and beautiful eyes . . . reaching out to touch his breast, as he had touched hers, with a gently questing finger.

He did not move. He allowed the touch. The thing's hand drifted to his face, explored, lingered so gently, so tenderly that he could barely feel her touch. His own hand rose, hesitated, then slowly reached to touch the face of the beast. The animal made no move to resist him. She moved closer, closing her eyes and quivering with pleasure at his touch. A surge of power swelled in him like flame rising to explode outward.

No man has done this! he thought. *No man has touched the wanawut and lived. No man!*

His hand moved, caressed the beast. Her eyes opened. He saw fear, confusion, and need in her face. Fear of the stranger.

Confusion in this new and astounding situation. Need to be comforted, to be touched . . . to be *loved*? Even by a man?

It was then that the madness took him. He knew it for what it was and did not care, for the need was suddenly as great in him as it was in the beast. He trembled at the thought of what he was about to do. No female was his equal. None had satisfied him. The beast was young. For the rising of many moons she had been alone, with only him daring to come to her, to feed her, to mouth utterances of her own sounds to her. She would not understand what he was doing now until his intent was accomplished, and even then she would not grasp that she had been mated.

Beast to man, flesh to spirit, Navahk to the wanawut—to *power*, to the very physical manifestation of all that men feared.

He lay the spear aside. He was afraid, but fear was sweet and stimulating as he cautiously moved into the nest with her. She did not stop him. He saw his image reflected in the eyes of the animal. Even with his ruined eye, he was as beautiful as the beast was ugly. No man in the world could equal him now—not Torka on a hunt, not Lorak at magic making, and not even Karana when it came to calling the spirits. For the power of the wanawut was in him; he could feel it pumping in his heart, surging in his arms and limbs, and rising in his loins. He had slain a wind spirit and danced in its skin, and now he would master the beast and teach her to respond to his command.

His smile became a carnivorous leer. "Come . . ." he invited, cautiously touching her, beginning to lead her, wondering if Sondahr also felt his touch, for within the flesh of the animal was the blood of the woman.

Not understanding, the wanawut leered back at him. "Kuh . . . mmm . . ." she repeated, and as he stroked her, her skin quivered again, the skin of an animal responding to the stroking of her own kind.

5

"It is early for such a hard freeze," observed Grek when they reached the Big Milk River. "This big river usually roars longer than most."

"The spirits are with us," said Karana.

"It seems so," agreed Torka, and he led them across the river.

They rested on its banks that night. They made no fire lest others see it or smell its smoke and thereby fix their position. Ahead of them lay the broad Plain of Many Waters. Under a clear, brutally cold sky, they ate dry traveling rations and observed the treacherous expanse of ice that lay between them and the country to the east.

"We dare not cross," said a weary Wallah. "Perhaps it is just as well. We could all do with a rest. Such an early cold cannot last much longer. Soon the ice will melt and—"

"Navahk will close the distance between us with ease," interrupted Karana, his tone stern with warning.

"But once the river thaws, they will have to journey far to the south to cross it," reminded Grek. "Besides, we have seen no sign of anyone. Perhaps no one pursues us after all."

"Perhaps," agreed Torka without enthusiasm, "but we will not stay to find out. Tomorrow we will go on, and the ice will be no hindrance to us."

He gestured to Lonit, who went to her traveling pack and brought out a pair of stone-studded leather nets. Before long Lonit had showed Wallah and the other women how to fashion their own special thong-webbed soles for their boots; studded with sharp bits of antler broken off from Grek's stalking cloak and bound securely across their insteps, these crampons allowed excellent traction on the ice.

The next day they crossed the broken, treacherous terrain of the Plain of Many Waters, glad for the frozen ground, and Demmi, riding with Aar on one of the two sledges, cried and pointed in frustration, wanting to join Summer Moon, who proudly high-stepped between Lonit and Iana in her own pair of ice walkers.

Straining to maintain her balance as she tried hard to keep up with Karana, Mahnie smiled to see the pride and joy in the little girl. "This morning Summer Moon told me that she is glad to be going home. Tell me about the forbidden land, Karana."

"It is far," he replied obliquely, looking over his shoulder as he often did, his handsome face grim with concern.

Her feelings were hurt. Again and again she tried to be a friend to him. He was never rude to her but merely preoccupied, except when she had mentioned her fear of Navahk after the way he had killed Pet. He had looked at her as though she had struck him, and for many hours he had spoken to no one but had walked on ahead, brooding and alone. She sighed. The bone barbs of her ice walkers snagged on a rough outcropping of muddy ice. She nearly fell. He caught and held her, but with less interest than he would have shown to his dog. She looked up at him, her feelings hurt until she saw the depth of his fear in his eyes. Now, for the first time, her confidence in her elders flagged. Memories swam within her. "Do you really think he will follow us? Grek says that the storm must surely have given us time to gain many miles on him."

"No storm will stop him. And if he finds us—" He stopped before he spoke words that he had no wish to conjure into reality. "You ask a lot of questions for a girl."

"I am not a girl!" she told him emphatically. "I am a woman!"

He looked her up and down. "If you say so."

"I do!" she declared, and in a huff pushed him so hard that his ice walkers went out from under him, and he fell down.

Lorak was dead.

Navahk danced in the firelight, in the skin of the wanawut, with all the assembled bands looking on. He danced as he had never danced before, whirling, leaping, the power of the beast in him. All who watched him were amazed.

Navahk smiled at the women, children, and elders. As the

hunters listened, he sang to the women of their brave men,
of past hunts and good winters, of full bellies and fires burning warm in the winter dark.

And then, with his staff in one hand and spear in the other,
Navahk circled the feast fire and chanted of Lorak, whose
body had been put out to look upon the sky forever.

"Great was Lorak! Proud will be the hunter whose woman
next bears a son into whose body the spirit of Lorak will
come! Who will this woman be whose man will name their
child for Lorak?"

The women looked meaningfully from one to the other,
and among the women of Zinkh's band, all eyes went to
Simu's young, pretty woman, for her time was fast approaching. Her face turned down. Her eyes stared with embarrassment into her lap.

Across from her, seated with the men on their side of the
circle, Simu was proud and troubled all at once. He wished
that Zinkh had never brought his people to the Great Gathering. Things had been bad in the encampment since the
banishment of the People Who Walk With Dogs. He had
been shaken by that; never in his life had he seen men
brutalized in the way that Torka and Karana had been. He
had liked and respected Torka and had learned more about
the hunt on one day's trek onto the tundra with him than he
had in a lifetime of hunting with Zinkh and the men of his
own band. He was glad that Torka's women had run away to
be with him. Simu hoped that his own Eneela would do the
same for him. He admired the strong old hunter Grek for
daring to risk his own family in order to help them, and he
wondered if he would be as brave as Grek had been—or as
unflinching before pain and certain death as Torka, or even
the youth Karana.

He watched the dance of the magic man and sensed a
falseness in him. But these shamans were all that way—aloof,
disdainful, overbearing, all show and sparkling fires and
strangely scented smokes. Having grown up in a band with
Pomm as magic woman, he believed with a certainty that her
healing ways were clever diversions.

Nevertheless, he wondered why old Pomm looked so nervous as she sat in the position of supreme rank in the center
of the women's half of the circle, next to Naiapi, who had
become old Lorak's woman during his last days. Pomm had
never made a secret of her longing to sit someday in that

spot, to outshine the legendary Sondahr. Now that Sondahr had died and Navahk had proclaimed the great powers of Pomm, Simu would have expected her to look smug. But instead her pudgy little hands plucked at her headdress of feathers in the way men and women pluck at the air when they fear that death is near. There was fear in her eyes as she observed the dance of Navahk.

Beside him Zinkh made a low guttural sound as he crossed his arms over his meager chest and shook his head. Simu saw his scowl and knew that he was not the only man feeling unenthusiastic about Navahk's display. True, there was not a band that would not covet such a shaman as Navahk; nor was there a man or woman who would dispute his right to become supreme elder in Lorak's place. But something set Simu on edge when he looked at him. He had not forgotten the way the man had threatened him. More, Navahk had blamed the death of Stam on Torka and his dogs. Yet Torka was long gone, and now Het was dead as a result of a freak accident in which he had tripped over air, it seemed, and fallen into Navahk's fire circle. The man had been so dirty, his clothes and hair so greasy, he had caught fire instantly and run through the camp. By the time anyone had been able to tackle him and try to smother the flames, it was too late.

Simu's mouth tensed. That was no fit death for a man. Yet others had died worse deaths since then: three old men and two old women among whom Navahk had generously portioned the meat of Torka's slain dogs. They had died screaming, like Sondahr. The magic men had not been able to heal them. In the end Navahk had commanded Pomm to end their misery, and after many hours spent in a trance, he had announced that bad spirits would walk the camp until Torka and his people were found and slain.

And now, suddenly, Navahk's dance changed. No longer chanting to honor the memory of Lorak, he set to loose fear within the hearts of the People, and when the bladder flask the men had been passing around came to Simu, he passed it on without drinking. Somehow, he sensed that to be drunk on this night would not be a good thing.

Yet the others drank as Navahk sang a dark song of bad spirits and an encampment that must be purged. His potent song caught fire in his listeners, and before Simu could fully grasp what was happening, the circle of watchers broke wide around him. Men, women, and children, urged on by Navahk's maniacal song, scurried to fetch their precious stores of bison and mammoth meat, to hurl their hard-won winter food supply into the communal fire.

"Torka has hunted this meat," cried the magic man, encouraging their madness. "It is bad meat, cursed by his bad spirit. All who eat it will die!"

Aghast at the appalling waste, Simu stood beside an equally incredulous Zinkh. How could the people believe what the magic man was saying? Sondahr had supposedly died of Navahk's own curse! Lorak had most likely succumbed to the infirmities of old age. Het had stumbled into a fire pit, and for days people had been eating bison and mammoth meat with no ill effects. Only those who had eaten of the flesh of the dogs had been . . . poisoned?

A coldness pricked at the back of Simu's shoulders as the young man understood. The flames, fed with fat and bone and dried flesh, grew high, giving birth to smoke that smelled rich and sweet with the aroma of roasting meat that would feed no one during the time of the long dark that was nearly upon them. In the wake of the storm, the land surrounding the encampment would yield little nourishment.

And still Navahk danced. At last he had the excuse to pursue Torka's people into the Corridor of Storms, where no doubt he would seduce others into helping him to kill them all.

The short, clouded days grew suddenly warm. Near the well-remembered River of Caribou Spring Crossing it rained hard, just as it had rained before. They passed old fire circles and the depressions of long-abandoned pit huts, and although there were no signs of recent camps, it seemed to Karana that they were being watched from the silent, bleak land. The tracks of many bands overlay each other, bleeding away into mud so that neither Torka, Grek, nor Karana could determine when they had been laid. Among them Torka found the footprints of two adults and a child heading east; and not far away, headed in the opposite direction, he saw the fresher prints of one of the same two adults, a male burdened with a heavy pack frame, if Torka was judging correctly by length of the stride and the depth of tracks. But even as he knelt to examine them, recalling the despicable Tomo and Jub and the pitiable little slave boy whom they had jerked along in their wake, the rain flooded the prints and pounded at them until they disappeared.

Torka rose, disturbed by his memories of the two slavers
and the frail, beaten-looking little boy. What had happened to
them? He looked around through rain and the gray, brooding
cloud cover. This was bad country. Like Karana, he felt
himself being watched. But by whom? The ghosts of Hetchem
and her malformed infant? He urged the others to move on,
and they walked quietly across it, not wishing to linger lest
they inadvertently offend the restless spirits of the dead.

For two days it rained lightly. Torka led relentlessly on
through the mist, avoiding the tundra barrens, which would
be a vast mud wallow now.

"The sky spirits behave as though they cannot make up
their minds whether it is spring or winter," commented
Lonit, eyeing the sky.

Walking beside her, Torka noted that despite their gruel-
ing journey, her step was sure. Indeed, it seemed that the
farther they went from the land of men and the closer they
came to the Corridor of Storms, the stronger she became.
Her bruises were healing. He looked at her with love and
pride, until Karana darkened his mood.

"It will be winter soon enough," said Karana grimly. "And
if Navahk catches us, for this band it will be winter forever!"

They took to the misted hills that climbed gradually through
scrub country and the thick, miniature forests of the Land of
Little Sticks. Here they rested as they looked back across the
land for any signs of followers.

Nothing.

"This would be a good place to camp," Grek suggested.
"For the sake of our women and the little ones, we *must* take
time to rest. And in these woods and clouds we could risk a
fire."

"We cannot rest until we reach the Corridor of Storms.
Not even Navahk will be able to convince others to follow us
there!" insisted Karana.

Torka saw exhaustion on the loyal, uncomplaining faces.
His own weariness was heavy in him. Once again he took
note of the vast, empty land that lay behind them. "We will
rest," he decided. "For a little while."

They raised a shelter against the rain and judiciously built a
nearly smokeless little fire beneath it, huddling close to eat
their first hot food in days. The women and children slept,
and Torka, Karana, and Grek took turns keeping watch over

the western land from the high hills. They saw no sign of life—not even of game.

"He *is* coming," said Karana, brooding and restless and unable to sleep except in spurts.

Torka nodded. "Yes, I feel it too. We will not stay long."

For two days they camped within the Land of Little Sticks, fishing, setting snares, hunting small game, replenishing their stores of meat and kindling moss, and gathering rare, precious wood and bark for the thousand tool-making purposes in which bone, less malleable than wood, was inappropriate.

Late on the morning of the third day, beneath clear skies at last, Summer Moon pointed toward what looked like a herd of large animals moving on the horizon far to the west.

From where he had been dozing at his lookout post, Torka awakened instantly and came to her. He stood watching in stoic silence, taking measure across the distance. Then he sighed with a grim resolve as he picked up his daughter, kissed her chubby cheek, and alerted the others.

"Will we hunt?" Mahnie asked, thinking that it would be wonderful to taste the good, rich flavor of bison or caribou.

"Look closer, daughter of Grek. It is *we* who are being hunted. Game animals do not walk upright on two legs."

6

It was the promise of meat that drove them.

Meat and the bold assurances of Jub that ahead of them, within the Corridor of Storms, all that Torka had claimed was true: There was game—so much that a hunter stood back from it in amazement. Wherever he threw his spear, Jub had reported, there was food—meat on the hoof in such numbers that women might never fear starvation for their children, and even in the dreams of men, such herds could not be conjured.

Jub had strode into Navahk's encampment on the western bank of the Big Milk River, his pack frame loaded with meat and prime skins. His eyes shifted from one headman to another, then settled finally on Zinkh because the little man was glaring at him with such open and obvious hostility.

"You in the funny hat—I remember you. You are still glowering like an old woman at a killing site with no teeth left to chew her meat. Look at someone else with doubt and dislike in your eyes!"

Zinkh did not appreciate the rebuke. "Where is your boy-using brother, slaver? And the little one who walked with you? Have you traded him to—"

Jub's dirt-crusted face wrinkled with indignation. "The little one was weak. Sickly. He cried too much. He was trouble to me. His spirit walks the wind. And I am one man since my brother Tomo died—spitted in a pit trap at the neck of a great and wonderful valley. Torka's valley, no doubt, the one he boasted of. And Torka's trap—the one he neglected to mention. Torka is to blame for poor Tomo's end, a bad end too. I would kill Torka for that. But one man alone was too dangerous."

Navahk stepped forward through the press of curious men, plus the women and children they had insisted upon dragging along. He eyed the dirty traveler with interest. "The Great Gathering has disbanded. Bad spirits walk the encampment of the mammoth eaters, so we seek a new place to encamp for the winter. It was the power of Navahk that called you here, for in the rain we have lost the trail of Man Who Walks With Dogs and know not the way to follow him."

Jub raised an eyebrow. "I heard no one calling me."

"No man hears the voice of Navahk. It is the power of my will that has drawn your spirit to this place, for we are of one purpose—to end the curse of the Man Who Walks With Dogs. You have seen him?"

"Yes. He was well on his way to the Corridor of Storms. I can lead you to his valley. For a price."

"Name it!"

"The pleasure of killing him . . . and possession of his woman! The one with the antelope eyes."

"Torka will die slowly by my hand after he sees his people die. But you can assist. Lonit is mine."

Jub accepted, then reconsidered. "He has a little girl—not the infant, the child. I would have the little girl to use if I cannot have the mother."

"Agreed," said Navahk enthusiastically.

Behind him the people of the various bands were silent, but their eyes showed disapproval. They were hungry and tired and afraid. Half the bands that had set out with them had turned back. The magic man had sworn that he would lead them to a better camp, but all he had done was lead them across the icy land to a great river, where they had encamped in a downpour while he retired into his tent to chant and make stinking smokes. They had seen no game, but some said they had seen the wanawut following in the rain mists. Everyone heard it crying in the night, and young Tlap claimed to have seen Navahk disappear with it into the clouds. But now it seemed that the magic man's smokes had conjured something, or some*one*, after all. Although they liked the talk of good hunting grounds, they did not like the talk of the infamous Corridor of Storms or of giving away children to such men as Jub.

The magic man sensed their reaction and turned to face them, his face radiant. "What is one girl child to the people of Navahk? The women who walk with me shall bear many sons! They shall walk proud and unafraid beside Spirit Killer into the Corridor of Storms. And when the people of Man Who Walks With Dogs are no more, we shall feast at a fire of celebration, for the forces of Creation shall smile upon us once more!"

And so they moved on. Although the meat in Jub's pack was not enough to feed them all, they were inspired by it.

That night Simu drew Zinkh aside. "I do not like it," he said emphatically, his face set and hard. "All my life I have been proud to walk with Zinkh. Always has Zinkh chosen wisely for his people. But now my woman weeps in the night and asks me how can I follow you. So I must ask my headman: How can you follow Navahk? Do you truly wish to see Torka dead? Or our people under such a man as Spirit Killer? When he commanded Pomm to stay behind, did you see how the poor old woman wept? My woman weeps at the thought of the forbidden Corridor of Storms. All your women are afraid."

"Pomm has wanted to be magic woman of the Great Gathering. Now she has her wish and must live with it. I say now to Simu that he is a man of little vision!"

"Simu will leave vision to such as Navahk. Simu will take Eneela and go back to the camp of the Great Gathering and—"

"Think!"

The younger man frowned. "I *am* thinking. That is why I have come to you this night. To try to convince you to lead our people back to—"

"To what? The encampment has no meat now. It was a place of death. This man will not live with such people!"

"Then how can Zinkh follow Navahk?"

"Because he will lead us to *Torka*, to whom this man Zinkh owes a great apology! If that man will look into the face of Zinkh again and call him friend, this man will walk with him off the edge of the world and be unafraid. Will you stand with me, Simu, as I will stand at his side against those who would destroy him and his good people? Do you understand now? Will you stop talking of weeping women and let this man get some sleep?"

At last the eastern wall of the Mountains That Walk loomed directly ahead of them beyond low, deeply cleft hill country. Grek paused. Wallah, at his side, slipped an arm through his.

"This man has not been so close to the white mountains in many years," he said, trying not to sound intimidated as his eyes took in the vast range of ice that stretched beyond the eastern horizon in glistening, tumultuous, glacial massifs two miles high.

"This woman had forgotten that they are such big mountains," added Wallah in a small voice.

"They are beautiful!" exclaimed Mahnie. "Are they so tall all along the Corridor of Storms?"

Torka noted that, like most of her queries, this one had been addressed to Karana. He smiled to himself. He liked the bright, sometimes brash young girl, perhaps because she was much like the bright, often brash Karana. They would make a pair, the two of them, when Karana's mourning for Sondahr was spent and he at last realized that though Mahnie was small for her years and possessed the curiosity and enthusiasm of childhood, she was a woman—and a very pretty and delightful one at that.

"Go ahead, Karana. Tell her what our world is like. We will all listen, and your words will pass the time and make our steps more eager."

And it was so. They went on into the hill country that had once been the land of the murderous Ghost Band. They bent into their heavy packs, dragging their sledges under clear skies, with Aar bounding ahead of them, marking the slowly ascending route that they must follow.

Karana was not certain when his words eased into a chanting cadence, but as the miles slipped away, his song seemed to bear him up. Time ceased to exist as he bore himself and his listeners onward—into the future where he longed to be, leading them forward through the past, through the years that had eventually brought them to this day, to this place, to this song.

He spoke of yesterdays long gone but well remembered, of adventures shared with Torka, Lonit, and old Umak; he spoke of the distant Mountain of Power, where he had lived as an animal until Torka had found him and taught him how to live as a boy again; he spoke of Manaak, Iana's brave husband, and her face glowed with pride, which, at last, overrode her sadness at her loss of that good and daring man.

He spoke of joining forces with Supnah's people to emerge victorious over the Ghost Men who had kidnapped him and Lonit after murdering Umak, Manaak, and Umak's old, brave

woman, Naknaktup; he spoke of pursuing the last of the
Ghost Men into a canyon toward which they now walked and
of facing the great mammoth Thunder Speaker where the
canyon opened into the river of grass, which ran ever eastward into the face of the rising sun between the Mountains
That Walk. When at last his song was done, he was surprised
to see that the day was also done.

That night, although frigid winds swept down from the icy
mountains, and the group made no fire in the bare, mounding hills lest those who pursued them see it and know their
route, Karana was warmed by the closeness of his people and
by the words of Lonit. She came to kneel beside him and
embraced him as though she were a proud and loving mother.

"Sondahr was right about you, Karana. The spirits have
given you a great gift. Through your speaking of their names,
Umak, Manaak, and Naknaktup are with us now, walking
with their people to a good land where they will live forever
in the children who will be born to us and given their names
. . . in a new world . . . beneath a new sky . . . beneath a
new sun!" She kissed him hard on the brow, then turned
quickly away lest he see the tears of love that had welled
within her eyes.

He saw them anyway and felt their warmth upon his cheek
as he lay back, bundled in his sleeping skins. He wrapped an
arm about Aar and gave himself to his dreams—troubled
dreams, of a golden land that trembled beneath the shadow
of a mountain that rained fire . . . of a white, one-eyed
stallion racing upon a burning wind, screaming its deadly
rage across the world while the wanawut howled and the
white mountains fell and the sky bled and drowned the
golden land in blood.

Navahk sat beneath his lean-to. He had not slept for days.
He stared out through the mist as Naiapi came toward him,
walking in the shaggy weatherproof robe of mammoth skin
that he knew she had taken from the hut of Sondahr.

Sondahr. She would have known what lay ahead. She
could have told him where Torka was now.

"Navahk, this woman would speak to you."

He grimaced. "Go away, Naiapi."

She knelt close, frowning. "You must heed my warning,
Navahk. Those who walk with you grow weak with hunger.
They are weary of the chase. The man Jub will lead us to the

valley of Man Who Walks With Dogs, and Torka and his people will be slain. What difference can a day make?"

The mists seemed to be roiling and settling within him. He looked up at Naiapi and smiled as he saw her recoil. What did she see that had caused her to draw back? What did they all see these past many days since he and the wanawut were one?

The power of the beast. That was it! It was in him now. He knew it. He felt it. For many nights he had gone out to the beast with food from his own meager rations and fed it as it fed him, then stroked it and joined with it and poured himself into it until it was his high, bestial howling of release that his people heard in the night—not that of the wanawut. The howling of the beast Navahk!

He laughed low and deep to think of it. Like thunder in distant hills, Naiapi heard the threat in it and started to withdraw, but he caught her hand. "It is good that you fear me; it is good that they all fear me. But tomorrow I *will* allow them to rest and hunt. But for my purpose, not their pleasure."

She saw the madness in his eye.

"You should not have killed Sondahr, Naiapi."

"I thought it would please Navahk."

"It did not please me. It pleased *you* to see her die . . . one who was to me what you could never be."

Her heart was cold, beating fast. "I would be your woman, Navahk. I would serve you, please you in all things."

"We will see. We will see." He laughed at her as he shoved her back into the mist and the night.

The next day they hunted. There was little meat in the rain-saturated barren lands into which Jub had led them, but the men took several steppe antelope and ptarmigan, and that night the people ate until the bones were stripped and cracked, and only the hair and horns, feathers and beaks were left of their kill. Navahk watched them, not sharing their feast. Instead, when all had returned to their sleeping skins, he stood alone, arms raised to the star-strewn sky, imploring the bad spirits of Torka to remain gone from the people of this camp forever.

With Eneela asleep and the baby drowsing at her breast, Simu rose to observe the magic man in silence. Zinkh came with him, and they stood together while the song of Navahk rose to fill the night.

"Your woman has eaten well?" asked the little headman quietly.

"For the first time in days, yes, and the baby sleeps contented. It is a good thing; I was ready to go off and hunt, even if he forbade it. But he has seen our need. There was no need to challenge him."

"Do not count on it. Walk carefully in the days to follow. And keep your spear at ready."

The next day they rested. By the following dawn they were traveling again, into deeply cleft hill country, the Mountains That Walk standing like clouds upon the eastern horizon.

Jub pointed. "Torka will be where the shadows lie. There's a deep canyon there. Beyond it the Corridor of Storms lies between the mountains, and five risings of the sun beyond that, the valley where Tomo was killed. Mark me, it is the finest hunting ground I have ever seen. Torka will be there."

Navahk urged them on, his pace ferocious, and for the rest of that day, although they walked with only brief breaks for rest, the mountains seemed no closer. It was nearly dusk when a small herd of camels was sighted. Many cheered Navahk, believing that his chanting of the previous night had put this game in the world for them.

He chafed against their words and told them that their destination was in sight, but the hunters reminded him that it was late in the day, time to make camp. In the meantime their appetite for the kill had been whetted. Seeing their eagerness, he told them that they might hunt.

The camels scattered when the first, a big male, was struck. It went down onto its front knees while howling hunters surrounded it for the kill. Several men took off after the other beasts, while two youths, Tlap and Yanehva, went after a young cow that disappeared into the deep, scrub-choked shadows that laked within the depressions of the convoluted hills. Several women expressed concern—the youths were not boys, but they were inexperienced hunters—and Navahk took up his spear and followed. The boys' mothers thanked him.

It was not particularly cold, but night was coming on fast, and the temperature was dropping. Navahk trotted into the clear, sharp air, smiling.

The camel had gone fast and far, and the youths were hot on her trail. Navahk had no difficulty following them. They were running close together for at least three miles over rolling, broken terrain, until the camel began to tire. Using sound strategy, the youths had separated, intending to come together from both sides of the animal and take it by surprise.

His smile deepened. This was perfect. Lengthening his stride, he trailed Tlap—the smaller, from the size of his footprints. Navahk would have to catch up with him soon if his plan was to work; he ran on, smiling, closing on his prey, moving as a shadow across the dusky, shadowed world.

Hearing movement behind him, Tlap turned and, a spear at ready, braced himself to take on whatever predator was following. But he saw no danger in the familiar, smiling form trotting behind him. He smiled back, flattered that the magic man would have wished to join him but irritated, too, because he needed no help to make his kill. Tlap shrugged and gestured Navahk forward, then ran on, into a deep shrubby depression, hoping to find the camel first so that his throw would kill their prey.

He made a small, gurgling cry of dismay and shock as Navahk's spear went through his back, pierced his lung, and propelled him forward onto his face. He could not breathe as he slapped his hands up and down against the ground; nor could he scream, for Navahk's foot slammed down onto the back of his neck, snapping it as he withdrew his spear, then plunging it deep again, straight through the youth's frantically beating heart.

He knelt then, listening. Far ahead he could hear the camel pounding on and the youth Yanehva crashing through the shrubbery after it. He put back his head and howled.

"Wah nah wah . . . wah nah wut!"

There was no sound from Yanehva now; he had probably stopped, no doubt in terror. Navahk howled again, and from within the dark and twisted hills the wanawut answered him. It would come now.

"Tlap?"

The call of Yanehva was the cracked pipe not of a young man but of a frightened boy.

"Tlap . . . where are you? We'd better get back. Did you hear it?"

Navahk was amused as he rose, walked a few paces, and called, "Run, boy! The wanawut walks these hills behind you. Go! Quickly! Do not wait for me. I will find Tlap!"

Silence answered him until he howled again, a high ululation that terrified Yanehva. Navahk heard the boy galloping away back toward the encampment as he stood hidden within the shadows, waiting for what he knew would come to him now.

That night the moon showed horns as the child moved with caution beneath its pale, silver light toward the man who had called to her. She came forward hesitantly because she smelled the rank odor of fear as well as blood and meat from the sprawled corpse. The child made a face. Had he killed it himself, one of his own? For her? She did not want to eat such meat!

The man was smiling in the moonlight, waving her forward, murmuring to her in the low, soothing way that he did when his hands promised stroking and his body promised pleasure.

Mother Killer.

Hatred was alien to her kind, and she found it hard to hate him now. But she did, in a small, scabbed nubbin of her heart that, in her need for companionship and affection, she was able to ignore. He was her mate now, as her mother had once had a mate, long ago, in a far land. It was good to be mated, to be stroked, to be held close and joined to the man, even though he was not of her kind and sometimes the savagery of their joining frightened her. The ugliness of the howling man sometimes disgusted her, so she howled back to override the sound he made and closed her eyes, pretending that he was one of her own kind.

Kneeling, leaning on his spear, Navahk offered meat.

She crouched before him, watching him out of her mist-colored eyes, her gray, furred body silver in the moonlight. Why did she hesitate? Why did she not eat? She *must* eat! The body of the youth must bear the marks of her claws and fangs if it was to terrorize the people. Once they saw what the wanawut had done, they would not wish to linger in the country of wind spirits; they would hurry forward to the Mountains That Walk, into the Corridor of Storms, and rush to kill Torka, whose bad magic had turned the wanawut loose upon them to slay one of their own living sons.

He smiled and spoke to the beast gently, cajolingly. "Navahk has brought this for you! Eat! Tear the body apart. Gorge yourself. And while you are not looking at me out of those all-too-human eyes, Navahk will thrust his spear into your heart. He does not need you anymore: I have mastered your power and made it my own. I will fear nothing in the world ever again. You are a hideous, repulsive thing, and it will be good to bring your body back to my people, gutted and on my back, as I wear the skin of your mother. Then they will know that I am a man whose power they will never question again!"

Her massive, bearlike head eased to one side. She was listening, trying to understand.

Impatient, he pushed the body of the dead youth toward her. "Eat!"

She knew the word. He used it often,' each time he brought meat for her. Yet there was something in his eye and smile and the eager way he thrust the meat at her that caused her to back away, then hunker down, trying to understand.

He was angry. With his bare hands he ripped open the youth's surplice, and with his spearhead he stabbed deep, opening the upper belly, reaching in, drawing out innards, holding them out.

"Eat!" he demanded.

She made a soft, questioning sound and, to his shock, uncurled the long, massive fingers of her right hand to reveal a dagger. With it, she imitated him, driving the dagger deep, in and out, looking up at him now and again, repeating the soft questioning sound as though she wished approval from him.

"No! Like a beast, not like a man!" Suddenly enraged with her, he struck the weapon from her hand.

As it flew from her palm, she cried out, startled, and jumped back, holding her hand, rocking herself, making cooing, confused sounds as she frantically rummaged through the undergrowth to retrieve the blade. She snatched it up, clutched it to her heart, and stared at him, breathing hard.

He righted his spear and held it out toward her defensively, knowing that even with his spear he had little defense against the beast if she chose to hurl herself at him. She was simply too big, too powerful. And in this moment, despite his bold talk, he knew that he was a man of fragile flesh and a heart full of fear. He had seduced the beast and mated with her. He had gentled her spirit. But he had not mastered her or understood her nature any more than he had been able to master or understand any other female in his life—except through pain and fear. But now *he* was afraid as he dipped the spearhead and prodded outward with the shaft, snarling at the beast, warning her away, hoping that his bluff would work as he advanced toward her.

She mewed, shocked and frightened and confused by his behavior, and suddenly hooting like a deranged owl, she whirled and fled into the night, leaving Navahk alone in the dark with the corpse that he had made.

No one dared to walk into the night in search of him. They built a smoky fire—there was little to burn in the soggy land—and cooked camel but had little heart to eat it. They called his name, and that of the youth Tlap, while Yanehva brooded, deliberately staring into the smoke so that his eyes would burn and he would suffer pain for having been so frightened that he had not stayed to look for his friend or to help the magic man fight the wanawut. He was sure that it had come to that, for otherwise Navahk and Tlap would have been back long before now.

At last they appeared, the magic man carrying the body of the dead youth. Tlap's mother threw herself to the ground and keened, and Yanehva felt sick with shame while the people listened solemnly as Navahk told them of how he had been unable to save the youth from the wanawut.

"We must not linger. Crooked spirits follow us, and not one man, woman, or child will walk in safety until we have killed the people of Man Who Walks With Dogs and claimed his valley as our own!"

But as the hunter Ekoh took the body of his son, his were not the only eyes to wonder at the shape of the wounds that had killed him. He looked at Navahk. "The wanawut did this?"

"What else?" queried the magic man, daring the man to challenge him. "With teeth and claws like daggers did the wanawut slay your son!"

7

The Mountain That Smokes lay ahead. In days that seemed like mere breaths of light, Torka and his people hurried forward, deep into the Corridor of Storms, anxious to reach the Valley of Songs before the time of the long dark was upon them.

They had covered their tracks well, deliberately leaving false trails, walking across talus slopes wherever possible— even though this meant taking the longer, more difficult route—carrying the sledges when the ground was soft and certain to carry the scars of their passing, step-hopping across tussocks, building no fires, and leaving no discernible refuse. Still they were followed. Karana knew it, even though Torka was beginning to have his doubts.

It had been many days since they had paused at the entrance to the Corridor of Storms and looked westward across the night to see the fire burning miles away in the country of twisted hills, and Lonit had wondered aloud if those who followed had not given up and were turning back. Why else would they build so great a fire unless they no longer found the need to conceal themselves from those whom they hunted?

Karana had no answer for that, but he knew Navahk well enough to know that even if everyone who walked with him abandoned him, he would come on alone.

Torka and his people walked under clouded skies. It rained again, but it was warm rain for this time of year, and when at last it stopped, the clouds remained and the temperature stayed well above freezing.

As they proceeded onward under the shadow of the Mountain That Smokes, the peak made low rumbling sounds that kept them from sleeping well during the night, and Mother Below was restless beneath them. By day the entire face of the land was different from how they remembered it. It was as though huge sheets of molten rock had poured out of the smoking mountain and across the earth, solidifying to form dark, steaming, brittle barriers that were hundreds of feet high in places. They tried climbing over the lower expanses of the strange rock, but the stone cut into the soles of their boots and bruised their feet. Soon they were all limping, even Aar. The women were forced to spend an entire day contriving new boots for them all out of the skins that formed their bedrolls.

"This will not do," said Torka. "If we continue over the flows of stone, we will measure the distance in the number of boots we wear out."

"We have not enough skins for the making of so many boots," Lonit told him, rubbing her feet.

"Perhaps the land is telling us that we are not welcome?" Wallah's suggestion was spoken softly. And ignored.

"We will walk around the flows," Torka decided. "The Valley of Songs is not far now."

They moved on, closer to the towering white massifs of the Mountains That Walk than they preferred to go. The mountains soared so high that they seemed to block off the clouded sky. They seemed to talk and grumble both day and night, and now and then avalanche mists rose from deep within dark blue canyons to cloud the ridges. Torka's people walked quickly, in silence and fear, looking up, half expecting the great peaks to fall upon them. It was with great relief when at last they put the lava country behind them and could stride out across the unbroken sea of grass again, with the Mountains That Walk miles away on either side of them.

Game was plentiful. They hunted and rested and ate over a small fire built within the sheltering windbreak of a grove of willows. There was fresh, sweet water in a spring that bubbled nearby. And as night came down, Torka looked back across the way that they had come and allowed himself a small smile of satisfaction.

"I do not think that Navahk will bring those who follow us beyond the flows."

They slept well that night, and although the dark was much longer than the day, they were in no hurry for the dawn as

they lay bundled gratefully beneath their furs, dreaming
untroubled dreams for the first time in many days.

Yet when Torka awoke at last, it was to see Karana crouching on his heels, staring across the miles, his traveling pack
rolled and ready at his side.

"He *will* come," he said, without turning to look at Torka.
"In the Valley of Songs we can stand against him. Here in
open country, we will be few against many. We must go on."

For two days and nights the child sat within the scrub
lands of the twisted hills, holding the man stone close, rocking herself, sleeping erratically, trying to understand why
Mother Killer had turned against her.

There was no understanding; there was only loneliness and
the terrible, aching need to be close to another of her own
kind.

But in all the world there were no others.

There was only the beast.

Perhaps if she followed him, if she called to him and
presented herself to him, if she turned up her throat and
allowed him to see that she was passive before him, he would
stroke her again and join with her again . . . and then the
loneliness would go away . . . and the hunger.

She was ravenous. She moved out of the scrub, back to
where the beast had left the corpse he had killed of his own
kind, willing to eat it now. But he had carried it off. She
followed the mixed scent of man and meat, sniffing the trail,
following day and night and another day until those scents
and the stench of rotting flesh led her through a dark, black-
walled canyon.

A lynx lay stinking and bloated in the shadows. A chunk of
disgorged meat lay within its gaping jaws.

The child hunkered near to finger the dead animal, to peer
close at the tiny skewers of sharp bone protruding through
the vomited piece of meat.

Bad and bony meat. The child made a face. The lynx
must have been starving to eat so greedily of such bony meat.
Her mother had taught her long ago to eat only of soft flesh
and innards, to crack bones and grind them thoroughly before devouring them—as she now devoured the lynx, opening
its skin with the man stone, eating only of the soft haunch,
avoiding the belly and gut, which must surely be full of bad
meat. She slept then, on her feet, and when she awoke, dawn

was coloring the distant river of grass between white mountains that reached into the clouded sky.

And then she howled a long, high, pitiable wail. She could see the pack of Mother Killer far below in the distance. Clutching the man stone to her breast, she followed.

It was the cry of the wanawut that caused the people to follow Navahk. They had reached the lava flows and had paused, discouraged by Jub's announcement that the valley of Man Who Walks With Dogs lay far beyond it.

"This man will take his family and go back!" Cheanah said, and his woman sighed with relief. Then the cry of the wanawut had her on her feet, drawing her littlest boy to her side.

"You said it would not follow us into this good land," Zinkh prodded Navahk, and Simu, Cheanah, and all the hunters muttered in agreement.

The magic man looked at the woman Naiapi as though the cry of the beast wanawut was somehow her fault. She shrank from him, her face white, until a slow smile of benevolent understanding came to the face of Navahk.

"Go back into the world of the wanawut if that is your will, Cheanah. And you, Zinkh, take your people with him. Navahk has not forgotten the death of poor Tlap. He would not lead his people to *that*. No, Navahk will go on to the valley of Man Who Walks With Dogs, where the wanawut will not follow."

"You said that it would not follow us here," reminded Simu.

Navahk looked the young man up and down with contempt. "Man Who Walks With Dogs summons the wanawut so that it will feed upon his enemies. When Torka is dead, Navahk will kill the beast . . . as I have killed its kind before. What man among you has done that? I, Navahk, walk now into this new land unafraid!"

And so he did, and they followed to a man, as he knew they would, for he was certain that the unknown country that lay ahead was less threatening to them than the land of the wanawut, which lay behind. But as they strode out, Cheanah joined the hunters of Zinkh's band, and as the little gap-toothed man in the incongruous hat spoke softly, Cheanah nodded and gestured to his sons and his woman to walk beside him.

*   *   *

As they walked on into the dark edge of day, it seemed the Mountains That Walk had done just that, for they were much closer than Torka remembered their being, towering on either side of the low hills that led into the Valley of Songs. Great rubble mounds of snow, ice, and boulders so obscured the entrance to their beloved valley that, had they not found the half-buried pit trap and the bones of the man within it, they would have turned back, believing they had come the wrong way.

"Tomo . . ." Karana spoke the name of the corpse.

Torka knew that he must have recognized it through his gift of Seeing, because carrion-eating birds had stripped the bones of flesh.

Lonit's hands flew to her face to stifle her cry at what lay ahead, and Torka stared, stunned, at the fouled leavings of the twosome who had encamped and hunted in this sweet place of memories and dreams that he had found and made his own.

It was not his own anymore. Bones of slaughtered animals were everywhere. The trees had been cut down and used as firewood. The pools were stinking quagmires filled with the refuse of the men's kills and body wastes, and with the bones of a child who had been drowned before its abandonment.

"We cannot stay in this place." Karana's voice was transformed by unspeakable anger and hurt.

Torka stood in stunned silence. A storm wind was rising beyond the ruined little valley and within the man. "Nor can we leave it . . . until the storm is over."

That night a sulfurous wind blew hard from the north. Navahk cursed the storm and his people. For days he had driven them; their fear of the wanawut was his prod. But now it was cold and snowing, and the foul-smelling wind was making them irritable. An equally exhausted Jub assured them that the way to the valley lay only a day ahead, but they moaned and dropped their packs, and not even Navahk's threat of the wanawut was enough to force them on.

All slept except Navahk.

He stalked the camp, bent into the wind, and circled like a lion trapped within a dead-end canyon. Of all who followed him, Zinkh alone lay awake in his sleeping skins, watching, waiting patiently for Navahk to do what he did every night— leave the camp to test the route along which he would lead his people the next day. It was uncanny the way the man could see in the dark with his one eye; like a nocturnal predator, Navahk needed no torches to light his way, nor was he afraid to be alone with the wanawut. Sometimes he would not return before dawn.

Zinkh hoped that tonight would be such a night as, rising to poke Simu into wakefulness, he crept in absolute silence to rouse Cheanah and his sons.

"Hurry. The time we have been waiting for has come," whispered Zinkh. "Jub has detailed the way that lies ahead. We must go now, before Navahk returns, or we will be too late to warn Torka. I will wake the others of this man's band. Wake your women. Gag your babies if you must! We go to join the Man Who Walks With Dogs!"

Torka and his people huddled close within their lean-tos, listening to the distant wind howling far beyond the valley. Above them the sky stirred restlessly and a dry snow fell, but there was little wind within the valley itself. Distant roarings rent the world beyond, and Mother Below shifted restlessly far beneath them. Through storm and wind and driving snow, they heard animals on the sea of grass crying, neighing, and trumpeting. Summer Moon buried her head in Lonit's bosom, as Iana held Demmi, and Mahnie comforted Wallah as though she were the mother. The men sat upright with their spears at ready, wondering what good their meager weapons of stone and bone would do against the forces of Creation.

At dawn they peered from beneath their snow-laden lean-tos. The world was unnaturally quiet and dark. It smelled of smoke and sodden, sulfurous ash. The snow that lay upon the land was black, as were the fine particles of ash drifting from the sky. Slowly they clambered out to look beyond the hills to the west, in the direction of the Mountain That Smokes, where roiling black and red clouds filled the sky and rained fire on the world. And, climbing over the tumbled glacial lobes of the Mountains That Walk, a group of disheveled, frightened people, covered with black ash, were coming toward them, led by the bandy-legged man in a huge and moldering hat.

"This man comes to name himself as friend of Torka!" proclaimed Zinkh, striding ahead of the others. He took a moment to catch his breath as Torka, Karana, and Grek gripped their spears defensively and eyed him warily.

"Put spears away. Put away, away!" demanded Zinkh, puffing out his meager chest as he looked proudly at Torka and his people. "Far has Zinkh brought people to stand with Torka against Navahk! Zinkh made big mistake to take up with that bad man. Many miles have we come ahead of a black and stinking wind to be away from him and the wanawut that follows him! Man Who Walks With Dogs will have need of men with spear hurlers to stand against Navahk and his many hunters! Zinkh's hunters and Cheanah thought we would be those men! Our people would be Torka's people, if Torka will forgive Zinkh for being less than a man in the face of his enemies."

Torka was amazed, grateful, and amused by the blustering apology. He could find no words except: "Yes, Torka will let it be so. Yes."

"Good thing!" proclaimed Zinkh, clearing his throat. He breathed deeply, decisively, and turned his gaze to Karana. "You. Lion Killer Karana. Zinkh brings to you something that you have left behind. Here: This man thinks that you have not been lucky these past days. Perhaps now you will believe Zinkh and wear this hat, and as brothers of one band, it will bring luck to us all!"

Karana met the eyes of the brave and stubborn little headman and understood for the first time that a man's size was best measured in the depth of his loyalty and the amount of his courage, not in the height of his head above the ground.

"I will wear the hat of Zinkh with pride," he said, and bent to allow Zinkh to set the hat upon his head.

The little headman looked around, eyeing the valley and the precipitous, ominously overhanging walls of ice. The way the earth had been shifting, those walls could jar loose and crash down to kill them all. "This is not such a good place for people to stay for one long time, I think."

"No," Torka agreed. "We cannot stay here. We must go on."

Navahk awoke. Buried within his sleeping skins, smothering in furs and hides, he fought for air, until at last, his face was free of them. He lay on his back, gasping in a world of suffocating black mist. Each breath was a burning agony as he slowly became aware of a low, constant, earth-shaking rumbling far to the west.

He sat upright, clutching at his burning throat and looking at the huddled forms of sleeping people around him. Suddenly he realized that most of them were not sleeping; they were dead. There was something deadly in the mist that had been loosed in the trembling night to sear the lungs and lull the brain into a lethargy that shrank the spirit until it was no more.

He had felt it the previous night but had not been aware of its incipient danger. As always, he had walked the dark tundra alone, unable to sleep, thinking of how it would be when at last he brought death to Torka and his people, wishing that the wanawut would come close so he could kill her and flaunt her skin before those who had begun to doubt him. At last fatigue drove him back to camp for fitful slumber; but last night he had returned early with a pounding headache and an uncharacteristic desire simply to lie down, close his eyes, and sleep . . . sleep. As he had slept, he dreamed that the world beneath him shook and roared, until now, fighting for every breath, he realized that he had not been dreaming.

He staggered to his feet, shaking his aching head to clear it of a thick, unnatural dizziness. His eye teared as though someone had tossed hot ashes into it. He looked around. Ashes *were* falling from the sky. He looked to the east. The sky was gray, as livid as a yellowing bruise, unlike any sky that he had ever seen.

It was not until he turned and looked west that panic bit deep within his gut and caused him to cry out. Above and beyond the soaring walls of the Mountains That Walk, the sky was black, and against it, the Mountain That Smokes was haloed in fire. From gaping rifts in its sides oozing rivers of molten mud poured out across the sea of grass, sending columns of steam high. The mud buried the snowy tundra, blocking the way back into the world of men.

Navahk's eye grew wide with incredulity. From the broken summit of the volcano an enormous cloud boiled upward for miles, its top torn by high winds that were dispersing its substance across the western sky, while lower winds skeined portions from its belly southeastward in long, thin strands of—Navahk's hand covered his mouth and nostrils as understanding dawned—poisoned air.

He stared, unable to move. Never had he seen anything like it. It was from the heart of the mountain that the rumbling came. And from the cloud, fragments of fire rained upon the land while bits of rock exploded upward. Although small when observed from this distance, the debris were the size of boulders as they hurtled upward into the cloud and then fell great distances—to hit the earth and the Mountains That Walk with devastating force. The magic man calculated. Fourteen times had the sun risen since he had walked beneath the shadow of that mountain, but even at this distance he felt the impact of the boulders' landings shake the permafrost beneath him.

He watched in horror as entire mountains of ice collapsed and swept outward onto the tundra in roaring waves of white spume. Desperately he tried to gather his thoughts. He must get away, far from the Mountain That Smokes! Quickly! To the east, where the sky was clearer of the deadly exhalations of the volcano. Then, without warning, the earth rolled sharply beneath Navahk's feet. He fell. To his relief, several of those whom he had believed dead now awoke and sat up, gasping, choking, holding their throats, grimacing against pain.

Suddenly the earth was still.

The few people who had survived the night of silent death gradually began to understand the extent of the devastating calamity. They could not rouse the others. All who had not slept with their heads fully buried under their skins were dead—women and children, young and old. The killing breath of the distant mountain had been impersonal and without compassion.

Again the earth rolled. The survivors—five men, including Jub, and only one woman, Naiapi—stared at Navahk, their eyes wild with fear as they clutched their skins and furs to their nose and mouth.

Panic bit his gut more deeply, but he tried to stand tall and bold. "Do not look at me! I did not bring this! Did this man not urge you to hurry?"

One of the men, an elder named Earak, dropped to his knees, threw back his head, and keened like a woman. "All are dead! My women! My sons! Where is the magic of Spirit Killer? Why did he not protect us from this?"

To the west the mountain continued to roar. A deadly silence settled as, for the first time, the absence of Zinkh, Cheanah, Ekoh, Simu, and the others was noticed.

Oga's man, a hunter named Rak, sank to his knees beside the corpses of his women and children. "Zinkh and his men have abandoned us! They have gone back. We should never have followed Navahk this far."

Naiapi was calm now. Her eyes flashing, she cut the hysterical words of the hunter. "The man Jub has brought us across this land, assuring Navahk that the way was good. If you would wail like a woman and fix blame for what has happened, do not blame Navahk, who has warned you all along of what must happen if you did not do as he commanded. Blame Torka for this black killing magic, and blame Jub. He is the one who has told us all that this was a good land!"

Jub stepped away from the others, his expression that of a cornered animal. He met the glares of those who faced him. "This was a good land when I left it. Do you think I would have come with you if I thought that this— No! You will not lay the blame for this on me, woman! It is Navahk who has brought us to this, with his talk of the wanawut! His need to kill the people of Torka!"

Jub saw his death in the faces of the others and would not stand still for it. He backed away, keeping them all in sight as he bent, picked up his spears, and slung his bedding over his shoulder. "I'm going back into the world of men! After Zinkh's people and Cheanah. Anyone who wants to follow, they can please themselves."

"The sky is poison, and the land burns ahead of you. Fire rains from the clouds, and the mountains fall. You cannot go back!" Navahk thundered.

"Nor will I continue on into the forbidden land!" Jub shouted, wheeling away and breaking into a run.

The others watched him go, then looked at their dead. In silence, drained by their grief, they went to their loved ones, made their final good-byes, and laid them to look at the sky.

"We will go on to the east." Navahk spurred them with the insistence of his tone. "Look: The sky is clearer there. We will find the people of Man Who Walks With Dogs, and we shall kill them all for what they have done this day!"

Rak looked at him with tired eyes. "No, Navahk. This man will walk with you no more."

His statement inspired the other hunters. To a man they proclaimed that they would walk west with Rak.

"The wanawut is waiting to feed upon those who challenge Spirit Killer!" Navahk threatened them.

Rak slowly shook his head. "What is the wanawut to us now? We have lost women, children, brothers, and fathers in this camp. How could it hurt us more than this?"

"It can kill you!"

"Then we will die—but not in this land. We will die on our way back to the land of our people. This land is not for men; it is for spirits . . . *bad* spirits. Come with us, Navahk. Let Man Who Walks With Dogs go his way. He is welcome to this land."

"I will see him dead."

"Then you will see him dead alone. Unless the woman stays with you."

Naiapi's head went up. "I am Navahk's woman! I walk at his side unafraid!"

Rak shrugged. "The choice is yours. But this man goes now." As one, the others muttered agreement and, without another word, took up their packs and spears and headed west.

"You will die! You will *all* die!" Navahk raged after them. "And this time it is the power of Navahk that shall take your spirits. Such weak and cowardly men are not fit to live!"

Shaking, he stood awash in a torrent of anger as he watched them hurry after Jub. They caught up with him. Without looking back, they strode westward.

Navahk's heart was afire, and his mind went round and round aimlessly, like a wolf biting after its own tail. The power of his life's purpose was ebbing in him. They had ignored his threats! They no longer believed in his power! They no longer feared him! If, by some small chance, they should make it back to the country of other men, they would tell how Navahk had lost his magic in pursuit of one whose powers were greater than his had ever been.

"They will not speak so of me," he snarled, then stalked to his sleeping skins and snatched up his spears and spear hurler. "I will kill them all before I allow them to speak so of me!"

Naiapi tried to clutch at him. "Navahk, come. We must go! Forget them! Look! The cloud from the west thickens, and we must go on ahead of it!"

He barely heard Naiapi's pleas. He shook her free, was loping out across the land, taking aim as he ran, until a wondrous feeling of calm slowly began to soothe his over-whelming sense of loss and betrayal. He stopped, stared ahead, and smiled. The power *was* still his.

Jub had led the others into the leading edge of the cloud. He could barely see them, but what he could see was enough to make him shout with delight. One by one, starting with Jub, the hunters were slowing their steps and dropping to the ground, clutching their throats, and dying!

He laughed aloud, and even though his throat still burned, he felt no pain. "I have killed them! Who will doubt the power of Navahk now?"

Naiapi stared at him as he walked toward her. For the first time she saw the utter madness in his eye. But it was too late to turn away from him. She *was* his woman now. And for the first time since she had set eyes upon him, she wanted no part of him.

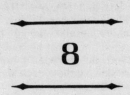

8

Before leaving the Valley of Songs, they took the bones of the
child from the fouled pool, and the women arranged them as
best they could. All gathered near to say gently words to the
spirit of the little boy who had known no kindness in his life.

But the bones of the man, Tomo, were half buried in over
thirty feet of glacial rubble that was an advancing frontal lobe
of the white Mountains That Walk. There was no way they
could have retrieved the body, even if they had wanted to.

"It was either Tomo or Jub that smashed the little lame
one's head and then discarded him in the pool," Torka said
grimly. "If the spirits of the white mountains want the bones
of either of those two, this man will not stand in their way."

They hefted their packs, the load lighter because it was
distributed among many. As they left the valley, Lonit lingered, falling behind the others for one last look at the sweet,
sheltering land that she had loved so much.

"In my dreams I never imagined this."

She was startled to find that Karana had come to stand
beside her. He looked so grave, so much older, so sad. She
longed to touch his face with motherly empathy, but he was a
man now, and with Zinkh and Cheanah and the others looking on, such a gesture would not be fitting. "Perhaps because
you have not dared to see?"

He frowned, recalling too many unwelcome dreams. Ice
. . . fire . . . the white stallion ripping the skin of the sky to
make it bleed . . . Yes, perhaps he had seen this, after all,
but had not understood. "It was good for us in this place. We
should never have left it."

Lonit could see the assembled people waiting at the ice-
choked neck of the valley: Mahnie standing close to Iana,

holding the hand of Summer Moon like a little mother and looking moon-eyed at Karana. A sweet realization, a deep sense of rightness filled Lonit. Mahnie would be Karana's woman someday. She did not need the gift of Seeing to know that.

They *had* done the right thing. Life had been hard and cruel to them, but if they had never left the beloved valley, Mahnie would not be here, and Torka's band would still be small and vulnerable before the forces of Creation. Now, in Grek, Simu, and Ekoh, in Cheanah and his sons, and even in bold, arrogant, preposterously vain little Zinkh, and the other hunters of his band, Torka had strong men to hunt beside him.

If they had never left the valley, Iana would still be a mournful mute. Now she walked with a new joy in life, a willingness to face whatever came. Her beauty shone once more, and all who looked at her were warmed by her bright smile.

If they had never left the valley, Lonit would never have found a friend in Wallah, nor would she ever have been fully assured of her own sense of worth. That had been a gift of the wondrous and wise Sondahr.

"We should go on now, Lonit," urged Karana, eyeing the soaring walls of ice that crouched upon the once soft and lovely hills. "It is not safe to linger here."

She lay her hand upon his forearm. "I must speak to you before we rejoin the others. You must not fear your dreams, Karana. You must face them. You must learn to use the gift of Seeing. It has always been a channel that allows the spirits to enter you, and through you, to speak to us all."

He shook his head. "The channel is forked and twisted in many places. It is too hard to see. Mists of blood and ice are everywhere beneath a sky that rains fire. It is not something that I want to see."

Her hand tightened on his arm. "Sondahr told me—a lifetime ago it seems to me now—that I must be a guide to you, Karana. But I know nothing of the way of dreams or of the Seeing gift. I only know my heart—my own feelings and my love for you, as though you were brother or son to me. I have seen the Seeing gift growing in you. Even when you were a small boy living by your wits on a distant mountain, you knew when the storms of life would come to us, and had we believed you, many of our trials might not have befallen us. Even this woman who has no Seeing gift has learned that many things are not what they seem and that those who look beyond the obvious—in life or in dreams—will find the truth if they really wish to see it."

Solemnly he confessed his fears. "The truth that underlies my dreams is not something that I want to see, Lonit, because when the dreams come to me, I am not a man but that same little boy living by his wits in a mountain cave, howling in loneliness at the moon, in fear of a world that is much too big and frightening for him."

She forgot that they were not alone and reached to hug him hard. "The time of the long dark will be upon us soon, Karana, even if we do not dream of it. Then the sun will rise, and the days of light will come. But only by dealing with the dark may we endure it to live to see those days of sun again." She drew away and, with both hands on his shoulders, looked at him squarely, wanting him to see her spirit, hoping that her newfound strength would also be his in the days to come. "Sondahr and Umak are dead, Karana. They have been your teachers. But they cannot walk with you now. For them and for us, you must be all that they believed you could be—Karana, spirit master, a shaman such as your father could never have been!"

The words jarred him, struck him as though a lightning bolt had scorched him where her hands lay. He stepped back, shook his head wonderingly. She had looked to the west and believed that Navahk and all of those who had followed with him must be dead. All morning Zinkh and his people had been saying as much. The clouds, the smoke, and the foul, fetid wind—it did not seem as though any man or animal could live in such a tortured world. Karana's main concern had been not for the life of his hated father, but the life of the great mammoth—Thunder Speaker, Life Giver—who had first led them to this land and who had raised his massively tusked head, lifted his trunk, and trumpeted in what had seemed a sad farewell, as though begging them to stay. Since entering the Corridor of Storms they had seen no mammoth sign at all, not even close to the dark, fragrant spruce forests where the herds were always found before.

Suddenly, within Karana, there was no thought of mammoth. The channel of Seeing abruptly opened wide for him, running beneath black mists and burning mountains, through narrow corridors of ice that pierced the sky. Under the sky

e fanged, white stallion ran, with a woman on his back, a
ast howling in his shadow, and his one eye spurting blood as
pawed the air with daggered hooves. Two black swans fell
earth, their bloodied wings entwined. Lost beneath the
ack mist and the burning mountains, they were Torka and
onit, always and forever.

Karana gasped. "No!" he shouted.

Lonit was frightened by his sudden pallor. "What is it?
hat have I said?"

He drew near and held her close, uncaring that others
tnessed his affection for her. "Navahk lives. He follows.
e must go. Now!"

The child stumbled on. She whimpered, confused and
ghtened, as she forced herself across the broken, trembling
d. Her nasal passages burned; it hurt to breathe. For the
st few days nausea had prowled in her belly, causing a
agering illness that had brought her to rest in a little cave
e had discovered beneath the crest of a low, tundral hum-
ock. Here she had lain in a hastily made but warm nest of
asses and lichens, sleeping, dreaming troubled dreams of
an and Mother, holding the man stone close as though it
ere a talisman of life, a thing made by those like Mother
ller, to take and give breath, to cut meat, and to gentle her
irit as she longed for summer to come again, for the hole in
e sky to bathe the world in yellow sweetness.

When the shivering earth and rumbling sky had drawn her
om her shelter, she had howled in terror; not in all the days
nce the breath had refused to return to her mother had she
lt such loneliness.

Now the cave lay far behind. Ambling forward, scenting
e troubled earth for signs of Mother Killer, she followed
m . . . and the female that walked with him, across the
nd.

The air grew cleaner and colder the farther they walked
om the western lands. Although he kept his thoughts to
mself, Torka was deeply worried as he led his people east-
ard into the Corridor of Storms. The sea of grass had
anged radically. The wide grasslands still rolled on end-
ssly toward the eastern horizon between the soaring Moun-
ins That Walk, but the mountains appeared so much closer
an he remembered them. In some places the changes were

subtle, barely noticeable—a now dry stream bed, its cours
diverted and the stream running elsewhere; a familiar penin
sular arm of a mountainous glacier extruding farther onto th
plain than before; a grove of scrub spruce that had onc
offered shelter from the icy winds now half buried unde
glacial debris.

"Have the trees walked to the mountain snow, my father
asked Summer Moon.

"No, the mountain snow has walked to the trees, litt
one."

She thought about this. "I do not like this land of walkir
mountains and fiery skies and black winds that stink. I wa
to go home to the valley."

"We have been there, little one. The spirits no long
smile for us there. We must find another valley, anoth
home."

He led his people on, and although the land grew increa
ingly strange and potentially hostile, he knew that it was th
only path for them now. Lava flows blocked the way to th
west, and death lay in the poisoned clouds from the Mou
tain That Smokes. They could not go to the north or sout
for the Mountains That Walk walled off whatever worlds la
there. There was only one world for them, and that la
ahead, into the face of the rising sun.

In the days that followed, they found no suitable place
set up a winter camp. Day was little more than a pale blus
of morning now. Hunting was poor, and the wind constan
growing increasingly colder. The deeper they went into th
unknown reaches of the Corridor of Storms, the closer the
walked to the mountains. In some places the sea of grass wa
less than a mile wide between the towering massifs of restle
ice. At night the world was alive with the sound of the
movement, and by day, everywhere they walked, there wa
evidence of icefalls and avalanches, as though the front
flanks of the mountains were collapsing in slow and inexora
ble tumult, advancing toward one another, rising up and ove
the hills, burying them, extending long, peninsular finge
out across the land.

Torka and those who followed walked on in silence. H
wondered if the world of trembling earth and fire-breathin
mountains behind them was worse than the country int
which he led his people.

"We could not have gone back into the world of men," said Lonit, wishing to ease his worry. "Surely the corridor must widen ahead of us! We will find a good place to camp soon. Game sign is everywhere! Soon we will find much meat!"

Torka appreciated her attempt to cheer him, but he was not cheered. The game sign—the tracks and burnable dung—was not fresh. No doubt the trembling earth had driven the animals on in the direction of the rising sun. But what lay there? Perhaps it was as the old men said, the end of the world, a great cold cliff of ice dropping into an endless dark, where he and his people would fall forever.

But no! For years the great herds moved east at the ending of the time of light. And for years, although the sun disappeared at the beginning of the time of the long dark, it always returned, and with it came the first of the herds. Where had they wintered? Wherever it was, they had survived! As he and his people would survive!

"It is as though the mountains would join, as lovers join, to become one." Lonit's voice was tremulous as she walked beside him. She looked back, making certain that Summer Moon was with Iana and Mahnie, and not within hearing distance. "If the mountains join, will they not bury the land . . and us with it?"

It was not like Lonit to ask such questions. During the past many days she had encouraged the hopefulness of the others. But time and distance were wearing on her. He reached for her hand and held it tight. "Soon we will be beyond the narrow land. Remember how it was for us, long ago, alone in the winter dark, a wounded hunter, a young girl, an old man, and a wild dog? The spirits were with us then; they are with us now. We are together, always and forever, and as long as we can say that, there is nothing for us to fear!"

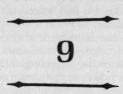

9

The land widened, and they all breathed more easily as they put the worst of the narrow country behind them and made camp in a little hollow between low hills bordered by higher, ice-free promontories of mixed rock and broken talus. On the highest of these Karana, wrapped in his robe, sat upon his sleeping skins and looked back. For days he had known what he must do. And for as many days he had pretended not to know because he was afraid.

It was early evening, but it had been night since noon. A red aurora colored the sky, granting light by which Torka had led his people until their weariness had dictated when they should stop and rest.

They were eating now, rations carried from yesterday's take of ptarmigan and squirrel. They would hunt soon, and the women would set their snares. Like owls, they sought the little movers in the night. And soon Karana must move, too, to hunt prey of his own.

He could not have said just when he realized that the fate of his people rested in his hands. Perhaps from the moment that he had drunk the blood of mammoth—his totem—within the hut of Sondahr, he had known that some act of penance would be required of him by the forces of Creation.

Karana stared westward, back across the long, tortured miles, his face awash in its glow, his heart burning with its cold fire.

Navahk was out there somewhere, following, driving the game ahead of Torka's people, sapping the powers of his son. Navahk was a man. He was a youth. As long as Navahk lived, he would be a shadow of death upon the people of Torka. Now, at last, Karana knew what he must do if the spirits of

Creation were to forgive his transgression against them and his totem.

"Karana, it has been too long since you have eaten. Torka told me to bring you this."

As though in a trance, he turned to see Mahnie clambering up the rocks toward him, a horn of some sort of brew dangling by a thong from her teeth. Aar stood below her, barking.

I will soon go from this place, thought Karana. *I will walk into danger, and I may not return. You may not come with me, Brother Dog, else you would die at my side. This time, old friend, I must face my enemy alone.*

"Here," said Mahnie, nearly breathless. "It isn't much. A horn of marrow broth and a few ptarmigan wings, but it will give you strength. I hope I haven't spilled it all!"

She seated herself beside him, expecting him to refuse the horn, smiling with gladness when he did not. She watched him drink and eat and told him that she knew that he was trying his best to make good magic for them and that it was not his fault that the forces of Creation were not listening.

"Do not be sad, Karana. Things will be better soon. You will see!"

She looked beautiful in the red glow of the sky. Young and eager to please him, her eyes shining, her mouth curled into a smile. He did not intend to kiss her, but he did. And when she threw her arms around him and kissed him back, he was amazed to find that he had no wish to end the kiss. He held her close and knew, in that moment, a strength and ferocity of resolve that he had not known he possessed until now.

I will come back! he promised. *And when I do, the dark magic of Navahk will be a thing of the past, and I, Karana, will be a spirit master at last!*

But the night was young and so was he, and the warm form in his arms *was* a woman. She trembled against him, and as he drew his robe around her, Mahnie yielded all of her love to him, while below the promontory, gathered with the others around the fire, Torka smiled, and Wallah and Grek put their arms about each other and were glad.

Long before dawn, in the shimmering, bloodred glow of the aurora, Karana climbed down from the promontory and, carrying his spears, headed west, leaving Mahnie and Torka's camp behind.

He went so quietly that not even Aar, asleep at the base of the talus slope, sensed his departure, nor was he missed for several hours, for when the girl awoke, she gave no alarm. Karana was always off somewhere alone. It was not until the camp was broken and the travelers were assembled and ready to move on that anyone even thought to call his name.

By then he was miles away. With no traveling provisions save for his spears and his wits, he was walking along a high narrow ridge of ice that granted him a broad overview to the west.

Now he stood dead still, a spear in his hurler, Zinkh's bison-skin helmet firmly atop his head, watching out of cold, steady eyes as Navahk and Naiapi made their way through the gorge below.

Navahk seemed barely aware of her presence these last many days. Naiapi had lied for him and killed for him, but he had found no need either to lie with her or hunt for her, since his own body had no appetite for mating and only occasional need of food. The driving force of his life was to move on, chanting to the spirits as he walked, until his voice was gone and exhaustion dropped him to his knees. Then he slept in brief, restless snatches while she lived on voles when she could catch them or scraped lichens and mosses from the rocks, boiled in a skin bag when Navahk unintentionally allowed her the time to build a fire.

Only once could he have been credited with having provided food for her, or for himself. A young, sickly sheep had skittered out of a stony, ice-clad canyon directly into their path, and Navahk had downed it with a single spear throw. He had eaten it raw, not taking the time to skin or kill it before he set to devouring it. She had watched him, waiting for her share, excited by his bestial manner, fascinated by the way he was able to keep the little animal twitching and making sounds of distress long after most of its flesh was gone, its body cavity emptied. At last it died. Navahk ate the heart and left her whatever she could pick from the bones.

He had slept soundly then, as sated by food and death as most men were by mating. She had gone to him and lain beside him, pressing her body to his, moving, wanting—only to be backhanded so hard that her nose had broken and bled. Uncaring, he had arisen, taken up his things, and stalked on without a word, even though it was the depth of night.

Terrified of being left behind, she had followed with barely
enough time to grab a handful of rib bones, which he later
took away from her. On these he had lived these past many
days, breaking them, scraping them free of marrow, discard-
ing them when all the nourishment had been sucked from
them, deliberately leaving her nothing . . . except resentment that had easily fermented into hatred.

Somewhere along the way into nowhere, in the cold, wind-
driven days and colder, wind-driven nights, Naiapi realized
that the man with whom she walked was not the man she had
loved and longed for all these many years. Somehow, perhaps
with the loss of his eye and his beauty, the spirit of the magic
man had fled away into the wind, leaving her alone in the
Corridor of Storms with a madman who did not care if she
lived or died.

Exhausted, her body aching and her heart pounding, Naiapi
looked up into the red sky, at a flame-red man. Not since she
had been a bride brought by Supnah into his encampment to
look for the first time at the glory that was Navahk had she
been so stunned by physical perfection.

It *was* Navahk. Half a lifetime of years dissolved as Naiapi,
disoriented by hunger, hardship, and fatigue, looked up out
of the shadowed depths of the gorge to see Yesterday standing above her as imperious and intent as the summer sun.
And as beautiful. She was suddenly young again, no longer a
middle-aged matron trudging behind the one-eyed magic
man.

In Naiapi's fatigued mind the Navahk she used to know
stood above her on the ridge . . . young, resplendent in the
daylit glow of the red aurora, his spear poised and ready,
aimed at the man who stood ahead of her.

On the ridge the young Navahk stared, his eyes locked to
the eye of the magic man below as he hesitated as though
unable to throw his weapon at . . . himself? Naiapi was
confused. Why did he wait? Could he not see that the magic
man had taken the backward step and was poised to spring
forward, to hurl his own weapon in an arc of death?

Karana saw. Karana stood ready. Yet he paused, aware that
the man who stood below him was more than his hated
enemy; Navahk was his natural father. Perhaps this was why
the magic man held himself in check?

"Navahk!" he yelled down. "Return into the country from

which you have come, or I swear by the powers of Creation, I
will spear you where you stand." His command allowed no
arguments. It was spoken in the voice of a man; the sound
did not surprise him. He had left youth and indecisiveness
behind him. Now the moment of confrontation was at hand.

Yet as Navahk looked up at him, Karana's eyes were caught
in the raptorial stare of the magic man, and he was suddenly
stunned and unmanned. His spirit was drowning, growing
small and young and vulnerable as the magic man smiled,
exulting in his power.

It was the smile of a thousand dreams and bloody nightmares. It was the white stallion with bloodstained fangs. It
was deadly. And it was a mistake. It reawakened the hunting
instinct within Karana.

Memories of the past strengthened his resolve: a youth,
driven out of the encampment of the Great Gathering by
torchlight and left to die; a child, cautioned by his mother to
be wary of the smiles and winning ways of one who would kill
him if he could; a boy, abandoned to death by Navahk's
command. He saw the faces of those younger and less strong
than he—frightened and confused. One by one he had watched
them die. Karana understood why. The reason was below
him now.

Navahk stood tall, smiling contemptuously, as the wind
whipped down from the heights on which Karana stood.
Karana hated him, seeing him for what he was. And with the
Seeing, the fears of a lifetime fell away. Now it was Navahk
who looked small and vulnerable. "Do not waste your smile
on me, Navahk. I am not afraid of you anymore. I *am* your
son. I share your powers. And I can see into your spirit more
clearly than you see into mine. Be grateful that for the sake of
our common ancestors I do not kill you now. So go! Go now!
Karana gives to Navahk, his father, the gift of life. Remember
that, and do not look back, or it will be into the eyes of your
own death, I swear it!"

But Navahk did not go back, nor did his eye leave the face
of his son as his smile reversed itself into a snarl of rage that
set panic loose within Naiapi.

"Navahk!" She screamed to warn youth and beauty just as
both men loosed their weapons, but the magic man's spear
was released first, and the youth on the ridge was struck. He
cried out, whirled around, grabbed for his arm, and then fell

back, back, and was gone. "No!" she shrieked. The youth's
spear had been released a second before he had been hit. It
came hurtling down and would have killed the magic man
had he not moved in time.

But he was struck nonetheless, propelled back and down
by the force. He lay stunned and staring for a moment, then
struggled to sit, his right hand grasping the shaft of the
youth's spear, which protruded from the flesh just above his
left armpit. His eye was wide with shock and incredulity.

The brow band that hid his disfigurement had slipped
down around his neck. Naiapi stared at the scarred and
empty socket. It was not the first time she had seen it.
Sometimes, when he slept, it lay bare, as ugly as the spirit of
the man beneath the otherwise unmarred mask of perfect
beauty.

Now that mask cracked into a snarl as Navahk glared at her
out of his one remaining eye. "You spoke my name, but it
was Karana you called!"

She stepped back from him as she tried to gather her
befuddled thoughts. Who had fallen from the ridge? Who lay
wounded upon the ground? Why did he speak of Karana?
Karana was a boy who had run away to be with Torka.

He saw the madness in her face and could not have imagined that as she looked at him, she saw the same in his. "You
two-faced, mindless, sag-teated sow. I should have known
better than to let you walk in my shadow." He was grappling
with the spear, grimacing, paling as he forced the head of the
weapon from his wound. Staggering against momentary weakness, he climbed to his feet, and levering the spear with his
left arm, advanced toward Naiapi with murderous intent.

Clarity returned to her in that moment as her instinct for
survival flared. She ran from him, but it was too late. He was
weak but well within striking distance. It took no special
effort to hurl a killing blow through her back.

Karana fell. The spear had pierced his clothing but not his
flesh. Its force had been enough to take him off balance,
causing him to stagger back. The ridge dropped away behind
him. He fell, struck snow, and tumbled head over heels in
the thin, cold air. He curled into a tuck, then slid on ice,
gaining momentum, instinctively cushioning his head with
his tightly folded arms, rolling down, down, into the mountain, it seemed, through the ice, inside of it somehow, slid-

ing, whirling, so dizzy that he would have been sick except
that, even with his hands gripping his head, something struck
him—or perhaps he struck it, and he fell again, suddenly
realizing that he had lost the lucky hat of Zinkh, feeling lost
and vulnerable without it, and then he felt nothing as his fall
took him into darkness.

Brother Dog was on his scent before they picked up his
tracks. Cheanah and the majority of the bandsmen and youths
had stayed behind with the women and children while Torka,
Zinkh, and Grek went west in search of Karana. Well-armed
but unencumbered by packs or sledges, they moved quickly
and quietly, with Aar sniffing the trail and showing them the
way.

"Why would he have left us?" Grek asked, unable to com-
prehend the motives of one whom he had expected to come
to him that morning to ask for Mahnie.

"Always that one Karana has funny ideas in his head," said
Zinkh. "But he took the lucky hat of this one man. All right
will he be."

Torka was not so sure; before he had led the others off,
Lonit had drawn him aside. Nearly beside herself with worry,
she had confided: "I fear that it must have been something I
said to him about his Seeing gift, about facing his dreams. We
all know that he dreams of Navahk following us, dreams so
troubling that he will not speak of them except to say that we
must go on. Can it be that he has gone to find Navahk, to
stop him, to—"

"Kill him." He had finished her sentence, as he finished it
again now, in silence, walking ahead of the others, following
the dog.

His left hand tightened about the hafts of his spears. His
right sought the bludgeon of fossilized whalebone at his side.
The weight of the weapon was comforting. How many times
had the bludgeon saved his life? Memories surged through
him of that vast, bewildering, salt-smelling land across which
he had come with Umak and Lonit, while a frightened little
boy named Karana had watched them from a cave. That cave
was high on a mountain that had groaned and shifted.

Torka stopped dead.

That mountain's ice pack had fallen. It had broken loose
and come crashing down, taking half of the mountaintop with

it, burying the entire eastern flank of the peak, including the cave and those who had taken it from Torka for their own.

Now his eyes swept the mountains of ice that rose in high, jumbled disarray on either side of him.

"What is it, Torka?" pressed Grek, frowning. "You look as though you have seen a spirit."

"I have," replied Torka. "A spirit of the past . . . a spirit of warning . . . we must walk quietly and find Karana as quickly as we can. We must not linger here."

They hurried on through the extremely narrow land that had troubled them days before. Less than a mile wide, the tundra was frozen through, from the uppermost edge of the permafrost to the top of its matted, tenuously rooted skin of mosses and lichens. With the mountains murmuring around them, they lost the trail and stood together as Aar circled intently, tail up and curled over his flank, nose to the ground, sniffing.

Not one of them saw the spear that struck Zinkh until he pitched forward, its shaft protruding through his neck and its head buried in the permafrost with most of his larynx. His spine severed, suffocating on his own blood, the sounds he made were those that no man who called him friend wanted to hear, and although Grek and Torka wanted to run to his side, both men knew that it was too late to help him.

Instinct propelled them back and away from the dying man. Torka grabbed the ferociously barking Aar by the scruff of his neck and dragged him into the protecting walls of the nearest icefall, where neither dog nor men would be vulnerable to attack from above.

Torka cursed himself. He should have expected this. He had come armed and ready to stand against predators such as bears and lions, but he had been so certain that Navahk and his followers were nowhere near, that he had allowed himself to be lulled into carelessness.

Yet as he stood beside Grek within one of many deep, narrow, vertically aligned fissures in the icefall, holding Aar in check beneath an overhanging cornice of blue ice, Torka looked back across the narrows to where Navahk stood high above them atop the opposite icefall and knew that he *was* looking at an animal.

His heart went cold as the magic man threw back his head and howled. Silhouetted against the towering glacial massifs that soared behind him, Navahk's high shriek of defiance was more like the cry of a wild and vicious animal than a man. It went out through the glacial canyons, and as it echoed across the miles, he delighted in its sound. He howled again, louder, more defiantly, hunkering down, then leaping high as he began to dance. The raw, savage power of the beast was in him. Beneath the dangling left arm of the dead wanawut, his own left arm hung useless at his side as he whirled and whooped and, with his good right arm, shook his staff at the sky as his howls continued to echo like thunder reverberating in the surrounding ranges of ice.

"He is alone," observed Grek in a whisper.

"And wounded," added Torka in an even lower tone.

"And as mad as a north wind sweeping down upon the tundra from the top of the world. Look: He holds only his staff. No spears. Do you think he's used them all?"

Aar strained to be free. Torka knelt, put a strong restraining arm around the dog's chest, and stroked him reassuringly with the other, wishing he could convey the same sense of calm to himself that he was trying to give the dog. Dread was growing in him as he looked at Navahk and his lack of spears. Against what had he used the spears? Or *whom*?

"*Karana!*" Navahk hurled the name as he would a spear.

It struck Torka to the heart. He could not breathe. The man had read his mind. The man had sensed his dread. The man had killed his son! Grek's strong body blocked Torka's forward movement.

"You search for one you will never find! Torka! Man Who Walks With Dogs! I have killed the one you seek, just as I have killed the dogs who once ran at your side! Just as I will kill your women and your children and all who are foolish enough to walk within your shadow! Come, Torka! Do not hide from Navahk! I have one spear left for you!" He threw down his staff, bent, and in one graceful, sweeping motion, turned, and retrieved a spear from where it lay behind him. "Come! Or are you afraid? You *should* be afraid! Now is the time of your death!"

"Hold, Torka! You cannot hope to win against him now. He holds the high ground. He will kill you if you do! You—" Grek's imperative warning stopped.

Deep within the permafrost the earth shook violently. Torka and Grek heard the icefall groan and crack around them as, from out of the mountains of ice, a roaring rose as though in

answer to the howling of the man. Beneath Torka's hand
every hair on Aar's back bristled as the dog went rigid.

Behind Navahk the mountains shook. One great tremor.
And then, as Torka and Grek and Aar stared in horror, the
icefall around Navahk shifted once more. Navahk was dropped
to his knees, and a wordless cry of disbelief and despair
escaped from his lips.

As they watched in macabre fascination, the magic man
clung desperately to the wall of ice and struggled to his feet.
He backed into a narrow vertical fissure and braced himself
with rigid arms and legs. The moment had passed. All was
quiet. The magic man relaxed and smiled.

"Torka! Now, Torka! I would kill you—"

With a crack that pained their ears, the icefall collapsed as
the leading edges of the Mountains That Walk began to fall.

10

They ran. They had no choice. The Corridor of Storms was collapsing behind them. Navahk was gone, buried in the rubble, still howling like the wanawut, still brandishing his spear toward the sky as he had disappeared into boiling ground snow and falling ice.

They ran, Torka and Grek together, sobbing against terror and the agony of leaving Zinkh and Karana behind.

On and on they ran out of the narrow land, with hearts pounding, lungs near to bursting, and muscles burning with overexertion, while the dog raced ahead of them. Behind them and on either side icefalls and cliff faces were tumbling, pouring across the tundra in clouds of white mist and falling glacial debris, forever closing off the western land.

At last the tundra widened ahead of them, opened into the bleak area of broad rolling hills and promontories of talus in which they had last encamped. But on either side of the low hills the Mountains That Walk were lost in spuming mists that were rising from uncountable avalanches. The sound of their tumultuous movement was nearly deafening, and as Torka raced forward, Cheanah had the band on their feet, pack frames on, and ready to move.

In spite of the pain in their limbs, Torka and Grek raced on beside their women, heads down, bent forward, gasping as Aar ran beside Mahnie's booted limbs and panted.

"Karana?" The unformed question came from Lonit and Mahnie at once.

Torka and Grek shook their heads, despair in their faces. Lonit and Mahnie came to a stop and embraced, sobbing. Lonit closed her eyes tight and held Mahnie close, wanting to comfort her; but there was no comfort in such a loss. Lonit felt as though her heart had broken. Karana's death would be a scar upon it forever.

Karana awoke to darkness and to sound, to a pounding headache and innumerable bruises. He lay on his side, a freezing little ball. He was so cold that he could not feel his fingers or toes. His hand drifted absently across his face and encountered a lump of ice that was on his nose. In the pitch blackness of the interior of the glacier, he sat up and rubbed his extremities until life came back to them.

Then he sat still, listening to the underground river rushing past him in the dark, while somewhere far above, the sound of distant roaring reached his ears.

It occurred to him that he might be dead. But then, as his fingers and toes and nose began to ache with life, he knew that he was still among the living. He hurt too much to be dead. His fingers explored the large lump on his head. He thought of Zinkh's hat, and memories returned in a rush.

Suddenly he was crying hot tears and choking sobs of anguish. He had not been able to kill Navahk. For a lifetime he had wished Navahk dead, and yet when he stood above him and could have thrust a killing blow into him, he had hesitated. He had sought the eye of the man who had tried to kill him so many times, the eye of the man from whose loins had poured the gift of his life, and had seen his own face looking back at him.

Father. Within his heart there had been a longing to call out that name, to forget the past, to heal the wounds that lay open between them. But then Navahk had thrown his spear, and Karana had loosed his.

Now, rubbing the lump on his head, he knew Zinkh's ridiculous hat had absorbed the brunt of his fall and probably saved his life, but it had fallen off after his initial impact, and it was gone now, into the dark womb of the world.

He drew a deep breath, held it, drew nourishment from it. He looked around and realized that never in his life had he seen such blackness. Straining in vain to see made his eyes throb. He closed them tight.

Now, within the cold and dark, he listened to the sound of water rushing away to his left. A river, shallow from the sound of it, but very fast. Where was it going in such a hurry? To the light?

He gasped again, short of breath, suffocating in the confining darkness. He rose too quickly. His head came up hard against a low ceiling of icicles that punctured his scalp as they shattered. They made light, crackling sounds as they rained down around him. He barely heard them as, stunned, dizzied, and disoriented, he staggered forward, tripped over he knew not what, and went sprawling forward into the river.

He screamed as he went down with a great splash and was swept away, away, through the blackness, choking, gasping, swimming even though he did not know how to swim, fighting every inch of the way, calling upon the spirits of Creation, upon the powers of his totem, Life Giver, to be with him, to hold him up, to strengthen and carry him away to life—to *life*—not to a lonely death in darkness beneath the ice where his spirit would be trapped forever, never to be reborn into the world of men!

"Thunder Speaker! Hear me!" he screamed, but as he did, water filled his mouth and ears and took him down, down, filling his nostrils, searing his sinuses. He could not tell if his cry had rushed on ahead of him above the water or if it was going down with him, drowning with him in the terrible roaring dark. "No!"

Holding his breath, he fought the river with all of his strength, found buoyancy, and forced himself up for air. Gasping, spluttering, he floated on his back, gave himself to the current, and felt his body rushing on, on, on through the endless dark. He could see the ceiling of the underground riverbed, fanged with ice, black and blue, slipping past him so quickly that he could not completely focus, and—

Light!

If there was light, it must be coming from the world of men! The forces of Creation *had* heard his plea! He actually laughed, until, for the first time, he felt the cold seeping through his now-saturated clothes.

He could fight the dark. He could fight the river. But he could not fight the cold. He tried, but it was an insidious and insistent predator. When at last the river came roaring out from beneath the glacier and deposited him at the edge of a broad, stony flood plain under the pungent shadows of a thick grove of spruce, he was barely conscious, so cold that he could not move, so cold that his heartbeat was a slow, unsteady murmuring in his chest, not strong enough to motivate his lungs to breathe.

Unable to move more than an eyelid, he stared at Death as

it approached, red, shaggy, a moving mountain of a mammoth. It would crush him and be a fitting death for one who had betrayed his totem, for one who had drunk the blood of a beast that he had named.

"Life Giver?"

He saw the scar on the animal's shoulder, the fragmented stalk that was all that was left of the shafted end of the projectile point. Torka's spearhead!

It *was* Life Giver!

He closed his eyes to the most impossible dream that he had ever dreamed and waited to die.

The mammoth came forward to stand over him. Its great body broke the back of the cold wind as Life Giver breathed the life-giving warmth of its breath through its trunk and onto the figure of a youth who had once stood before him and bravely named him Brother.

Exhausted, Navahk lay on his back in a rubble of snow and ice, his left leg still buried up to the hip in the debris of the icefall. For hours he had dug and worked himself up and out of what at first he had been certain would be the end of him. But there had been pockets of air trapped within the collapsed icefall, and the mountain snow that had fallen over this had fallen as powder, in oddly shaped blocks that might have crushed him had they fallen directly upon him. As it was, the icefall had sustained the weight of their impact, allowing him space to maneuver up through cracks and spaces, twisting his body in contortions that half dislocated his joints, squeezing himself through fissures that would have wedged in a mouse. But he was Navahk, and the power of his will was extraordinary. He had dug his way to life, scraping with his fingers until the nails were split and the tips worn raw to the bone. What was a little blood and pain compared to slow and certain suffocation? He had worked consistently, losing all track of time, and now, at last, he lay exhausted and too weak to try to remove the last blocks of ice from his leg.

Later. He would do it later. There was plenty of time. Now he must rest, sleep. He succeeded for a few moments, but the wound in his shoulder was aching. He had forgotten all about it, his last gift from his son.

Karana. He sneered at the thought of the name, then smiled and stared at the sweet, living sky of night. It was red with bold, auroral rivers of light. How beautiful they were to him now, when he knew how close he had come to never seeing them again. His smile became a leer of satisfaction. Karana would never see them again; he had seen to that. At last! Karana was dead, and he had killed him! And soon, when he had freed his leg and recovered from his ordeal, he would follow Torka and Lonit, and he would kill them, too, and their children. Yes. First the children.

The child saw him and hurried forward. For hours she, too, had been digging herself from potential death within the suffocating masses of snow. She was glad she had paused to feed off the female that Mother Killer had left behind to be meat for her. The meat had given her the strength to free herself, and the man stone had allowed her work to go quickly. Now she held it, curled in her fist, close to her breast. She had not slept but had hurried on the moment she had freed herself. Her thoughts were focused entirely upon the beast as she mewed and cried softly to herself. If he were dead, she would be alone.

Alone. The thought was more terrifying than the premise of her own death, more terrifying than the world around her that had suddenly shaken itself, then had collapsed in roaring, tumultuous fury.

But there was Mother Killer, lying in the snow. Her heart beat faster at the sight of him. He would hold her. He would stroke her. He would take away her fear.

He did not move as she came to kneel in the snow beside him. He was so still. So very, very still.

Beneath her sloping, bony brow, her prominent lids narrowed over her gray eyes. Fear and perplexity moved in the grayness. Why did he lie motionless like that in the snow? Men did not sleep buried in the snow. Men slept under the skins of the animals they killed.

Troubling memories rose within her. Painful memories. She whimpered softly, remembering her mother . . . so still . . . so very, very still, and then not breathing, not moving, not living! She leaned over Mother Killer, sniffed his face, and hunkered back, relieved and yet still troubled. He was alive! He *was* breathing, but so shallowly that she feared that any moment he would stop, and then he would never move again. He would never come to her to speak to her, to stroke her, to take away her loneliness.

She frowned, noticing for the first time that there was

blood in the snow just above his shoulder. She leaned close again, sniffed it, and drew back. It was *his* blood. The long, powerful, hairy-backed fingers of her right hand flexed about the man stone while her other hand reached to flick the bloody snow away from him. She did not have to lean close to see that, beneath the snow, there was a wound below his shoulder. She had seen its kind before, in her mother's breast. A wound made by a man stone.

Thoughtfully she uncurled her fist and appraised the lanceolate stone. Stones took away the breath from beasts and from mothers. Perhaps they could give back what they took. It had not been so with her mother, but her mother's wound had been much worse than that of Mother Killer. His was only a little wound. If she used her stone deftly and surely, perhaps she could put the strong breath of a healthy beast back into his body, and he would rise and stroke her and—

Navahk screamed and awoke in horror to see the child straddling him, stabbing him again and again, driving a dagger into his wound at an oblique angle that took it deep into his chest cavity and toward his heart. She was looking at him out of her guileless eyes, making cooing sounds to him, softly and gently, as though loving him at the very moment that she was killing him. He felt his heart leap madly as it was pierced, and he screamed again and tried to pull away, but his leg was held fast and he could not move as an amazing, awesome lightness filled him. He fell back, staring, witnessing his own death reflected in the eyes of the beast.

She drew back, puzzled and frightened, cocking her head as he fell back. She stared. She went close and sniffed his nostrils and gaping mouth. This time there was no breath. No breath at all! She breathed into him. She stabbed him again, more insistently now, trying to revive him, but the man stone that had served her so well at cutting and skinning meat refused to serve her now. In her frenzied attempts to revive the beast, she cut herself, drawing blood and pain, and howled in frustration as she threw the stone away, then crouched and howled and sucked her wound.

Although she stayed with him for hours, all through the long, cold night and into the brief, cold, sunlit dawn, Mother Killer did not awake to breathe or speak sounds to her or stroke her or join his body to hers. She held him in her arms and lifted his hands and tried to make him stroke her, but he would not. She grew lonely and slept at last, still holding him, hoping that when she awoke, he would be breathing again, and she would not be alone.

Sunset came before noon. Mother Killer did not move. His one eye was glazed. She put him down and went to search the tumbled snowdrifts for her stone. She found it and held it, then stood looking toward the east, where the other beasts had gone, into the face of the rising hole in the sky. She would go there. Perhaps one among them would hear her howls and know that she was lonely. But now Mother Killer was dead. It was time to dance in his skin.

They walked for many days across the eastern land, beneath the red sky, beneath the rising of the winter moon. Swans flying high against the brief glow of dawn led them to a valley where great herds grazed upon the rich, snow-dusted tundra grasses, and the trumpeting call of mammoths brought them across the broad flood plain to where Karana waited, wearing the hat of Zinkh that he had found along the bank . . . as the great mammoth Thunder Speaker had found him and given to him once more the gift of life.

He raised his hand in welcome as Torka's people ran toward him. Lonit wept, and Aar leaped in joy to see him, but it was Mahnie who embraced him as he looked at Torka and said: "What has taken you so long? Karana has been waiting many days and nights in this good land to greet his father."

Author's Note

It has long been the belief of the author that fiction is most absorbing when it is rooted in fact, because fact is, as the old cliché contends, more astounding than fiction. And no period of human endeavor is more astounding than that of the Age of Ice, in which our ancestors struggled to survive and, against all odds, succeeded.

Ongoing geological studies confirm that the Age of Ice was not one but several long protracted periods of cold. At least four times during the last two million years the climate of the world has cooled, allowing the growth of great continental ice sheets, which, during the coldest times, formed one vast, earth-crushing wall across North America—a wall two miles thick, over a thousand miles wide, and spanning the continent from coast to coast.

This mass of ice reshaped North America, drew into itself two-thirds of the moisture of all of the world's oceans, and lay seabeds bare, allowing Man to walk out of Asia and into North America across the exposed floor of the Bering Strait. In *Beyond the Sea of Ice,* Volume One of the First Americans Series, it was across this now drowned land—which once stretched for a thousand miles from the Arctic Ocean, across the Chukchi Sea, then to the Pacific Ocean—that Torka led his people out of the old world and into the new to become the first Americans. They would have remained upon the rolling, thousand-mile-wide tundra grasslands of Beringia, however, had they not been big-game hunters following the great herds of the Pleistocene as they migrated ever eastward.

But where did these first Americans go? How could they proceed into that frozen and inhospitable world if it lay buried under ice two miles thick? They walked through the

Corridor of Storms—a real place, not a figment of the author's imagination.

Throughout all but the coldest periods of the Ages of Ice, the continental ice sheets that blanketed the northern latitudes was not one mass, but two. During the most recent glaciation, these glaciers were known as the Laurentide and Cordilleran ice sheets, and where they met, along the eastern spine of the Rocky Mountains, a corridor lay open into the heartland of the Americas. During each epoch of ice the Corridor of Storms was there, a place of rich summer grassland and savage winter storms.

In Torka's time, over forty thousand years ago, the corridor may have extended farther north and west than during the last glaciation. At its broadest this ice-free tundral rangeland was never more than a hundred miles wide between the soaring, two-mile-high frontal flanks of the ice sheets. During those periods when the ice sheets were merging, it takes little imagination to visualize what it must have been like for those men and women who dared to follow the game between the Mountains That Walk into the Corridor of Storms from which this novel has taken its title.

Over six thousand years ago, when hordes of conquering Asian nomads swept out of the taiga to force the peaceful proto-Eskimo reindeer hunters of the Siberian steppes farther east—eventually to people the Aleutian Islands, venture across the shallow Bering Strait, and continue into the vast, rolling tundral barrens of northern Alaska—Paleo-Indians of various tribes, the descendants of earlier immigrants, were there to greet them. The Paleo-Indians' ancestors had dwelled in the "new" land for countless millennia and had established a "new" race and "new" cultural and linguistic groups from Alaska to Tierra del Fuego—because, in a time beyond remembering, a handful of men and women followed the vast herds of the Pleistocene out of Siberia, across a thousand-mile-wide bridge of steppeland, and into the high barrens between the Brooks Range of Alaska. Onward they trekked, through the Yukon River valley, into the broad delta of the Mackenzie River, along a wind-scoured, ice-free corridor that lay open between the ice sheets beneath which most of North America lay entombed.

It has been the hope of the author not only to entertain the reader through the fictitious adventures and travels of Torka's people, these first Americans, but to offer a journey back into time—that most elusive of corridors—a journey upon which an epoch might be seen and experienced with as few diversions from known historical fact as possible.

For those who may be curious as to whether the "child" in this novel is fact or fiction, the author will only say that myths of half-human, half-spirit creatures abound in the Americas. Although the bones of Neanderthal Man have yet to be unearthed in the New World, the wanawut is drawn from various native American legends that strongly hint of the possible presence of such a being inhabiting the continent in ancient days; its name is taken from the Chumash Indians of southern California, who recounted that in ancient days their people came from the far north, from the land of the wanawut, where "fear was born."

Once again the author must credit the staff of Book Creations, Inc., for invaluable and timesaving assistance with the editing and often painstaking research that was necessary to complete the construction of this novel. In particular, thanks to Betty Szeberenyi, Librarian, and to Laurie Rosin, not only because she is an incomparably *patient* Senior Editor, but because she has been an interested and involved sleuth on my behalf as well!

William Sarabande
Fawnskin, California